"HOLLYWOOD AS SEEN [...]
WHO HAVE EARNED THE RIGHT TO WRITE
THIS BOOK."   —David Geffen

"Obst and Wolper have "been there, done that"
as the Australians say. DIRTY DREAMS is a
great read. Readers will love it."
                    —P. J. O'Rourke,
                         author of *Modern Manners*

"AUTHENTIC AND SEXY . . . BEHIND-THE-
SCENES HOLLYWOOD."   —Kirkus Reviews

"Carol Wolper and Lynda Obst's insights about
the entertainment business are more entertaining
than the business itself."
                    —Barbara Benedek, co-author of
                         The Big Chill

"This is Hollywood today—fevered, frantic, and
libidinal. Lynda Obst and Carol Wolper capture
all that."
                    —David Freeman, author of
                         A Hollywood Education

DIRTY DREAMS

a novel by
Lynda Obst
and
Carol Wolper

A SIGNET BOOK

SIGNET
Published by the Penguin Group
Penguin Books USA Inc., 375 Hudson Street,
New York, New York 10014, U.S.A.
Penguin Books Ltd, 27 Wrights Lane,
London W8 5TZ, England
Penguin Books Australia Ltd, Ringwood,
Victoria, Australia
Penguin Books Canada Ltd, 2801 John Street,
Markham, Ontario, Canada L3R 1B4
Penguin Books (N.Z.) Ltd, 182-190 Wairau Road
Auckland 10, New Zealand

Penguin Books Ltd, Registered Offices:
Harmondsworth, Middlesex, England

Published by Signet, an imprint of New American Library, a division of
Penguin Books USA Inc. Previously published in an NAL Books edition.

First Signet Printing, June, 1991
10 9 8 7 6 5 4 3 2 1

REGISTERED TRADEMARK—MARCA REGISTRADA

Printed in the United States of America

PUBLISHER'S NOTE
This is a work of fiction. Names, characters, places, and incidents either are
the product of the author's imagination or are used fictitiously, and any
resemblance to actual persons, living or dead, events, or locales is entirely
coincidental.

We'd like to thank Erica Spellman, Michaela Hamilton, Jim Wiatt, Owen Laster, Dawn Steel, Stacey Sher, Debra Hill, Nora Ephron, and David Freeman.

Also, special thanks to Oly

—L.O.

and . . .

David and Gloria

—C.W.

THE
HOT
WINDS

1

There were two cars ahead of Carolyn Foster's beat-up VW convertible as she approached the gate to Millennium Studios. Impatiently she tapped the steering wheel. It was already five of nine. The studio both intimidated and excited her. When she'd first driven past it, on moving to L.A. three years ago, she'd stared like a tourist at those privileged few who were permitted to cruise through the checkpoint. Today she realized that she was being eyed in the same way by some passersby in a dusty Chevy pickup. How easily fortunes change in this strange place, Carolyn thought.

As the cars in front of her advanced, she pulled up to the security station.

"Carolyn Foster," she informed the guard on duty. "I'll be working in the executive building."

He checked his list. "Follow the green line all the way to the end, then follow signs for lot D. Park only in an unmarked spot." He was so official, she had the urge to salute.

This is going to take more than five minutes, she thought, knowing the green line was not a short one. She quickly drove ahead, forgetting there were strategically placed speed bumps in the road. Her old Beetle rattled as it sped over one of them, causing the rearview mirror to fall to the floor, "Not an auspicious beginning," she mumbled to herself.

She slowed the car and tried to stem her anxiety by

inhaling deeply. So I'll be a little late. At least I know my
way around the studio lot.

She'd been working at Millennium for three months as
a secretary for an in-house producer. He was successful,
judging from the many on-air series for which he took
credit, but he was not a man looking for bright new
ideas. At least not from Carolyn.

For her, the only bright spot was the other secretaries
she met. Over lunch at the nonexecutive commissary,
they'd all jokingly commiserate about doing the kind of
dull work that kills brain cells. Or, as Carolyn put it,
doing hard time in minimum-wage prison.

More important, though, this lunch klatch taught her
who was who around the lot. When a job was about to
open up in Executive V.P. Nicole Lanford's office, Carolyn knew about it before Nicole did. Nicole's departing
secretary had become a friend, and paved the way for her
replacement. For Carolyn it was an early lesson in team
nepotism and one that brought her closer to her goal.
Working for Nicole would teach her how to develop
movie ideas, something she'd have to perfect if she was
ever to become a screenwriter.

Besides, at thirty-five, Nicole Lanford was the most
visibly powerful woman in Hollywood and Carolyn's role
model. Though she'd never met her, she admired her
accomplishments and style. She considered her part of
the new breed of Hollywood women: tough, sexy, and
way beyond feminism. Through studio gossip she'd heard
that some men complained about Nicole being too tough,
something they never said about each other. But even
Nicole's enemies grudgingly conceded she had to be taken
seriously. They called her a player, a high compliment in
an industry that thought of itself as a game.

As Carolyn made her way on foot through the maze of
back alleyways, she became self-conscious about her earrings. They were two-inch-long pink-black-and-white primitive dancing figures that swung dramatically as she loped
across the lot. It occurred to her that maybe they were a

bit too avant garde to wear to her first day on the job in the executive wing. But as she cut over to the main thoroughfare, she saw a girl with a Peewee Herman haircut walking with a guy wearing a "Sex Fiend Band" sweatshirt. What am I worried about? she thought. This is Hollywood.

Carolyn sat in the anteroom of Nicole's office suite and breathed in the heady atmosphere. She knew that it wasn't unusual for Nicole to fire a new secretary after just one day. Trial by fire was her technique. And since Nicole couldn't abide "temps," Carolyn didn't get to start off fresh, nine A.M. on a Monday, but as Nicole's need dictated, on a Friday before the Fourth of July weekend.

Carolyn scanned the room. A gallery of framed pictures of Nicole with movie stars of the moment adorned the walls, mixed with action shots of Nicole with her director on the set of Millennium's fall blockbuster. She's all business, Carolyn concluded as the door to Nicole's office swung open.

"Come on in," this petite but formidable-looking woman commanded, leading Carolyn into her office. Nicole had an alluring face crowned by a mass of thick curly auburn hair. From one angle she looked elegant, from another almost coarse, and it was this combination that proved captivating. As she settled into her desk chair, she leaned back and crossed her arms in a battle-ready pose that had become her trademark.

"We've got to hit the ground running. I have a short but busy day. I expect a lot from my secretaries, whether or not they're new. Sit down." Nicole pointed to a couch, upholstered in chintz to appear cozy. "Take notes. There are only two calls you should interrupt me for, no matter what. The first is Kevin Holberstein. He's the president of Millennium, and my boss. His secretary's name is Shelley—be nice to her. You'll be talking to her all day. The other person is Ted McGuiness. He's chairman of the board. Kevin reports to Ted, who frequently works out at his beach house. If and when he calls, let me know immediately. If I tell you that I need him, call his secretary, Adele. She's screening calls down the hall."

Nicole was striding around the office as though she were working out her anxiety aerobically. Carolyn's fast notes were struggling a beat behind. Nicole paused for a second and then picked up the phone sheet from her desk.

"I'll always take calls from inside the studio first. That includes marketing, distribution, publicity, and business affairs. But not from my creative executives David Beach and Bambi Stern." Carolyn had heard a lot about these two "snakes," whose collective offices at Millennium were referred to as "the Reptile Wing." She also knew, from the secretarial grapevine, that Nicole had reluctantly inherited the two of them last month as part of the deal that promoted her to executive vice-president.

"They will each call all day and in any manner possible attempt to persuade you to let them get through to me," Nicole warned. "They are always on their private little agendas, so ignore them. Also, when those two sidle around your desk, watch my phone sheet and any loose papers." She stopped, aware that she might be giving a wrong impression. "Information is their currency," she added. "Getting it is their job, but their bloodhound routine has got to be kept in check. Anyway, I'll return their calls at the end of each morning and each afternoon. Other than that, screen the agents and the producers. In-house producers get first priority, or any producer currently shooting with us, and the list of films in production is on file. Schedule writers for pitch meetings or lunches, and directors for dinners. I will breakfast with producers, but only if they've made a picture. Be sure to ask for credits, nicely. The rest of the meetings should be handled by David Beach or Bambi."

Nicole, winded, stopped talking for a moment and focused her attention on her daily calendar book. Suddenly all the energy that had been radiating toward Carolyn was spent. Not knowing how to respond, Carolyn shuffled her notes and made movements to leave. This provoked Nicole to continue her instructions, but now with an oddly pinched look on her expressive mouth.

"My most important meeting for today is at three o'clock, with Millennium's most powerful producer, Lance Burton. I assume I don't have to fill you in on how important he is to the studio."

Carolyn shook her head. "Five blockbusters in a row."

"He's definitely been on a roll," Nicole agreed. "However, when it comes to appointments, he's been known to show up anywhere from an hour early to an hour late or not at all. I want you to doublecheck with his office about the time, and mention that the meeting is to be here. Explain to his secretary that I have to get out of here by five o'clock. Oh, and confirm table number two at Morton's tonight. Dinner for two at eight." Then, in the same breath, she added, "What's your name?"

"Carolyn Foster," Carolyn responded softly.

"I don't like surprises, Carolyn, so keep them to a bare minimum." Then Nicole handed Carolyn the phone sheet from the day before. "Roll the calls marked in yellow."

Carolyn assumed that this order was her cue to move to her desk in the anteroom. She grabbed her notes and her purse and headed for safety behind Nicole's now-shut door. She scanned the list, and placed the first call to NBC's Mike Ovitz.

With Nicole temporarily at bay in negotiations with the head of a network, Carolyn could relax for a second and reflect on the tornado she had just witnessed. How could this short Jewish girl from Bayonne, New Jersey, be so intimidating? she wondered. And why did it seem that everyone successful in show business was short? In fact, Carolyn thought, Nicole Lanford was the first woman she'd ever met with a Napoleon complex.

*   *   *

Three calls lit up the phone all at once. Carolyn put the first two on hold and took the third. It was Michael J. Fox and Carolyn guessed it was a call Nicole would take immediately. After buzzing her boss, she hit the middle button. It was someone calling about a party Don Henley was giving for a city-council candidate. Had Nicole received the invitation? Was she planning on attending?

Don Henley? *The* Don Henley of the Eagles? Carolyn wondered. She sorted through a stack of opened incoming mail and located the invitation. Not only was it obviously *the* Don Henley, but *the* Warren Beatty was co-hosting the party. Carolyn checked Nicole's calendar and saw that she had penciled in the event. "Yes, she is planning on attending," Carolyn replied, "but there's an outside chance she'll be out of town." Having covered all bases, she hit the last lit button. It was a very persistent Bambi Stern. Carolyn held firm and took a message.

After hanging up, she leaned back in her chair and took a moment to slow down. She checked her Swatch watch. It was five to two. She took another quick glance and decided she didn't miss the Rolex she'd sold last week to pay some bills. To her surprise, pawning her jewelry had not been the humiliating experience she'd imagined it would be. Andrew Spencer, her new boyfriend/obsession, had come with her and turned it into a kind of madcap lark. They playfully haggled over the selling price, delighted to raise it a hundred and fifty dollars above the first offer. Immediately they celebrated by going to Prego's for a dinner of exotic pasta and champagne. Andrew, my Andrew, she thought with a smile.

The late-afternoon sunlight made the glass bookshelves in Nicole's office glisten. As her eye narrowed to pan her office, Nicole took pride in her taste, which had kept pace with her accumulation of leverage and power. She was pleased with the marble desk she had chosen, as well as the sleek Italian armchair. Arranged fresh flowers graced a beveled glass tabletop, reflecting the Hockneyswimming-pool-light-blue walls. The wet smell of the paint was a reminder of her recent promotion. A huge palm tree stood guard to the right of the door, cautioning those who entered to speak briefly and cogently to the queen. That's what they called her, the queen of the five-minute meeting.

She didn't care all that much what they labeled her. The fact was, she was executive vice-president. There was only one of those in a sea of vice-presidents. The possibility was strong that she could one day be president. She was reminded of something the masterly Brandon Tartikoff had recently said to her. "There are a lot of boxcars in this town, but only a few engines." That's what made Nicole different from other women in Hollywood. She intended to be an engine.

Nicole had felt tense all day. She'd been anxious since yesterday when she'd received Lance's call.

For all her career, Nicole thought, surprise calls from Lance had been watershed ones. The first, five years before, catapulted her from publicity into production. At that time Lance was producing his second film for Millennium. The first one had been a breakthrough movie. Lance was the golden boy, full of instincts and energy. Nicole brilliantly orchestrated the multimedia campaign that opened the movie, and Lance had been duly impressed. Spotting a potential ally, Lance privately talked her up to Chester Baines, his friend on the board of directors, pointing out what a good P.R. move it would be to have a "visible woman" in feature production. So, years ahead of her schedule, Nicole made her move up the corporate ladder. Now it was up to her to decide which ideas would be turned into screenplays, which screenplays would become movies, and who would direct them and act in them.

For five years her life had consisted almost exclusively of her desk and her bed and the five-mile drive that separated the two. But for Nicole this responsibility, with its awesome pressure, was nirvana. The problm was, she knew that what Lance had given, he could take away. Her fears were only increased by this meeting, hastily scheduled on a Friday afternoon before the July Fourth weekend. Lance knew damn well that everyone left the studio by lunch, so there was no way this meeting meant anything but bad news.

It was way past three o'clock. Lance was deliberately late. So what if she wanted to leave early to pick out an outfit for her dinner with a hot Australian director? What did he care that she had to reschedule a pitch meeting and that two writers' weekends were ruined by her cancellation? She knew Lance's lateness was deliberate because she knew in her bones that with Lance nothing was unintentional, that his every whim had an underlying objective. Now, dying to get out of the office, she was in his control, a captive audience with no captor.

"God damn him," Nicole quietly cursed as she checked the time again. She was in no mood to wait around.

She buzzed Carolyn. "Has Burton called?" Without waiting for an answer, she impatiently shot off a series of orders. "Call his office. See if he's left yet. If he has, find out how long ago. If not, tell his secretary . . ."

Then, unannounced, breaking the rules even in his entrance, Lance Burton burst through Nicole's closed door and strode up to her desk. He sat on its corner, pushing her important memos out of the way to clear his seat. He looked like a Hollywood outlaw in his denim shirt, black Levi's, and Tony Lama snakeskin boots. His brown eyes seemed especially bright and his attitude suggested he was ready to take on anything or anyone. Nicole shifted in her chair, looking up in a defensive posture that reflected Lance's usurpation of her territory.

"So, sweetheart, what can you do for me today?" Lance grinned, and Nicole fought against her natural attraction.

"Lance Burton." She tried to pull a relaxed smile from her collection. "What brings you to Millennium? Slumming? Ferrari out of the shop?" They laughed at their private joke. Lance's excuse for their last four canceled lunch dates was that his Ferrari was in the shop.

"Seriously, Lance. You haven't actually booked an appointment over here for over three pictures. And now it's in my office, not yours. You must want something badly."

'How perceptive of you, Niçole. But then, you didn't get this job by being stupid."

She acknowledged his backhanded compliment with a toss of her hair.

"I'm here to talk about *Dirty Dreams*. You know what it means to me, don't you? Or have they drained the passion out of you already? Are you still getting laid?"

She took a deep breath. "Slow down, Lance. No one is talking about sex. We're talking, I believe, about a script in development here, that we have financed to the tune of five hundred thousand dollars—through four, or is it five, drafts. A script that, as far as Kevin and I are concerned, still doesn't work. It's not that I haven't tried, Lance. I can't count the hours that I've spent in story meetings on *Dirty Dreams* alone. Sometimes you just have to stop and reconsider the whole thing. Maybe there's nothing sympathetic about bound-and-gagged women—maybe it's too decadent to be a mainstream-movie idea." She swallowed hard at the end of her brave declaration.

"Idea? Excuse me!" His tone was blistering as he leapt up from the desk and stormed around her office, picking up paraphernalia—picture frames, scripts, a Tiffany paperweight engraved HBO—and tossed them from arm to arm. "You are going to talk ideas with me? *Me*, whose ideas, I surely needn't remind you, have grossed this studio its entire operating overhead for the next decade? Don't insult me!"

Nicole mentally played out strategies to calm him down. She went for an old standard. "I'm not quibbling, Lance. You know I know how brilliant you are. I learn more by watching you than anyone. I never would have gotten my

first script out of development without your patronage.
But more than that, I love working with you. It's just
that Kevin and I—"

"Don't give me that Kevin-and-I shit. What are you?
Rocket scientists? America's demographics? You think
you're tapped into the mainstream but you're really drowning
in your own bullshit because you have no guts. Maybe
you two actually are the lowest common denominator!"
A half-sneer, half-laugh punctuated his diatribe.

"Please, Lance. Don't get vicious. We are all friends.
We can discuss this with marketing—whether or not there
is an audience for this picture and how to find it. Until
then, you should look for a new writer. And it better be
a good one, because nobody decent is going to direct this
the way it reads now, and you know I need a major
director to even try to get this one made."

"That's what I came here to tell you. I've made a
decision. I'm going to direct *Dirty Dreams*. No one else
can direct this picture but me. It's my life's work. It's out
of my goddamned private fantasies. It's my invention, my
vision, my art."

Nicole fought to suppress a giggle, though Lance's
back was, for the moment, to her. He pivoted, to catch
her off-guard, and gathered up the silence. Like a coiled
cobra, he awaited her response, his laser beam of attention
directed to her face. Nicole sensed the delicacy of
the moment. Perhaps Lance is *really* crazy, she thought,
not just movie-business crazy. She had to be careful,
lighten it up. "But, Lance . . . if you direct, you'll have
to come to work. You'll have to take phone calls, deal
with agents, stars, people you hate. You'll have to show
up!"

Her attempt at humor was not playing. "Listen, Nicole,
and if for some reason you can't hear me, read my
lips." He talked with deliberate pauses. "If I say I'm
ready to direct, I am. I'm not a fool, nor am I bluffing.
This movie is in my blood. It is a movie that will define
me and create my place in film history. And no one

knows more about female sexuality than I do. I know things about women that you don't yet, my dearest, and if you can't take the heat, Nicole—of a controversial, potentially groundbreaking film—then you shouldn't be in your position."

He gestured as if the whole office were his stage. "You would have tried to stop Bertolucci from making *Last Tango in Paris*. It's your type, the know-nothing-scared-to-lose-your-job P.R. hacks turned executives who are killing the creative spirit in this town."

The tirade was taking its toll on Nicole. Her office was in shambles and it was obvious that she'd need Thorazine and a team of shrinks from Cedars Sinai to talk this maniac down.

"Look at me," Lance demanded. "Look at me carefully. I am dead serious about this. More serious than you've ever seen me. I am giving this studio two weeks to pay or play me as director of this film, at a fee of two million dollars. After that, I am taking this deal to Fox, and you know I'm not bluffing. I think Ted has some friends in New York who wouldn't be happy about me making my next deal elsewhere. So take my advice, Nicole, if you've never taken it before. Don't stand in my way or a tidal wave will bury you. You're just the first cog in a wheel I intend to turn."

Nicole gathered her thoughts, trying to come up with the right strategy to diffuse the crisis, or at least one that would buy her some time.

"Calm down, Lance. I hear you. We can deal with this. Just give me a chance to think this through. I will reread the script and come up with some new ideas. I'll get things rolling in marketing. If there is a way to make this movie work, we'll find it. We know how valuable you are to Millennium—you never have to remind me of that."

Before her speech had ended, Lance was out the door, bounding down the hall, flirting with secretaries. From the elevator, Nicole heard him call to her, "See you at

the B-B-Q, sweetheart. Be there or be square," he howled
with laughter.

Carolyn opened her drawer, looking for a package of
Emergen-C. "The champagne of nutritional drinks" was
how it was advertised on the package. "Health-food cocaine" was what the junior executives at Millennium
called it.

As she stirred her Emergen-C into a cup of Sparklettes
water, Nicole buzzed. "Hold all calls and get me Kevin."
Before Carolyn could comply, another line lit up. Maybe
it's Andrew, she hoped, but it was an agent with another
deal to pitch. "Nicole is on a conference call," she lied.
The agent wasn't happy. All afternoon, people had been
frantically calling, trying to push through some last-minute
business and escape from the office early. Pre-Fourth of
July performance anxiety, Carolyn thought as she waited
on hold for Kevin's secretary, who jumped back on the
line and informed her that Kevin was out at a meeting
but due back any minute. Carolyn relayed the message to
Nicole and then reached for her vitamin concoction.

As she took a sip, she found herself staring over the
top of her glass at a familiar face . . . familiar because it
had looked out at her from dozens of magazines. He
didn't introduce himself. Burt Reynolds didn't have to.
Before she had a chance to make the polite inquiries as
to how she could help him, the door to Nicole's office
flew open. As if by radar, Nicole had sensed the arrival
of a visitor, and was unhappy to find it wasn't Kevin.
Carolyn watched her boss quickly and effectively cover
her disappointment with a smile and gracefully usher
Burt into her inner sanctum.

Burt Reynolds! Carolyn was in a daze. He wasn't David Byrne, one of her rock-and-roll idols, but Reynolds
was a name she had grown up with. Her mother, a
small-town woman who rarely went to the movies, was a
Smokey and the Bandit fanatic. When Carolyn brought
boyfriends home, her mother's most typical comment

was, "He's no Burt Reynolds." Back in her hometown, the depressed factory city of Fall River, Massachusetts, having actually seen, let alone met, Burt Reynolds was worth a notice in the *Herald News*. When she had left the east coast and come to Hollywood three years earlier, her father had said, "You're no Farrah Fawcett." Her mother had said, "Get Burt's autograph."

The phone rang again. It was the same agent with a message to Nicole that Paramount was interested, so if Millennium wanted to make an offer, they should schedule a meeting ASAP. Carolyn felt as if all the day's telephone voices blended together into one tense monotone demanding immediate attention. Deals seemed on the verge of coming together or falling apart. The pace was so fast it was hard to focus. Like motion sickness, Carolyn thought, jotting down the phrase in the notebook she used for her story ideas.

Just then Burt reemerged from the inner office. He planted a quick good-bye kiss on Nicole's cheek before rushing off to get his own three-day weekend in gear.

With his departure, Nicole slumped into a chair across from Carolyn.

"I can't believe that was Burt Reynolds," Carolyn said, thinking about how impressed her mother back in Fall River would be.

"If one more person pops in when I'm dying to get out of here . . ." Nicole knew she sounded shrewish but couldn't help it. At work she frequently donned a tough attitude in order to avoid any visible lapses of self-confidence. Sometimes she felt sorry for the secretaries who had to put up with her rough edges, but she couldn't explain to them that this was the only way she knew how to march forward.

Impatiently she sorted through a stack of papers on Carolyn's desk. "Where are my breakdown sheets?" Finding them, she stared blankly at the weekly totals, her concentration drifting back to her meeting with Lance. She knew somehow that this problem was bigger than

Lance's mere egomania, and bigger than his desire to direct this movie, but she didn't know quite how.

The phone rang and Carolyn caught it on the first ring. She nodded yes to Nicole's unspoken question: Is it Kevin? "On line two," Carolyn announced, and immediately Nicole was galvanized into action. Her finger shot down on the lit button.

"Kevin," she said, "just don't move until I get to your office. I don't care who's in there, get them out. We have to talk about Lance."

She dropped the receiver and bolted out of the chair. Frantically she gathered up her notes for the weekend, her linen blazer and handbag.

"Carolyn," she demanded. As Carolyn snapped to attention, Nicole realized her voice had tightened. In fact, her entire musculature was tense. She forced herself to soften a bit, if not in her words, at least in her tone. "Stop letting people just pop into my office. Lance almost gave me a heart attack. You're my first line of defense, and we're losing. If anyone calls, I'm gone for the day. And don't forget, call Maxfield's again and tell Tommy I'll be there. I've got to pick up something to wear tonight."

"Don't worry, everything's under control," Carolyn assured her.

If only that were true, Nicole thought as she headed down the corridor to Kevin's office. If only that were true.

As Carolyn sat at her desk working to update Nicole's Rolodex, she worried about whether or not Nicole would keep her on and what would happen if she didn't. She had an irrational fear of turning into a fat old telephone operator with varicose veins. This picture brought her thoughts back to Fall River.

I didn't get Burt's autograph, she realized. On the off-chance that he might have stopped at another office, she dashed down the corridor to the reception area, but he was gone. The only person around, David Beach (who for some reason was always referred to as David Beach— never just David), was picking up some scripts left at the front desk. He noticed Carolyn's Converse All-Stars pink high-tops.

"Nice shoes," he said.

"Thanks," she replied, somewhat surprised. Although she'd seen David Beach around the lot a number of times and in fact had been introduced to him once by her former boss, he'd never before acknowledged her. She'd learned through the studio grapevine that he and his cohort, Bambi, were known for their snobbishness. The joke was that they had only two modes. Depending upon whether you had less or more power than they did, they were either at your throat or at your feet. Still, as Carolyn headed back to her desk, she was pleased by David Beach's comment. Especially since her look was not one that earned her many compliments around Millennium.

Stylistically, she was a combination of Elvis Costello (the haircut) and Audrey Hepburn (the pearls). Although twenty-five, Carolyn could pass for nineteen. She still had a cheerleader's cuteness about her—sparkling green eyes, blond hair, cupid-bow lips, a physically fit five-foot-six-inch-tall body, and lots of energy. What she didn't have was a cheerleader's attitude. Her enthusiasm was for writing and a style of dressing that celebrated the pop culture. Only she did it in a neochic way. She could wrap strands of fake pink pearls around her arm or wear mismatched earrings and somehow make the accessories look like something out of Italian *Vogue*.

Though she got a charge out of creating her look, she knew that no matter how cute her Beat Four sunglasses from L.A. Eyeworks or how unusual her T-shirt designed by a New York graffiti artist, the look was not enough to earn her much notice around the studio. The bottom line was, she was a secretary, and the general consensus was that secretaries ended up in one of two places. Either they stayed in the service end of the business or they married one of the executives they worked for. In which case they'd be accorded token respect as long as they remained legally attached. But until the day that one became a Mrs. Somebody, she was almost unanimously considered a Miss Nobody.

Carolyn imagined that if Bambi and David Beach knew that she'd been living with tennis star Paul Easton for the last two years, they'd be impressed. However, the fact that she intended to break up with him tonight when he returned from his latest two-month-long road trip would affect their evaluation of her. Let's see, Carolyn thought, having had a pro tennis player as a boyfriend could probably earn her five points on the Bambi/Beach grading system. But then, leaving Paul, regardless of the reason, for a destitute aristocrat, even a cute one like Andrew Spencer, would cost her ten. What was worse was that from that point on she'd be known as Paul's ex. Carolyn couldn't understand women who based their entire credibility on being someone's ex: Elvis's ex. Rod Stewart's ex. Prince's ex.

Thinking about this absurdity gave her an idea. She jotted a note to herself to develop a character who hated her ex-husband but constantly dropped his name because it was the only way she could get any validation. As she closed her notebook, Nicole buzzed.

"Did you reach Tommy at Maxfield's?"

"Yes," Carolyn replied. "He said he can't wait, but he put aside several outfits that are perfect for you, and Sandy will be there to help you."

Nicole chuckled. "Thank you, Tommy, and fuck you, Tommy." She knew for a fact he'd waited two hours for Lesley Ann Warren last week. "Call him back. Tell him I'm on the corner of La Cienega and Santa Monica."

Carolyn made her fourth call of the day to a store which was the mecca of fashion for those to whom it was commonplace to pay $350 for a blouse. She wondered if anyone at Maxfield's found these calls from Nicole excessive, but when she relayed the message to Tommy himself, he seemed to be expecting it.

With this call out of the way, Carolyn settled back, noticing with relief that as furiously as the phones had been ringing earlier, they were practically dead now. The studio was quieting down. The weekend was under way. Finally she was idle.

All day she'd had an urge to pick up one of the countless scripts that were lying all over the office. Taking advantage of the lull, she selected one of them, but then she hesitated. This and all other submissions to Nicole were her competition, and she wasn't sure she was ready to discover just how stiff that competition might be. The truth was, she had almost zero self-confidence in her work.

Slowly she cracked open the script she'd arbitrarily chosen. The first twenty pages set up the story of two old people who break-dance, die, go to heaven, and are sent back to earth to compete in a break-dancing competition of the 1996 Olympics. Carolyn couldn't believe the lunacy of the plot, and the dialogue was like something lifted from a child's comic book. There was a memo attached to the title page from an agent at William Morris. "Dear Nicole," it read, "I think you'll enjoy this script, which has a Capraesque time-warp theme with a *Rocky* ending."

Carolyn read another five pages of this compound genre before chucking it. Well, at least she'd done it. She'd cracked open a script by a so-called serious writer, and not only didn't it make her feel like a lightweight, it actually gave her hope. I know I can do better than that, she thought.

2

It was almost dusk when Millennium chairman Ted McGuiness got out of his Jaguar in front of his favorite beachside restaurant. In the gentle light he looked considerably younger than his fifty years. The gray streaks in his hair were less apparent and the lines on his handsome face seemed to come from character, not mileage.

His mood was upbeat as he stepped inside La Scala, Malibu's most popular hangout for the rich and famous. The place suited his style. He liked that it was a small, intense, almost self-effacing haunt, but for the subtle first-rateness of its brass-and-mahogany appointments. He felt at home with its checkerboard-tablecloth casualness and was impressed by its grand name and equally grand maître d's imported from the original La Scala in Beverly Hills.

Immediately he was spotted by Guido, who had known Ted for years, through two marriages, including the one to Bebe, the manic-depressive Scientologist TV starlet he had most recently shed. Guido was not a fan of Bebe's. Now, neither was Ted. In fact, Ted was so off Bebe that ever since they had broken up he felt tired of women in general, but for the occasional convenient quickie with a young actress or junior executive.

"What, Mr. McGuiness, no movie star on your arm tonight?"

"No, Guido. Tonight's work only."

"I thought you told me that you were getting too old to work too hard. That's why you hired that young guy, that

26

what's-his-name. So you could stay out here more with us."

"Holberstein, that's his name—and I was right. He's exactly who I'm having dinner with. So I can hear what horror shows I missed at the studio this week. The casualty report."

Guido nodded knowingly as he led Ted over to his usual corner booth and handed him the menu Ted knew by heart.

"Can I get you some *pinzimonio* to snack on?"

"Nah," Ted declined, opting for a breadstick instead. Alcohol and carbohydrates were his idea of dinner.

"A drink?"

He was about to order when he saw Kevin enter the small restaurant. "In a minute," he decided.

Guido nodded again, signaled to a busboy to bring over some water, and went off to greet another guest.

Ted watched Kevin cutting a swath through the casual beach atmosphere with his nervous energy, not waiting for Guido or anyone else to show him the way.

As he got closer, Ted noticed that Kevin appeared lost in thought. Ted called it his fireman look, because it was the expression Kevin wore when he was putting out fires, nipping in the bud the multiple breaking crises that were the life of a production chief.

"You look relaxed," Kevin complimented Ted as he slid into his side of the booth. Neither of them needed to mention that the observation was not mutual.

"You'd look relaxed too, Kevin, if you had you working for you. Maybe you should get yourself a place out at the beach. Unwind for a change. It wouldn't kill you."

It was true that Kevin resisted relaxation as if it were a sign of defeat. If it wasn't for the tenseness that he wore like a badge of honor, his innate boyishness would have given him an almost cuddly quality. He had a twinkle in his ice-blue eyes, which, along with his red hair and Ryan

O'Neal freckles, suggested his mother's Irish background. But it was his Jewish father's serious nature that he most often displayed. He was known as a consummate realist who always took into account the length of the game. Endurance, Kevin believed, was the secret to success in Hollywood.

"You want the bad news or the bad news?" Kevin opened.

"I don't seem to have much choice," Ted replied nonchalantly.

"*Norsemen* didn't open, not even in the cities where we have reviews. It doesn't look like we'll clear three million over the weekend."

"What does marketing say?"

"We should have done a video, they want to change the print ads, they're changing markets on the thirty-second television spots, and the sixty-second ones suck."

"What's new? Don't recut the sixty-second spot. Don't even think about the video. This asshole went two million over budget on the feature. Let them jerk off with new print ads."

"Exactly what I'm doing. So, are you ready for the really bad news? Lance pulled a number on Nicole."

Ted knew what was coming. He'd been suspecting something like this for a week now—ever since his last conversation with Lance. He'd sensed then that Millennium's star producer was gearing up for some kind of confrontation, and he'd taken that as his cue to step back. Twenty-five years in the business had taught Ted to wait and see where the pieces fell before making a move.

"Why Nicole?" Ted asked, curious as to Kevin's take on the move.

"I think he's saving his strength for you and me. Opening round, trial balloons. Order a drink before I tell you all this."

Ted waved Guido over. A vodka martini, very dry, appeared. And for Kevin, a Perrier, no ice.

Ted smiled. Kevin's moderate life-style was so extreme, it had become something of a joke. Everyone knew Kevin hated alcohol and drugs. Apparently he'd never smoked a joint in his life, and appeared not to have an iota of bohemia in his blood.

"Here's the bottom line," Kevin stated. "He wants to direct *Dirty Dreams*. He's giving us two weeks to pay and play him for two million dollars. If we don't, we can forget about renegotiating his deal. He's threatening to move over to Fox."

Ted took a long sip of his drink. "Just what we all need. Lance directing his trashy fantasies for a stab at celluloid immortality. Did Nicole remind him that the script isn't ready?"

"Of course. And he called her a cretin, an imbecile, an asshole P.R. hack who is single-handedly ruining the aesthetic standards of Hollywood. The question is, does Millennium want to lose its star producer?"

Ted snapped a breadstick and considered the options. If Lance won and the picture got made, that was okay with him. Ted had seen so-called sure things bomb and clunkers catch the public attention. Anything was possible. If Nicole and Kevin won, then it was them and not him who'd alienated Millennium's biggest money-making producer. Distance would keep him clean. He decided to avoid Kevin's question.

"Did Nicole appease him?"

"Tried to. She has good instincts in the ring. She bought time. Told him we'd all meet to discuss the script and take it from there. I don't know how you want to play this out."

Ted's response was automatic. "You and Nicole get together, sketch out options."

"There aren't many. We need to know if you're ready for a knockdown, drag-out with Lance. You know he's got allies in New York and is itching for—"

"My job," Ted finished Kevin's sentence.

"All our jobs."

"And I'd give it to him gladly, if only I could." Ted dismissed the ploy. "Anyway, I'd rather deed it to you, Kevin. Go on. We'll get back to this, I'm sure."

Kevin persisted in spite of his boss's evasiveness. "What if the movie bombs? What if it's another *Ishtar* or *Heaven's Gate?* With Lance in control of the budget, we know it will easily cost over forty million. For one thing, we already have a half-million in costs up to now. He wants the cinematographer of *Ishtar* to shoot it. The construction costs alone will run in the millions. To get a star to open the movie could cost up to six. And schedule? Lance hasn't even glanced at a schedule. You know full well that up till now Lance has derived his power from being in control of his productions and his directors. But who's going to be in control of him? It's the fox guarding the chicken coop."

"So now he's an artist," Ted mused. "Being a millionaire producer was boring. It's intellectual credibility he wants." Ted hid his extreme irritation at Kevin's getting so wound up about this. The problems Kevin hated most were the ones that hard work couldn't solve. If work was ninety percent perspiration and ten percent inspiration, Kevin's weakness lay in the inspiration department. Where he carefully strategized, Lance shot from the hip. They were as different as fire and ice.

"Maybe you and I and Nicole should meet tomorrow and put together some kind of crisis-control strategy," Kevin pressed.

"No," Ted replied. "I prefer to hold off on this one. Let's talk to Lance at his B-B-Q Monday and see if we can't get another script revision."

Kevin wanted to laugh. Nicole had predicted that Ted wouldn't want to touch this one. Exactly which one does he want to touch? Kevin thought. Resigning himself to his own inevitable showdown with Lance, he decided to get on with the rest of his studio report.

"We offered *Gutbusters* to Stallone and he asked for twenty million, guaranteed. The man's a walking vault. We said yes, he turned us down. I think they used us to establish a new price."

Ted shook his head and finished off his vodka martini. "I remember paying Paul Newman and Robert Redford one million dollars and going nuts for weeks. Those seem like the good old days, and it's not even fifteen years ago."

"They cost seven now, and a piece of the gross," Kevin remarked as Guido brought drink number two to the table.

"Let's toast to a piece of the gross," Ted laughed. "You and me, kid, we'll never see gross points. We'll define them and give them away, but we'll be lucky to see rolling break-even in our lifetime."

Kevin wondered if Ted really thought this was funny. "If I'm in charge, you'll see gross points," he assured both himself and Ted, alluding to the inevitable day when the reins of power would be handed to Kevin and Ted would take the movie business's golden parachute.

"Let's toast to the blissful state of indie-prod," said Ted, looking ahead to the ultimate independent-production deal. Someday, as a former studio head, he'd negotiate . . . well, his attorney, Ken Ziffren, would negotiate for him, a position with all the same perks as before but none of the responsibilities. As his vodka glass clicked Kevin's goblet of designer water, Ted felt himself click into a little peace of mind. He felt a tinge of his old determination. Lance's pornographic movie would not bring him down. No way. He'd have his golden parachute. All he had to do was carefully play both sides. A little conversation with Chester Baines was clearly in order.

On the drive back home, Ted formulated his morning phone call to the chairman of the board in New York. He did his clearest thinking on the Pacific Coast Highway.

"Chester," he'd begin, "I'm afraid Kevin Holberstein is sandbagging our friend Lance." Something like that, he figured, as the remote-control button opened the gates to his private ocean retreat.

3

Nicole straightened the shoulder pads in her Jean Paul Gaultier jacket, touched up her lipstick, and turned her baby Maserati over to the valet parkers at Morton's, the chic restaurant on Robertson and Melrose that was practically a clubhouse for Hollywood moguls.

"How much this baby cost?" asked one of the Guatemalan valets. "Thirty? Thirty-five?"

Why is it that everyone in L.A. thinks it's okay to ask how much your car costs? Nicole wondered. She never knew how to answer. What a good buy at twenty-eight thousand? That was a little absurd. But the car was great for the high-profile-getaway scene after dinner at Morton's. She remembered how she hated to have her big-name dates watch her get into her old Datsun ZX.

"Something like that," she said to the valet as she rushed past him for the door, wishing she wasn't always running late.

Pam Morton greeted Nicole with a kiss on the cheek and assured her that her table, the coveted number two, was ready. Despite the pleasure she inhaled from this privileged entrance, Nicole was still not immune to the anxiety she'd always felt, coming into this hotbed of action. Passing the throng waiting to be seated, she was afraid she'd trip before she got to her table. The assemblage of players so overloaded her computer that it was difficult for her to focus on her dinner date, who was standing right in front of her. His name was Peter Gibson: an Australian director she'd spoken to but never met.

"Miss Lanford?" he inquired.

He's divine, she thought as she registered the maverick looks she loved: cowboy boots, jeans, and a fabulous forties tattersall jacket. His complexion was pale, with a ruddy glow from recent California sun. There was a ruggedness about him. He was like a gust of fresh air from the Australian frontier—so unlike the power wimps this town had to offer. Men like him made her feel the weight of her aggressive persona. She sensed the expression on her face shift, and at once craved a mirror.

"So, please sit down," she said disarmingly. As they did so, she noticed that he was drinking a beer (of course).

"I got here a little early, so I'm a drink ahead of you," he said.

"Actually, I'm late, but it's nice of you not to make me feel guilty." She smiled. Then, turning her attention and her smile to her favorite waiter, who came over to take her order, she said, "A greyhound, as usual."

The waiter smiled back. "You got it." Nicole appreciated the good service but she was under no illusions about what motivated it. The guy was a struggling actor.

"What's a greyhound?" Peter Gibson asked.

"Ah," Nicole said coyly. "It's grapefruit juice and vodka. Healthy and potent. It's probably not the kind of thing I should order at a business dinner. You may end up having an unfair advantage."

"From what I hear, I'll need every advantage I can get with you," he replied flirtatiously.

"I suppose I'm meant to be flattered by that." She was melting now. She could tell because she broke into English cadence whenever she felt like a heroine in a novel.

"You don't need flattery from me, I'm sure. I'm just a bloke with a camera, trying to get the likes of you to pay for my film."

"Your film, your cast, your cameramen, your sets, your ads, your prints. Guys like you are insatiable."

They were both laughing now, enjoying the playful one-upmanship as Nicole's drink was placed in front of her.

"And what about ladies like you?"

"I've been thought to be insatiable, but only by men with limited resources."

As the first sip of vodka hit her, Nicole had to coax herself to pep down and relax. She didn't want to lose control of her objective of the evening. She was here to convince him to direct a movie, that was all. But that wasn't really all. She couldn't help but hope her business savvy would not only convince Peter Gibson to sign on for a project at Millennium but also, more important, intrigue him enough to want to initiate a relationship with her. The thought of being seduced by an Australian cowboy was definitely intriguing. But Nicole also knew she had to temper her hopefulness.

She'd been around and had heard all the lines and excuses before, her favorite being, "I love you but my shrink says you don't help my self-esteem." She'd been rejected for being too motherly and for not being nurturing enough; for being too independent and for being too dependent; for giving too much and for giving too little. Powerful women were simply not attractive to men the way powerful men were to women. Sometimes she thought she'd priced herself out of the erection market.

"They don't make ladies like you in Australia. I could bottle you up and make a fortune. Aussie ladies need spice," Gibson was saying.

Nicole licked her lips and thought about what it would be like to kiss him, really kiss him.

"I wish you could meet my woman," he went on. "She would really like you, you'd be a good influence on her."

Nicole's smile withered to a cold professional clench. She could feel the luster evaporate from her eyes. The descent to disappointment gave her stomach the bends, and her mind scurried to protect itself.

"I've spent a year and a half developing this script for you. You are my favorite director." Move this to work, she instructed herself. Go home with something, if not someone.

"Still," Gibson asked, "even after I turned down *Dirty Dreams?*"

"I can't blame you for that one. It's a hot potato."

"Who did you get to direct it?"

"Don't ask, and don't ask why. Anyway, I'm here to talk to you about *Soothsayer.*"

"Tell me the premise of the film," Gibson replied.

Nicole put on her best garment-center-salesman-pitch tone.

"It's an incredible story—and true. It's based on a guy I read about in *Psychology Today,* who was a psychic in the voodoo world of New Orleans. He was a very powerful mind reader who infiltrated the New Orleans police department and one by one compromised its key players for his own insidious purposes. It's kind of film noir meets *Witness.*"

Nicole knew about directors. There were two things they couldn't resist. True stories, and film noir. She threw in *Witness* because it was a safe bet that every Aussie wanted to be Peter Weir.

"I'm crazy about film noir," Gibson said. "How did you know that was what I was looking for?"

"Adult movies are back, thank God," Nicole answered, reeling him in like a fish. This was another line no director in her experience could resist—a line that implied the conspiracy of the intelligentsia.

Although the conversation was back on safer, more familiar ground, Nicole still needed to regroup her thoughts.

"Would you excuse me for a moment?" she asked, getting up to go to the ladies' room in the front of the restaurant. "And order me another greyhound."

*   *   *

Across the restaurant, Bambi Stern sat alone at a table for two. She had been elated to get a call from Lance Burton, inviting her to dinner, even if it did come at six-forty-five. When he asked, she hesitated. *If I say yes, he might wonder why I don't have my own plans for Friday night, but if I say no, I'll be passing up an opportunity to have a date with a man I'm not only attracted to but a man who can also help my career.* Sexual stimulation and job advancement were too tempting a package to jeopardize by playing hard-to-get. Bambi resolved her dilemma by saying no and yes. *No, I'm not free, but yes, I will see you tonight.* She told him she had a couple of parties to go to, but wasn't really in the mood, so missing them would be no sacrifice. When she hung up, she hated herself. Pretending to cancel something to have dinner with him was too accommodating, potentially a worse move than just having accepted in the first place.

She had arrived ten minutes late and had been waiting another fifteen. Fifteen long uncomfortable minutes. To keep from appearing ill-at-ease, she concentrated on all the reasons she had to feel good about herself. *I'm pretty. I'm only twenty-six, and I make more money than a lot of the Phi Beta Kappas I went to school with.* She took a deep breath. The knot in her stomach was still there. Clearly the positive imagery wasn't working. She considered checking her answering machine but decided against it. She'd checked it just ten minutes before, and there'd been no word from Lance or anyone else.

She'd been trying to reach Ted McGuiness all day, and the fact that he hadn't called back did not bode well for their very discreet affair. In the beginning, the phone calls were frequent and exciting in their secrecy. She imagined that he would be her guide, teaching her the shortcuts to the top, advising her, and then, when the moment was right, he would promote her. She had insisted on secrecy because she expected rapid promotions and didn't want anyone saying she fucked her way to the top. Ted insisted on secrecy because he said privacy was the only luxury he really valued anymore. It seemed like a bizarre reason to Bambi, but it was compatible with her desires, so she didn't give it any further thought.

As she took a sip of her Evian water, she noticed Andrew Spencer sitting at the bar. She knew he'd been trying to reach her all day, asking for five minutes, just five minutes to pitch a development deal. This afternoon he wasn't a priority. Now, with Lance late and Morton's full of people who knew her and saw her alone, being in Andrew's company suddenly gained in importance. Besides, he looked especially appealing tonight, she thought.

Andrew was a blond Englishman with a strong jaw and penetrating brown eyes. Something about the way he was nursing his drink with such intensity reminded Bambi of those self-possessed men in Ralph Lauren ads.

She tried to catch his eye so she could invite him over, but soon realized there was no choice but to go over to him.

She stole a quick look in her compact mirror to check her raspberry-glacé lipstick and her smoky-topaz eye shadow. She noticed her blond streaks needed a touch-up, but was otherwise pleased with herself. She adjusted the oversize belt around her white linen dress and hoped that the soles of her new Walter Steiger high heels wouldn't be too slippery for the restaurant's tile and wood floors. Leaving her handbag on the table, she carefully walked toward the bar, keeping an eye on the door, just in case Lance should appear.

"I know the English like to drink alone, but you're in Hollywood now."

Andrew turned around and broke into a grin. No matter how preoccupied he might be, he could always force himself to cheer up and perform when a potential deal was at stake, especially when his checking-account balance was dwindling at an alarming rate.

"Bambi, my favorite mini-mogul. How wonderful to see you." He gave her a warm hug. "Yes, we English are a pensive sort. I was actually thinking about you."

"The term is *baby* mogul," she corrected him, "and what were you thinking . . . not about work, I hope."

"Struggling young producers always think about work. It's not very healthy, but I'm told that's the way it is here. To the English it seems that in Los Angeles everything is work. Even sitting by the bloody pool and getting a suntan is work."

He was trying hard to be entertaining. Although Bambi wasn't really listening to him, she saw how flirtatious he was and enjoyed how he exerted himself to win her approval. He put his arm around her in a gesture that was affectionate and, apparently, harmless.

"Is that true for you too, Bambi? Is everything work for you? You know, one must also live a life."

"Live a life," she repeated thoughtfully. "I love your expressions."

He checked his watch and nervously wondered how Carolyn's "talk" with Paul was going. He missed her.

"Is your dinner date late?" Bambi asked playfully.

"Not really," he replied evasively. He reached for his glass and then stopped. "I'm terribly rude, not offering you a drink. Will you join me?"

She was tempted. It's about time someone plays up to me, she thought. For years she'd been playing up to men like Ted, adapting herself to their needs for her own job security, and she was getting tired of it. I'll have to explore this Andrew connection at a more convenient time, she promised herself.

"I can't. I'm meeting Lance Burton here any minute," she replied, fully savoring the effect caused by dropping his name.

Aware that his time with her was limited and that a relationship with her was worth cultivating, Andrew switched into second gear. "It's a shame we can't talk. I tried calling you this afternoon—"

She held up her hand. "No work talk tonight. One must live a life." She thought that repeating his phrase was cute, but Andrew had a hunch that she was about to incorporate it into her vocabulary and that he'd be hearing it for the next six months.

"It'd be uncivilized to spend the entire evening talking business unless you were a young producer who had to hustle a deal to pay the rent—in which case, it would be perfectly legitimate." He laughed good-naturedly. He got away with telling the ugly truth because he didn't seem to take it seriously. "Well, we should get together to talk some other time." He paused, trying to figure out the best strategy. Lunch was all business and dinner was too intimate. "Let's meet for drinks." Drinks could be interpreted either way.

"Drinks sound good to me. When?" She turned to check the door to see if Lance had shown up, and in so doing came face-to-face with Nicole, passing the bar on her way to the ladies' room.

"Kiss, kiss, Bambi. Anything up, sweetheart?" This was Nicole's name for Bambi. Bambi perceived it as hostile and patronizing, but it was intended innocently.

"Waiting for Lance," Bambi said.

Nicole understood immediately that regardless of what Bambi might think, Lance's motives weren't social. It made her nervous to think of Lance's diabolical mind teaming up with Bambi's raw ambition. As best she could, Nicole covered her nerves with a flippant reply.

"Aren't we all, always. We can count on our beloved Lance to keep us waiting. Later, sweetheart, see you at the B-B-Q on Monday."

"Of course, Nicole, and . . . oh, your outfit is fabulous. Maxfield's?"

Andrew watched with irritation as the two of them exchanged fake pleasantries. Bambi didn't bother to introduce him to Nicole or include him in their chitchat in any way. This shutout annoyed him. He thought it shortsighted of Bambi not to treat him with more respect. Only someone as self-absorbed as this lightweight could be oblivious of his privileged heritage, he concluded.

Andrew had been bred on both sides of the Atlantic,

the Mayfair section of London and the exclusive Montego Bay side of Jamaica. (His maternal grandfather was the British ambassador to the island.) His appreciation of the more casual Caribbean culture mitigated the stuffy mannerisms he'd picked up at English public schools. However, nothing could mitigate his sense of superiority. The fact that his family had entirely depleted the fortune left by his great-grandfather and that the last trickle was barely sufficient to get him through Eton had not dampened his self-image. All it had done was to galvanize him to fully embrace the challenge of refilling the empty ancestral coffers and restoring himself to his natural position of status and ease.

As a testament to his personal power, he'd already, at twenty-five, convinced a goodly number of people of this inevitability. In this effort, he cited his talents as a writer, director, producer, agent—everything save his talents as an actor, which was probably his best suit.

He returned to nursing his drink, and began to analyze these "Hollywood princesses"—so unsophisticated, no matter how many French lessons they'd had or how many ski trips to St. Moritz. It annoyed him that Bambi thought he hadn't earned the right to be part of their "elite club." *She's so provincial,* he thought. *She doesn't realize I was born into the bloody club.*

Nicole's mind was racing as she resumed her trip to the ladies' room. Lance . . . Bambi . . . dinner? *What does that pervert have on his mind? He doesn't waste dinner with an executive on her level. Was he planning to charm Bambi out of any information she had on the Dirty Dreams project? That'll take all of two minutes,* Nicole thought, considering Lance's power of persuasion.

She stepped into the ladies' room and put her bag down on the counter. She pulled out her lipstick and powder and halfheartedly redid her makeup. She was feeling more and more anxious about the way she'd handled Lance's ultimatum. Though Kevin had calmed her fears and supported her position, her intuition told her she had plenty to worry about.

She considered calling Lance to set up a casual meeting over the weekend. Maybe if she could reestablish the rapport they had once had, she could defuse the mounting tension.

At times like this she deeply missed having a man in her life. She thought about how nice it would be to have someone to go home to, someone who would hear her out, offer a perspective, and if worse came to worst, remind her that there was more to life than Millennium's position on the box-office charts.

The door to a toilet stall swung open, interrupting Nicole's reverie. Out walked a classic Beverly Hills housewife, dripping in informal jewelry. Someone's ex-secretary who had scored big, Nicole thought as the woman dropped her purse on the counter next to Nicole's and proceeded to recoat her eyelashes with mascara. This is the kind of woman that powerful men love, Nicole realized. Women they can control with their credit cards. At that moment Nicole knew that no matter how lonely she felt, she wouldn't trade her life for theirs. Alone, she controlled her own destiny. Alone, she made decisions and the world confirmed her. Being a woman mogul might have its romantic drawbacks, but the exhilaration that competence and success brought her could not be bought with credit cards.

"Is this mine of yours?" the classic asked, picking up Nicole's black woven-leather Bottega bag.

"Mine," Nicole answered.

"We all have the same pocketbook," the classic giggled.

Nicole smiled. Yes, but the resemblance ends there.

By the time Carolyn entered the restaurant she was in a frenzy. Immediately she spotted Andrew at the bar. The two of them were practically telepathic, like giraffes, sensing each other's presence, even when out of range.

She brushed past Pam Morton and in her hurry didn't notice her new boss finishing dinner at table number two.

She came up quietly and kissed Andrew's check.

"How'd it go?" he asked, his face showing concern as he waited for her words to support his natural optimism.

"He didn't show," she exclaimed. "He called to say he'd be arriving sometime in the next few days. He wasn't sure when."

She sat on the bar stool next to Andrew's and tried to catch the bartender's attention. She knew she was about to cry, and looked for some distraction that might stem the tears.

"Did you tell him you were moving out?" Andrew asked.

"No," Carolyn replied softly. "I can't have that conversation with him over the phone. We got into a fight as it was."

The bartender was busy making a margarita, and Carolyn's efforts to wave him over went unnoticed.

Andrew gripped her arm to pull her attention back. "Darling, you can't postpone this thing. Paul could drag out this breakup for weeks, maybe months. It's not in your best interest."

Andrew wasn't happy with Carolyn's reluctance to call it quits. He didn't doubt her intention to leave Paul, but he'd seen too many girls opt for security over passion. He needed her to break off cleanly and irreversibly.

"I know, I know," she agreed, "it's just that—"

Andrew cut her off. "It's just that he'd rather put you on hold to make his life more convenient. Isn't that what he's always done? You started a new job today. I bet he didn't even ask you about it."

"No, he didn't," she admitted, "but I didn't really give him a chance to."

Her defense of her soon-to-be-ex infuriated Andrew. "Carolyn, for the last four weeks you and I have been together every day and night. We've started something together. Paul is your past. You don't need his blessing to get on with your new life. You don't owe him anything but the truth."

"I just can't move out while he's gone," she argued.

Andrew sighed. "Darling, do you think he's going to bed alone at night? When was the last time he invited you to join him on one of his road trips?"

Andrew knew he was being a little too blunt. It wasn't his preferred way of operating, but he had been counting on a different outcome to the evening.

"It's not easy . . . not easy," she repeated, her eyes tearing. "Oh, great," she apologized. "Just what you always wanted, to be at Morton's with a girl who can't keep from crying."

Andrew put a consoling arm around her and picked up a cocktail napkin to catch the tiny tears that were welling up in the corner of each eye. He kept his frustration in check and tried another approach.

"Did I ever tell you how attached I am to you?" He was using his storytelling voice. "Did I ever tell you I am going to capture you and take you off to a castle in Scotland, make you bear my children and wait faithfully for me to come back from the wars?"

Carolyn smiled through her tears. "I think I've heard that a few times."

"Can I get you anything?" It was the bartender, intruding on their private moment.

"Some Visine and Valium," Carolyn joked.

"A bottle of Perrier-Jouet. Put it on my tab," Andrew instructed. "We'll take it with us."

Carolyn looked at him questioning. His tab? A dangerous thing for Andrew to have. She wondered how he had talked Peter Morton into that one. And buying champagne at a restaurant? Not a very budget-conscious move, she thought, but his spirit delighted her.

"Where are we going?" she asked.

"To dinner, but not here. Unless you really want to."

"You've got something else in mind?"

"How about some fried chicken from Maurice's Snack 'n' Chat?"

"Really?" She perked up. "You'd do that? You hate fried chicken. I thought it was too greasy for your refined tastes," she teased.

"Fried chicken and champagne. A nighttime picnic," he suggested.

"Let's see . . ." She feigned indecisiveness. "I can have my favorite fried chicken under the stars, with the man I love, or . . . I can stay here and have goat cheese on lettuce in a room filled with agents who were rude to me on the phone all day. Hmmmm. A tough choice."

Andrew laughed. "Is that all it takes to make you happy? Fried chicken?"

"It's a start," she replied, slipping her arm around him. "What can I say? I admit it—I'm a love junkie."

"My love junkie," he corrected.

"Where are we going?" Carolyn giggled as Andrew drove his Fiat convertible up to the chained entrance of the Neiman-Marcus parking structure. It was late and Carolyn had been looking forward to collapsing onto Andrew's California king-size bed. Between first-day-on-the-job exhaustion, her disquieting conversation with Paul, and the champagne picnic, she was ready to crash.

Andrew answered her by inching the car forward. With his left hand he reached out, grabbed the chain, and held it up over the windshield.

"Could you get your side?" he asked.

Carolyn, already complying, asked, "What *are* you doing?"

Andrew carefully accelerated until the car slipped beneath the chain and he'd successfully maneuvered them inside the barrier.

"This is Beverly Hills. Beverly Hills is big on security," Carolyn scolded. Being there reminded her of her overdue Neiman's bill. It had been sitting on her kitchen counter for weeks because she couldn't face the damage she'd done. On an impulse last month, she'd charged six pairs of pink socks, a forty-dollar jar of Sisley face cream, and a great Chanel scarf. Shopping could boost her mood, but the jolt lasted only fifteen minutes. In retrospect she decided she could have lived without the scarf and socks.

Andrew shut off the headlights, his only concession to her concern about their trespassing. With the streetlamps lighting the open-air parking structure, he continued up to level two. The sound of the tires screeching around the sharp corners bounced off the walls. Carolyn looked about, expecting to see a flashlight, a policeman, a Westec Security guard, or a lunatic. Even Beverly Hills had its share of bag ladies, bums, and crazies. Andrew, unfazed, drove all the way up to the roof before stopping. He lowered the back of his seat and gazed up at the stars and half-moon. The noise of a Ferrari careening down Wilshire Boulevard pierced the silence.

"I like it up here," he said. "I don't know why."

"Do you come here often?" Carolyn asked. Has he been here with other girls? she wondered.

"Never," he replied. "I've driven down this street a hundred times, and it never occurred to me—"

"It never occurred to you to sneak under the chain of a deserted parking structure?" she teased. "I can't imagine why not."

He laughed, opened the glove compartment, rifled through the contents, knocking out a half-dozen parking tickets before he finally found the key he was looking for. He jumped out of the car and unlocked the trunk. Digging through towels, books, and a beach chair, he pulled out an old red jacket and tossed it to her. Gratefully she took it and put it on.

Warm and cozy now, she pushed down the back of her car seat. She relaxed with her legs stretched out and her feet resting on the dashboard. She did kind of like it up here, she decided . . . up on the roof, their private island in the middle of Wilshire Boulevard. Expecting Andrew to join her, she was surprised when he opened the door, pulled her out, and pushed her up against the back side of the Fiat.

He embraced her, his hands slipping underneath the jacket. As tired as she was, she loved his touch on her bare shoulders and the way he confidently took hold of her. She cuddled closer, still distracted by the possibility of someone discovering them. Was that a light that just flashed in the Mitsui Manufacturing building across the street? She turned her head away, nestling her cheek on the soft cotton of his pale blue shirt. Her sleepy eyes traced the curve of his neck. She loved every inch of his body. His effect on her was so potent that she was able to conjure it up even when they were apart. Portable eroticism, she called it.

Suddenly Andrew's hands were in her hair and his lips eagerly sought hers. They kissed, a long slow kiss, delaying for a moment the desire surging in both of them. Unable to sustain the limbo, Carolyn became the aggressor. She grappled with the zipper of his pants while he undid the jacket and pushed up the front of her T-shirt. Like a souped-up Corvette, their sexual frenzy could go from zero to sixty in ten seconds. They knew how to bring each other along fast, and, once there, knew how to control it. Sixty to a hundred could take all night if they wanted it to.

The light in the Mitsui building flashed again, but Carolyn ignored it.

"I've made love on beaches," she whispered. "I've made love in a park, I've even made love in an olive grove, but this is—"

"You slut," Andrew growled in a tone both provocative and dirty.

"Yes, I am. All for you, everything and anything for you," she agreed as she pulled up her short denim skirt.

Sometimes their attraction to each other was so intense it seemed to border on obsession. Were they two lovers consummating a passionate craving? Or was it more like two addicts getting a fix? Whatever, Carolyn knew Neiman-

Marcus would never be the same for her. No longer would it be a place she associated with great socks, Chanel scarfs, and fancy creams. Now it would forever be a reminder of Andrew's face in the half-moonlight, the feel of the Fiat against the back of her thighs, and the realization as he pushed inside her that nothing else mattered. Whatever doubts she might have had about leaving Paul, one thing was indisputable. She couldn't imagine ever giving up Andrew. That's it, she decided. Tomorrow is moving day.

4

The minutes alone at the table were piling up like demerits on Bambi's public report card. It wasn't like Lance had stranded her at a low-profile table. No. She had to be stood up at table number one. And she'd already exhausted everything she could think of to do to look busy. She'd flirted with a hopeful, taken out her agenda and jotted down notes. She'd waved to other development executives and kissed the cheek of every agent in the room. She wished she could just slip out quietly, but had ruined that option by bragging to Nicole about dining with Lance. It seemed that everyone was looking at her, about to laugh.

Pam Morton approached Bambi's table with a sympathetic nod. "Lance is calling."

"Can you bring the phone to the table?" Bambi asked.

"This is not the Polo Lounge, Bambi. You can take the call at the desk."

Anxious not to stir too much attention, Bambi headed to the reservations desk. She brightened her smile as she picked up the blinking line, just in case anyone coming out of the bathroom might be watching.

"Where the fuck are you?" Bambi drawled, almost southern.

"On my way out of town, sweetheart. Sorry. Emergency came up. Business."

"Aren't I business, Lance?" She was still pushing.

"No, Bambi. You are pleasure, pure unadulterated pleasure."

Lance made it hard to stay mad. Even over the phone he eroticized her.

"But everyone who is anyone in this town is watching you stand me up. If it's not business for you, at least appreciate that humiliating me in public is business, bad business for me." There. She'd stood up for herself, she thought.

"Cute, very cute," Lance said. "But very conventional. Come on, you're not one of those silly development sluts who think work is a popularity contest. Your ambition forces you to be unconventional. That's what I've always liked about you. That's what makes you hot."

This made Bambi purr. "Unconventional." She liked the hook of it. She was thrilled that Lance viewed her as different from the others, different from Nicole. But Lance's compliments didn't help her get enough courage to march back through the dining area. To collect her purse, she still had to run the gamut of inquiring agents and competitors.

"What do you suggest I say?" she asked. "Lance had better things to do?"

"Say fuck you. See you in court. Have your people call my people. Eat my dust. You'll think of something."

"But, Lance . . ." Bambi pleaded, "there was so much I wanted to talk to you about . . . ideas I had for *Dirty Dreams*—"

Lance interrupted sweetly, "There will be plenty of time for that, Bambi. You and I are going to play great together, because we're two of a kind. See you at my house Monday. You're coming to the barbecue, aren't you?"

"Who could refuse you?" she replied coyly. "I'll be there."

Bambi sat in her 450 SL in gridlock traffic in front of the Roxy, watching people line up for the late show. She figured that the congestion on the street meant it would take another twenty minutes to drive the eight blocks home. She sighed anxiously. Ever since leaving Morton's, over an hour before, she'd been driving around aimlessly, not able to call it a night.

Talking to Lance had left her in a highly charged sexual state. She altered the vent on the air conditioner and turned on the fan so cool air blew up her ultra-sheer-stockinged legs. The breeze made her even more aware of her garter belt and the reason she'd put it on in the first place. She had dressed in anticipation of undressing.

As the traffic crawled ahead slowly, all she could think about was what might have been. She imagined telling Lance how much she hated it when people told her what to do, but how willing she was to do whatever he wanted. She imagined a scene where he got her so crazy with desire that she begged him to fuck her. She remembered that she had once gone into the Pleasure Chest to buy a joke present and couldn't believe what a supermarket of sex toys the place was. She wore big dark aviator sunglasses so she wouldn't be recognized, and was embarrassed by all the gadgets and leather. She wondered if Lance shopped there. If he did, maybe he could teach her how to work some of the sexual paraphernalia.

The thought of it actually induced a sensation between her legs, and even though she was sitting at a red light in front of Tower Records, she had an urge to touch herself there. One part of her brain told her that to do so was wrong. But another part of her brain told her that it was merely "unconventional," Lance's word.

She slid her hand up her thigh and allowed her fingers to gently explore her G-string. The light switched to green, but the intersection was still jammed. A bus inched up alongside of her. The passengers had a vantage point that allowed them to see right into her Mercedes. Quickly she put both hands back on the steering wheel. She looked around at the other cars stuck in traffic. For the first time in her life, she craved anonymous sex.

Up ahead, she saw a car stalled in front of Le Dome. The traffic behind was at a standstill. Next to her was a

convertible filled with teenage boys from the Valley.
Their radio played "Little Red Corvette." She located
the station on her own radio and upped the volume. She
buzzed her window down all the way. The boys turned to
check her out. She knew she must be a vision of sophistication to them. One of them tried to get her attention by
shouting out lyrics . . . something about what he wanted
to do to her love machine.

Normally Bambi would have stared straight ahead and,
at the first opportunity, changed lanes and accelerated
away from their adolescent leers. But tonight she was in
the mood to be "unconventional." She threw them a
smile before forging ahead through the traffic.

By the time she finally reached Sunset Plaza, where
she was supposed to turn off and head up into the Hollywood Hills to the cozy bungalow her daddy had bought
her, she'd free-associated herself into a condition bordering on nymphomania. She dwelled on Lance's expectations
of her and felt compelled to live up to this new image.
Right in front of a No U-Turns sign, Bambi cut in front
of two honking cars and one beeping Honda motorcycle
and swung back onto Sunset, facing the direction she had
just come from. She checked her watch. It was eleven-
ten. If she drove really fast, she could make it to Ted's by
twelve-thirty and be in bed with him by twelve-forty-five.
I'll surprise him, she decided, stunning herself with the
confidence of her decision.

When she arrived at the beach house, she parked out
front and peered over the fence. Ted's car was in the
driveway and there was a light on in the living room. The
house was a contemporary design, white walls with a
curved glass-brick entrance. Bambi quietly opened the
gate and headed down a flower-lined path. The sound of
an early reveler lighting a firecracker somewhere along
the Pacific Coast Highway made her jump.

She tiptoed around to the side of the house. She felt
like a "backdoor girl," which intensified her excitement.

Through the window she could see him. He was reclining on his pony-skinned Le Corbusier lounge chair, reading the trades. His video recorder replayed dailies from something. She tapped on the window, startling him. When he saw her in the plate glass, Ted's first thought was that there was a problem at the studio.

"What are you doing here?" He was at the door, talking in a loud whisper and looking confused and sleepy in his gray flannel robe.

Bambi forced herself to cross into a verbal territory she'd never explored before. "I need to see you. I'll make it worth your while."

"Worth my while?" Ted studied her as she took a moment, like an actress, pausing, preparing herself for a monologue.

"I've got an uncontrollable desire to do a striptease for you. I've been thinking about it all night."

Ted could not believe what he was hearing. She sounded like a second-rate player in a fifties sleaze film.

"Are you crazy, Bambi? Are you on a drug? Did you take an ecstasy pill?"

Boldly she turned on some music. Tempted to choose Ravel's *Bolero*, she rejected the idea as being much too derivative. She settled for an oldie from Sade's first album, "Smooth Operator," a song she thought could have been written for Lance. "Sit back, Ted. Come on, I know you'll love this."

Does she think she's some kind of sex kitten? he wondered.

She unbuttoned her dress, stepped out of it, and left it in a heap on the floor. She moved with the music, trying to imitate Melanie Griffith in *Body Double,* the closest thing she'd ever seen to a porno movie. She was wearing the expensive lingerie that she'd put on for Lance—a lacy ivory camisole, matching G-string and garter belt.

She looked appealing enough, Ted thought. Her petite body with sizable breasts had always been his ideal type. But other than the obvious sexual attraction, he felt absolutely nothing for her. He didn't want her spending the night, but he wouldn't turn down a quickie. Without committing himself, he encouraged her. "You seem quite prepared for this."

"I've been thinking about you all day," Bambi lied, giving him her best Playmate-of-the-Month coy smile. "I want you to get turned on like you were getting turned on for the first time." She removed her camisole and massaged her nipples.

She was beginning to feel like an erotic dancer, as if the lid to her libido had been slipped open and the "Flashdancer" in her was emerging. Bambi bent over in front of Ted and stuck out her ass. This is a rehearsal for my nights with Lance, she thought. She imagined how Lance would take control of her. Nothing would be off limits. He'd massage her, spank her, lick her all over. With each mental image, she felt herself letting go of twenty-six years of inhibitions. Forget her Grace Kelly dream. At the moment she was more interested in being Grace Jones.

She faced Ted. Her breasts fell in front of him. She offered them to his mouth while her hand moved down his body. "How hard are you?" Her body looked appetizing and Ted felt ready to plunge into her, but he couldn't shake the awareness that her "act," once over, would appear pathetic.

She opened his robe and reached between his legs. "Tell me you want it," she demanded.

He didn't need to answer. He pulled her on top of him, pushed aside the narrow bit of lace of her G-string, and thrust inside of her. He was not really fucking Bambi, he realized. He'd abstracted her. Turned her into a nightcap, nothing more. As Bambi built toward an orgasm, she tightened the grip of her legs around his waist and dug her perfectly manicured nails into his back. "Hold my hands back," she ordered him. "Hold them back."

Ted didn't respond immediately. Lance would have,

she thought, as Ted belatedly pulled her arms behind her arched back.

"Yes, yes," she cried out. She rode him, first sitting up straight, swaying back and forth like a child on a rocking horse, and then bucking furiously up and down, wild with lust. She came in a wave of excitement that began like a mild tremor and escalated to a crescendo that had her screaming with pleasure.

She lifted herself off him. He was harder than she'd ever seen him and she wanted very much to satisfy him like a courtesan would. She licked his chest and worked her way down. Ted roughly grabbed her hair and controlled the rhythm of her mouth with his grasp until he exploded. The two of them, still breathing heavily, sat motionless for a couple of minutes.

Bambi was the first to move. She got up and retrieved her clothes, pleased with herself. She headed for the bathroom to freshen up, passing a hallway bookshelf stacked with scripts. Surreptitiously she checked to see what Ted was reading this weekend. At the bottom of the stack she found *Dirty Dreams,* and quietly slipped it into her purse. My homework for the barbecue, she gloated, doubly pleased.

When she emerged fully dressed, Ted was surprised. Clearly she had no intention of hanging around. She strutted toward the bemused Ted. "This is not the Bambi you're used to, is it? I'm very modern these days."

Ted was speechless. "Modern" wasn't exactly the adjective he would have chosen.

Bambi emerged from the beach house exhilarated by her unconventionality. She got into her car but didn't switch on the ignition right away. She sat there with the door open, taking in the sea air, invigorated by it and the certainty that whenever the call from Lance came, she would be ready to perform.

5

Joey Martucci was ready to talk. Though he was not usually an avid conversationalist, the two lines of cocaine he'd just done had put him in a social mood. As he sat in his penthouse suite at Caesar's Palace in Las Vegas, he fiddled with the remote control to the TV.

"Look at this," he said to Al, his assistant. "Cops-and-robbers crap. Hollywood doesn't know shit about the street. This is a fuckin' comic book."

"Tell me about it." Al understood that his job called for him not only to be an errand boy but also to shore up his boss's ego.

Joey tried another channel—a love scene from some dated movie of the week.

"Look at those tits," he said.

Al nodded. "She looks like the stripper you used to play around with. What was her name?"

"Darlene," Joey replied. "Wasn't it? Or was it Donna? Can't keep track," he laughed. He enjoyed this image of himself as a playboy, but the truth was he was never very comfortable with that role. Though he was the son of a New York Mafia don, Joey's big-city upbringing had not given him the cavalier attitude toward pleasure that most of his peer group had. Too many early years in catechism with Sister Mary Theresa (who lectured on how all men must ultimately suffer for their sins) had robbed him of much of his fun. Her words had been drilled into him and had embedded themselves into his consciousness, and now, like a low-grade infection, kept him from ever feeling really well. He could have a lot of laughs on a Saturday night, but inevitably woke up the next morning feeling like the Fredo Corleone of the family. Only around Lance did Joey feel in top form. In Lance's world, Sunday morning—time of penance and regret—never came.

"What time is Lance's plane due?" Joey asked, switching from the movie of the week to MTV.

"Nine-thirty," Al replied. He hated Joey's habit of listening to heavy-metal music. It gave him a headache.

"Who's he bringing, again?" Joey asked.

"Someone named David Beach. I think he works at the studio."

Joey lowered the volume on the "Guns 'n' Roses" song. "You ever been on a studio lot?"

"Naah."

"Naah? What does that mean? You don't like movie stars? You don't like hanging out in Tinsel Town?"

Al shrugged. "Not my kind of place. People out there put goat cheese on their pizza. They drink decaf espresso."

Joey laughed. He liked this older man who seemed to want nothing more than to keep his job and on his days off spend time with his family in Queens.

"You wouldn't move out to L.A. if I set up some business out there?"

"You thinking of doing that, boss?"

Joey leaned over the glass table and did another line. "Could be," he said as he inhaled the fine white powder that took the edge off his confusion. "It depends," he added, his mind playing out all the variables it in fact did depend upon. He switched the channel back to the cops-and-robbers show. "Is everything set up for tonight?"

"All set," Al replied. "Poker game'll start around one. Your dinner reservation's at ten-thirty and there are some broads on hold if anyone's in the mood."

Although Joey had asked for this recap, he hardly paid attention to the response. His mind dwelled on a more important matter. "I've got some business to discuss with Lance," he blurted out. "You'll have to entertain this

David Beach guy for a half an hour or so." He pulled ten
one-hundred-dollar bills out of his pocket and dropped
them on the table. "Let him roll some dice."

"Sure, boss."

Joey was tempted to fill his trusted aide in on more,
but held back. He wanted to be sure the information he
had on Kevin Holberstein was worth something before
he started bragging about it.

He leaned his head back on the couch and thought
about what it would be like to get out from under the
yoke of his father and brother and have his own scene on
the west coast. He was tired of New York. He was tired
of Vegas. He was hungry for a change.

For all his efforts to pass himself off as someone who
wouldn't shy away from adventure (he'd even bought a
Harley), the truth was, David Beach was afraid of flying.
From the second he set foot on a plane, to the second the
aircraft touched down, David Beach had to struggle to
keep his anxiety under control. Much to his surprise, that
wasn't (yet) the case this time. As he relaxed in his cushy
leather seat on Millennium's twelve-seater jet, he felt
completely calm. While he waited for Lance, the only
other passenger, to board, he perused the list of videos
that were part of the plane's film library and nibbled on
the fruits and cheeses that the steward had presented to
him on a platter.. The door to the cockpit was open and
he was aware that the pilot and copilot were going through
their preflight preparations. Surprisingly, this didn't un-
settle him. David Beach had the feeling that on this
well-serviced company plane, nothing bad could happen.

"Nothing like it, pal, is there? This your first time?"
Lance asked as he ambled in and took his seat across
from David Beach.

As he spoke, the steward closed the door behind them
and the captain began to taxi slowly onto the runway.

"Being a junior executive doesn't qualify you for these
kinds of perks," David Beach replied.

Lance smiled. He liked playing David Beach's guide to the big time. He also liked keeping this ambitious young executive off balance. "I just spoke with Bambi," he said.

"What's she up to?" David Beach was trying hard to sound carefree.

"She's at home," Lance lied, "rereading *Dirty Dreams* and making a list of casting suggestions."

David Beach paled at the thought of Bambi becoming an active part of Lance's team. Quickly he sought to even the score. "I've been meaning to talk to you about a location I found for the nightclub scene in *Dirty Dreams*," he said. "There's a place called Tangiers in South Hollywood, opens at two A.M., closes at noon. I call it the place where the yuppies meet the junkies. You can go up to the bar and order a Corona and two lines, no questions asked."

"You're kidding?" Lance was impressed with David Beach's thorough coverage of the after-hours scene.

"You should check it out," David Beach suggested.

"I'll have to stop by on my way to the studio some morning," Lance laughed.

David Beach felt relieved. Bringing up Tangiers was a good move, he decided. Maybe he and Lance could even hang out there together. David Beach had long understood that hanging out with the right people was the best job security in the world.

Lance gazed out the window as the plane pulled into position for takeoff. "You spend much time in Vegas?" he asked.

"Not much," David Beach admitted. "A couple of wild weekends, bachelor parties, that kind of thing."

"You ever hear of a guy called Joey Martucci?"

"He sounds like a native of Vegas," David Beach answered, trying to be clever.

Lance chuckled. "You might say his forefathers were early settlers, and for the next twenty-four hours you're going to see just how the natives play."

Lance enjoyed his connection to the Mafia. He was fascinated with their unaccountable power and wanted access to it. He felt it would be the ultimate insurance policy. No one in Hollywood would fuck with him if his connection to Joey's family was known. He wasn't worried about any possible negative backlash from this hoped-for association. In fact, he romanticized the alliance. There were precedents that validated this kind of thing. Historically, some of the best-known performers and studio heads had befriended members of the "major families," especially in the early days of Vegas. It suited Lance to have one foot in that tradition and another in the club of young mavericks who were defining the New Hollywood. Besides, Joey was someone who appreciated a good time. Lance could easily get into that, especially since it helped him establish a tie to what he considered Mafia royalty.

As Lance hooked on his seat belt, David Beach's eyes were fixed on the digital speedometer located on the wall outside the cockpit door. He'd never seen a gadget like this one, which allowed the passengers to know just how fast they were traveling. As the plane's speed increased and its wheels left the ground, David Beach's usual anxiety was nonexistent. What a difference top-of-the-line equipment makes, he thought. Maybe money can't buy happiness, but at times like this it can sure buy peace of mind.

By the time Lance and David Beach finally arrived at the penthouse suite, Joey was tongue-tied. While waiting for them he'd had a few shots of vodka and had rehearsed in his mind a number of different ways to bring up the subject he was obsessed with. He thought about just casually mentioning to Lance that he'd been thinking about investing in the movie business. Then he considered being more forthright and asking Lance outright how he should go about setting up shop in Hollywood. He even toyed with the idea of pretending that someone had already approached him about getting involved with the financing of a project. Maybe that, he hoped, would inspire Lance to do the same. He mulled over all these possibilities without zeroing in on any one of them.

And then there was the Kevin Holberstein business. Joey had lured Lance to Vegas with a promise of some interesting information he had for him. Would it be interesting enough to expect some favor in return? Joey found his game plan getting fuzzier and fuzzier, and the situation wasn't helped by this David Beach kid, he decided.

At first glance, Joey took a dislike to him. He was everything Joey wasn't. He was blond and blue-eyed and glib. Joey had slicked-back black hair, dark eyes, and was talentless when it came to repartee. David Beach looked much younger than his twenty-six years, whereas Joey looked older than his age of thirty-three. Though only seven years separated them, David Beach had the sensibility of the Brat Pack while Joey operated like one of the now-extinct Rat Pack.

For the last twenty minutes while they sat around in the suite having a drink before heading downstairs to dinner, Joey's agitation had increased. Normally he wouldn't have cared who Lance brought with him—the more the merrier—but tonight, at least for a half-hour, he needed Lance's undivided attention. He was about to signal to Al that it was time for him to show their young guest around when David Beach, trying to impress all present, launched into a Hollywood anecdote.

The story was triggered by a Prince video showing on MTV.

"Did I ever tell you about the meeting I had with Prince last year?" David Beach addressed this question to Lance but didn't wait for a reply. "He submitted this treatment to Millennium which, I tell you, made no sense at all. So I called for a meeting and he showed up with *three* managers. One was, get this, his interpreter. Can you believe that? Anyway, Prince walks in wearing emerald-green toreador pants, a green sequin vest, tuxedo jacket, and green snake cowboy boots. Ted turns to me and whispers, 'Thank God, I was going to wear that today.' Anyway, I spend twenty minutes doing a treatise on why the treatment isn't a movie and how to fix it. I wait for a response. Nothing. So I said, 'Well, Prince, what do you think?' He looks down and says, 'I wear green shoes.' We all look blank. 'What does that mean?' I ask. Prince then points to his interpreter for decoding. Can you believe that?"

Lance feigned a baffled look. "Didn't that same thing happen to David Geffen?"

David Beach panicked. In fact, it was David Geffen who had told him this story, but it wasn't a widely known incident so he'd foolishly gambled on being able to pass it off as his own. "Well, maybe it did happen to him too," David Beach explained. "I mean, anything is possible with rock stars."

Joey knew this was his moment for action. The mood had been broken and the timing was right. "Hey, Al," he said as if the idea had just occurred to him, "you should show David Beach around the casino." Turning to his guest, he added, "Lance and I will meet you at the restaurant at around ten-thirty."

David Beach couldn't conceal his disappointment. He knew he was being dismissed and didn't like it one bit. He looked to Lance for a cue.

"Try your luck," was all Lance said.

"Or change your luck," Joey added.

David Beach looked over at him, wondering if that comment was meant to be as subtly insulting as it sounded.

Joey smiled. "All I'm saying is, you can't win if you don't play."

David Beach decided to handle this scene by doing what he did best—riding the horse in the direction it was going. "I'll see you guys at ten-thirty and don't be surprised if my pockets are full. Blackjack's my game."

With that he turned and followed Al out of the suite.

*   *   *

The minute they were alone, Joey pulled a plastic bag out of his pocket and poured out more than an ample amount of cocaine. He did it to buy time. Now that he had an opportunity to talk to Lance, he wasn't sure how to begin.

"What are you trying to do, turn me into a fast-lane casualty?" Lance laughed as Joey measured out four very thick lines. Lance joked about the amount of drugs present, but he wasn't kidding. He'd seen too many friends, cokeaholics, turn old overnight. He was too vain not to be moderate about substances that affected his appearance, but he also knew Joey was counting on him to be in a party mood. *I'll be moderate back in L.A.,* he decided as he inhaled his half of the powder laid out on the tabletop.

"Smooth stuff," Lance declared.

Joey beamed.

"You always have the best," Lance added, knowing Joey needed these kinds of strokes.

"Yeah, well . . ." Joey replied. He didn't know how to handle the compliments he craved.

Underneath this small talk, both of them knew a bigger issue was at stake. Lance was the one who finally brought it to the surface. "So what's up, Joey?" he asked. "Your phone call definitely intrigued me."

Joey poured himself more vodka but didn't take a sip. He laid the glass down and sat forward on the edge of his seat.

"Remember a couple of weeks ago when I was talking to you about *Dirty Dreams,* 'cause I'm kinda interested in the film business?"

"Yeah," Lance replied somewhat coolly. He knew Joey was anxious to get a foothold in movies, but it wasn't a topic that fascinated Lance.

"Well," Joey continued, "you were talking about the assholes at the studio you got to deal with, and you mentioned a couple of the executives. I'm not great with names, but this Kevin Holberstein name sounded famil-

iar. Only I couldn't figure out why, so I didn't say anything. But I kept thinking about it, and checked out a
couple of things, and turns out maybe I know something
that could be useful to you."

"You know Kevin Holberstein?" Lance was amazed.

"He's around thirty-five, right?"

"Right."

"Red hair?"

Lance nodded.

"Kevin Holberstein from New York . . . a fag."

"What do you mean? Kevin's not gay."

"Well, he was when I first heard of him."

"Who told you?"

"Told me? I saw. The family has videotapes of Kevin
and some guy in a hotel room in New Jersey."

Lance was looming over Joey now, his intensity and
energy turned on full blast. "Tell me everything."

"Well, you know about Kevin's career in politics?"
Joey was relishing his role as a teller of tales for a
change.

"Career?" Lance was dismissive. "He considered running for some local office. Dropped out during the pri-
maries. Said he wasn't interested in eating chicken Kiev
and making no money."

"That's not the way I heard it," Joey said. "Kevin was
making a name for himself, building a following, getting
a lot of attention for his campaign promise to crack down
on the mob. One day my father gets a call from one of
his boys who works down on the docks. He says he-
knows-a-guy-who-knows-a-guy kind of thing. Turns out
Kevin's got something going with a trick who hangs out
at a bar near the docks."

"So, they made tapes?" Lance was pressing now.

"Knowing something means shit," Joey reminded him.
"Proving something means everything. So," Joey went
on, relishing the attention he was getting from Lance, "I
get the assignment. I gotta get the evidence. It just so
happens I knew a guy who worked in the hotel in Atlan-

tic City where Kevin and his boyfriend used to meet. It's not hard to set up a hidden camera. Shit, the government does it all the time," he laughed.

"Then what?" Lance asked impatiently. "Once you had the evidence."

Joey took his time with the dramatic punch line. "Well, then, you might say, Kevin was inducted into the service."

The realization that Kevin had been the mob's man in Hollywood shot through Lance's system like the pure pharmaceutical cocaine he used to free-base in the old days.

"Where are the tapes now? Can you get them? Have them sent to me today?" Lance's words were coming out like artillery.

For the first time since he'd brought it up, it occurred to Joey that maybe he'd blurted out something that was confidential family business, not just some gossip he could parlay. The doubt made him uneasy. "I don't know, Lance. It was, I don't know . . . maybe ten, twelve years ago."

"Joey, my friend . . . look." Lance tried, but failed, to tone down his aggressiveness. "One day, that's all I need. Get me the tapes for twenty-four hours. No one will know. It's a small favor to ask, but I won't forget it."

"I'll see what I can do," Joey gave in. "What's in it for me?"

"Call now," Lance pressed harder.

"Jesus, Lance, it's Friday night."

"So what?" Lance replied.

Joey massaged his eyes as if that would ward off what looked like trouble on the horizon. It wouldn't be long before he started to slip into the night's downward spiral. Already he was beginning to feel the accumulated effect of his indulgences.

Lance had traveled this spiral with Joey many times before. He reached for the quickest antidote to the fatigue he now saw in front of him. He handed Joey the rolled-up fifty-dollar bill he'd used to do the coke.

"So what do you say?" Lance asked as Joey partook of another dose of instant stimulation. "A little business between friends? After all, if you're going to be executive producer of *Dirty Dreams*, we've got to get used to being in the trenches together."

"Executive producer. I like the sound of that." Joey grinned. Maybe, he thought, I'm not being a chump. Maybe this is the way business gets done. "I'll track the tapes down in the morning," he agreed.

By the time the two of them walked into the restaurant downstairs, they were laughing and looking like the brothers Joey truly wanted them to be.

6

Melrose Avenue in Hollywood was a novel in motion, so it was natural for Carolyn to love having a writing office there. She loved what she called "the fifty-seven varieties of fanatics" right outside her window. There were fifties fanatics shopping at Cowboys and Poodles, sixties fanatics reviving the paisley/madras look, seventies fanatics covered in glitter, and eighties fanatics wearing pounds of junk jewelry. Even so, it wasn't the view outside her window or the convenient location, upstairs from Tommy Tang's Thai Restaurant and across the street from Johnny Rocket's diner, that sold her on the space. It was the pink walls. They were the most beautiful shade of pink she'd ever seen. Just being in that room made her feel peaceful.

Paul had rented the place for her. It was yet another one of his generous gifts. He'd kiddingly claimed he did it in self-defense. The apartment they shared had become cluttered with books and papers, and one wall was nearly covered with the index cards she used to plot out a screenplay. She had dozens of stories she wanted to write, and planned on finishing them all inside her new pink space. She had stories about Frankie, the small-time Mafia lord from her hometown. Stories about Dougie, the Newport, Rhode Island, preppie who dated her girlfriend before falling in love with an Upper East Side hooker. Stories about Nancy, the most popular girl in her high school, who, now, at twenty-five, was married to a gas-station attendant, had three kids, and was having an affair with a nineteen-year-old ex-con. Stories about Antoinette Wilkes, a classmate from Brown and a candidate for the Edie Sedgwick self-destruction award. Paul was always amused by these stories, but never considered them anything more than a hobby. The writing office might have been generous, but it was no different from humoring a weekend photographer with a Hasselblad.

All afternoon on this oppressively hot Saturday, Carolyn and her best friend, Lou, had been organizing and packing everything into moving boxes. Lou excelled in packing, having been through six boarding schools before she got to Brown, and three dorms and three apartments before graduating from the university. Her octogenarian father and her fifty-year-old stepmother considered her a "problem" and thought it best that her trust fund not be given to her until she was forty. This announcement had only one effect on her. It made her even more committed to being a self-supporting stylist. Someday, hopefully, she'd do movie sets, but in the meantime she already had some success with her hole-in-the-wall Fixtures shop on Melrose.

Lou took a swig out of her bottle of sparkling apple juice and did a quick inventory of what had to be moved. A typewriter, a rickety table, two white plastic chairs ($3.98 apiece at Builder's Emporium), a few posters, papers, pens, stacks of notebooks, a pink cassette player, a dozen or so tapes, and boxes and boxes of books.

As Carolyn taped up one of the book boxes, the door was suddenly swung open. Paul stood there with a look that immediately made Carolyn feel like a villainess.

"Nice, Carolyn, really nice," he said, his voice full of sarcasm. "I love coming home to our apartment and seeing all your stuff in boxes waiting to be moved out. That's a respectful way to end our relationship."

All the doubts that Carolyn had suppressed in Andrew's company now consumed her. She couldn't blame Paul for being angry. He was right: they should have talked first. "I tried to tell you on the phone," she replied.

Paul looked over at Lou accusingly, as if she were responsible for Carolyn's sudden decision.

"Lou had nothing to do with this," Carolyn pointed out quickly.

"I'm going downstairs to get an iced tea," Lou said, knowing she had no place in this scenario. She picked up a copy of *Rolling Stone* that was in one of the open boxes. "Take your time," she said to both of them. She meant it to sound impartial and understanding, but to Paul it sounded snide.

"Thanks, Lou," he shot back as she headed down the hallway. "I wouldn't want to interfere with your busy life."

"You don't have to be rude to her," Carolyn said softly. "I'm the one at fault. I should have told you I was moving out."

"So tell me now, Carolyn, and I'd like the truth, not just something that reads well."

"The truth is . . ." She paused. "The truth is, I want us to be friends."

Paul laughed. "Friends? Does that mean I get to stand up front on the sidelines and watch you go off with someone else? Not my idea of a fun time."

"Well, our relationship hasn't been a lot of fun for me lately," Carolyn said.

"Now, what is that supposed to mean?"

"It means we don't work together. It only works at all when I'm the one standing on the sidelines cheering you on."

"Are you telling me that's why you're leaving?" Paul demanded. "Are you telling me there's no one else in the picture?"

Carolyn had hoped this would be a two-step process. First they'd break up, and later on she'd tell Paul about Andrew. She didn't want to link the two choices, but she couldn't ignore Paul's question.

"I have been seeing Andrew Spencer," she admitted.

Paul's eyes flashed with anger and then he let out a bitter laugh. "Andrew Spencer? Are you kidding me? What is this, something you're doing to get back at me for a couple of meaningless flings I had on the road? Do you have any idea what kind of reputation he has?"

"You don't understand." Carolyn searched for the words that would communicate what Andrew meant to her without implying some deficiency in Paul. "He's a source of detoxification in my life," she blurted out, hating how pretentious that sounded.

"What the fuck are you talking about?" Paul stood in the middle of the room, his body, taut, aggressive, ready to do battle.

"It means . . ." She halted. How could she explain that the relentless pessimism that haunted her childhood simply vanished in Andrew's presence? That she admired Andrew's breeziness, his ability to turn a difficult situation into something that seemed only marginally consequential? "I'm trying to say," she went on, "that it's not easy to live here. L.A. is a very toxic place, and I'm not talking about the smog. Andrew helps me deal with that."

Paul stepped away in anger, only to immediately return. "That's great, Carolyn. He helps you with the smog, and what do you help him with, his rent?"

"Oh, please, you can't be serious," Carolyn replied. "If Andrew was looking for financial aid, he wouldn't be with someone who makes a dollar-fifty."

"Have it your way," Paul replied, ready to give up the fight, until another thought popped into his head. "You know you have a unique mind but terrible survival skills."

At first Carolyn laughed, amazed at his arrogant judgment, but she couldn't brush off the remark. "I survive fine," she insisted, as much to herself as to him.

"Yeah, you were doing so well when I met you. That room you were renting in that hellhole apartment in the Valley—now, that's what I call surviving."

"Survival isn't just about living in a fancy apartment," she shouted. "Survival is—"

"Is this the beginning of a sermon?" Paul interjected. "The world according to Carolyn Foster. Spare me."

Carolyn thought about walking out without uttering another word, but couldn't bring herself to do so. At the same time, she wondered if she was crazy to think the conversation could have gone differently. How fair is the truth? she wondered. Seeing how hurt Paul was, she suddenly felt very protective. She wanted to tell him that she still felt such tenderness for him, as if he were a brother. No, closer—a twin. She looked away from Paul. Her eyes fixed on the few mementos still tacked up on the wall. Her favorite photo of the two of them stared back at her. People always said that she and Paul looked like they belonged together—and in this photo, particularly, they seemed like the perfect couple. But time had taught Carolyn that they were in fact very different. He's so all-American, she realized; he could never appreciate my bohemian side.

Breaking the silence, Carolyn attempted to inject some levity into the situation. "I guess we're just two passengers on the love *Titanic*."

Her humor fell flat. "Don't make me a character in one of your little stories," Paul replied.

"Dammit, Paul. That's not what I'm doing. I'm just trying to make the point that we're incompatible. Look," she said, "you're a professional athlete. You've always been very self-motivated, and on those days when you don't wake up with the right spirit, your coach fires you up. I guess I'm not such a great self-motivator, and I've never had any coaching. Maybe I need a little help."

"Grow up, Carolyn. I want to be your boyfriend, not your father."

"Andrew's not my father, and he gives me that kind of help."

Paul didn't even try to hold back a laugh over that

one. "Andrew Spencer—some call him a coach, some call him a gigolo."

"Forget it," Carolyn screamed. "I can't talk to you."

"No, you can talk, Carolyn. You just can't listen," Paul shouted back.

"You're the one who isn't listening," she replied. "Paul, I got tired of being a groupie. At first I was overwhelmed— trips to Paris, London, I didn't notice what was happening. I can't become a writer if I don't take myself seriously, and I can't take myself seriously when you and everyone around you treats me like my function is to look cute and be there when you need to unwind."

Paul was not swayed. "Carolyn, the only person who thought of you as a groupie was you. You're carrying around some kind of inferiority thing from your child-hood that you can't let go of. What are you trying to prove? That you're just as good as the rich college kids you went to school with? Or that you're better because you started off on the poor side of town but you'll beat them all yet? Let it go, Carolyn. Get rid of the master plan and just live your fucking life."

He stormed out onto the tiny terrace that overlooked Melrose Avenue.

Carolyn slumped back, leaned her head against the wall, knowing Paul was right about this too. She was constantly judging herself by a blueprint she'd drawn back in Fall River.

Things had started out according to plan. She'd es-caped her hometown. College was her ticket out. But her scholarship to Brown was not the express ride to the more prosperous end of Route 195 she'd expected. She had been certain that her Ivy League education would bring her new friends, important jobs, and a lifetime guarantee to never slip back into a working-class exis-tence. Both socially and economically, this forecast proved false. Except for her girlfriend Lou, the avant-garde black sheep of her Darien, Connecticut, family, Carolyn's pen-etration of the "in" crowd had been occasional at best.

Her intelligence and inherent style made her attractive to this crowd, but she couldn't afford them. The weekend would come and they would head off to New York because some "dear friend" was throwing a party. Spring vacation would arrive and they would be off to meet their fathers and stepmothers in Florence. Naturally, everyone was fluent in a second language picked up after spending summers abroad.

But most intimidating of all was their attitude. They weren't worried. Even if things got rough—broken heart, too many drugs, flunking out. It was just a bad patch. Whatever fell apart could be put back together again in Westchester, on Park Avenue, in Georgetown or Lake Forest, inside the secure fortresses they called home. Jealously Carolyn had watched them become deeply passionate about social and political issues, or radically irreverent about absolutely everything without ever risking anything consequential. When it came time to go out into the world, there'd be shrinks for those who lacked direction, and positions in the family company for those who didn't.

Around them, Carolyn had felt like an ambitious misfit. She told herself things would change after graduation. A degree and a good job would provide her with a firm foundation from which to operate. She set off for L.A. with a notebook of ideas and visions of screenplay assignments dancing in her head, confident that her academic accomplishments would be rewarded. What a fantasy that had turned out to be. After a month of steady job hunting, she was forced to conclude that without the right connections, an honors degree—unless it was from Harvard or the USC Film School—meant nothing. She found she was just another dreamer, alone in Hollywood, living in a dump, eating mashed potatoes and broccoli. No one was coming to her rescue.

For a year she spent her evenings writing and her days working as a receptionist for a fledgling cable news station. She was slowly working her way out of debt and depression when she met Paul. It was a Saturday afternoon at Fred Segal's, an emporium of shops selling everything from jeans to luggage to bath oils to lingerie, shoes, candy, magazines, radios, and toys. It was the kind of place where you might find Tina Turner buying earrings, Eddie Van Halen checking out the sweatshirts, or teenage girls from Encino trying on miniskirts. Sometimes the place had a frenetic energy about it; other days it was as laid-back as the dated "see/feel/love" motto printed on all the stores' shopping bags.

Carolyn hadn't been looking for a savior that day. She was looking for the perfect white T-shirt and a pair of Keds, which along with her pink high-tops were the staples of her wardrobe. Amazingly enough, she found both at Fred Segal's, no small feat considering it was a shop known primarily for its zebra-striped high heels and rhinestone blue jeans. After shopping, she stopped for a snack at their indoor café, feeling a little better than usual. The T-shirt, the Keds, a salad . . . she could subsist on small treats as she worked hard to improve her screenwriting skills. In the meantime, she was intact, at Fred Segal's on a sunny Saturday afternoon, keeping her anxiety at bay with a seafood salad and the latest issue of *Vanity Fair*.

It was then that she noticed Paul. He was standing in front of a shelf filled with high-tech portable cassette players and eyeing her shyly. He had an appealing midwestern macho quality, a toned athletic physique, and a healthy complexion. At first sight, she loved his sandy hair, well-defined jaw, high cheekbones, and the careless smile that had made him a high-school heartthrob back in Ames, Iowa. But it was his deep, penetrating brown eyes that captivated Carolyn. Eyes that suggested a sensibility and intensity closer to Sam Shepard than Bruce Jenner.

She pretended to concentrate on reading until she looked up to find him in front of her, holding a Sony and a Panasonic.

"What do you think?" he asked. "Which should I get?"

She put down her magazine. "I think guys don't ask girls which gadgets to buy, so you're probably asking me something else, but the answer to your pretend question is: I'd go for the black one."

He ended up picking the gray one and buying her dinner.

Remembering their early sweet days now motivated Carolyn to join Paul out on the terrace.

"I'm doing what I have to do, Paul. I know that's not a very satisfying explanation, and I'd probably want to throw a lamp at someone who said it to me, but it's the only explanation I have."

He reached out and rested his hands on her shoulders. "So what is this? A stage you're going through? Is this I-love-you-but-I-can't-be-with-you-right-now? Okay, I know everything wasn't perfect with us, but there's a lot that was pretty terrific."

He took her in his arms and she buried her head in his chest. Although she no longer wanted to live with him, the thought of not having him in her life at all terrified her. I'm not being fair, she thought. This is not fair to Paul and it's not fair to Andrew.

She pulled back. "I have to be honest. There's no way in the foreseeable future—"

He stopped her, his hands firmly gripping her arms, his eyes steadily seeking hers. "I know guys like Andrew Spencer. They're in love with the idea of love. *You* don't matter. No one will take care of you the way I have."

His words hit exactly the nerve he'd intended. His accuracy off the court was just as deadly as his accuracy on-court. She could be jeopardizing a solid affection for a fraudulent passion.

She turned away from him and looked out over the railing.

"You know, Carolyn," he continued, "they say we get the President we deserve. And we get the religion we deserve. Maybe we also get the lover we deserve. Maybe the truth is that I deserved this and you deserve Andrew."

She took that verbal punch silently and kept her focus on the traffic moving steadily below. Other people do it, she told herself. They dare to take a chance. I can do it too. I have to. She whirled around to face Paul. "Maybe the truth is: I'm so fucking tired of being afraid."

"Have it your way," Paul said, giving up. Then suddenly something occurred to him. "Where are you moving to?"

"Andrew's," Carolyn said defiantly.

Paul shook his head in disgust and walked past her. Before stepping out the door, he called back, "Your era of pink walls is over, kiddo."

7

At first, Andrew Spencer thought that a smoke alarm had gone off, jolting him upright in his bed. Once awake, he realized there was no sound at all. It was only his anxiety reaching out from its well-protected daytime hibernation. He glanced at the clock on the bedside table and saw that it was four A.M. It wasn't the hour you could keep anything from yourself. The hour of the wolf, Andrew thought. Ingmar Bergman's words.

He nestled closer to Carolyn. Her tender embrace couldn't soothe the feelings of emptiness that gripped at him. He realized that she couldn't hold him hard enough to make him believe she wouldn't go away. Thoughts zipped through his brain. Could he offer her enough to keep her? Would she start to miss the kind of life that Paul Easton offered?

Last night they'd celebrated Carolyn's moving in. Andrew was in top form. He'd won. Carolyn was his. They had a quiet dinner and then hit the clubs. Andrew wanted to flaunt their romance. Although Carolyn seemed to be enjoying herself, at times Andrew detected a reflective mood beneath her frivolity. These somber flashes came and went so quickly, he didn't consider questioning her about them. Nor did he quiz her about the details of her conversation with Paul. Last night, these details had seemed insignificant, but now, in the light of day, without the first rush of victory and expensive champagne to cloud his vision, the details assumed a greater importance.

Restless, he pulled away from Carolyn and that mysterious bond between them that made him always want to possess her, own her, cover her completely with himself. Defying that magnetic pull, afraid she somehow knew and understood the uncertainties that had jolted him from his sleep, he got out of bed.

He walked out past the genteel apartment buildings that lined his street, watching for the dawn to poke through the horizon. Like all L.A. neighborhoods, this one was a mixed bag of architectural styles. But at least here most of the buildings were old and substantial, structures that were made when plaster, not dry wall, delineated rooms. This detail appealed to the traditional side of Andrew's personality. As did the fact that there wasn't one shopping-plaza strip mall anywhere nearby. He liked the quiet and serenity of his early-morning walk but couldn't figure out why he was having trouble sleeping. He never had insomnia, not since his school days.

As he passed a neighbor's yard and plucked a freesia from the garden, those nights right before holiday at Eton came back to him with the force of a rugby stick in the face.

Two days before holiday, like clockwork, the parcel would arrive, the beginning of an elaborate family charade. Buried beneath sweets (his favorites) and books (his mother's), would be the dread letter, the one that he'd hoped would not arrive. "Sorry, love: So wish we could spend this time with you . . . but Mummy has to help Princess Grace with a charity ball in Monaco, and Daddy's skiing in Gstaad. He'd love for you to join him, but there isn't enough time . . ."

Andrew knew better. Mummy wasn't in Monaco arranging anything. She was in Paris with a new boyfriend—and most likely she didn't even know where Daddy was.

Andrew wouldn't open the parcel when it came, as if denial would change the facts. No one must know that he had nowhere to go for his holiday. Its arrival would commence the endless nights in which he'd lie awake planning cover stories. He had to decide where he would tell everyone he was going, but first he had to ascertain everyone else's travel plans, careful not to claim to be anyplace where anyone might try to ring him up.

As he researched his alternatives, his imagination drew vivid pictures he longed to be part of: dinners by the roaring fires of baronial mansions . . . romping on the beaches of the Mediterranean. Andrew hated envy, but what he hated more was being pitied. So every precaution was taken during these long calculating nights to protect the lie. It became a kind of game to him: to elude being caught in his lie was to win, and winning was something that could always make Andrew Spencer feel better, whatever ailed him.

The morning would arrive with long cars driving processionlike up to the front hall. Then the protracted farewells began, full of laments of separation, promises to ring, and reports of parties to reunite them.

"Next holiday you're all coming hunting at our house in Scotland!" Andrew's voice would ring out cheerfully. "Yes! Yes!" they'd exclaim, dying to see this legendary place. The house in Scotland was now, too, part of the elaborate family charade. There wouldn't be any idyllic vacations with his school friends there. The house was no longer theirs because his family couldn't afford the taxes. Even the furnishings—the family crests, the boars' heads, the wonderful tall dining-room chairs he had gotten lost in as a child—had been auctioned this year to pay his tuition.

Everyone understood that Andrew's car was always late; his family's driver had long ago become the butt of jokes about tardiness. As Andrew would watch the cars depart, for a moment he would almost expect this apocryphal driver to appear, full of ridiculous explanations.

Then it would hit him. He would be staying alone at school for a fortnight, amusing himself by charming the headmaster's wife and dallying with some local girls. He was amazed by how easy it was to fool everyone. I've pulled it off again, he would laugh to himself. Not until every last car was gone would he return to his room to take the brown-wrapped parcel from under his bed and open it. Nibbling his almond bars, putting away his new walking shoes, he'd read the rest of the bloody note.

The pain of this memory gripped Andrew physically, connecting him with a hole inside his soul that, until Carolyn, had informed his deepest fears about himself. He stopped, overcome with pain, and sat on the concrete steps outside his apartment. He'd forgotten how far away he'd always felt from real love, how little he'd really expected it, despite the outward image he had of being a romantic. Sometimes he felt so hard, as if his heart had turned to muscle. But Carolyn penetrated his glinty armor and exposed the emptiness inside. That was why he couldn't sleep. If she left him, the pain would be unbearable. He reluctantly admitted to himself that he hated that she had ever loved Paul, that she had ever loved anyone besides himself.

The aroma of frying sausages and fresh brewing coffee filled the apartment. Andrew had returned from his walk, finished the L.A. *Times*, and arranged the stolen freesia on the wicker tray he carried into the bedroom.

"Breakfast for my lady," he announced.

"What a treat, my darling," Carolyn said. "What a nice way to wake up."

She heard the strains of Bach's *Well-Tempered Clavier* coming from the living room. "It feels like London, the south of France, Italy."

Andrew sat at the foot of their bed. "Places we'll be together," he promised. "Only the beginning of the places we'll go."

He loved how she looked in his heavy cotton Eton rugby shirt. When she had first started spending the night, Andrew wished she'd wear something more lacy and extravagant. But now the sight of her firm breasts in his public-school T-shirt was beyond erotic to him.

"Let's put on Bryan Ferry," she teased, fully aware of his distaste for rock and roll in the morning.

"Let's not." He inched closer, rubbing her neck. "Why is it that I live with a hard-on since I met you? Eat up so I can have you."

He picked up a sausage with her fork and placed it to her lips. She took a bite and picked up the next sausage with her fingers.

"We don't eat with our fingers, darling, do we?" he asked.

"Are my manners too working-class for my little lord?" She licked her fingers, one by one.

He loved when she busted him, when she pricked holes in his stuffy English veneer. It was a relief not to have to maintain the upper-class claptrap that had infatuated most of L.A. She instinctively understood in him both the decadent aristocrat and the hustling con man, and begrudged him neither.

Carolyn was the first woman in his life who aroused him mentally more than physically. With her vixen face, she was not as beautiful as some of the other women he'd been with, but she was somehow more compelling. He'd never thought of himself as a man who lived for sex; he'd believed in the pursuit of higher truths. Lust was common. But with Carolyn, it was another matter. He wanted to take her in the bath, on the couch, in his Fiat, at a red light.

He removed the dishes and tray from the bed and pulled her close. "I'm mad for you," he said, pulling up her rugby shirt.

Giggling, she slid under the covers, eluding him. She loved morning sex with Andrew more than she had ever known was possible. Ignoring the papers strewn all over the bed, he followed her under the tent she'd made of their sheets. He found her lips and they kissed long and deep until both of them were breathing so hard it felt as if steam was rising inside the tent.

He climbed on top of her and kissed her cheek and

neck and ears. "I love you I love you I love you, my baby," he whispered.

"Tell me you love me, tell me you'll never leave me, tell me, tell me . . ."

When they finished making love, Carolyn, shining with sweat, kissed him softly on the freckle on his shoulder. Her tongue carved "I love you" on his arm. She drifted peacefully, almost back to sleep, as Andrew lifted himself carefully from her and off the bed.

He began tidying up in order to keep his mind off a sense that something was still wrong. He carried the tray and dishes back to the kitchen and picked up the newspaper. The sports page stared him straight in the face with its news of Wimbledon and tennis reawakening his worst fear. In spite of all Carolyn's reassurance, he didn't believe that Paul was a dead issue. And now the sight of an article about an upcoming tournament in New York, featuring an interview with Paul, roused Andrew's hostilities to the breaking point.

Andrew marched back into the bedroom. "Tell me everything you and Paul discussed yesterday. Everything."

Carolyn was stunned to hear the edge in his voice. He stood at the corner of their bed, staring intently into her eyes. For a second she almost laughed because Andrew's posture looked like he was about to deliver a soliloquy.

"Tell me, Carolyn. Not the abridged, approved version you can live with. Everything."

"There's nothing to tell. We both know it's over. He knows I'm in love with you."

Andrew paced around the small room. "Exactly. I want to know exactly what you said."

"I told him that I don't see any way in the foreseeable future—"

Andrew pounced on the hedge. "Goddammit, Carolyn. How could you betray me like this? You know he's still in love with you and you've given him reason to wait." He took the sports page and hurled it across the room.

"Terrific, Andrew." Carolyn was livid. "If we're throwing things, I could do with fewer pictures of your Eurotrash ex-girlfriends all over your goddamn apartment. Why don't you throw a couple of them too? I'm not leading Paul on—"

"Then what the hell is 'in the foreseeable future' supposed to mean?" he shouted. "Is there a chance in the unforeseeable future?"

"It means that I made a choice for you," Carolyn said. "You want it in blood?"

"You didn't leave Paul for me." Andrew played psychologist. "He wasn't right for you and I was merely the proof. You were climbing out the window and I opened the door."

Carolyn got up and stormed around the room throwing on her clothes, searching for her baggy socks, retrieving her high-tops from under the bed. "If that makes you feel less responsible, in a way you're right," she fumed. "Though I've never seen someone want it both ways like you before. I had to choose this. I am responsible." She stopped to look him squarely in the face, unintimidated by his anger. "I can't give you up . . . this feeling up. If I could have, I would have. I had to go for it, knowing that it could easily turn out to be the stupidest decision of my life."

Andrew was not appeased. The insinuation that her choice was a risky one meant that his prospects were doubtful. He crackled like kindling. "I want you to call Paul tomorrow and tell him to bug off in the bloody foreseeable future. It's never, and I mean never."

Andrew was ignited by this power struggle he'd created, and insisted on being victorious. Brinksmanship permeated the room. He took Carolyn by the shoulders and held her hostage to his demands. "I want you to burn your bridges." His voice grew husky. Again he felt aroused, just pressing his body next to hers. He pushed her onto the bed. "There's no safe passage, Carolyn."

She struggled with him, one ear to his messages. She

hated him for physically controlling her, but she felt his sexy breath coming in shorter spasms, and in spite of herself, he turned her on. She bit his tongue inside her mouth and hissed, "You just want to punish Paul for loving me, you monster."

He tore off the jeans and T-shirt she'd just put on, and pressed her back against the bed. "You're mine." He grasped her hands in a tight grip under her back. "Mine, mine, mine."

8

Five minutes had turned into fifty, and with them went Nicole's hopes of "containing" the Lance problem. She'd spent all Sunday afternoon mulling over how best to deal with Lance. Finally, as the evening approached, she'd called him and asked if she could come by the next day an hour before the barbecue. He'd agreed readily enough, but now it was apparent that the relationship-maintenance meeting she had hoped for was not to be.

"Sorry, he's still on the phone. Would you like another mineral water?" Brett Holston, Lance's houseboy, was doing his version of a Malibu socialite.

"I'm fine," Nicole assured him.

He leaned against the door frame. "Well, I'm crazed. Do you believe that two of the girls with the Valley Girls Valet Parking Service can't drive stick?"

"Really." Nicole wasn't up for small talk.

"And the floral-art pieces for the tables aren't done and the party was called for . . ." He checked his Rolex. "Five minutes from now."

Just then the buzzer on the intercom rang. Lance. They both felt his long arm as Brett picked up the receiver. "But I was going to do that later," Brett pleaded. "Sure," he acquiesced. "I'll do it now." He hung up the phone. "Attention must be paid to the boudoir/cabana/ gazebo," he snapped. "I guess Lance is planning one of his late-night gatherings."

Left alone, Nicole could feel her uneasiness building. She wondered if Bambi had wangled an invitation to

Lance's post-party inner circle. One thing was certain. Nicole was no longer a part of Lance's studio clique.

At one time she had even thought she might be more than just part of his clique. That was over a year ago when she'd run into him at the Boss Club. It was a rare night for Nicole, because she had chosen to do something completely unrelated to work. She'd joined some non-industry friends for some Springsteen music and simple relaxation. No studio politics. No zooming, which was the current Hollywood lingo for some old-fashioned networking. Five minutes into her drink (a greyhound), she spotted Lance. It was a rare night for him too. He didn't have a MAW (model-actress-whatever) on his arm. He was actually behaving like a regular guy.

He sought her out, stealing her away from her friends with flattery and attention. He convinced her to join him at a small neighborhood sushi bar for some sake. In a talkative mood, he confessed his growing weariness for the bimbos he'd been dating. He claimed intelligence turned him on. Nicole laughed. But in spite of her cynicism, she found herself flirting back. When he spoke of his respect for her and his inability to succeed at a relationship of substance, she began to wonder if maybe he was at a turning point. She could feel herself letting go. Somewhere into the third hour and her fourth sake, her hand fleetingly brushed his thigh. In response, Lance took hold of her hand and guided it back under the table and between his legs. It was a gesture so unexpected and so pornographic that Nicole had had no quick comeback. The only thing going on in her mind was how excited she was, and she wasn't ready to admit that. Through his jeans she could feel how hard he was, and that awareness sent her own body into overdrive. Her stiff nipples were visible against the cotton of her Millennium T-shirt. Provocatively she hiked her skirt up a couple more inches. The juxtaposition of porno fantasies and power fantasies was fast becoming the combination that silenced all reason. Lance finished off his drink, left a fifty on the countertop, and affectionately took her arm. Together they walked out of the nearly empty sushi bar. Catching sight of their reflection in a storefront window outside, Nicole thought: We look like a couple. Her hand slipped back down to his thigh, and this time there was no timidity in her reach. I want this, God, how I want this, she thought. They stopped alongside his Ferrari and Lance leaned her against the car and slid his hands all the way up her skirt.

"I can't believe you live all the way out in Malibu," she said, assuming that that's where they would spend the night. She locked her arms around his neck and pressed her body against his. When she had fully committed herself, making no secret of her desire, Lance abruptly stepped away. "Where's your car?" he asked.

"Across the street. No problem," she replied. "I can leave it there until the morning." Her eyes invited him to continue what he'd started. That's when she had glimpsed another facet of Lance, the one manifested in his quasi-sadistic grin.

He leaned over, flashed what he'd call a smile, and gave her a quick kiss on the cheek. "Well, drive safely," he said before completely disengaging, getting into his Ferrari, and taking off.

He left Nicole standing alone, stunned, on Sunset Boulevard at midnight with the words "Drive safely" echoing in her brain. Where did the heat go? she wanted to know.

The next day she realized that she, like everyone else, was a private amusement for Lance. He would never sleep with her because that kind of intimacy might reveal too much about him. He needed to humiliate her by getting her to admit her desire. Lance lived for total control. That was the point of sex.

She checked the time. An hour had passed since she'd arrived. She had to face the obvious. Lance had always intended to blow off this meeting. Forget about it for now, she advised herself. Downshift. Switch gears. The party's about to begin.

Party? Not quite the word for it. What would appear to be just a holiday get-together would in fact be work masquerading as play. Even a workaholic like Nicole couldn't abide all these pleasantries masking self-interest. What made this particular gathering interesting was the drama of whom Lance would be working.

She stood at the window and looked out across the expansive backyard area. She knew Lance had just spent a small fortune on redesigning his pool. What had once been a large blue expensively tiled rectangular pool was now a long narrow black expensively tiled pool, perfect for laps. The fact that Lance never swam was beside the point. He also never sat in any of the plush upholstered lawn chairs, and never walked down to the ocean from his castle up on the cove.

Three young men from the catering crew exited the guesthouse at the far end of the backyard. This one, where the afternoon festivities would take place, was a petite version of the whitewashed ultramodern main house. Brett was supervising the catering crew as they set up their equipment—rib racks, charcoal-igniter guns, serving platters, tongs, spatulas, brushes, alder chips, mesquite chips, hickory chips, and oak chips. But he panicked when he saw that they were about to start up the custom ebony Weber barbecue grills.

"Not yet, not yet. We have hors d'oeuvres and drinks first," he shouted.

Nicole turned away from the scene. She thought about how much she hated three-day weekends. On an impulse, she picked up the phone, punched in a New Jersey number and her calling-card code.

"Hi, Dad, it's me."

"Hi, honey. I've been thinking about you. Everything okay?"

Why did those two words spoken by her father have

the power to undo her? She fought to steady her quavering voice. "I'm fine."

"Your mother and I finally saw that picture *He's a Rebel* your studio made. We really enjoyed it."

Nicole smiled. Her dad was always so supportive. He became a cheerleader for any project she had anything at all to do with.

"Thanks, Dad. Millennium doesn't do many small-budget movies, but this script was too special to pass up."

"Hold on a minute, will you? Your mother just walked in."

Nicole could hear him calling out, and strained to hear her mother's muffled reply.

"What'd she say?"

"She wants to know when you're getting married."

"Tell her tomorrow," Nicole said. When would her mother give her a break?

"Honey, don't get upset. You know she's proud of you, she's just being a mother."

Nicole knew she had to change the subject or she'd scream. "Are you taking care of yourself, Daddy?"

"I'm fine." He sounded tired.

"You exercising?"

"Don't worry about your old man. Semiretirement agrees with me."

The thought of him aging made her feel vulnerable. "Daddy, I've got to run. Just wanted to say hi. Miss you. Give my love to Mom. See you soon."

As she hung up, she felt so alone. There was no comfort to be found in turning to her parents, and no comfort to be found anywhere else. She looked out the window at the perfect sunny day and felt like an alien in this land of happy endings. She fought to hold back a wave of self-pity. I need some air, she decided. I need some of that priceless ocean air.

*   *   *

As Nicole emerged from the house, she saw that Kevin Holberstein had arrived, predictably on time. His wife, Peggy, accompanied him with their young daughter, who was wearing a Laura Ashley pinafore. As Nicole hastened over to greet them, she overheard Brett comment to one of the waiters, "That child hasn't been well-dressed for this occasion as much as well-marketed."

Nicole saw immediately that Kevin was uncomfortable mixing business with a family outing and that Peggy probably would be happier in her own backyard. But, consummate mogul's wife that she was, she could breeze through this event effortlessly. Nicole envied their self-contained family unit and envied Peggy her cool self-contained style. Today she had on simple baggy black cotton Bermuda shorts, sandals, and a traditional white button-down-collar Brooks Brothers man-size shirt. It was an outfit that cost far less than Nicole's Claude Montana sundress, and one that, in its own way, was no less attractive. Nicole knew Peggy was from one of those well-to-do New York families that didn't believe in wearing their wealth. The Carlyles were not the type to follow trends. Peggy stuck to the basics and always looked crisp and appropriate. She didn't need to wear a denim miniskirt to look young and desirable. With her healthy glow, lively brown eyes, and dark blond hair pulled back into a ponytail, she appeared closer to thirty than her actual age, thirty-seven. They make a great team, Nicole thought, watching Kevin and Peggy together.

After hellos all around, Kevin got to the point. "Did you talk to him?"

Though he had advised her to forget about the *Dirty Dreams* problem over the weekend, Nicole had left a message on his machine saying she thought a casual talk with Lance might help.

"What do you think?" Nicole shrugged.

"A no-show?"

"Apparently he's on an important call. No one's even seen him all morning."

Kevin pondered that fact for a second. "I wonder what he's up to."

"I live for another one of Lance's surprises," Nicole said.

Kevin stared out toward the main house of the ranch, where Lance was sequestered, as if the answer could be found there.

"Calistoga, mimosa, or margarita?" Brett interrupted them to take an order.

"Calistoga," Kevin answered.

"Do you want lime in it?" Kevin and Nicole hadn't acknowledged his presence, and Peggy had stepped away to greet another mogul's wife. The houseboy seemed offended by this lack of attention. He audibly sighed.

"No lime, thanks."

"No lime it is, then," Brett said, marching off.

Kevin looked baffled at this behavior, but Nicole explained his pathology. "Brett thinks anyone who doesn't want to share life experiences with him is homophobic."

"It isn't good business to be homophobic in Hollywood," Kevin said, and then, with a trace of an impish grin, he added, "Is that one of Ted's lines?"

"I think David Beach's," Nicole answered with a smile.

All at once a flurry of guests appeared and Nicole braced herself for the circus that was about to begin. Across the pool she watched as industry groupies ogled industry heavies. "Lance is even pulling them in on time," she observed, knowing this crowd was habitually late. "Ah," she sighed. "The power that is Lance."

Ted steered his black Jaguar XJS up the sloping driveway and around to the valet parkers. Only two Mercedes were ahead of him, and he dreaded that he might be early. Nothing worse, at one of these events, he thought. Some frustrated producer, or an old lover, could corner him. He handed his keys to one of the Valet girls, hoping she wouldn't pop the clutch.

As Ted put on his sunglasses, he heard a voice behind

him inquire as to the whereabouts of their host. The
accent had the slightest Bostonian ring to it. Harvard
Bostonian.

With a smile, he turned to greet the surprise guest. "Well,
well. Steven Lloyd. I thought Wall Street boys spent the
Fourth of July sailing off the Vineyard?"

Steven Lloyd greeted Ted with a friendly grin and an
easy but not informal manner. His bearing distinguished
him from the California crowd. Steven's attitude said
East Coast Reserved, and his style was the authentic
one—khaki pants, pinstriped shirt, blazer, and loafers—
that Ralph Lauren had built his empire upon. Like a
forty-year-old preppie, he seemed to be both young and
wise. His healthy complexion and ready but not overused
smile suggested that those forty years had been privileged
ones.

"I haven't seen you in ages," Steven said. "When was
it? The Fourth of July? Liberty Weekend? On that wild
boat?"

They both laughed, remembering the night the movie
business rubbed noses with the power elite at sea.

"So," Ted pressed, "does your presence in town mean
those rumors about Millennium being on the block are
true?"

Steven was noncommittal. "There have been rumors
about possible buyers for Millennium almost as long as
there have been rumors on the street about you. Rumors
that you're about to quit. Life's too short, and any day
now you'll announce you've just signed a lucrative
independent-production deal."

Ted laughed. "I just want you to know that if I see you
having dinner with any high rollers shopping for a Hollywood acquisition, I'm going to draw the right conclusions."

Steven held up his hands, a gesture that said: You
didn't hear a thing from me.

Ted smiled. He was happy to have run into Steven. He
felt comfortable with him, as he did with all men who
needed nothing from him and sat solidly on their own

power bases. As he escorted Steven toward the front door, Lance's houseboy, Brett, welcomed him as if they were old army buddies. Brett handed Ted a frosty drink.

"Here's the first margarita of the day, Ted, but follow me to the pool and I'll introduce you to the bartender. I've got pull."

Brett thought this was hilarious, but Ted hardly acknowledged the joke. He steadily moved through the house that had all the warmth of a museum, and out toward the agapanthus-and-lily-striped path to the pool. He was anxious to find a lounge chair in the shade, near the bar, and to ensconce himself there with Steven Lloyd. Perhaps he could even avoid Lance today, he thought.

"Hi, Ted." The enthusiasm in the voice registered at least four decibel points.

Ted knew it had to be Bambi.

"Who's your new friend?" She turned to Steven. "Hi. I'm Bambi Stern. I work for Ted."

Bambi had dressed to assure attention. She had on bright yellow toreador pants and an oversize blue-and-yellow V-neck sweater worn backwards. The clack of her bejeweled sandals announced her approach, yet she hid behind huge Yves St. Laurent sunglasses.

"Bambi, this is Steven Lloyd. An old colleague from New York."

"Colleague? Does that mean you're in the movie business? Like our east-coast cousin or something?"

"Not exactly." Steven Lloyd wasn't used to people talking business this quickly, particularly when they had nothing to say.

Steven's reticence didn't deter Bambi. Ted was astonished by her complete lack of subtlety. Why hadn't he realized before what a Kewpie doll she was?

"No, Bambi. Steven is in finance." He said this as if saying to a child: Run along now, the grown-ups want to talk.

Bambi stood awkwardly. She didn't understand people who didn't love to talk about the business. But she knew someone who did. "Where's Lance?" she asked Ted.

"I'm sure you'll find him," Ted allowed as he steered Steven toward a shady front-row seat. At that moment he was the last person at the barbecue who cared where or with whom their host might be mingling—and conspiring.

As Nicole approached the margarita bar, a stranger standing nearby caught her eye. He was tall, she observed, and slightly overdressed. Definitely not L.A., more Bridgehampton. His face was manly and his attention was direct, intelligent, and slightly bemused. He was definitely staring at her. Usually this would make her uncomfortable. But he wasn't staring in a usual way. He didn't seem to be a usual guy. She liked the way he took her in. He was more than looking at her, he was assessing her.

"Do I know you?" she asked, stopping in front of him as if they were playing musical chairs and the music had just stopped. She felt corny and light-headed. Suddenly they were both smiling wickedly for no reason.

"We haven't met formally, but I'd like to meet you. I do know who you are."

This comment always rattled her. She didn't mind being spotted at the cleaners or restaurants, or when she spoke to students at Hollywood seminars. But with out-and-out strangers whom she couldn't place in any known hierarchy, the one-way recognition made her feel at a disadvantage.

"You're one up on me. I don't know who you are."

"I'm Steven Lloyd. See, that means nothing to you."

"Steven Lloyd. Steven Lloyd." She even liked the sound of his name. "Nope. Not on my directors' list. And I know you're not on my comedy-rewrite list."

"I'd like to see your comedy-rewrite list. I've never seen one before. What does it look like?"

"A little like the lists of partners in a law firm. Teams of funny-sounding names. I'm Nicole Lanford. Nice to meet you, Steven Lloyd."

For a moment they stood speechless. Then, as if by

unspoken consent, they navigated themselves toward the more private space of a flower-lined path between two beds of lilies.

"What do you do?" Nicole knew the question sounded stupid, but she couldn't go on being unable to place him. As two acquaintances of Nicole's passed by and nodded hello at both of them, she realized that, oddly, dangerously, she felt like part of a romantic twosome walking with Steven.

"Oh, I'm a numbers man. Wall Street type. Buy companies, sell them. Make improvements for their stockholders, that sort of thing."

"It sounds like you're wheeling and dealing like me, but on a more abstract level. How do you know Lance?"

"Styvie Pell introduced us," Steven replied.

Nicole tried to place the name. "Of the Detroit Pells?" she guessed.

"Same, except Styvie lives in Los Angeles now," Steven replied. "In fact, he's due here this afternoon."

"Really," Nicole said, trying to piece together this new puzzle. Was Lance just expanding his network of movers and shakers or was he putting together some kind of alliance? Casually she asked, "Are you out here on business?"

"I'm advising Styvie on a couple of things."

"Must be serious," Nicole teased, "to bring you all the way to Hollywood."

Steven Lloyd was about to answer, carefully phrasing his response to be both true and politically unexplosive, when from virtually nowhere Lance appeared with his genius timing.

"Lance!" Nicole said. "You're like an apparition."

She turned to Steven. "Lance is like a cop. Never around when you need him, but he suddenly appears when you're contemplating getting into trouble."

Steven Lloyd laughed a laugh that implied he knew much about his host that Nicole need not explain. Lance, for the time being, was nonplussed. He collected himself to reply.

"Nicole, don't let me stop you from getting into trouble. That would certainly destroy my reputation. This barbecue is expressly designed to facilitate trouble, so let me know if there's anything I can do."

Lance and Nicole embraced as though an issue had been resolved.

"So how have you had the foresight to meet the eminent Mr. Lloyd without my introduction?"

"Oh, that was entirely my doing, Lance," Steven said.

Lance shifted his gaze, searching for a new diversion. The scene had begun to bore him and he was in need of a power fix of some kind. Nicole sapped him because he couldn't punch it out with her as he would a guy. Just in time, he caught sight of two latecomers making their entrance. With a wink, he turned to Steven. "Styvie Pell," he said as if in answer to a question. Steven, Nicole assumed, was in on the secret. Then, as quickly as he'd appeared, Lance was gone.

Nicole regarded the new arrivals from a distance. Even if Steven hadn't filled her in on Styvie's lineage, she could have guessed he was important. Lance's reaction and the waves of activity that radiated from other well-wishers in the crowd made that apparent. Nicole zoomed in for detail. Styvie was about thirty-eight, average height, lean, with blondish-brown thinning hair. He seemed reticent, shy or snobbish, and ill-at-ease.

His companion, on the other hand, stood in relaxed stance. Her long blond hair was slung casually over her shoulders, and Nicole could tell, even from a distance, that she was covered in fine pieces of jewelry, gold and diamonds by the yard.

She watched Lance embrace her as though he'd known her for life. "Okay, I'll bite. Who's Lance so excited about?" Nicole asked Steven.

"Her name is Christie Collins. She's Styvie's girlfriend."

Nicole noted the way Christie carried herself, as if her every move were being recorded for posterity. "Let me guess: she's an actress."

"A seasoned amateur and an aspiring professional," Steven corrected her. His comments were not a put-down of Christie but simply a clarification of her status.

He definitely has the precise mind of a numbers man, Nicole thought.

"So," she pressed, "what does Styvie Pell do when he's not busy being the heir to an automotive fortune?"

"He sails and buys boats. Some say he's shopping for a studio."

"He could buy a studio?" Nicole was impressed. This was definitely how to leverage yourself into business, she thought.

Steven laughed. "He could buy two. His ex-wife could buy one." He took her elbow, distracting her. "Let's walk."

Ted watched Nicole with fascination. She was full of crackerjack energy, with a smile so bright it almost neutralized the rough edges of her power. He could see that she wasn't aware that she was being evaluated by Steven, thinking the attention was a flirtation. Ted knew that for a guy like Steven, assessing part of the manpower of any studio was a reflex action. Ted wondered if Steven would mention that he was out here gathering information for Wall Street. The more Ted watched the two of them together, the sorrier he felt for his executive V.P. Her vulnerability showed when men dealt with her like a man and she responded like a woman. Ted wasn't generally attracted to career women like Nicole. Who wanted to talk treatments at two A.M.? Nonetheless, he had great sympathy for their complicated sexual conflicts. Unlike this bimbo next to me, he thought, looking at Jasmine, an exquisite young woman who was getting her first taste of an industry party. At her side was Lisa Sapien, personal manager to a number of celebrities, who got where she was by working the inside track. Lisa had perfected the art of being best friend to the stars, buying their confidences with lavish attention and flattery and, when the situation called for it, being a matchmaker.

At times Lisa seemed fueled by negative forces, as if she'd made a deal with the devil and was comfortable with how the negotiations had gone. Her eyes reflected her core of coldness. They were a beady blue that made her appear unapproachable until she flashed her smile, which dispelled all thoughts that she might be a modern-day witch. She sucked people in with that smile and got them hooked on her pretty face and enigmatic personality.

Ted knew that Jasmine was a New York model and one of Lisa's newest clients. "Perfect for *Dirty Dreams,* don't you think?" Lisa had said on introducing the two of them.

"Could be," Ted had replied. He wasn't interested in casting Lance's movie, but he was drawn to this extraordinary-looking face with flawless skin, high cheekbones, and green eyes. Jasmine was too slight to fit into Ted's preferred type, but something about her appealed to his undernourished father side. And, thankfully, she didn't appear to be on the verge of breaking into an audition.

She was instead imbibing giant strawberries laced with liquor and now she was getting giggly as juice dribbled provocatively down the corners of her lips and chin.

"I'm here to be with Lance, but I've barely seen him," she confessed. "So I'm not sure where I belong."

"You belong right here with me, my dear, watching from the sidelines."

"I don't think I belong in L.A.," she continued aimlessly. "New York is my town, though I'm from Chicago. Well, not exactly Chicago . . . Libertyville, Illinois. But only since I was fourteen, because before that it was Lincoln, Nebraska." She gulped down another cognac berry. "These things are delicious. They don't make these in Lincoln."

"I bet not." Ted glazed over as the midwestern patchwork quilt that was Jasmine washed out before his eyes.

"Here, take a bite." She was leaning toward him, offering half a strawberry.

"I'm off sweets," Ted declined. He was beyond temptation.

Jasmine giggled again, but this time with a hint of hysteria. "Do you want to know my real name?"

Where is Lisa? Ted wondered. Then he spotted her nearby. She was busy chatting with Diana Ross. They were sitting in the shade of a eucalyptus tree discussing a cable television faith healer's views on media celebrity.

"The reason I make such a big thing about it is . . . Are you listening?" Jasmine nudged Ted. "It's Karen Joy Spaight. Did you hear me?"

She looked at Ted as though this was supposed to mean something, but whatever it signified escaped him altogether.

"My guidance counselor in ninth grade told me it sounded like the name of a victim of a mass murderer."

She giggled uncontrollably and then suddenly burst into tears. Ted silently agreed that her name *did* sound like that of a mass murderer's victim, but wouldn't stoop to admit it.

"Now, stop it. Don't cry. You're only upset because Lance hasn't been around. You may be his victim, but it's only Lance. And whatever his faults, he's not a mass murderer. At least, not yet."

Jasmine had gradually regressed to Karen Joy Spaight, and now sat gaga at Ted's feet.

"What do you do, Ted?"

Here it comes, he thought. Get me out of here, home in bed with some scripts. Or, even better, no scripts.

"I'm studio head at Millennium. This week," he added. A stab of humility? Humor? His edge escaped Jasmine altogether.

"That sounds like the most wonderful job in the world. How powerful you are."

I am too old for this conversation, Ted thought.

"Let me tell you a joke, Jasmine. It may help you understand my job."

A small crowd gathered around Ted. He looked expansive, and everyone loved an expansive studio head.

"One day a mogul left for work at his usual time, and drove off merrily in his Porsche. When he arrived at his office, he saw that it was padlocked, and all of his belongings had been packed and boxed outside his door. Panicking, he ran downstairs to the pay phone on the lot and called his wife at home. 'Honey, you're not going to believe what just happened. I've been fired . . . all my belongings are being shipped back to the house. I know we can get through this, we can handle ups and downs, but it means we're going to have to put off the condo in Aspen and summer in the south of France. . . . Honey . . . are you there?' There was a silence at the end of the line. A quiet little voice answered, 'Yes, I'm here.' 'We'll get through this,' the mogul reassured her. 'We love each other . . . you love me, honey, don't you?' Then she answered, her voice, sweeter than sweet, 'Of course I love you, darling . . . I'll miss you, but I'll always love you.' "

Lance settled down next to Styvie Pell and his girlfriend, Christie Collins, with a plate of the best Tex-Mex barbecue food found north of the Rio Grande. His guests had already finished dessert, but Lance had been distracted by another of his "behind-closed-door" calls.

"That was Chester Baines," he announced to Styvie. "I told him I was busy entertaining Millennium's future."

Styvie shifted in his seat. "I don't know about that."

Lance wasn't concerned about how low-key Styvie's interest in Millennium appeared to be. After a string of hits, most of them produced by Lance, the studio was perfect for Styvie, who was seeking a stable foothold in Hollywood. It was also perfect timing for Chester and the rest of the board, who felt it was a good time to sell. Lance had psyched Styvie out as a billionaire with a big ego and something to prove. Ultimately, he figured, that could be the factor that clinched the deal. Lance also considered the reserved billionaire a closet exhibitionist.

Why else, he reasoned, would he be interested in the film business? There were more lucrative investment possibilities everywhere, especially when you were part of the illustrious Pell family. No, Lance concluded, underneath Styvie's rigid snobbishness was a man looking for a little glitter.

Evidence of that was his choice of girlfriend. From the moment they arrived, Christie had been courting attention. Lance noticed she frequently gestured with her right hand, which just happened to sport a significant emerald ring. He also noticed she avoided eye contact with him. He considered secretly saying: Christie, sweetheart, relax. I won't mention that I knew you when. He had to give her credit for her tenacity. Five years before, in Miami, she'd had a faltering career as a yacht-groupie/call-girl. Now she was a paramour to a billionaire, decked out like a *Town and Country* socialite.

"Does the coastal commission give you much trouble about building out here?" Styvie asked, purposely changing the subject.

"Interesting that you should bring that up," Lance replied. "I've had my run-ins with them, which is why I've hired a new attorney from Manatt."

"Chuck Manatt's firm," Styvie said. "My family helped him out with some Democratic Party fund-raisers."

"I thought all you Pells were Republicans," Lance said.

"We are," Styvie responded. "But good business necessitates backing both parties."

Lance nodded approvingly. This flattery was part of his strategy. He knew Styvie needed others to treat him as an astute businessman. In return, Styvie would appreciate Lance for having the intelligence to see his brilliance. It would be a mutual-admiration fraud. One that Lance intended to use to his benefit. In the event that Millennium did change hands, he wanted the guy at the top in his pocket.

"What about you, Christie?" Lance asked. "Do you

get involved with politics?" He could think of a few
senators she had had dalliances with in her "other life."

"A . . . well, not really. I'm busy with my acting classes
and I'm also designing a line of pool jewelry," she primly
replied.

"Where do you sell your line?" Lance asked, enjoying
the little game.

"I haven't gotten to that stage yet," she said. "It's
really more of a hobby."

Lance finally caught her eye and he saw her unspoken
fear. Silently he reassured her that her past would go
unmentioned. A serene expression crossed her face. She
settled back in her chair and let her emerald-rich hand
rest on top of Styvie's. Lance smiled. Her grip reminded
him of a velvet vise. Poor very rich Styvie, he thought.

"And the acting, is that a hobby?" Lance asked.

"It's more like a passion," she answered.

"Hollywood is always looking for beautiful passionate
actresses." Judging Styvie to be the jealous type, Lance
was careful to make the compliment sound polite, not
flirtatious.

Christie beamed. "Well, thank you. I hope Hollywood
finds me."

"In fact"—Lance leaned in—"I'm about to start reading actresses for my new movie." He was about to further ingratiate himself with Styvie by respectfully offering
Christie a chance to audition, when he was interrupted
by Brett.

"I can't find the key to the screening room, and it's
locked."

"It's to stay locked," Lance instructed him. "Until I'm
ready, until we're all ready for what I've got planned."

By the time the credits rolled and the lights came on,
Lance's B-B-Q party had been in progress for seven
hours. Nicole ached to get out of Lance's screening room.
He had insisted that she and Ted sit with him in the back
row, and for an hour and a half while the latest summer

action movie played, all she could think about was what Lance really had up his sleeve.

Now that the second phase of his July Fourth festivities was completed, she watched him do inventory on the remaining crowd. Everyone was there except for Styvie and Christie. But just the fact that Styvie was at the barbecue at all was a clear message to Millennium. At the very least, Lance was saying: I have access to independent financing. And at the most, he was saying: Your boss-to-be is my buddy.

Before the guests had a chance to think about stretching their legs, Lance hit a button on his Sorriano Memphis-designed chair. The room was plunged into darkness.

"Oh, shit," Ted mumbled to Nicole. "Who does he think he is? Prospero bringing on the tempest?"

Lance hit another button and the movie screen rose up into the ceiling. People shifted in their seats, unprepared for the turn of events. Nicole wished she'd been able to sit with Steven, who was on the other side of the room next to Kevin and Peggy. Not only did she thoroughly enjoy his company, but she also had a dozen questions for him. Earlier, while watching Lance bid a warm goodbye to Styvie, it had occurred to her that she was way out of the loop when it came to the corporate side of the business. She'd never worried much about a takeover of Millennium. Why worry about something so completely out of her control? But now she wondered if she shouldn't be better-informed about the politics of a Wall Street deal.

Before she could dwell on this further, a third button released a melody from four powerful speakers. It was a Jann Hammer/*Miami Vice*-type synthesizer piece and it assaulted Nicole's end-of-the-day, too-much-sun, and one-margarita-too-many fatigue. The driving pulse of the music put her back on red alert.

"I should have left earlier," Ted whispered. "Before being a guest at a Lance Burton party started to feel like being a prisoner."

"I wouldn't be surprised if he's locked the door," she whispered back as the soundtrack changed tempo to intoxicating rhythms counterpointed by sensuous breathing.

At that moment Lance held a tiny microphone up to his mouth and flicked on a switch.

His voice filled the room. "An erotic adventure awaits those ready to leave their fears behind."

He pressed another control. A beam of light danced around the room, darting everywhere, landing for a split second on a now-dry-eyed Jasmine, her face restored to its former state of cover-girl perfection. Finally it held on what had been hidden behind the now-raised movie screen. The beam of light widened to encompass a large poster suspended by wire so thin it appeared to defy gravity as it floated in space.

The image on the poster was a crescent moon. Attached to the bottom of its tip was a scantily dressed girl, her wrists tied together by a scarlet silk scarf, dangling from this position of bondage. Superimposed over this image, in large red letters, was BURTON FILMS PRESENTS. In a flash, the words were gone, replaced by the title *Dirty Dreams*. The music picked up, now almost all bass line, punctuating each new revelation. The anticipation in the room snowballed as PRODUCED BY LANCE BURTON prompted sporadic applause. The next credit elicited unanimous shock and plenty of cheers. There, up on the screen for what felt to Nicole like an eternity, was the announcement: DIRECTED BY LANCE BURTON.

She was furious at Lance for breaking the rules, and disappointed with herself for not foreseeing this possibility. She turned to get Ted's reaction, but he was already out of his seat, stealing his way in the dark toward the exit. She watched him turn the knob, and could imagine his relief on finding it unlocked.

By the time COMING TO YOU FROM MILLENNIUM STUDIOS hit the screen, Nicole was outraged. She knew that Lance's move was directed at her and her administration. Handling this project was her responsibility. Mishandling it would not only make her look bad but also reflect poorly on Kevin, who supervised her. She wasn't worried about Ted. He'd ride out this storm; that was his specialty.

Her heart pounded. She realized that as soon as the lights went up, all attention in the room would be focused on her, and she was notoriously bad at hiding her emotions. If she didn't control her temper, this sandbag could turn into an out-and-out public fiasco.

She grabbed her handbag off the floor, readying herself to flee, when Lance, from his position at control center, hit a succession of buttons that cut off the audio and visuals and turned back on the lights.

He smiled, looked over at her, and said, "It's called squeeze play. Get used to it. This is how the big boys get things done."

"Ah, yes, the big boys," she replied sarcastically.

She stood up, all set to escape, but the aisle was blocked by casting agents seeking Lance's attention. She looked over to Kevin for support, but he too was receiving his share of congratulations. Like the aspiring politician he once had been, he expertly hid his feelings. A handshake and a smile now. Later—tonight, first thing tomorrow—he'd tackle Lance. One step at a time. Nicole knew Kevin's technique, which she struggled to imitate. She politely pushed her way forward, but was stopped by an agent who tapped her on the back.

"Kathleen Turner. You've got to consider Kathleen for the lead."

She managed an attentive but noncommittal response. But it was difficult when Bambi's loud voice, just a few feet away, was proclaiming *Dirty Dreams* to be a "breakthrough concept." And no less annoying was David Beach, whom she overheard referring to *Dirty Dreams* as a "fab script."

Nicole made another move toward the door, but didn't get far.

"I'll set up a meeting with Michelle Pfeiffer," an ICM agent offered.

His agent trainee chimed in, "She's got incredible range. From a nun to a nympho, she can play it all."

"Interesting, interesting," Nicole agreed. She appeared relatively calm, considering that she was seething inside. Lance is enjoying this, she thought. Now he gets to play coach and pick his team.

"Hey, look, I want your suggestions. Collaboration is what makes a hit movie," Lance preached to a swarm of agents.

On hearing that, Nicole knew she couldn't stick around any longer. Forget trying to be like Kevin. Forget trying to be polite. She wanted to grab the microphone and announce to the assembled that Lance's idea of collaboration was giving orders and having others carry them out.

Finally she broke out of the web of well-wishers and made her way to the exit. For some unknown reason, she stopped a minute and looked back. CAA superagent Mike Ovitz had grabbed Lance's arm in an implicit acknowledgment of their special camaraderie.

"I'll give you a call this week."

"Tomorrow morning," Lance insisted.

"I'll be in a meeting till noon."

"Fuck the meeting," Lance said gleefully. "This train has already left the station."

The Valley Girls Valet Parking Service was taking forever to bring Nicole's car around. Thankfully, having been the first to break away from Lance's celebration, she could at least wait and agonize in private. How dare he confront me like that? Whatever you do, do not cry, she instructed herself.

She felt bad about leaving Kevin to deal with this mess alone. But she knew that she'd be more of a liability to him if she couldn't contain her emotions. She tenaciously held back her tears, as if her crying would be a setback for all working women, not just a personal failure. She wiped at her eyes with the back of her hand and struggled to calm down.

She felt an arm tug at her shoulder and whipped her head around in the animal instinct of fight or flight. It was Steven Lloyd.

"I can't talk now," she said. "It's a very bad time. I have to think."

Ill-at-ease with her discomfort, Steven sought a safe topic. "Have you been waiting long?"

"A lifetime," she answered.

Just then they heard a car barrel up the driveway and Nicole breathed a sigh of relief as her Maserati pulled up in front of them.

Steven walked around to the driver's seat to hold open her door.

"I want to see you again." His tone was serious. "Can we have lunch?"

"Of course." It was Nicole's automatic response. "Call me at the studio sometime."

"But I'm leaving tomorrow night," he replied.

Nicole was far too distracted to parry. She tilted her head toward him in a minor concession to flirtation.

"Then I lose, I guess," she said.

He helped her close the car door, and as she turned the ignition key, he took a step back.

"Well, drive safely."

She snapped off the ignition and faced him. "Do me a favor. If we ever see each other again, don't say, 'Drive safely.' It's nothing personal. The phrase just makes me crazy."

She turned the ignition back on and released the emergency brake. She slammed it into first and accelerated ten yards before hitting the brakes. She stuck her head out the window and called out to Steven.

"I'm sorry," she said sincerely. She didn't want to lose this connection just because she was losing her patience. "It's not a good day and I'm sorry if I've made a bad impression."

"Don't worry about it," he reassured her as his own rental car appeared. "It won't scare me away."

*   *   *

Jasmine slipped the terry-cloth robe, the required mode of dress in Lance's hideaway gazebo, off the top half of her body. Slowly she ran a wet facecloth over her chest. Too much anxiety and too many lines of coke were eating away at her cool. She'd already lost it once that day; twice would be demoralizing.

What was she doing here anyway? she asked herself. Originally she'd come to L.A. to take a break from the east-coast humidity. When Lisa had suggested she meet Lance, she started to think. Lance could put her in his new movie. That would make up for losing the Revlon account, a slight she'd been brooding over for months. Though she hadn't read *Dirty Dreams*, she had no doubt she could do the part. Lisa said all the role called for was a beautiful, sexy young woman. Well, she was beautiful, sexy, and young. Why shouldn't she get the lead in the movie? Last month her psychic had told her that her career was about to take off. On first seeing Lance, a week before, Jasmine had felt that *Dirty Dreams* was her destiny, but now she wasn't sure. She couldn't get a beat on what Lance was thinking. The way he touched her was very intimate, but he hadn't tried to fuck her yet. Was tonight supposed to be the night?

Exasperated, she threw the facecloth into the sink.

"Take this," Lisa instructed, choosing a pill out of the stash Lance kept in a compartment behind a mirror. Of those who had attended Lance's after-hours party, only they were left.

"What am I taking?" Jasmine asked, examining what was definitely not an over-the-counter drug.

"It's a relaxant. A mini-lude."

Jasmine complied, washing it down with some water Lisa poured for her. Out of habit, while downing the pill, Jasmine examined her reflection in the mirror. She made a mental note to get her hair trimmed. From the corner of her eye she noticed that Lisa was studying her body, and when she became aware that Jasmine had noticed, she didn't turn away. Instead she grew bolder.

"You've got a beautiful body."

"Thanks," Jasmine replied weakly. She wasn't feeling all that well, and it wasn't because of the drugs, champagne, or that afternoon's deadly liquor-filled strawberries. This was a very specific kind of discomfort she felt when things were happening too fast. It was like she was on some crazy merry-go-round and her body rhythm couldn't get used to the speed. She'd wanted to leave before the screening, but Lisa had convinced her to stay, cajoling her out of her depression by chatting about clothes, men, and restaurants.

God, she didn't know what she would have done without Lisa. She'd never met anyone like her before. Though they hadn't known each other long, Lisa had a way of making Jasmine feel as if she'd been her manager and friend forever. In addition to how quickly she had insinuated herself into Jasmine's life—giving her advice on everything from what music to listen to, to what kind of mascara to buy—she'd also acted as Jasmine's guide through the business and pleasures found in L.A. Staying at Lisa's house meant having a ringside seat to a nonstop parade of problems and propositions. Yet no matter how crazy things got, Lisa's ability to turn everything into girl-talk made it all seem acceptable.

Now Lisa was off on more girl-talk. Locker-room girl-talk. Health-club locker-room girl-talk . . . comparing bodies.

Lisa stepped out of her robe, completely naked and completely comfortable. She too checked herself out in the mirror. "I've got to start going back to the gym. When I was doing free weights, my arms were so much stronger." She pivoted, eyeing her figure from a side mirror. "And so was my back. I love a muscular back. You've got a good one." She reached out and lightly traced the curve of Jasmine's spine. "I've got a great masseuse you should see. She really knows how to get all the knots out." As she spoke, she caressed Jasmine from her shoulders down to her waist, and then brazenly pried her fingers inside the folds of the draped robe. Jasmine went rigid with this unexpected invasion and quickly moved away, ostensibly to refill her water glass.

"Did that bother you?" Lisa asked. "I didn't mean to scare you away. There's nothing wrong with our appreciating each other."

Jasmine pulled her robe back over her chest and dropped into a chair set up in front of the makeup area of the white-tiled countertop. She picked up a hairbrush and worked through some tangles. She wanted to come up with an easy out, but Lisa gave her no time to think of one. She knelt by the chair, her hands on Jasmine's knees in a posture of forgiveness. "I'm sorry. I just wanted to make you feel good. That's all. It's not a big deal, you know."

Jasmine tried to smile with understanding. She looked straight into Lisa's eyes to reassure her that the apology was accepted, and then, unintentionally, her gaze wandered down to Lisa's full smooth breasts, which heaved slightly with her accelerated breathing. Jasmine had an urge to touch them and at the same time an urge to push Lisa away. But the greatest urge of all was her desire to sit there and drift off into a safe sleep. Was the mini-lude beginning to have an effect? She leaned her head back and let her mind wander. When she felt Lisa's hand brush against her legs, she drifted happily into soft-focus reality. When Lisa's fingers climbed up Jasmine's thighs, she snapped out of her dream state.

"What are you doing?" she demanded.

Silently Lisa continued her exploration.

Jasmine squirmed and pushed away Lisa's hand. "What do you think you're doing?" she said. Something made Jasmine look up toward the open door. There she saw Lance, sipping frozen Stoli from his perch on a bar stool, perusing the action as if it were his private floor show.

"Baby," Lance cooed, coming toward her as though he

had just become aware of her displeasure. A quick look sent Lisa out the door and left Lance in charge. He held Jasmine's hand and listened attentively to her complaints.

"Tell her to stay away from me. I'm not a dyke. I'm not interested in women. I can't handle this." Her tears ebbed as Lance stroked her hair.

He guided her over to the side of the steaming turquoise spa, sat her down, kissed her feet, and placed them carefully, lovingly, into the water. Then, with an almost Japanese austerity of movement, he wiped the beads of anxious sweat from her brow and lightly massaged her temples. Slowly her face gave up its look of pinched hysteria. She told herself that she was with a well-respected man. This wasn't some loser from the low-rent side of Lincoln, Nebraska. This was a man who collected art. A man who had a higher aesthetic. A man who served his cocaine on a silver dish from Cartier. She felt protected by him and so she allowed him to take her robe.

"You're a beautiful little girl and an exquisite woman, all in one."

Jasmine smiled politely. She was used to compliments, and this one was not original enough to spark a more enlivened response.

Lance pulled her face toward his. "No, you don't get it. I'm not talking about what you look like."

Jasmine's mind scrambled for the correct answer. "You're talking about sexuality."

He let go his grip on her. "Sexuality. You make it sound clinical."

He walked away from her as if he were disappointed. But it was really just part of his game plan. He wanted to throw her off balance, to break the pattern of her automatic responses. Once he'd stripped her of her confidence, then he could lead her wherever he felt like going.

"Then what exactly do you mean?" she asked, confused.

This time she sought his eye, but he got up to reach for a Baccarat pillbox which sat on the ottoman in front of a leather futon—the recovery area for the Jacuzzi.

"Do you trust me, Jasmine?"

"Sure I trust you, Lance," she said much too quickly.

"I don't think we're talking about the same kind of trust." He pulled a tiny white pill out of the box. "I need you to really trust me."

"But I do, Lance. I really do. I mean, you're the only one here I feel comfortable with and want to spend time with and everything. You're the reason I stayed after the barbecue."

He stepped closer and placed the pill up to her mouth as if testing her declaration of trust. She opened her lips and swallowed it, her obedience made easy by the mounting effect of the first mini-lude.

"I'm talking about wanting something badly, wanting it totally . . . being willing to beg for it."

"I do want it, Lance," Jasmine admitted. From the moment they'd met, she was attracted to him, even though he was not her usual type. At five-feet-ten, he was a little too short, his arms were a little too muscular, and for her New York taste, he was a little too tan. But she had noticed his great ass. But now, at this moment, it wasn't his ass or any other physical attribute that eroticized her as much as it was something intangible. His power? His nonchalance? Jasmine wasn't sure. But she saw him as some kind of professor from whom she was determined to earn high marks.

Trying to control her jerky movements, hoping to appear enticing, she slipped her back onto the futon and offered her body to Lance as proof of her willingness to surrender. With his hand, he gently pried open her legs. Using his fingers to tickle and tease, he probed inside of her, making her moan. He kept at it, probing deeper, making her more and more hungry for him. Then, abruptly, he stopped. Deprivation made her moan louder as Lance leaned in closer.

"I saw you looking at Lisa's breasts. You wanted to touch them, didn't you?"

Jasmine tried to divert Lance by reaching between his legs, but he blocked her hand.

"Jasmine, trust me with your secrets."

She teetered on the line between giving in and pretending to give in. "I didn't mean to look at them," she said, her voice growing babyish.

Lance gripped her fingers as if testing her resistance. "But you did, and you couldn't help but wonder what it would be like to touch them, could you?"

She felt her temperature rise as she strained to control the thrill that was building inside of her. "Yes," she whispered. "I couldn't help it."

Gently Lance turned her head to the side so she could view Lisa, who was standing nearby observing them. Immediately Jasmine understood what was about to unfold. Lance, the conductor, backed away from the podium, replaced by the first violinist. This change seemed rehearsed, as the transition was made seamlessly. Lisa approached Jasmine and resumed stroking her body as Lance had.

This time, Jasmine was too far gone to protest. Lisa lowered her head so her thick blond hair swept Jasmine's breasts like an erotic duster. She wet her lips and lowered them to Jasmine's chest, kissing and caressing her with abandon. Jasmine tried to pretend that it was Lance who was fondling her, and she heard his voice comfort her.

"That's my beautiful little girl. Let Lisa love you, let yourself want her."

Lance watched admiringly as Lisa performed her role. She was good, he thought, as well as smart. Most of the Hollywood women he'd had a fling with were never invited back, but Lisa made him aware that she could be of service in other ways. He knew that what she got out of these evenings wasn't only a scene that fed her desire to flirt with danger. It was also a scene that fed her desire for safety. Knowing other people's secrets was Lisa's version of an insurance policy. It made her feel an inte-

gral part of their network. As long as she didn't abuse his
trust, Lance was happy to have Lisa be a part of his inner
circle, with all the perks, favors, and gifts that went along
with that status.

Jasmine turned her head sideways and saw how aroused
Lance was. His pleasure released her from any remaining
hesitation. With her mind now in sync with the desires of
her body, she reached out for Lisa's breasts, bringing
them to her lips and relishing this new sensation.

Lisa, following Lance's lead, intentionally kept Jasmine off balance. Denying her the gratification Jasmine
yearned for, Lisa sat back, leaving her would-be lover
with a wild look in her eyes. Lisa's hand lightly touched
Jasmine's stomach and traveled over her smooth thighs.
This time knowing it would be granted, she looked to her
for permission before proceeding.

"Yes, yes," Jasmine murmured.

With this now articulated, Lance moved in closer and
tapped Lisa's shoulder, signaling that he was ready to
take over.

He walked toward a console built into the wall and
opened the third drawer. In it were neatly stacked priceless antique Chinese scarves, each one exquisite and
unique. He pulled one out and turned deliberately toward
Jasmine.

He announced his presence by grabbing her hair and
pulling it tightly. Jasmine's eyes opened in surprise.

"Slow down, love. Lance is here. Listen very carefully
and don't be afraid. I know where I'm going. Trust me."

Lance took her hands into his. "God, you're beautiful.
You're what *Dirty Dreams* is all about." He saw that she
was completely malleable now, and slowly he began to
bind her wrists together with his elegant scarf.

9

"Something's up, I know it is." Kevin Holberstein was in his office talking to himself a he paced back and forth on his Persian rug. He'd known something was up since he'd spoken to his secretary this Tuesday morning and discovered that Lance had left a message on the answering machine at seven A.M. He knew that Lance had seen this hour from the other side, and in this frenzied state of mind had booked himself for nine A.M. Kevin imagined a wild animal pumped up on chemicals and full of demands. There was something ominous about this wake-up call. This was more than one of Lance's rank-and-file tirades, of which Nicole was currently the chief recipient. Kevin had been waiting for the shoe to drop since the screening, expecting that sooner or later Lance would turn on him.

"Lance Burton is here." Kevin heard the reverberations of the message over the intercom. He pressed his foot on the door release under his desk. He sensed that for some reason he would always remember this moment.

He immediately noticed two things: Lance was carrying something and it looked like he hadn't slept.

Kevin's second confirmation that something was wrong was that Lance was acting strangely demure. Though unshaven and slightly disheveled in appearance, Lance was calm. Too calm. There was a frightening reserve of leverage oozing from him.

Slowly Lance placed three VCR tapes on Kevin's marble desk. They were copies of the ones he'd gotten from

Joey. He spoke very reasonably. "You know what this is?" Lance's eyes were fixed on the tapes. "This is the jugular, Kevin. Compliments of Jerry DiLeo. Am I tapping your memory banks?"

Kevin couldn't speak.

"The Surfside Hotel in Atlantic City? Does that help? A young trick named Billy Weathers? A drummer?"

Kevin dropped to his seat. His mind, his body, his heartbeat, all on halt.

"Nice weekend with the family?" Lance changed the subject, as everything necessary had already transpired between them.

The facade of Kevin's strength collapsed like a dying star. He felt himself living the moment he'd always dreaded.

The power of this fear had compromised Kevin with the east-coast gangsters who had entrapped him when he was twenty-five. He'd been ready to leave his secret dalliance on the docks of gay New York behind forever. He'd gotten married to his politically well-connected wife and under his father-in-law's tutelage was becoming a power to reckon with in the state Democratic machine. The mob put an end to all that.

When first confronted with the evidence, Kevin instantly knew that he could never let his wife or her family know about his past. They could not handle the humiliation. He'd have to get out of the limelight, abandon politics as a way of abandoning his blackmailers. Hollywood struck him as a place free of moral watchdogs. People there cared less about a man's past and more about his current industry status. Kevin believed he could safely start over three thousand miles away. But he had miscalculated the mob's possessiveness. He was their guy: east coast, west coast, didn't matter. In fact, Hollywood was a good place for Kevin, they decided. He had no choice but to accede to their wishes.

Not that he'd done anything really bad for the mob— but few would appreciate these distinctions. His role had been benign: exert a little pressure on the teamster contracts, get some "machers" invited to the Academy Awards, screen-test some bimbos, and protect some local informers he'd had to hire. But his in-laws, the squeaky-clean Carlyles, would never understand, and he knew there was no reason in the world he should expect them to.

He felt a piercing stab of pain, as though he'd literally been knifed in the back. He struggled for stability. Something to hold on to. He was looking out the window as if saying good-bye to the privileged view.

Lance strolled around his office, reading stray memos. The room was filled with heavy air. My daughter would be more devastated if I killed myself, Kevin realized, than if I lost my job and went to jail.

He looked up at Lance as if he were turning to a priest for absolution. Lance smiled kindly at him, as though from a vast height.

"Don't worry, Kev. No one has to know. It'll be our little secret. A scandal could hurt Millennium, especially now that the studio is in play."

Kevin knew this did not mean he should feel relieved. He waited for Lance's postscript. He watched him stroll toward the door, and then, sure enough, as he passed Kevin, he stopped. "Oh, by the way, we're going to make *Dirty Dreams*," he said. "There's a lot of work ahead and I don't want any interference from Nicole. In fact," he added with just a hint of a grin crossing his face, "I think our executive V.P. wields a little too much power. You might want to correct that. Got it?"

"Got it," Kevin answered softly.

"Good," Lance said as he made his move for the door. Once again he stopped. "And don't look so scared, Kevin. Smile. This is going to be fun."

THE
FIRES

10

Nicole checked her Rolex and realized that, as it was Tuesday, her weekly development meeting was scheduled to start in five minutes. She knew that the edginess she was feeling came from a combination of pressures. Starting late meant that every meeting was exponentially delayed by the one preceding it, until there was no way that she could complete all her phone calls. It was a pace she often complained about, but it was also one she'd have been lost without. Charging through the day with no time for anything but meetings and crisis control meant there was no time to dwell on what was missing in her personal life. Today, however, would be especially demanding because of the escalation of the Lance problem. The word all over town was that *Dirty Dreams* was in preproduction. To make matters worse, Nicole couldn't get Kevin to even discuss the situation. For over a week, since returning to work after the Fourth of July break, he had been strangely aloof. He claimed to be too busy to have a meeting with her. Without any guidance, Nicole racked her brain to come up with the best way to proceed. So far, the only thing her solution-oriented mind had come up with was to prepare a confidential memo for Ted and Kevin, one that laid out Millennium's options. As she jotted down a few key points, Carolyn buzzed her on the intercom.

"Bambi and David Beach are here. Do you want me to send them in?"

"Send in the clowns," Nicole called into her speaker box. "And interrupt us if this goes on too long. I've got to dictate a memo before lunch."

The door to her office swung open, revealing Bambi, perky as ever, in an overaccessorized dress-for-success suit. Behind her, David Beach sauntered in, wearing his Guess jeans, open white tuxedo shirt, and black blazer.

"Why do I feel we should hold our story meetings in Maxfield's?" Nicole asked as the natty twosome took their seats around her pitch table.

Armed with memos and scripts, the junior executives shuffled their papers, signaling the commencement of their most important meeting of their week. The game they played was getting a script or a pitch they'd heard approved by Nicole for development. Which one of them had more projects in the works was a tally the two privately kept. The agents always knew who was winning.

At times, Nicole was amused watching them jockey for position, harpooning each other's ideas at critical moments, lending surprise support, so the favor would be returned in the next round. It was a sport she once had excelled at, but it seemed shrill to her now, and a little ridiculous.

"Let the *Gong Show* begin," Nicole recited in their traditional exchange. "I'm running late, so we have to stay focused today."

"Well, I'm prepared," Bambi said. "I read thirty scripts over the weekend."

Nicole was stunned. "Bambi, tell me, how is it possible to read thirty scripts in two and a half days? Didn't you go out? Eat? Go to the gym?"

"I went out every night," Bambi replied. "And I work out at the Sports Connection every other morning. I still have plenty of time. I can read a script in fifteen minutes. I read them between phone calls."

David Beach couldn't resist. "How far apart are your phone calls?"

Nicole laughed. "Bambi, don't ever let a writer hear

you say that." She turned her attention to David Beach. "How was the CAA package you read over the weekend? Don't we have to respond today?"

"Yeah, it's in multiple submission. But I wouldn't race to the phone. It's about a Mother Teresa type who gets involved in a plutonium heist to save her flock. They'd have to bring Lassie out of retirement to get cornier than this."

"Isn't Vanessa Redgrave doing Mother Teresa as a mini-series?" Bambi loved to look plugged-in.

"Bambi . . ." David Beach started in a mocking tone. "This is called fiction."

"Thank you, Professor Beach," Bambi shot back.

"How's the writing?" Nicole asked. "Is it an Alan Pakula picture? A Sidney Lumet/Jane Fonda special?"

David Beach tried to recall what the reader had told him that morning. "The writing is serviceable, the plotting sort of falls apart in the third act, but basically, I think it's a ludicrous premise."

"Pass," Nicole said.

"I got pitched a terrific high-concept musical," David Beach said as he continued down his list. "This new writer, out of USC, a protégé of Spielberg's, wants to do a piece about a motorcycle gang that forms a band. It culminates in an action blowup against their rivals in a battle-of-bands sequence in the finale."

Nicole strained to visualize what sounded like a musical version of a Nintendo video game. Not wanting to admit that the post-MTV universe left her feeling her age, she reserved judgment. "Sounds like a Walter Hill piece to me. Check it out with ICM, and if the agency thinks he'd be interested, I'll buy it for scale."

Bambi saw an opening. "Walter Hill is unavailable. He's got two pictures at Fox." She smiled at her scoop.

"But that doesn't make him unavailable for a development deal," David Beach countered. "I'm seeing him at a screening this week and I'll talk to him about it." Now he'd one-upped her and could smugly endure the rest of the meeting.

"Anything else, David?" Nicole's tone made it clear that she didn't really want to hear any more.

"No, the others can wait," David responded, passing his hand to Bambi.

"I want to do a remake of *Singin' in the Rain,*" Bambi said.

"You've got to be kidding," David Beach said under his breath. "You can't do an old-fashioned musical these days. Give me a break."

"Well, I figured out how to do it. I was talking with Herb Ross and—"

Nicole cut her short. "Save this one for when we have more time." She tried to be conciliatory. "If you're concentrating on remakes, Bambi, I'll tell you what I'm in the mood for. I'd like to see a hip *Pat and Mike* piece, something Hepburn/Tracy-like that we can package with Kathleen Turner and Harrison Ford. A romantic comedy with a very modern point of view."

David Beach scrambled mentally through his list, looking to adjust one of his old ideas to meet Nicole's new criteria.

Bambi beat him to the punch. "I've got a cross between *Charade* and *Three Days of the Condor,*" she began. "It takes place in Vietnam, in the beginning of the CIA, called the OSO or something, and a debonair bachelor—"

Nicole interrupted her again. "I want it contemporary. Not period." She closed the leatherbound notebook she used for story ideas. "At our next meeting I want each of you to come up with three or four different remake ideas. Check our library and see what rights we control. We'll pick this up next week. Now. Anyone read the Forman script for my two-thirty meeting? Milos is coming."

Bambi fiddled with her gold bangle bracelets and adopted a presumptuous tone. "No, Nicole. You have the only copy. Don't you remember, you said it was an exclusive submission that might leak if you made Xerox copies. But I know that Paramount is meeting with him this afternoon."

Bambi's needling found its way to Nicole's nerve endings. "This meeting is over. I've got to finish the script. Out."

Without further discussion, David Beach and Bambi left the office, David Beach in a considerably better mood than his counterpart. Nicole organized the papers on top of her desk, but her mind kept returning to the Lance problem and a nagging picture of Bambi's newly adopted attitude. She knew that normally Bambi was too ambitious, too political, and too manipulative to be overtly competitive with any boss. Therefore, she reasoned, if Bambi now felt safe being less than a team player, it must mean that Nicole was inconsequential to Bambi's job security. Bambi's possible "chummy" connection to Lance sprang to mind again, as it had several times over the last week. God damn this system, she cursed to herself. Two years ago Bambi had come up with a halfway decent idea for a movie that Paul Newman liked but had not yet made. That move alone had turned her into a credible force in development. It wasn't even an original idea, just a book that had been gathering dust on many studios' "pass" shelves. Bambi had parlayed that one suggestion into a fairly high-profile career. No telling how far she could parlay an alliance with Lance. I can't deal with her now, Nicole reminded herself. I've got to write this memo.

She tapped the button on the bottom of the speaker box to bring it to life. "Could you come in here," she called to Carolyn, who sat behind her door ten feet away.

Carolyn popped up from her desk, grabbed a steno pad and sharp pencil, and bit her lip. "I do fast notes, not shorthand," she warned.

"Don't sweat it. This should be short and sweet."

Nicole got up from behind her desk and moved slowly around the room. "Carolyn, I have something important to discuss with you. What I'm about to dictate is extremely sensitive. Let me repeat. It is of the utmost secrecy. When you're finished typing this memo, tear up the notes. I want you to personally hand Ted and Kevin their copies. Instead of putting mine in the outer-office *Dirty Dreams* file, slot a copy in my personal legal file. And be very careful in the Xerox room because some of these overzealous secretaries are out to get a raise by stealing memos for their bosses. This is currency, and it could mean my job. Can I trust you?"

Carolyn felt the curious exhilaration that is addictive in Hollywood. She was inhaling the "inside" where everyone wanted to be. She looked Nicole in the eye. "I have no interest here but to work for you as your confidential secretary. I take that responsibility seriously."

Nicole nodded her acceptance of Carolyn's directness and began dictating.

To: Ted McGuiness/cc: Kevin Holberstein.
From: Nicole Lanford.

With respect to Lance Burton's preemptive announcement of *Dirty Dreams*. I fully expect to hear that Burton is making offers to actors this week, pledging the studio's money. We are all aware of the dire repercussions likely to follow any effort on our behalf to halt preproduction on *Dirty Dreams*. Given Lance's grand-scale plans, we are also aware that this kind of expensive noncommercial production can seriously damage the studio financially. I suggest that we counter Burton's moves indirectly, taking a uniform attitude. To Burton, business affairs, the other creative executives, and the community, we should act as if Lance's actions are supported by Millennium. We should also allot something on the order of a million dollars to be made available to him to crew up. We must buy time to deal with any political problems in New York before we can publicly pull the plug on this project. Because we will also have to pay or play him, the total abandonment costs are likely to be very high. We already have half a million dollars in development costs, so I think we should be prepared to tell New York that we may end up having to write off somewhere upwards of three million dollars to get rid of the Burton problem. The strategy for buying time can be the standard delaying tactics—approvable lists of stars, budget fluctuations, the regular wildgoose chases. With this in motion, I figure we can buy two or three months. With the studio apparently in play, this is not the time to do anything that will make us look unstable and affect our price on the market. Hopefully two or three months down the line, we'll be able to kill this project without causing a high-profile confrontation. Please advise.

N.L.

The relief Nicole had hoped to get by putting her thoughts in writing eluded her. She'd come up with the idea of the memo after fruitlessly trying Ted on the phone last night. Unable to find him, she fell into a fitful sleep punctuated with nightmares about Lance. At four A.M. she'd finally cajoled herself back to her pillow by inventing the strategy she'd just composed in the memo.

"Okay, Carolyn, type it up, and remember what I said. Deal?" She looked at Carolyn with an uncertain smile, fraught with vulnerability, like that of someone only learning how to like other people. Then she stretched out her arm in a handshake.

Carolyn returned the gesture. "Deal."

As she turned to leave, she noticed that Nicole's phone lines were flashing silently. Answering the first one, she said, "Nicole Lanford's office."

"I have to read the Forman script before lunch, so hold my calls," Nicole cut in softly.

"Who may I say is calling?" Carolyn paused. "She's

unavailable right now, Mr. Lloyd. Can I tell her what this is in reference to?"

Steven Lloyd's name caught Nicole off balance. "No, Carolyn. I'll take this one. Get messages from the rest."

Their eyes momentarily locked into a women's recognition. A new man.

"Excuse me, Mr. Lloyd, she just stepped back in," Carolyn announced into the receiver. She then put the phone on hold and left, closing Nicole's door behind her.

"Well, well, well," Nicole said as she picked up the extension. "I hear it's another hot, humid day in New York City today."

"I wouldn't know," Steven replied. "Right now I'm on my way to Avenue of the Stars. Great street names you've got out here."

"When did you get back?"

"Last night."

"Couldn't leave L.A.'s hot winds behind?" Nicole asked playfully.

"Couldn't leave something behind, that's true. I'm calling to set a lunch date. We made a tentative plan, remember? Though you were rather distracted when we said good-bye."

" 'Distracted' is one way of putting it," Nicole admitted. " 'Panicked' is another." She couldn't believe how intimate she felt talking with this man, and she knew almost nothing about him. Slow down, she warned herself. "So, what can I do for you, Mr. Lloyd?"

"Don't get formal with me, Nicole. What I like best about L.A. is that it's not stuffy."

"Oh, that's right," Nicole said. "It's a land of happy laid-back people. You can vacation here and drop all your inhibitions. Perhaps change your name and get your aura cleaned while you're at it."

"What I'd like to do is take you to dinner tonight. Possible?"

"Dinner? Where?" She'd meant it to sound affirmative, but it came out as hesitation.

"Is everything with you a negotiation?"

They both laughed at his intentional misreading. He'd saved her from sounding too eager.

"No, Steven, anywhere is fine."

"How about if I pick you up at eight-thirty for chili and crab claws at Chasen's?"

"Chasen's?" Her tone said it wasn't her favorite.

"Too old-guard for you?" he guessed.

"No, it's okay. I did say anywhere, but . . ." She paused.

"No, really, Nicole, continue. I'm not offended that you're critiquing my well-planned-out evening."

"I'm sorry, it's fine, but—"

"I've got an idea," Steven said. "Let's forget about Chasen's. Trust me to come up with another idea. Let the tourist show the native around town."

"Okay," Nicole agreed. "It's in your hands."

"Now all I need is your address," Steven said. "We can't assume too much, you know."

"Hutton Drive, off Benedict. Twenty-three-thirty-two. At the end of a very windy road, the white guesthouse in the back."

"Till then," Steven closed.

Nicole placed the phone down on its cradle very gently and brushed back her hair, almost in slow motion.

Her usually abrupt movements seemed rhythmic and controlled, like a dancer's. Suddenly she realized it was time to leave for her lunch meeting and she hadn't glanced at the Milos Forman script. "Oh, shit," she said out loud. She considered canceling lunch, but the two writers she was meeting were undoubtedly already waiting at the commissary.

She buzzed Carolyn again. "Come on in, we've got to talk."

With steno pad in hand, Carolyn rushed into Nicole's office and took her seat.

"Look, Carolyn. I'm incredibly behind today, as you know, and I haven't been able to get to the Milos Forman script. I have a meeting with him when I get back from lunch. I don't want anyone in the story department to know I haven't read it, so I can't get it covered that way. Can you read it and type up some quick notes on what it's about . . . how to fix it . . . perfect casting, et cetera?"

"Oh, God, sure, absolutely, I'd love to." Carolyn was thrilled to get a chance to use her brain, but realized her gushing response made her appear unprofessional. "I mean," she rephrased, "I've been reading some of the submissions whenever the phones are quiet, and it's exactly the kind of work I really enjoy doing."

Nicole eyed her secretary carefully, trying to size up this person she was forced to entrust. "Second week on the job, Carolyn, and you're already privy to your boss's secrets."

Carolyn knew she was being tested. "No one will know," she promised.

"Deal," Nicole said for the second time that morning.

11

Bambi had Andrew right where she wanted him, sitting across from her in her office, working hard to sell her an idea she had no intention of buying. She sat in a comfortable upholstered chair, while Andrew was delegated to the armless, practically backless couch. He looked as if he were adrift on a raft, his direction subject to the currents, or, in this case, the whims of the territorial waters he invaded. He did his best to navigate.

"Jamaica would be a wonderful setting for a movie, and Millennium's never done a book like *Wide Sargasso Sea*. The author was considered one of the best English novelists and I don't see how a story about the first Mrs. Rochester wouldn't have wide appeal. Think of all the people who loved *Jane Eyre*. To take a minor character from that book and write a novella about her was a brilliant idea, and the movie we can make from it will be a work of art. It was all set to go, but the Italian money fell through."

Bambi was tired of hearing novice producers talk about the Italian money falling through or the Cayman Islands money falling through or the Rio de Janeiro money. She'd learned from experience that in situations like this, no matter what exotic locale the money was coming from, it in fact never came.

"What about copyrights?" Bambi asked.

"The author's estate is willing to sell to me. We've mutual friends in England, so it's just a matter of the studio putting up the money."

132 *Lynda Obst and Carol Wolper*

Bambi wrapped her Chanel necklace around her fingers. Chanel accessories had become popular again in Beverly Hills ever since Princess Stephanie of Monaco had been photographed at a party at Vertigo's with her little black Chanel bag slung over her shoulder. Bambi's coverage of the society page was considerably more extensive than her coverage of English novelists. As for *Jane Eyre,* she knew it was a love story. Or was she confused? Was she thinking of Heathcliff and what's-her-name? I hate the classics, she wanted to announce to Andrew, but held the thought in and kept twirling her Chanel pearls.

"Have you ever had conch fritters and ginger beer?" Andrew asked.

"Conch fritters," Bambi repeated, as if they were something you called Western Exterminator about.

"When we start shooting, you'll come visit the set. I'll take you to see this amazing Jamaican woman who used to be my nanny. She makes the best conch fritters in the Caribbean. Then we'll go to what was once my grandfather's plantation. The gardens there, even now, when they're not properly cared for, are a botanist's dream . . . frangipani trees, exotic orchids in colors more brilliant than anything Gauguin ever painted. The sunsets from the top of Strawberry Hill are second only to those in Kenya."

Andrew was a good salesman. He could romanticize a visit to a decaying family manor until Bambi almost forgot the nightmarish logistics of shooting a movie in a third-world country. It was his voice which worked this magic. The same words written in a letter would seem pretentious, even silly, but spoken in his deep resonance, they had the power to cut through layers of superficial concerns and engage even the most shallow person in poetic dialogue.

"I've been to Jamaica," Bambi stated, trying to gain a firmer footing in the conversation. "It *was* beautiful," she agreed, not mentioning that it was a Club Med vacation and she never left the hotel. "But then, politically, things got dangerous there. And all those Rastafarians. I've never understood why they don't comb their hair. What's that got to do with religion?"

"I'm going to give you a Bob Marley record," Andrew said. "Listen to 'Natural Mystic' and you'll begin to understand the Rastas. And you must listen to 'I Don't Want to Wait in Vain for Your Love,' " he added with the sincere enthusiasm of a fan.

"I like the title. Send it to me." Bambi smiled, assuming, incorrectly, that his choice of a love song was no accident. "Is it on compact disc? I only have a CD player at home."

Andrew leaned forward and sat on the edge of the raft. "My God, Bambi," he scolded, feigning impatience with her princess attitude. "How about if I bring you the tape and a cassette player to hear it on? It may not be the best sound, but then, Bob Marley never had a CD. The people in the shantytowns of Kingston didn't have CD's, and their reggae music ignited the whole bloody country."

He delivered this sermon with a grin to let her know that although he thought of her as a spoiled brat, she could get away with it.

"Well, so bloody what?" She grinned back. She was enjoying this immensely. She believed that people let you get away with things only if you were a "special case" —extraordinary in some way—and her fear of being average made her crave this validation. "What's the point? That I should have inferior listening systems in my home?" she asked defiantly.

"The point is, Bambi, that you will fall in love with Jamaica."

"Maybe," she said. "May . . . be." She looked at him intently, noticing that behind the twinkle in his eyes was a drive that would slow down for nothing and no one, a drive not unlike her own.

"How would you like to come to a fund-raiser with me?" she offered. "It's one of those big industry galas at the Beverly Hilton. Black tie. Sometime next month. It'll give you a chance to meet some people you should know."

"What kind of charity?" Andrew was stalling, trying to figure out the appropriate course of action.

"I don't know. The blind. The deaf. Something. It's an industry gathering. They're all the same."

Making contacts was exactly what Andrew needed. "I'd love to escort you," he agreed. The word "escort" made it seem like less of a date and he was able to convince himself he wouldn't be betraying Carolyn.

"Terrific." She looked at her watch and stood up to get a piece of paper, but also to signal the end of their meeting. What's your number?"

"It's 555-9001," Andrew answered. He was still floating on his raft, his destination still in question. "And what about *Wide Sargasso Sea?*"

"I'd love to see you do some work on it and bring it back with a bankable director."

Development, Andrew wanted to shout. Your job, Bambi, is *development*. Look the word up in the dictionary. It means you help something grow. If I had a bankable director, I wouldn't need to meet with a junior executive. If he'd been brought up differently he might have told her she was wanking him off, but etiquette prevailed. He even managed to keep some of the twinkle in his eyes as he jumped off the raft.

"I'll do that," he lied.

"Wait, I'll walk you to the elevator," Bambi said.

"I thought only stars got that kind of treatment from you," Andrew joked.

Bambi took his arm in hers as if they'd just forged an agreement. "It's true. I don't do it for just anybody."

"I'm sure you don't," Andrew replied, a weariness creeping into his charm.

* * *

Carolyn worked the keys of the IBM Selectric with renewed purpose. Even the ringing that constantly interrupted her couldn't dull the vigor with which she attacked her mundane task. She sat forward in her chair, and when she proofread, her feet tapped out a rhythm and her hands turned a pen-and-pencil set into drumsticks. Every part of her body was awake, primed like a racehorse at the starting gate.

She knew her notes on the script for the Forman meeting were good. She'd identified the theme, pointed out the pacing problems, and come up with a list of safe casting choices as well as creative ones. She'd watched Nicole and Milos walk down the hallway together after the meeting, and could tell by Nicole's relaxed attitude that it had gone well.

Just then she heard Nicole approaching, laughing at some comment someone had made. Hearing this levity, Carolyn knew the meeting had gone *very* well. She hoped for some small acknowledgment from her boss, but what she got was more than just an appreciative nod.

Nicole stopped at Carolyn's desk and glanced at the incoming-call side of her phone sheet. Without looking up she said, "Suggesting Robbie Robertson for the lead was really inventive."

"I've been a big fan of his for a long time," Carolyn said. "I even liked him in *Carny*. And I think his performance in his 'Somewhere Down the Crazy River' video proved he's still compelling on-screen."

Nicole put down the phone sheet and leaned against her secretary's desk. "Are you one of those people who live and breathe movies? One of those who know all the trivia from some obscure Bogart movie to who the assistant director on *Police Academy Five* was?"

"No, I've got major gaps in my film knowledge," Carolyn admitted. "I've never seen a Godzilla movie. In fact, I can't watch horror movies at all. I don't understand why the characters in those movies always walk *in* the direction of the scream."

Nicole laughed. "I've got a proposition for you. Instead of answering phones, how about, on a trial basis, being my personal reader? No change in pay, for a while, and probably longer hours, but you can take over the empty office at the end of the hall."

Carolyn tapped a package that had just arrived that morning from William Morris. "I'll start on these scripts today and have the coverage on your desk first thing in the morning."

"Before you do anything, call personnel and get them working on finding me another secretary," Nicole instructed.

"Right away," Carolyn replied eagerly.

Nicole smiled slightly at the gung-ho spirit she remembered from her own early days on the lot. "Welcome to the movie business, Carolyn. Things can happen fast around here. Feast or famine, that's the way it seems to go."

Carolyn had no comeback to that line, nor did she need one. Nicole had walked off without waiting to hear a response. "First thing first," Carolyn said to herself as she looked up the extension number for the personnel office. Before she could make the call, she was distracted by a familiar voice calling out.

"How's my little love button?" This was Andrew's abbreviated version of "You're cute as a button and I love you."

In a second, Carolyn shot up and sprinted from behind the desk. "You won't believe it," she said, excited that he was there to share her good news. She took hold of his arm, and in spite of Bambi's firm grasp on the other side, she drew all his attention her way. "Nicole just hired me to be her reader."

"Sweetheart, that's fabulous. This calls for a Lawry's celebration." He gave her a quick but tender kiss.

"Isn't that fabulous, Bambi?" Andrew asked.

"Un-huh." Bambi was in shock. She had had no idea that Andrew and Carolyn were an item. That really did it. She wasn't thrilled with Carolyn to begin with. "She's so unprofessional-looking," she'd complained to David Beach. Secretly she was intimidated by Carolyn's self-invented style and creative way of dressing. She hated it when girls like Carolyn looked great without spending a lot of money.

"Yes, let's definitely celebrate at Lawry's," Carolyn agreed.

The intimacy between them made Bambi uncomfortable. She let go of Andrew's arm. "Lawry's? Lawry's on La Cienega? On Restaurant Row? Only tourists and people from the Valley go there."

"It's refreshing," Carolyn tried to explain. "No nouvelle cuisine, no pastel paintings on the walls, no stone tables."

"It's the best place for the last two meat eaters in L.A. to go to," Andrew added.

"Andrew's love of Yorkshire pudding and beef Wellington makes him a freak in the tofu capital of California," Carolyn jokingly said to Bambi.

"It's my kind of menu," Andrew admitted. "Plus they've got these great old-time professional waitresses. Real characters. They're completely into their job. They're there to wait tables, not look for husbands or meet casting directors."

"Nice," Bambi said dismissively. Then, in an effort to recapture some of Andrew's attention, she added, "You know, I was a reader when I was twenty-one."

Andrew caught only part of what she said. "You were a dealer?" he asked with amazement.

"No . . . a reader. A reader. Five years ago I did what Carolyn's now doing."

Andrew laughed. "I was thrown for a minute there, Bambi. I couldn't quite picture you weighing out the grams."

Carolyn giggled at the absurdity of the miscommunication but Bambi looked glum. Andrew had glossed over the point that Carolyn's promotion was no big deal.

"Your phone is ringing," Bambi commented at the completion of the first ring. Carolyn leaned across the desk to get it, and Bambi studied her outfit: white leggings, droopy socks, full skirt, a lacy T-shirt, short boots, a dozen thin black bangles and an airplane pin. She memorized these details as if they were part of a recipe she could later follow.

She then looked to Andrew to see if she could catch his eye. Would he flirt with her while Carolyn was busy jotting down a message? No chance, Bambi realized. His gaze was locked on Carolyn, who glanced up from her notepad and exchanged with him one of those looks that pass between two people dying to make love.

Bambi had to ask herself why she was still standing there. Was she a masochist, forcing herself to witness the kind of happiness between two people she not only had never experienced but had done a pretty good job of convincing herself was unrealistic? She tried to think of an exit line. "I've got an important meeting" was always a possibility, but like a compulsive gambler on a bad streak, she was incapable of cutting her losses and walking away.

Carolyn finished the call and turned to Andrew. "And I get an office. A teeny one, without a window, but still . . ."

"Show me," Andrew insisted, taking her hand and pulling her away from her obligations.

"I can't," she protested. "What if the phone rings?"

"Bambi will take a message. Won't you, Bambi?"

Bambi shot him a look that said: Think again, buddy . . . think again.

"No, no, I can't," Carolyn said as the phone buzzed and once again she was trapped.

"Be right there," she said. She put down the receiver

and picked up her notepad. "Nicole," she explained, affectionately touching Andrew's arm as she moved past him on her way into her boss's inner office.

"She'll be stuck in one of the small rooms down the hall," Bambi pointed out to Andrew. "Nothing special."

She was pissed at him for having a girlfriend and angry at herself for caring. He's just a struggling producer with a lot of charm. Do I need this in my life? No, she decided. But that didn't make her feel better. She'd been counting on an affair with Andrew ever since running into him at Morton's, and felt unjustly punished by this setback.

Andrew was oblivious of her aggravation. He was perched on the edge of Carolyn's desk scanning the headlines in the trades. He tossed the papers aside and addressed Bambi's comment.

"Carolyn's promotion is quite a nice show of support from Nicole. Don't you think?"

Oh, pul-eeze, Bambi thought. "The problem is, so many people just get stuck in the grind of reading," she replied. "But," she added, "of course it beats answering phones."

Her initial dislike for Carolyn was quickly escalating into an overwhelming desire to discredit her rival. Although Bambi was aware that this reaction was juvenile, she justified it. Arrested development was the driving force behind too many major moguls to be considered a liability.

"It's a step in the right direction," Andrew pointed out. "That's the important thing to keep in mind."

What I need to keep in mind, Bambi decided, is my leverage. I can't let a cute guy who talks a good game make me feel rejected.

She struggled to come up with the perfect exit line. Something short, sweet, and ambiguous would be perfect.

Finally she caught Andrew's eye and, with a look, let

him know that there was a lot more the two of them needed to discuss.

"We'll talk," she said before turning away. It was a statement designed to imply everything, commit nothing, and leave him thinking. As Bambi strolled down the hall to her spacious, prestigiously situated office, she had no idea that Andrew had already moved on to another thought and another agenda.

12

So far, Steven Lloyd had gotten Nicole to do two things she never did: leave the office early and go to a restaurant she knew nothing about. Calling back in the afternoon, he had convinced her to go along with him on a whim of his to dine at a place called Plow and Angel.

"Plow and Angel," she repeated when he suggested it. It sounded so sixties to her, so unlike the present crop of eateries—Chaya, Trumps, Spago. When he informed her it was a two-hour drive up the coast and they'd have to leave L.A. by six, she, who hated being cooped up in a car and hated things being sprung on her, almost vetoed the whole idea. Something inside her, some voice that hadn't been heard from for a while, overruled her usual inclination to control. This time she allowed him to chart the course, at least as far as dinner was concerned.

As they drove through the gates, past a sign that identified the location as the San Ysidro Ranch, she recalled that though the restaurant might not be familiar, this ranch certainly was. It was a place she'd heard about before. The peacefulness found here was supposed to be ideal for writers who wanted to get lost in their work or lovers who wanted to get lost in their romance. She'd always wanted to come here for the weekend with some "very special guy," but none of her past relationships had evolved to the "very special" stage.

When she studied the menu, she was surprised to read in a short history of the place printed on the back cover that this was where Sir Laurence Olivier and Vivien

Leigh were married and where JFK and Jackie honey-
mooned.

Looking around, it was hard to imagine them here.
The dining room was so down-home, cozy but nothing
more. It wasn't Nicole's taste, but the place worked its
charm even on her. She was amused by the pattern on
the wall-to-wall rug. It was designed to look like a hardwood floor. There was nothing *trompe l'oeil* about it,
though. It clearly looked like a rug with an image of
wooden planks stamped—not even woven—into the wool.
How cutesy, she thought, as was the doormat at the
dining-room entrance, which greeted guests with the message "Meanwhile . . ."—the dot-dot-dot implying "back
at the ranch." That reminded her of the Saturday-morning
TV cowboy shows she'd loved as a kid. Thoughts of Fury
the horse mingled with thoughts of Steven sailing off
Cape Cod as she listened to him describe his favorite
getaway spots.

He talked about the house he used to rent on Indian
Hill Road, the blueberry jam his next-door neighbor
made, and watching the day break over Vinyardhaven
harbor. The places he mentioned—Menemsha, Chilmark,
Tisbury—evoked a serenity and beauty, but had he been
talking about Central Avenue, One Hundred and Twenty-
fifth Street, or Denny's Coffee Shop, Nicole would have
been equally enthralled.

"Have you ever seen *Fast Times at Ridgemont High?*"
Nicole suddenly blurted out.

Steven took another sip of wine. "Spicolli," he said.

"Right," Nicole said. That was the name of Sean Penn's
character. "So you did see it?"

"No, my daughter named her dog after that character,
that's all I know."

"Well, I bring it up because there's another character
in it, Damone. And in my favorite scene he gives his pal
his five-point plan for scoring with girls of all ages. Point
three was: Act like, wherever you are, that's the place to
be. And I started thinking about it because you manage

that point simply because you have natural curiosity and acute observations." As Nicole completed this point, it dawned on her that what she'd just admitted was that Steven was successfully scoring with her. What was I thinking? she asked herself as she noticed that they'd finished a whole bottle of wine.

"Shall we get another bottle?" Steven asked as the wine steward waited for instructions.

"Not for me," she replied. "I think it affects me like sodium pentathol. If you don't watch out, I'll start reciting from my journal."

"Another bottle," Steven ordered; then, turning back to Nicole, he said, "I'll have to rent the video, see what the other four points of Damone's plan are."

"I'm not expressing myself correctly," Nicole said, seeking safer ground. "I simply wanted to compliment you on what a good storyteller you are. I think I've sat through too many script meetings. I find that I'm constantly making analogies based on movies. Maybe I better start reading some books for a change."

"I think," Steven began as the steward refilled their glasses, "and this is just my biased opinion, that when *Fast Times at Ridgemont High* is your frame of reference, that's definitely your cue that you need a vacation."

He was joking with her, but she felt like she'd strayed too far off her corporate image. "I couldn't take a vacation now, even if I wanted to. There's too much to take care of at the office."

"Problems at Millennium?" Steven probed.

"You tell me. Is Millennium in play?"

"Yes, it is."

"What exactly does that mean?"

"The board of directors would welcome being bought out."

"Why?"

"I assume because the studio has had a number of successful seasons. The board believes the stock is topping and it'd be a good time to sell."

Nicole considered the information carefully. "Is Styvie going to buy it?"

Steven smiled. "You know I can't tell you that. That's insider trading."

Nicole moved on to what was really on her mind. "Did Lance bring him into the picture?"

"Nicole . . ." Steven gently cautioned.

"Does Ted know?"

"Nicole . . ."

"Okay, okay." Although Nicole agreed her questions were out of line, she was hit by a wave of paranoia. Was this dinner simply a fact-finding mission? Had she once again misread the signals?

"Why did you bring up Millennium?" she demanded.

Steven saw her defensive posture snap to attention and sought to reassure her. "Because it's your work, a part of your life."

Nicole resisted his sincerity.

"And the kind of shape Millennium's in these days is your work too, isn't it?"

"Let me explain something," he said. "The thing that impressed me the most about William Randolph Hearst was not his San Simeon, but the fact that he never discussed business at the dinner table. When the workday is over, it's over. I like spending my evenings getting away from talk about leverage buyouts and the SEC. I'm asking about you, not Millennium. I'm curious"—he emphasized the word—"about whether you like your job, how you worked your way up to executive V.P., where you grew up, what your favorite movie is, do you like being a role model." He paused. "I sound like Phil Donahue, don't I?" He shook his head. "I didn't ask you to dinner so I could milk you for details about Millennium's current status. Now, if I'd invited you to lunch . . . Just kidding." He grinned.

It's a good thing he's a legitimate investment banker, Nicole noted. A smile like that on a hustler would be dangerous.

"And do I get to hear the Steven Lloyd story?" she asked, softening.

"If you like," he agreed, "but I have a hunch yours is a lot less predictable."

Nicole waited for the waiter to refill their glasses before responding.

"Are you one of those people who went from the right prep school to a picturesque Ivy League college, Harvard Business School, first job at a prestigious company, brownstone on the Upper East Side, marriage . . ." She stopped, letting the sentence dangle on the word "marriage." Not that it was any secret. Steven's wedding ring made no pretense that he was unattached.

"Actually, the marriage turned out to be unpredictable."

"Is that good or bad?" Nicole asked.

"I don't know what it is."

The vulnerability in his face wedged a crack in Nicole's armor. She slowly unraveled her autobiographical thread, giving him sketchy details of her childhood. Quickly she got to her favorite part, the chronicle of her rise up Millennium's executive ladder.

"When I was first hired to work in development, we'd have these staff meetings every Friday morning. I worked so hard to be prepared, but once the meeting started, I was a blob of jelly, intimidated, afraid of being judged. The self-doubt made me clumsy. I remember bumping into chairs, dropping my notebook. Once I knocked over an ashtray . . . and the rug was beige. I didn't stutter, but came close to it. Then one day I got angry. I got angry at myself and at my bosses for making me feel like a second-class citizen. That particular day, as I sat in the meeting, I remembered something that had happened to me when I was ten. I was at a school carnival and they had an egg-throwing contest. They paired kids up, and after every round they made you take a step back so it would be harder to catch the egg. There must have been a hundred kids when the game started, but it narrowed down to four. I was one of the four and as I threw the egg back and forth to my partner, I knew we could win. I saw us winning. I pictured us getting the prize, and the picture frightened me so much, I dropped the egg. Classic stuff, I know—fear of success and all that—but that particular Friday morning, in the development meeting, I felt like I was on the verge of dropping the egg again, and it infuriated me so much that I forced myself to take control. I remember I argued persuasively for a particular change in a script and they went along with my idea. That's when I learned that the one in the room with the most conviction wins."

"You west-coasters have an evangelistic strain in your point of view," Steven noted. "This isn't a criticism, Nicole. In a way I envy you for it. There's always a new horizon out here. In New York, the person in the room with the most money wins."

"I don't buy this cynicism," Nicole replied. "You're too cheerful."

"That's because I moved into my own 'room,' so to speak," Steven explained. "You were right about the first job at a prestigious New York company. Problem was, it was my father's firm. For a while I had visions of a future that would read 'Lloyd and Lloyd'—classic expectations. I started off with an MBA from, I'm almost reluctant to admit, Harvard. I was full of ideas about creatively expanding my father's investment firm. 'Innovation' was an important word for me in those days. But my father wasn't about to change what he considered the formula that had made him successful. I won't bore you with the details. The broad strokes are: I'd go to work in the mornings talking structural decision-making and computer modeling, and I'd be assigned to oversee some small real-estate transaction. When I started I was one hundred percent confident that my theories and instincts about the financial marketplace would translate into profits. Eight years later, I looked around at the next wave of MBA-ers, and I wondered if I'd missed my chance by wasting time on ten-unit condo deals or if I'd been delusional all along. Maybe my talents were no more remarkable than anyone else's."

"You definitely are an overachiever. You even had your mid-life crisis early," Nicole said. "So, obviously, you did something about it."

"Actually, the first thing I did was quit, the second thing I did was go fly-fishing in Wyoming, and the third thing I did was come here to this ranch to figure out how I was going to suport myself."

"Cut to," Nicole added, "your own company. Another good story with a Hollywood ending, I might add. Prodigal son proves his father wrong."

"You make it sound heroic."

"That's my expertise," Nicole replied. "Seriously, though, breaking away from a static situation isn't easy. No blueprint for that kind of thing."

"You just blindly do it." He stopped a moment, trying to recall something. " 'Find the light at the end of the tunnel and just keep walking in that direction.' That's Bruce Springsteen's advice, or so my daughter tells me. She reads all his interviews. She's at that age, fourteen, when her philosophy of life can be reduced to a slogan by her favorite idol."

"What's her name?" Nicole inquired. She noticed that Steven's face changed when he mentioned his daughter. What she read on his countenance was delight.

"Alison. Her name is Alison."

"Alison Lloyd, a very blond name," Nicole remarked. She could imagine a young teen, her golden hair held in a schoolgirl braid down her back. Nicole saw her riding a white Peugeot bicycle, a colorful knapsack on her back, making her way skillfully through Upper East Side traffic as she headed for her private school.

"She's not what you might think. She's an unusual girl. I can't describe her. You'll have to meet her."

"I'd like to," Nicole replied.

"You will," Steven said, and at that moment there was

no doubt in either of their minds that this was not idle chitchat.

It was not Nicole's habit to get involved with married men, but she couldn't deny that the immediate kinship she'd felt for Steven, and seemingly he'd felt for her, put them on a collision course destined for complications. But that was the big picture, and tonight she was interested only in the picture with the San Ysidro Ranch as a backdrop.

She would see him again. That thought allowed her to unwind and become more lighthearted than she'd been in a while. Dinner passed in a kind of suspended animation. A freeze frame.

"Can we go outside?" Nicole asked impulsively. "This looks like the kind of place that might even have an old-fashioned porch swing somewhere. It's such a warm night. Would you mind?"

"Not at all. I know just the place. You think they'll care if we borrow a couple of their glasses, or would finishing up our wine outside give us away?"

"What does that mean?" Nicole asked.

"It means, in case you wanted to maintain an impression of a business dinner, it'll be a little difficult if we're seen finishing off a bottle of wine in the middle of a garden at midnight. Even in Hollywood, I doubt if people negotiate their deals in that setting."

"I've never negotiated anything in that setting." Nicole thought that over for a moment and added, "That's one of the deprivations in my life I've been meaning to do something about."

Steven wasn't kidding when he said "the middle of the garden." There they sat on two chairs Steven had taken from the bar, amid daisies, pansies, irises, and sunflowers that were five feet tall. The fact that there were perfectly good, civilized, wrought-iron chairs in a clearing nearby made Steven's choice even more whimsical.

"Tell me," Nicole asked, "is it the wine? There must

be a reason why I don't feel awkward sitting here, and there must be a reason you chose this spot. It's like something out of an Italian movie. . . . There I go again, analyzing everything in terms of movies."

Steven smiled. "I thought it was the next-best thing to a porch swing, which unfortunately they don't have."

Their chairs were very close, but the invisible line had not yet been crossed. There had been no touching except for the polite kind, handing a glass, steadying a chair, and once Steven had lightly brushed off a leaf that had fallen on Nicole's shoulder.

"I was here about a year ago," he said, "and there was a young couple up here to get married. The manager had set up a champagne bucket and table down near the entrance to the garden, but the bride and groom decided to get married right here. I could see them from the bungalow I was renting, and I watched them marry in what was no more than a five-minute event. There were no guests, just a judge, two witnesses, and the couple. One of the witnesses, who was also the photographer, and obviously not a professional one—she was using one of those inexpensive yellow plastic waterproof cameras—had to stop the ceremony because she didn't know how to change the film. The groom happily obliged and then went back to saying 'I do.'

"The next day, I saw the newlyweds at the pool. They looked very much in love and I wondered about them. Where were their families, their friends? Was this marriage an elopement? Had they known each other long? As the afternoon went on, I managed to strike up a conversation. I found out that they'd been together for six months. He was only twenty-three, she was thirty-two, and although their families weren't opposed to the marriage, they weren't elated. When I asked why they decided to tie the knot then, that weekend, they both agreed that they wanted to get married when they were in a state of intoxicating optimism.

"I thought to myself: How far away my world is from

theirs. Where I come from, people marry suitable mates. The choice is a cold, sober, analytical one. The engagement and the events leading up to the wedding are planned down to the minutest detail. In my world, the intoxication comes after the 'I dos,' and optimism isn't a consideration."

He took a long breath. "There was a spirit about that impromptu ceremony in this garden a year ago that impressed me. I often wonder about the two of them, if they're still happy, if the optimism, though tempered by everyday life, is still alive, or if all that passion came to nothing. What is that line about hot blazes turning to smoke? Another line Alison likes to quote."

Nicole's pulse raced. If she were alone, she would have said: Don't do this to me, God. Don't make me want someone I can't have. Don't set me up for the big letdown. She gripped the sides of her chair and came up with an unrevealing reply. "Alison's certainly got sophisticated taste in music."

"She does," Steven said. "She read somewhere that Prince was a Joni Mitchell fan, so she decided to study her work. That's exactly how she said it—'study her work.' Hearing that really got to me. She sounded so grown-up."

Nicole wanted to delve into all of it, his feelings about his child, his implied dissatisfaction with his life-style, and tucked between his lines, maybe an implied dissatisfaction with his marriage. But she wasn't ready for that two-way street that called for her to reciprocate with details of her own past relationships. She couldn't trust that what she traditionally reserved for girl-talk wouldn't become boy-talk when Steven and Ted, or, worse, Steven and Lance had lunch together one day. She was ready to sit in the middle of a garden with Steven at midnight, but she wanted to take one careful step at a time.

"I have yet to feel intoxicated with optimism, except about work," she confessed.

Steven jumped at this opening. "A particular project?" Purposely he led their conversation away from his own autobiography.

Nicole took another sip of wine. She inhaled the fresh air scented by the fires burning in the wood stoves found in each of the ranch's cabins. It was nice to smell a safe fire instead of the charred odor that hung over L.A. after one of their devastating brushfires.

"Years ago when I was promoted to junior executive, I thought: Great, no more meetings with the lowest echelon in town, no more unanswered phone calls, no more hustling to make contacts. The last thing I considered was how I'd handle the unestablished writers and directors who would be knocking on my door. About eight months into the job, I happened to pick up a treatment for a movie that had been left along with a stack of scripts on my secretary's desk.

"It was the story of a teenager from the slums of Boston who learned how to play the saxophone, and how he started exploring not just jazz, Miles Davis stuff, but everything—pop, rock, even classical. It was a story about how music saved him. How it gave him a frame of reference bigger than anything he could pick up in his neighborhood or school.

"I won't give you the long version of this story—and believe me, most stories about how a movie gets made are long ones—but I not only championed the project, I got involved with it through every stage. I swear it was better than a vitamin-B shot for boosting energy. I believed in this movie and the talent that went into it so completely. It was teamwork and it was a team without stars. The writer and the director were unknowns, and the actors, at best, recognizable faces. We all worked hard to put this story on the screen, and the process was the closest I'd ever come to a feeling of being 'intoxicated with optimism.' "

"Did it go on to become one of Millennium's blockbuster youth movies?" Steven asked. "You have to excuse my ignorance. Unfortunately, I'm not up-to-date on movie plot lines, just names and totals."

"No," Nicole said. "It got great reviews and won a prize at the Cannes Film Festival, but it did lukewarm at the box office. It was a lesson in the importance of timing. If it had come out even six months later, when audiences were getting tired of high-concept comedies, it would have done a lot better."

As Steven was about to ask if it was on videocassette, his question was halted by a clicking sound. A split second later, water forcibly poured out all over them from a half-dozen spigots stuck in the ground.

In one decisive motion Steven crossed the invisible line. He took Nicole's hand and, holding tight, pulled her away from the sprinkler system. Drenched and weak from laughter, they spilled out onto the drier main walkway of the ranch. Steven had the wine bottle in tow and Nicole was still clutching her half-filled glass. A foursome of sedate late diners maneuvered past them, mistaking their gaiety for drunkenness. A silver-haired woman showed her disapproval with the ladylike expletive "num-nums." This only made Steven and Nicole laugh harder. They were still only a shared glance or word away from another outburst of giddiness as they stood at the front desk of the office requesting towels.

The young man working the late shift couldn't reach anyone at the laundry extension. "They won't be back until seven tomorrow morning," he explained, "and I don't have a key to the supply room."

Steven looked down at the floor, trying to think through the problem. He noticed that the water dripping off the sleeve of his sport jacket had created a small puddle. Nicole noticed it too, and the sight of it triggered more giggles.

"What about vacancies?" Steven asked. "Do you have any?"

The young man nodded. "Number ten is available until Thursday."

"Well, aren't there any towels in there that we can use?"

"Ah . . . ah . . ." The young man hesitated. "I don't know if that's within the rules."

Steven noticed that when he took a step his shoe was not only wet but also squeaked. There was no time to debate.

"How about if we rent the room? I'll pay you the full price for one night but we'll only use it for at most an hour." Steven took a beat. "Wait, I better rephrase that. We want a place to dry off a bit before continuing our drive. If there are towels in number ten, we'll take it."

The young man sprang into action. "I'll check it out right now." He handed Steven a short sign-in form. "Could you fill this out, and will that be cash, check, or credit card?"

Steven tossed a credit card on the desk and felt himself cross another line. It was possible his wife would discover this charge on the monthly bill and drill him about it. If she did, she did, Steven resolved. Maybe it would provoke a conversation that was long overdue.

The second the door to number ten closed, the silence between the two of them was explosive. Nicole could have said something about the old-fashioned quilt that covered the brass bed. Steven could have commented on the fire, already ablaze in the potbelly wood-burning stove, courtesy of the young man behind the desk. Neither one of them gave in to their inclination to be glib, to be safe. Nicole sat on the edge of an armchair and Steven stood nearby, leaning against a wall.

He thought about the events that had led up to this moment and wondered if he had unconsciously choreographed them. From his introduction to Nicole at Lance's barbecue, he'd known he wanted to know more about her, but he hadn't admitted to himself that he wanted an affair. Now that it was within reach, he realized it wasn't an affair he was after. It was much more. The longing he had was for a relationship, a companion, a friend, a lover.

In fifteen years he'd cheated on his wife, Elaine, only once, and that was because she had impulsively taken off to the Bahamas for three days, claiming she was under unbearable stress and needed relaxation. He knew all about Brando, an Italian furniture designer who had come into favor with the *W*-magazine socialites his wife spent her time with. He knew that Brando was in Nassau, and he assumed his wife was involved with him.

She wasn't a very good actress. When she started taking cooking classes to learn how to make pasta from scratch, he suspected something was going on. When she, who rarely exercised, hired a trainer, he deduced it was another man. Brando's name popped into his mind when he found a receipt for $285 worth of trashy lingerie he'd never seen Elaine wear, which she'd unwisely left in the desk drawer where Steven kept the spare tapes for his Sony recorder.

Elaine's shopping habits were to buy lots impulsively, decide carefully at home, and send back the rejects, which usually amounted to at least two-thirds of the merchandise. She liked to joke that she'd replaced her eating disorder with a shopping disorder. "My shrink says I've got shopping bulimia," was a line that had gotten laughs for her at quite a few parties.

To clinch his suspicions, Elaine announced over dinner that she'd enrolled in an extension class at NYU . . . Introduction to Contemporary Italian Design. "I need to broaden my scope," she explained.

Steven didn't care enough to lose energy in a hostile discussion. He let her depart for her three-day break without challenging her excuse for going.

During her absence, he spent an afternoon in a room at the Plaza with the younger sister of an old college roommate. It wasn't done for revenge. It happened because the situation presented itself, and when he asked himself why not, no voice argued against it. The "why not" came to him as he rode the elevator back down to the lobby. He simply didn't need to be physically inti-

mate with someone he had nothing to say to, other than
to play catch-up on where mutual friends from Steven's
Cambridge days had ended up.

His train of thought got back on the main track as
Nicole disappeared for a second and reemerged from the
bathroom with a towel around her neck. There was something so familiar about her, yet she was nothing like the
women Steven usually came into contact with. Her style
was so much more casual. There was no carefully crafted
image to work his way through. He watched her move
over to the fireplace. Her hair was still damp, and she
dried the ends of it delicately. Steven walked over to her,
took the towel, and lovingly resumed the task. As he stood
behind her, he saw her shoulders rise and fall to the
rhythm of her breathing. He discarded the towel, but his
hands continued to play with her beautiful thick hair. His
fingers massaged and then caressed her neck. She turned
toward him, her arms engulfing his broad frame. He
touched her face. She looked innocent, vulnerable, with
all traces of makeup washed away by the garden sprin-
klers, but her dark almond-shaped eyes seemed alive with
mystery.

He put his arms around her, loving the feel of her strong
back and narrow hips. She fit perfectly into his embrace.

"Where were you fifteen years ago, Nicole?"

Her gaze met his. "I've been meaning to talk to you
about that."

"It's not too late," he said.

"Really?" she asked, her voice serious with the plunge
she was considering.

"Whatever it takes," Steven replied.

His hands moved up her back and gently caressed her
neck. He sought out her mouth and they kissed hungrily,
greedily, like two people who weren't afraid to take what
they needed.

Sometime between five and six A.M., while the air was
still cool, before the sun had risen and brought with it the

heat that unfailingly engulfs Southern California in summer, Nicole, still asleep, shifted her position and pulled around her the lightweight comforter that adorned the bed. As she did so, her leg rubbed up against Steven's. The feel of his skin brought out a moan from the dream she floated in. She shifted again, turning away from him but maneuvering her body into his, like spoons. He embraced her, and working his way back to consciousness, lightly traced the skin between her shoulders, and kissed her there. She shifted once again, this time to face him. In the early grainy light of dawn, she looked at him with her wide-awake body. He pulled her closer.

Two Mexican maids wheeling a cart of cleaning aids and fresh linens passed by the window of number ten. Nicole heard their foreign words, felt an empty space next to her in bed, and awoke with a start. There was no sign of Steven. *I cannot fall in love at midnight and have my heart broken the next morning. I couldn't survive that,* Nicole thought. She threw the covers off the bed, wrapped a sheet around her naked body, and opened the door a crack.

She knew by how hot it was that it was late. She was afraid to check her watch. She'd had a few lost weekends in her life but never a lost middle-of-the-week. She found her Rolex underneath the room-service menu. It was nine-forty-six. She grabbed the phone, called her office, and was relieved when Carolyn answered on the first ring.

"It's Nicole. Cover for me until twelve." As she hung up, she peered out the window for a sign of Steven. The Mexican maids were talking to one of the gardeners. Nicole tried to remember the Spanish she'd learned in her senior year of high school. "Man" was *"hombre."* "With" was *"con,"* but she couldn't recall the words for "dark hair." *"Les cheveux brun"* kept coming to mind, but a smattering of French was useless here.

She picked up the phone again, this time to call the ranch office, but reconsidered. *I'll be reasonable,* she vowed. I'll think this through. "He went to get some coffee. He went to buy a newspaper." She rattled off these possibilities aloud because hearing her own words helped her analyze the situation. "He went for a walk. He went to pay the bill."

From behind her Steven's familiar voice said, "No, he went to get you some papaya juice." She spun around. There he stood in the doorway with a glass of freshly squeezed juice on a small tray.

"I didn't know if you'd want a big breakfast. People in L.A. seem to be into the kinds of diets that allow only fruit before lunch."

The tension was erased from Nicole's face as she reached for her fresh-squeezed treat. "At the risk of sounding like a typical L.A. fanatic, I have to admit, I've been thinking about starting that kind of regimen."

Steven embraced her, and the feel of her body under the thin sheet made him wish they had more time.

"So, how did two predictable people like us find ourselves in such unpredictable circumstances?" he said.

"Unpredictable?" Nicole asked. It didn't have the same ring to it as last night's "whatever it takes."

Steven read the concern in her eyes. "Don't look so worried, Nicole. I'm not going to let anything happen to us."

"Sure, sure. No guarantees in life," Nicole reminded him.

"No, but if we don't act like there are, we'll end up with nothing. I'm not a religious man, but I think that's called faith."

"You talk like a born-again romantic," Nicole joked as she started rounding up her clothes. They'd have to ignore the speed limits to get her back to Millennium by noon.

"Could be," he replied, "but a fruit-diet fanatic I'm not. While you were asleep, I had apple waffles."

Before stepping into the bathroom to freshen up, Nicole asked coyly, "Think our two different approaches to breakfast can coexist?"

Steven smiled. "If not, I'll consider giving up the waffles."

For Nicole, driving south from San Ysidro meant gearing up for reentry. L.A. was never an easy place to return to. The city appeared dull, empty, a lazy giant. It was hard to locate its lifeline, and in fact, Nicole had learned, it could only be done as an inside job. It was only after living here for a while that she'd gotten a sense of the show-business network that surprisingly never slept. But it took daily interaction to stay plugged in.

She looked over at Steven and felt supercharged. Love was responsible for this elevated mood and the I-can-do-anything headiness that came over her. It was the best mental shape to be in, to return home to the city that demanded self-motivation. Out on this coast, it was self-motivation or no motivation at all.

Turning east along Santa Monica Boulevard, she spied a billboard advertising Millennium's latest flop, *Norsemen*. Thinking about work provoked a reappraisal of the Lance crisis. In her new frame of mind, Nicole confidently looked ahead to following up Tuesday's memo about *Dirty Dreams* with a strategy meeting with Kevin.

As they stopped at a red light in Westwood, she watched two little girls, about ten years old, cross the street. They carried a giant red plastic bat and ball.

"Girls of Summer," Nicole observed.

"Is that what you'd call a high-concept movie idea?" Steven asked. "Or has 'Girls' Little League' already been done?"

"Actually I wasn't thinking about movies when I said that." She smiled. "Some things do change."

She looked out the window at a topless jeep that had pulled alongside them at the stoplight. "And then again, some things don't ever change, do they?" A young all-American couple were sharing a can of diet cola with the same fun-loving air of actors in a Pepsi commercial. Sunshine, a jeep, and a cute date wearing Ray-Bans.

"The stuff teen dreams are made of," Nicole said, which made her think of the last line of *The Maltese Falcon*, which, minus the word "teen," was identical.

"It's amazing," Nicole admitted. "It's easier to remember scenes from films than scenes from my own life. The past seems to evaporate. Memories don't stick in L.A."

"Very profound, Nicole."

"Don't worry, the profundity won't last," she said. "I've got to start thinking about what I can wear to work. It wouldn't look good to show up at the office in yesterday's suit."

Steven glanced up at the time flashing from the sign outside the Imperial Bank. It was 12:02.

"What time is your plane?" Nicole asked.

"I'm hitching a ride on the Warner jet with David Wolper. He wanted to leave by twelve-thirty."

"You'll just make it," Nicole said, wondering whether or not she should bring up when they'd see each other again.

"I'll call you tomorrow," he promised, reading her mind.

From where? Nicole thought. A phone booth? A friend's house? The rules governing an affair with a married man, even one who wanted to break that bond, called for some subterfuge, which could go from being exciting at first to a drain on the purest passion.

"Don't you think we can sustain it?" Steven asked, guessing the source of the anxiety on Nicole's face.

Tapping into her own brand of religious positivism, she managed a smile. "I have faith we will."

13

From L.A., Steven had made plans for his car and driver to meet him at the airport and take him straight out to East Hampton. As soon as the plane landed at Kennedy, he called his wife and told her he'd be arriving in a couple of hours.

"But it's only Wednesday," Elaine said.

He didn't have to be there to know a look of disappointment had come over her face. "I want to talk to you," he said.

"About what?"

She would have been a great chess player, he thought. Everything was a move. "I don't want to get into it over the phone."

"I have plans," she stated. "I won't be back till very late. How was I to know you'd be driving out? I didn't even know you were in New York. Your office didn't know your plans. I figured you got detained in L.A." She shot the word "detained" out at him as if it were an accusation.

"Can you cancel them, Elaine. Or leave early?"

"Cancel my plans? It's an intimate dinner party. I can't cancel at the last minute. It'd be rude."

He heard the ice clicking against glass and knew she was sipping a cocktail.

"I'll wait up till you get home. We'll talk then." He was trying to compromise, which only made her madder.

"Oh, wonderful, I get to be anxious about this mystery

conversation all through dinner. Lucky me, I get to worry about what disaster awaits me. Is it a financial crisis, a health crisis, a—"

"It's about us," he interrupted her. "I want to talk about us."

There was a silence on the other end.

"Elaine? . . . Elaine?"

"Well, Steven," she finally said, "I guess we'll have your little talk whenever you get here." Her tone was composed.

"Okay, I'll see you in a couple of hours."

"See you." She hung up first.

Steven held on to the receiver, his mind darting back to waking up in San Ysidro.

"Are you okay, Mr. Lloyd?" His driver broke him out of his flashback.

"Yeah, I'm fine. Let's get going."

It was almost eleven when Steven reached the house. Elaine was not only there, she'd called one of the gourmet specialty shops and ordered food brought in. He hadn't realized how hungry and tired he was until he found himself back in familiar surroundings. The *gamberetti marinara* and *ziti* in basil and tomato sauce were perfect. A glass of wine and the Hampton sea air worked like a tranquilizer. All through dinner, they had steered away from "the topic," talking instead about a review of a new Broadway show, that night's news report, and Alison, who after warmly greeting her dad had retired upstairs to, in her own words, "hopefully stay awake long enough to see *David Letterman,* even though it's a repeat."

Elaine explained that Alison was exhausted from an afternoon of marathon tennis. As she updated her husband on their child's activities, Steven had to acknowledge that Elaine was a good mother. Her only fault in that area was the pressure she put on Alison to "make

the right connections," and Steven was pleased to see
that her efforts were in vain. Alison did not emulate her
upperclassmen, whom *New York* magazine had once labeled "The New Snobbery." When her mother brought
up the Junior International Club, Alison's reply was,
"Let's get real."

Elaine also was not a mother *in absentia*, Steven knew.
Even when she'd taken off for her Nassau rendezvous
with Brando, she'd called Alison every day. As Steven
settled back with his cup of Colombian/Viennese coffee,
he also admitted to himself that in some ways Elaine was
a perfect wife. She knew how to maintain a home—or,
better said, the external manifestations of a home. The
house was decorated with lilacs in April, tulips in May,
roses in June . . . always the appropriate touch. She
stocked the linen closets with hundred-percent-cotton
sheets, the cupboards with cases of salt-free mineral water, and the refrigerator with berries, buying the New
Zealand imports when the local crops were out of season.
Steven appreciated her dedication to these details,
though he never lost sight of what motivated them.
Elaine kept hoping that one day her phone would ring
and it would be John Fairchild asking if they could do
a piece on her for *W*. Seeing her living room splashed
across the front page of her bible would be the culmina-
tion of years spent researching and developing the right
life-style.

"I came to a decision while in L.A.," Steven said.

Elaine studied her husband closely. In her gut, she
knew what this was about. What she needed now was to
ascertain the amount of damage. Would she have to fight
for what she called a marriage, but in her heart knew was
no more than an arrangement?

"A decision about us?" she asked.

Steven braced himself. "It hasn't been a real relationship for a long time. I think we should admit it, accept
the failure, and go our separate ways."

"The decision just came to you? Out of nowhere?" Elaine was trying hard not to sound bitchy, but his words made her want to lash out. "Did someone help you see the light?"

Steven didn't want to bring Nicole into this discussion, or Brando, or the others he suspected were sprinkled through Elaine's past. Already he saw the conversation giving way to a scene. The tension in the room had risen sharply in a few seconds, though they were still speaking in hushed tones. He regretted not waiting until tomorrow, when Alison was out at the beach. He didn't want her waking up to arguing, and he saw that Elaine could easily explode.

"Don't tell me you haven't seen this coming," Steven reminded her. "Aren't you tired of being married to someone you're no longer close to? Half the time we don't even sleep in the same bed because you claim you have insomnia. Come on, Elaine, we both deserve better."

"Don't give me that we-both-deserve-better crap. Don't give me that pious I-care-about-you-too attitude. Don't try to sugar-coat what's going on here. What did you do, pick up a starlet out in Malibu, someone who makes you feel like you're twenty-five again? I thought you were smarter than that."

Her hand nervously played with the corner of her bottom lip in the gesture she unknowingly displayed whenever she was in one of her strategy sessions.

"This is not about entrapment," Steven said. "This is about what we've lost over the years."

She sat forward in her chair like a debater who had hit upon a new angle. "Why didn't you ever mention it before? Why didn't you come to me and try to work through these problems? You say nothing, and then one day you show up and it's a fait accompli."

He knew she had a point and he also knew that coming to her sooner wouldn't have made any difference. "Is that what bothers you, or is it that you're comfortable with the way things are? You never did like change very much."

Elaine wanted to scream at him: You're playing by new rules. Suddenly change is in and stability is out? When did that happen? She had to call up all her power to rein her emotions back into line. Forget everything, she counseled herself, except keeping him, whatever that takes. Keep him at least for a while longer.

She altered her approach. "It hasn't been easy for me, you know. I've made a lot of mistakes, but I've always struggled to keep our marriage intact. I know how hard you work and I always made sure our home was an oasis for you. I never burdened you with my problems. I kept them to myself. It's the way we've both been brought up. There were times I felt so alone . . ."

As she got lost in her monologue, unwittingly she tapped into a sadness that had as much to do with past hurts as it did with the present one. To her astonishment, and Steven's, she began to cry, tears pouring out of her, rendering her unable to speak. The only sounds she uttered were gasps as she sought to regain her equilibrium.

Steven had never seen her like this. Torn between his desire to comfort her and his fear that anything he did now would only cause her more pain, he attempted to hold her. She pushed him away, got up, ran into the bathroom, and locked the door.

Left alone, Steven remembered the hopes they'd both had for this second home and had to admit that until tonight it had been a place of tranquillity. Newly built, just a year old, it had provided them with the visual and audio privacy that was such a welcome contrast to the overstimulation of New York.

Tonight the moon was full, and the garden outside was clearly visible.

Steven turned off the lamp alongside his chair, waiting in semi-darkness for Elaine to reemerge. He thought about the sensation of letting go—letting go of tranquillity, letting go of things, houses, people. That's what divorce is about, he thought, and in a different sense, it's what falling in love is about—letting go, a condition, he knew, that, like his wife, he had been bred to avoid.

He heard the door unlock and turned quickly. Elaine was standing in the doorway.

"I'm tired," she said. "I'm going to bed."

"We can talk again in the morning," Steven suggested.

"Wonderful," she said sarcastically.

"Don't play martyr," Steven countered. "You're not a victim. This third act was co-written by you."

"And isn't that a convenient way for you to see it?"

In spite of her sarcasm, Steven could see she was like a wounded creature and wished he'd kept the "martyr" comment to himself.

He strove to make her understand. "Elaine, I have a lot of love for you, I always will—"

She cut him off. "It's just that you're not in love with me."

Two tears slid down her face. She dabbed at them with a Kleenex. Two more appeared instantly. Unable to stem the tide, she sat down on the bottom step of the staircase and buried her head in her arms. Steven sat next to her and pulled her close. This time she didn't resist. They sat like that for twenty minutes, saying nothing. Every so often, she would move, to grip his hand, to sink deeper into his shoulder. He stroked her hair. He held her until he felt her heart quiet down, until her convulsive sobs had subsided. Worn out by emotion, she could have fallen asleep right there. But Steven pulled her up, took her hand, and led her to their bedroom.

As she followed, she counted her blessings. We have fifteen years together. We have a daughter. We have a life. Besides, she told herself, "realities change." She'd read that in an article in *Vanity Fair*. At the time, the words had unsettled her, but now they brought hope. I'm not going to let him go, she vowed. Things will be different tomorrow. If I have to be reduced to a vulnerable hysteric to save my marriage, I will. She despised Steven for what he had put her through tonight, but she clutched his hand as she had during their courtship.

Realities change, she kept telling herself as he sat her on the edge of the bed.

"Stay with me, Steven, please stay with me," she pleaded. A digital clock visually screamed out 12:52—that was 9:52 in L.A., Steven thought, seeing Nicole and then pushing the vision away.

Elaine pulled back the sheets. "Steven," she whispered. "Tomorrow, can we spend the day together, you, me, and Alison, as a family? One day without talking about our future, or the past. A reprieve for us, a one-day reprieve. We'll have waffles in the morning, drive out to Montauk, stop at the tennis club . . . nothing big or fancy, but the three of us together."

"I've got to get back to the office," Steven replied.

"All that way just to drive out again Friday evening?"

Her question carried a loaded subtext. Would he be coming back out to her for the weekend?

"I'm wiped out," he said as he lay back on the bed. She cuddled next to him. Letting go, Steven kept thinking. That's what it takes. But he didn't. He cuddled back. He knew the right thing to do would be to walk away, make a clean break, but he didn't have the coldness for that act of kindness. Everything seemed subject to interpretation. Was making love to his wife fair to her? Was it betraying Nicole? Was it a way of showing Elaine he cared about her? Was it the last fuck, a necessary rite of passage before separating for good? Was he seeking a brief solace from the chaos he'd created? Was he trying to help Elaine make it through the night? These questions were smothered by their hugs, which became gropes, and Steven found himself pulling open his wife's shirt as she reached inside his pants. With kisses, they filled the unknown with the familiar, blocking out New York, L.A., and everything that went before and everything that might follow.

Maybe this is a mercy fuck, Elaine thought when she had her husband all the way inside her. If it is, it is. At least it means I've still got a hold over him, even if it is through guilt. That's one charity I don't mind accepting, because it buys time and . . . given time . . . realities change.

14

Nicole careened around the long curve on Sunset as Beverly Hills turned into Bel Air. The day was fresh, beautiful, and promising. Not only because it was eight-thirty in the morning but also because it was Thursday, and Steven had promised to call. Although it was early, the temperature had already reached eighty-five. Today will be a scorcher, Nicole thought, wishing she were still in breezy seaside Santa Barbara with her lover. It was odd, she thought, that Kevin had insisted on meeting at his house. Not that she minded it at all; in fact in many ways she preferred this setting for some of the things she wanted to explain to her mentor. She had to excuse her unscheduled absence yesterday morning, but felt that he would understand. Kevin always said his family's affection enabled him to survive the madness of the Hollywood shuffle, and frequently advised her to be more concerned with her personal life. Of course, Steven was married, and Kevin, family man that he was, wouldn't approve of that part. He would warn her about being hurt in the end. But Steven's feelings toward her were so persuasive that she knew with deep certainty that this relationship was the furthest thing from self-destruction she'd ever known. It was self-construction, she thought, smiling. As she neared the formidable Bel Air gates and turned right on prestigious Bellagio Drive, Steven was fast receding from her consciousness and work was taking its place.

She downshifted and accelerated as she rounded the

final turn. She could feel her face falling into its usual serious mask. I'd like to know what the hell Lance has been up to, she thought. She hadn't heard or seen him since the B-B-Q. His absence made her uneasy. It reminded her of a particularly quiet night that had preceded her first earthquake experience. Lance imitating nature. There was a cheery thought. She was sure that today, at least, she was competent to ward off any arrows he could cast her way. She was stronger than ever before. Someone really loved her.

Peggy Carlyle Holberstein held up a California sun-dried tomato between her fingers before cutting into it. "Look at that. Perfect, wouldn't you say?"

"Irvine Ranch Market?" Nicole guessed.

"Do you shop there too?" Peggy asked.

"I've got orange juice in my refrigerator and Cup-o'-Soup in my cupboards," Nicole replied. "That's about as much shopping as I do."

"Coming from New York, I'll tell you Irvine beats the tiny Gristede's at Sixty-seventh and Park," Peggy said.

She scrambled six eggs into the lightly sautéed onions and delicately added sheared strips of salmon. "I never cooked until I got married. And, let me tell you, it was a long slow road from making bad beef Stroganoff to finally mastering the recipes in the *Ma Cuisine* cookbook."

Nicole took another sip of coffee and wondered why Kevin, who was never late for a meeting, was late for this one.

"I think of you as being a natural at stuff like this," Nicole said, making small talk.

Peggy smiled. "My father used to say a natural is just someone who does his homework."

She reached over, pulled loose a cream-colored invitation that had been tacked to a small bulletin board near the sink, and handed it to Nicole. "My father, a man who always does his homework, is the guest speaker at the

California Bar Association next month," Peggy said proudly. "And Kevin's the introductory speaker."

"Very classy." Nicole was impressed, though less by the Bar Association dinner than by Peggy herself. Here's a woman who knows how to be with a man without clinging to him, she thought. Nicole could easily see what attracted Kevin to his wife. She was the kind of woman he could commit to without feeling like he was going to be swallowed up with a lot of needs and demands. Their marriage was a true partnership. Nicole had heard several stories about what a dynamic duo they once had been in the political arena. Back in the early days of their marriage, when Kevin was seriously considering running for a seat in the New York state congress, Peggy used every connection and influence her family had to drum up support. But somehow—Nicole wasn't sure of the details—in spite of the solid endorsements and the extensive coverage Kevin was getting in the press, he decided to come to Hollywood. As it turned out, their partnership flourished on the west coast as well. Anne Archer playing a young Jackie Kennedy was how Nicole often described Peggy. It was her way of saying Peggy Carlyle Holberstein was both sexy and proper and comfortable with that combination.

"I envy you," Nicole admitted. "You've got all the important pieces in place."

"I hope so," Peggy replied as Kevin finally made his entrance. He was dressed casually in a pink Lacoste shirt and comfy old chinos, not his usual office attire.

"Aren't you going to the studio, hon?" Peggy asked.

"Not till later," he said. Addressing Nicole, he got to the point. "Shall we start?"

"Sure," she agreed, surprised by his chilly greeting. "That's what I'm here for."

Peggy had set the table beautifully. Blue-and-yellow hand-thrown plates and pewter tableware were complemented by straw place mats and pale yellow linen napkins. Fresh orange juice was poured to the brim of the Baccarat glasses. Nicole loved this dining room with its rectangular knotty-pine table and straw chairs covered in Pierre Deux blue and green paisley cotton. Against its pale pink walls was a Welsh pine dresser where Peggy kept her collection of Provençal primitive pottery. The French windows, adorned by French lace, caught brilliant slivers of the intense morning sun.

"Do you have meetings out of the office all morning?" Nicole asked.

"I'm not sure what time I'll get to the studio," he answered.

"I'm sorry about getting in late yesterday. I tried calling you but you were nowhere to be found."

"Meetings," he explained.

"I wanted to tell you, I got detoured by my future husband." She laughed when she said this, expecting at least a smile out of him. For years they'd shared jokes about Nicole's apocryphal future husband.

"Well, I hope it works out for you," he said. He seemed more interested in buttering his toast than listening to what she had to say.

"Kevin, am I boring you? Excuse me for taking up time with this silly chatter. Let's get down to business. What meetings do I need an update on?"

Kevin was scarily taciturn. "Nothing of any significance."

"Anything happen with Lance? Did you read my memo?"

"He put an offer out to Bruce Willis. There's a chance he'll be available in a month and a half. I think it's a good idea."

Nicole put down her fork. "In a month and a half? Are you saying you think *Dirty Dreams* will be and should be in production by then?" Her heart was pounding rapidly to the soundtrack of her undoing. How could this be happening? At the B-B-Q she and Kevin had been in sync on this issue. What irony, she thought. On her way into town yesterday she had been so happy. She believed she had her job under control, a strategy to deal with Lance, and at the very least, a nonfictional future boyfriend. Well, "Just when you thought it was safe to go back in the water . . ." The cynical approach was helping. She felt her steely determination rise from her gut to combat today's surprises. Meanwhile, Kevin still hadn't answered her question. She looked straight at him, with the edge of a smile in her eyes.

He glanced away. "Did you ask me something? My mind was wandering."

"Are you feeling okay, Kev? You seem off today."

"I'm fine, Nicole. I just have a lot of work to do and I'm a bit distracted. What were you saying?"

"I can help out with the work. Just tell me what you need."

"No, thanks. Nothing. I'll handle the meetings." Succinct. Just like that.

Nicole pushed. "What meetings?"

"Nothing I can talk about. Couple of directors. Couple of agents. A few of the guys are in from New York."

She felt the serenity she'd brought back from the San Ysidro Ranch receding. These were her meetings too. "Which directors?"

"Nicole, will you slow down and eat? You're giving me a headache."

"Okay." Her tone was icy. "Let me finish up breakfast and get to the office. I have a lot to follow up on myself. Just give me the point of view on *Dirty Dreams*, because I know half my phone list will be about it, and I want to be in line."

"Lance has done some work on the script and I think it's much better. We're trying to put some casting together."

Nicole felt a lump the size of one of the sun-dried tomatoes growing in the back of her throat. No way she could eat.

"The script has gotten that much better in less than two weeks? I find that hard to believe."

"Calm down, Nicole. We've got other points to cover. I read your proposal for new development projects and I am going to turn them down. I don't want to put anything into development right now, until we know what the budget for *Dirty Dreams* is. No deals, understand? Even scale deals."

This was worse than she could have anticipated. Development had been her domain, and now she couldn't buy a script. It would take her off the market. Erode her power base. Finish her. She wiped the corners of her lips carefully. "Am I to understand," she said, "that the budget of *Dirty Dreams* precludes new development?"

Kevin stared out the window. From the kitchen the phone rang. Quietly he said, "Yes."

"So this studio is going to make *Dirty Dreams* regardless of what a disaster it's likely to be. Lance Burton has got us utterly by the balls."

With that, Peggy, cheery as usual, tiptoed into the room to talk to her husband. "Phone, honey."

"Who is it?"

"Lance," she said. "He's calling from your office. He wants to have lunch."

Nicole felt as if a terrorist's bomb had detonated in her career as Kevin exited the dining room to take the call in private.

I've somehow lost my job, Nicole realized. I'm done with. History.

15

By six-thirty Nicole had placed three calls to Kevin, and none had been returned. She stared at her desk calendar, painfully aware that over a week had passed since the ugly breakfast meeting at Kevin's house, and since then he'd hardly spoken to her. She was hoping he would come with her to the screening of Peter Gibson's movie tonight. After all, Millennium was courting Gibson and she took it for granted that Kevin and she would check out his latest work together. Can't take anything for granted around here anymore, she realized sadly as she faced the fact that she was dateless. What's going on? she wondered. Why was Kevin behaving this way? She tried to distract herself by placing other calls, calls she would have ignored—in local parlance, blown off—on any other day. Now she made them, in a compulsion to make contact, but no one was around.

"Toast," she could imagine people whispering about her, meaning a person soon to be fired. The ones whose projects she'd passed on would be the smuggest of them all. Burnt toast is what she already felt like as she realized the screening would start in an hour and it was a half-hour away. Get it, she told herself, you're going alone.

"If Kevin phones," she called to Doreen, the secretary who had replaced Carolyn, tell him I'll meet him there. Any other messages for me?"

As Doreen shook her head, Nicole heard the plaintive sound of her own question, and it made her feel pathetic.

"Damn Steven," she muttered as she pushed her chair back from her desk and stood up to go. "Damn men in or out of Hollywood."

Nicole's Maserati joined the line of Porsches, Jeeps, and BMW's making their way through the underground parking garage that was attached to the Academy of Motion Pictures screening room. A famous agent and his producer wife slipped into the space she'd had her eye on. The agent represented virtually an entire generation of comedy directors, the bread and butter of the business. She craned her neck to catch his eye and wave. Breezily he and his wife returned the greeting. Nicole thought about how happy and settled their lives must be, married with children and out to a screening together. Seeing them brought Steven back to mind. Where the hell was he? Why hadn't he called? He was supposed to have called a week ago and all she'd heard was a message left on her machine three days ago when he knew she'd be at the office. "Nicole, things got busy back here. I'll be in touch soon." The waiting was driving her crazy. Seeing an illegal parking space, a handicapped slot, she decided to grab it. Surely no one, at that moment, felt quite as handicapped as she.

Nicole walked across the street, where a crowd mingled. Could she pretend she was meeting someone? She determined to stride quickly forward, as though she had important plans. She adopted a shield of arrogance as she passed a few minor agents and a writer she had recently heard despised her.

Ahead of her, a group of executives was chatting up Hollywood's favorite flavor of the week—director Peter Gibson. As her farsighted eyes made out the key players, she felt her chest constrict. It was Kevin and Ted, working the relationship they knew she had been cultivating. In the center of the throng was Bambi, aglow in reflected power.

Nicole waved weakly to the threesome. No one waved

back. Each one of them glazed over, as if she were invisible. She pretended they didn't see her, in case anyone had witnessed the snub.

She made her way inside the hallway and moved purposely toward the water fountain at the bottom of the stairs to the theater. I'm getting out of here right after the screening, she decided. No party.

"Nicole," someone called out.

Nicole turned to find Carolyn with a good-looking young man. The two of them were also kind of hiding out, but in their case it was because they were at that stage of being in love when whispering together in a corner was far more appealing than making small talk with acquaintances.

"Hi, Carolyn. I forgot you were coming tonight," Nicole said with an edginess to her voice. Seeing them together made her think of Steven, and thinking of Steven made her even more anxious than being alone at this screening.

"Thanks so much for getting my name on the list," Carolyn said.

"Yes, thank you," Andrew joined in.

"Oh, God, excuse me for being such a klutz at social graces," Carolyn apologized. "Andrew, this is Nicole. Nicole, Andrew."

Andrew extended his hand and Nicole shook it.

"I'm delighted to finally meet you," Andrew said. "I've heard so much about you from Carolyn, and of course everyone else."

"Nice to meet you," Nicole mumbled. Carolyn's boyfriend is the only person playing up to me, she thought to herself. At least he doesn't know.

Across the lobby, Andrew spotted Bambi. He turned his head to catch her eye. It would be perfect to have Bambi see him talking with her boss, Andrew calculated. Good for the deal.

"Andrew!" Bambi's shrill voice beckoned. "Come meet a wonderful director!"

"Will you excuse me?" Andrew said to Nicole. "Bambi and I are working on something together." His eyes tried to look apologetic, but the bounce in his step betrayed him.

Carolyn smiled weakly to Nicole. She was stunned that Andrew would be so rude to Nicole, to walk away from her in the middle of a conversation in order to play up to Bambi. They stood silently together, watching Andrew across the room, gesticulating broadly and laughing. His persona was in high gear tonight.

"I guess he pitched her a project or something," Carolyn rationalized. She looked to Nicole for reassurance. But Nicole wasn't up for being the big boss tonight. She had no advice. About men or anything else.

"I've got to find someone I'm supposed to meet, so if you'll excuse me," Nicole said, stepping away from the hideaway, which hadn't made her feel safe but trapped. "Enjoy the movie," she added.

As she took her chances and strode back into the thick of things, she felt a tug at her shoulder. It was Charlie Dooley, a campy popular producer she often enjoyed gossiping with, who now felt like her only safe harbor.

Charlie had something of an updated beatnik about him. His squared-off wire-rim glasses accented his intellectual scowl. His stylish baggy pants and thrift-shop jacket made him look like a new-wave poet.

"Kiss, kiss," he greeted her. "Guess Bambi's got the boys in tow."

Nicole turned away from his offered cheek.

"Nicole, is something wrong? I was only kidding."

Nicole realized she was overreacting, and this alone could create controversy. She had to lighten up. "No, my sweetheart, I'm just distracted. Looking for someone."

"Anyone I know?"

She felt cornered. "I think we missed calls. I don't know if he's coming."

"Are you all right?" Charlie asked, clearly not referring to her health.

"Don't be so sensitive," Nicole said. "Of course I'm all right. Now, tell me the goss. What's up?"

She wrapped herself in his protective presence as David Beach approached from across the room. Nicole sensed that he was trying to decipher the same set of hieroglyphics she was, and was no happier about Bambi's sudden public coziness with the bosses. As David Beach steered closer, Nicole steered away.

She and Charlie weaved their way down the center aisle of the spacious screening room and grazed the room for information. Clusters were forming throughout the center rows of plush theater seats. Nicole tried to catch the eyes of a woman writer-director she liked, but lost her to a conversation with Warner execs.

"Does anyone really like anyone in this town?" Nicole asked Charlie. "Or is everyone zooming everyone at all times?"

"You're *not* all right."

She forced a smile. "Don't be ridiculous," she responded. "I'm great. Let's find some seats before we have to separate."

As the two of them wound their way across the front aisle into two unoccupied seats, Nicole felt her eyes chase faces around the packed room. She hated the nervous glancing about for recognition she referred to as ocular darting, and yet here she was, like a work slut, fishing around for reassuring nods from the room filled with names from her Rolodex.

"What did Gibson bring this in for?" she asked Charlie, though she was more likely than he to have a reliable figure.

"I heard fifteen," he answered. "It will have to gross forty-five million in rentals to break even. Weren't you after him for something?"

"I'll let you know in ninety minutes," she replied, holding on, in words at least, to her last vestiges of power.

Halfway through the movie, Nicole checked her watch

for the third time. The pacing of the movie felt like the Australian crawl. "Is this the fifteen-hour Holocaust movie?" she whispered to Charlie, who was completely engrossed in the character drama. Her anxiety dilated time and she wished she could doze off until the lights came up again.

Finally the synthesizer score rose like a chorus, and she knew the end was near. She couldn't begin to remember what the movie was about.

Rows of whispering agents poured onto the plushly carpeted aisles, and she found herself standing behind the head of Fox, whom she'd tried to get on the phone that afternoon. A couple of weeks ago he'd teased her about moving over to his studio, and she'd dismissed his comment as idle flattery. Now she needed him, but he was deeply engrossed with Peter Gibson. She let herself fall four people behind until she could compose something clever to say.

The screening was followed by a kangaroo party in the reception room. Meat pies and blue shakes were being served on twelve red-white-and-blue tables, and the lines were already long at all of them. Nicole spotted the bar at the other end of the room and made it her destination. She took hold of Charlie's arm. "Let's get a drink."

"Drinking on the job, Nicole—this isn't like you."

"Give me a break." She laughed. "Work ends sometime, doesn't it?"

"Not in this business, darling."

Ahead of her she saw the executive producer of the movie, who always acted like he had a crush on her, but probably wanted a development deal. "Hal," she said to the lanky Australian, "you must be so happy."

"Hello, Nicole," he responded. She saw his hands shake beneath the cool facade. "Did you like the movie?"

Nicole was stuck, but she had a collection of responses for just this tight squeeze. She chose one appropriate for a producer. "Every dollar is up there on the screen," she said.

Nicole stepped closer to the bar, where a friend of hers was standing. He was a handsome bearded Louisiana boy with a soft-spoken voice to go with his sharp wit. Nicole often wondered why he never asked her out.

"How ya doing?" He brushed her cheek with a kiss.

"Well, work is good," Nicole lied.

"Work is all there is!" he volleyed back.

"You know," Nicole said, trying to crank up a good flirt, "if I were a guy, I'd believe that too, and life would be so simple."

"You *are* a guy!" He laughed, and with that, was gone—suddenly engaged in a new conversation.

Nicole moved on to look for Charlie, who was lost in the throng. She thought he might be over near the area set up for dancing. The music, coming from somewhere, was inviting, but few people in the room seemed to notice. She passed Bambi talking to Peter Gibson.

"Hello, Bambi," she said.

"Hi," she answered, not looking at her boss. "You remember Peter, don't you?"

"Nicole and I are old friends," Gibson said, and turned to Nicole. His expression was both cocky and scared.

"You've got a lot of guts," Nicole said, knowing how macho he was. "Quite a picture." Pretty soon she was going to run out of benign double entendres.

"You know just what to say to make a guy feel good," Gibson replied, getting her off the hook. Then he turned back to continue his chat with Bambi.

Nicole moved toward the meat-pie table. She was annoyed with herself for having given in to her aggressive need to network. Going home would have been better for her soul, but there was one more person she looked to to elevate her mood. Spotting the head of United Artists helping himself to a snack, Nicole stood in line next to him. For weeks he'd been courting her to join his new team, and now she could use some of that attention.

"Hi, Jack," she said, interrupting his conversation. He and a friend were discussing Friday night at Helena's.

"Oh, Helena's," Nicole said as though she were bored instead of anxious. "Looking for love in all the wrong places?"

"Where do you look for love, Nicole?" he challenged jokingly.

This is not starting right, Nicole decided. Do not insult this man's pastimes. You need him. "Oh, all the wrong places," she answered, and then added, "I've got to run, I've got about twenty scripts waiting for me. Can we talk for a second?"

"Sure," he replied. "Did you fire your readers or something?" Everyone laughed, including Nicole, who regretted her faux pas. No one, save maybe an overworked Disney exec, read that many scripts—particularly in the middle of the week.

"About that lunch you wanted . . . how about next week?" Nicole tried to cut the desperation from her tone.

"Jeez, Nicole," he said, looking away. "I'm all booked next week. Why don't you have your people call mine tomorrow. I'm sure I'll free up in a couple of weeks."

"Fine," Nicole heard herself say. She averted his inquiring gaze. "I'm out of here, check you later." This time she was determined to exit. A couple of weeks? Her eyes stung at the insult. This guy knew damn well that in Hollywood, a couple of weeks was a decade—so far away that it was essentially irrelevant.

Nicole geared herself up for a hasty retreat. She walked past recognizable faces, avoiding eye contact with most of them, and faintly smiling hello at those she couldn't avoid. She felt all eyes were upon her, noting her departure, early and alone. She wasn't up for faking gaiety. Her reserve of strength used for "saving face" was practically gone. She pushed the glass door open, to the fresh air of the street, and once again bumped into her reader.

Carolyn and Andrew were leaning against a car, laughing at some shared secret.

Nicole would have avoided them too if she could have,

but the three of them were the only people out on the street.

"This was great," Carolyn said. "A movie and a blue milk shake—it was a whole new experience." She was actually holding a glass with the remains of the concoction in her hand.

"You've been to screenings like this before, haven't you?" Nicole asked.

"Not really," Carolyn replied. "It's a real perk. Actually I think this is the first job I've had that's even had perks."

"And we're about to go get a real drink somewhere," Andrew interjected. "Would you like to join us?"

"No," Nicole said, suddenly feeling old in front of this couple who were all about beginnings. "Thanks for the offer, but I ve got to get home. I'm expecting a call."

Carolyn smiled as if to say: I understand. It's Steven. The new man in your life.

Nicole smiled back, confirming Carolyn's misconception, and then headed off to retrieve her car from its handicapped spot.

Back home, Nicole took a bath, fixed herself some hot milk, and tried to lull herself into quiet. If only Steven would call and tell her he loved her. She opened the sheets to her bed and slipped between the covers. She closed her eyes and imagined his face again. Trying telepathy, she concentrated as hard as she could on communicating her need to him, praying that their connection was so special that he would respond. She replayed their first meeting, and their glorious night together. I'm acting like a frigging teenager, she thought, and like a love-crazy teen, she pounced on the phone when it rang.

"Hello."

"Hi, it's your mother."

Fear shot through Nicole. Eleven P.M. L.A. time . . . two A.M. east-coast time. "What's wrong?"

"Nothing's wrong, I can't sleep. I'm doing the *Times* crossword puzzle. I knew you'd still be up."

"I was just falling asleep," Nicole lied.

"I was waiting for you to call me about the tickets."

Nicole rubbed her tired eyes. She'd completely forgotten she was supposed to get her mother tickets for a Broadway show. "East-coast publicity hasn't gotten back to me. We've been crossing calls."

"I'd do it myself through a friend of Aunt Sophie's, but you did offer."

Nicole was constantly trying to share the perks of being a Hollywood executive with her parents. Since she hadn't given them the grandchildren they wanted, she tried to make up by using her connections to get them house seats as status symbols. "I'll call again tomorrow," Nicole said.

"Well, let me know how much they cost."

"My treat," Nicole said.

"You know you don't have to."

"I know. I know."

"Well . . ." Her mother's voice trailed off and there was a deadly silence on the other end. "Well," she picked up again, "I'm sending you a package, a few things I got in the city. Bergdorf's was having a sale."

Nicole was acutely aware that the two of them compensated for their deteriorating communication by giving each other presents. She did not want to dwell on the thought.

"Mom," Nicole stopped her before she could go off on a long tangent, "I've got to get off the phone, get some sleep. I've got an early breakfast meeting at the Polo Lounge." She regretted adding the last detail. The fiction of a breakfast meeting was bad enough, but dropping references to the Polo Lounge to impress her mother was ridiculous.

"Okay, Nicole, we'll talk later, then. Sleep tight."

"Yeah, you too."

Nicole hung up, feeling even more depressed. Talking

to her mother made her more aware of her solitary life. "Enough," she said to the walls. "Enough already." This heartbreak pain was getting old. The same hurt over and over again. Why, goddammit? What lesson was she supposed to learn from it? Never need a man? Never need anyone? She couldn't pull that off, though God knows she'd tried.

"Ring goddammit, ring," she shouted at the phone. Silence. A silence that seemed so unrelenting she couldn't take it. Everything was falling apart. Tonight's screening had made it clear it was no longer business as usual at Millennium. She had seen the domino theory at work before, when one big move led to many. The season of change was upon Hollywood again, and more than ever she needed a friend.

Desperate, she picked up the receiver. She knew she was out of control and calling him was wrong, but she had to.

"Information in Manhattan. Lloyd, please. Steven Lloyd," she told the operator. She got the number, memorized it instantly, and prayed for him to be there. After five long rings, he answered. A sleepy, gruff hello.

"Steven, it's Nicole. You said you were going to call. I thought . . ."

"A . . . oh . . . yeah. I was planning on taking care of that tomorrow."

Her heart sank at the impersonal response.

Hang up, she told herself, just hang up, but she held on to the receiver as if it were her lifeline.

"I'm sorry, Steven. I guess I forgot about the time change," she lied. "It's been a grueling day. I seem to be in the middle of some new studio shuffle, and . . ." She paused to gain her composure. "I really need to talk to someone."

Her words came out like a plea, not a request, and she could feel herself approaching the breaking point.

"Unfortunately, I can't help you," Steven replied calmly.

"The problem is too complicated to go into over the phone."

Nicole grabbed a pillow and clutched it to her stomach as if having something to hold on to could stem the tears that flowed down her face.

"My mistake for calling," she said.

"Don't worry about it," Steven said. "I'll talk to you in a week, Ted."

With that, he hung up, leaving Nicole feeling like a fool. Worse, she felt like a one-night stand. She had to face facts. To Steven she was just some girl he had picked up on a business trip. And a stupid girl at that, one who didn't understand the rules of the one-night game. Get it through your head, Nicole chastised herself. He's married. His wife is lying next to him at this very moment.

She squeezed the pillow tighter and cried.

16

Back at Lance's Malibu ranch, houseboy Brett Holston was howling with a bad case of the naughty giggles as he flounced on top of his boss's imposing bed. With him was Digby Butler, an owlish-looking Oscar Wilde type, the entertainment-gossip writer for the *Tribune,* also Brett's hoped-for conquest of the night.

Brett had been planning this for five days, ever since Lance told him he'd be in New York for the weekend. Brett figured he deserved this break from what had been a hectic two-week schedule. First there had been the Fourth of July B-B-Q, which had started Lance's current manic phase. Since then Brett had had to oversee three dinner parties, including the one the week before for Bastille Day. Of the fifteen guests, not one was French. The only thing French about the party was the food and champagne. The music was pure American rock and roll, and the drugs pure South American. Brett felt like he'd been going nonstop, trying to keep up with Lance's demands, so if he was now taking a few liberties while his boss was away, who could blame him? Besides, he wasn't sure he could have gotten a date with Digby without including an invitation to the ranch.

Brett was attracted to Digby because he was so hard to impress, not like those senseless pretty tricks he'd been feasting on for years in the back alleys of Melrose Avenue and Santa Monica Boulevard, the area commonly known as "Boys' Town." It took the inside of Lance's bedroom to excite Digby, who was frequently invited to the most important of the "Velvet Mafia" parties. Brett had yet to be invited to one of these in-crowd celebrity gatherings of the rich show-business gays, but he had no doubts he'd fit right in. He knew some of the boys who frequented those events. He'd met enough of them at the bars to see for himself that they were no better than he was, no more chic or socially acceptable.

Digby Butler was powerful enough to be his escort through this party town, and Brett knew that with the help of some of Lance's champagne and perhaps just a hit or two of his boss's special stash, Digby would come to see how acceptable Brett really was.

"So where is your infamous employer? And what would he do if he caught us here lolly-dollying in his private playpen?" Digby smiled.

"If he were high enough and the scene got crazy enough, he might join in," Brett responded.

"No way, Brett. Of the many things I've heard about Lance, no one has ever accused him of being gay. Maybe a subliminal closet case acting out his homosexual fears by beating up women, but not out-and-out gay.

Digby was pumping for information, but Brett chose to be evasive. "I've seen enough groups leave here at six A.M. to assume anything and everything," he replied, sensing it was time to stop talking about Lance or else it would be his boss Digby was eroticized by instead of him.

"Why don't we take a look through his porno collection?" Digby suggested. "I bet you one wish that there are gay men and gay women mixed in with the standard bondage stuff. I'd like to see what Lance's viewing pleasure is." Digby was enjoying this privileged and illicit entrée into the inner life of L.A.'s most controversial producer. Cultivating this flirtation with Brett wasn't a bad idea, after all, he thought. He was certain of getting something out of it.

Brett sorted through the titles in the extensive video library. *"White Women and Black Men . . . Handcuffs and Pain"*—he read off the titles as if he were scanning the movie section of *The New Yorker*. "Here's one without a label. I wonder what old Lance is hiding on this one."

"Let's put it on and see," Digby replied, cuddling up to Brett now, in tone at least, if not in fact.

Brett rigged up the VCR, attached to a fifty-four-inch screen, as Digby relaxed against a half-dozen king-size pillows. He straightened out the brightly colored Santa Fe blanket in preparation for Brett's return to bed. He wanted not a moment's discomfort to postpone the presentation at hand.

Grainy blankness greeted their excited anticipation. For a long two minutes they considered that perhaps the tape had nothing on it at all, but neither one of them suggested turning it off. Unevenly, a picture came into focus. Evidently the camera that had made this video had been set in one fixed location aimed at the bed in what looked like a hotel room.

"This must be a homemade one," Brett said. Had he gone too far? Treading on Lance's territory could be more danger than fun.

"It seems old to me," Digby added. "Perhaps an example of Burton's early work," he joked.

Suddenly a boy came into view, a rather good-looking one. It was immediately clear to both of them that this hunk wasn't straight.

"Well, well, well," Digby murmured. The implications here were fascinating, if this was indeed Lance's handiwork. Then with a force lost on Brett, but stunning to Digby, a body naked from the waist up entered the picture. Kevin Holberstein, president of production at Millennium Studios, was unzipping his fly. The camera's fixed focus recorded every detail, the images rendering Digby astonished.

"Is that . . . ? No, it can't be." Brett tried to make out the face. "But he does look familiar. I think he's been here for a party or something. I think he's a friend of Lance's."

Digby realized immediately what he'd stumbled upon. This is the scoop of a lifetime, he thought. I can't let Brett know how valuable this is, or else he'll freak, the little wimp. I have to play it cool.

Slowly, demurely, like Marilyn Monroe, he smiled and turned toward Brett to distract him from the screen. He placed his arm under Brett's neck and put his mouth close to Brett's ear. "Now, what was the one wish you wanted me to grant you? Because I'll grant you one if you grant me one back." His lips grazed Brett's cheek.

"I'll take a rain check on my wish," Brett answered, suddenly afraid that Lance could unexpectedly return. There was something menacing in the air, and he couldn't fathom what it was.

Digby persisted. "Here's my wish. I want to take this tape with me and bring it back first thing in the morning."

"I don't know, Digby. I could get into trouble." Brett was starting to feel cold, very cold.

Digby was not about to let this opportunity pass. The moment he saw straitlaced Kevin Holberstein in a compromising position with a boy hooker, he understood everything and could virtually write the scenario. The release of this tape would cost Kevin his job and a whole new administration would wash its way into power. Lance, Digby surmised, was trying to keep this coup as his private reserve—for what purposes, he could only guess. This is going to give me some Hollywood clout, Digby realized. This is my ticket to ride. This will get me more than just a job in development like every other compromised two-bit L.A. journalist.

"Honey," Digby crooned in a mock camp tone, "let me put it this way. Either you give it to me and I'll return it before Lance gets back, or I'll just take it and never return it at all."

"Okay, okay . . . but you'll return it first thing tomorrow morning, right? And you'll owe me a wish, right?"

"Sure," Digby said, thinking: This piece of evidence will put me on the fucking map. "I'll give you your wish right now, honey. Turn over."

*   *   *

Ted hated being interviewed. The thought of it put him in a testy mood as he drove east along Sunset Boulevard. A low profile had always been his rule, but in this particular case he knew refusing to make a statement would carry more weight than a statement that basically revealed nothing at all. Though he'd finessed his way around enough journalists in the past, he felt anxious about meeting with Digby Butler, a reporter known for asking provocative questions. He'd only agreed to the meeting because he knew it was critical to appear to be in control of the studio, in the midst of persistent rumors of a shake-up at the top. But leaving his beach hideaway and going into the studio was a prospect that unnerved him. Drop-ins could ambush him for an answer on some issue he wasn't fully apprised of, and he'd be drawn into the political infighting created by Lance Burton. His experience in the business told him that his best approach was still the wait-and-see one. When the full picture came into focus, then he'd do what was necessary to escape unscathed. Besides, he was eleven days away from August 8, the start of a two-week vacation, and he didn't want studio problems interfering with his departure date. Why was he always having to dance around land mines placed by his inferiors? Moments later, he was pulling into his designated and usually vacant parking space.

His secretary, Adele, greeted him, carrying a silver tray with a glass of iced coffee and morning trade papers.

"Your appointment is due here in ten minutes, Mr. McGuiness. Can I get you anything else?"

"I'll just check out the trades, Adele, thanks. And hold him for at least ten minutes when he arrives. Tell him I'm talking to the east coast."

Ted picked up *Variety* and the *Hollywood Reporter* and perused them for gossip. He checked out Army Archerd's, Martin Groves's, and George Christy's columns for amusing news of his ex-wives. Just as he was starting to get comfortable, Adele buzzed him.

"Ready?"

"As ever," Ted replied.

Digby Butler was dressed to be taken seriously. Entertainment reporters rarely showed up for interviews in conservative gray suits. He looked as if he belonged in *Business Affairs*.

"May I sit down, Ted? I have rather important news."

"Be my guest. Would you like something to drink?"

"Let's dispense with the amenities," Digby said. "I'm not here to interview you for just another industry update. I would shut the door if I were you."

Ted touched his magnetic door release, and his office became a private sanctum. "What's up, Digby?"

"I am in possession of very incriminating evidence about Kevin Holberstein's past. As I have great respect for him and do not want to see his career destroyed, I decided to bring it to your attention so that we might arrive at a mutually beneficial strategy."

"What kind of information?" Ted asked.

"A tape that shows him engaged in homosexual acts with a male prostitute."

Even for someone as jaded as Ted, this news took him by surprise. He had occasionally wondered about Kevin's private life, but never had sex entered into his speculations. To his credit, in spite of the shock, Ted showed no emotion. Through years of playing cards with the boys, he'd mastered a poker face that not even a scrutinizing mind like Digby's could decipher.

"I'm sure no one cares about Kevin's sexuality, past or present." Ted was closing in on a game plan.

"I'm sure the board of directors of a public corporation, especially one that spends millions every year promoting a clean-cut image for its products, would find these revelations sufficient to dismiss him. And I'm sure that's not something you personally would want to see happen. Especially not now when the 'team' is so vulnerable."

"We are all adults, Digby, and can handle whatever

comes our way. What is it that you're suggesting we do to alleviate this?''

"Vice-president of production—Digby Butler. It would never look unusual with all the journalists in Hollywood taking jobs at the studios. And I'll destroy the tape."

Although Ted found Digby's aggressiveness offensive and felt sorry for Kevin's predicament, he decided he wouldn't touch this mess with a ten-foot pole. No up side. If the studio needed to get rid of Kevin to protect themselves, well, let them. As long as he ended up with a check and no lawsuit, Ted could live with the outcome of any crisis. "I'm afraid there's nothing I can do for you, Digby," he concluded.

"You'd let Kevin blow in the wind?" Digby persisted.

"Kevin will handle the situation masterfully, as he does everything. Now, if you're finished, I have a pressing appointment."

"Oh, come on with the pressing-appointment bullshit. Everyone knows you'll just leave for the beach again. Do you want to run this studio alone? Or worse, have a new administration imported from New York, less supportive of your life-style?"

Ted summoned his most charming smile and extended his hand. "Good morning, Mr. Butler. A pleasure, as always." With that, he turned his back on Digby and headed for his private john.

Alone in the cavernous office for a minute, a stunned Digby absorbed his collapsed initiative. Doesn't Ted give a damn about Kevin? About anyone? He didn't even ask to see the tape for proof. Maybe he already knew? Digby's mind was reeling. Fuck 'em all, he decided. Let them read about it in the headlines.

17

Nicole felt conspicuous sitting on a park bench at noon. Why in the world did Kevin insist on meeting here? she wondered.

She looked across the grassy play area at some toddlers and their moms, recognizing one of the women as a former legal secretary who had married her boss. Nicole had met her at some dinner party a year ago and remembered the woman being a bitch. Nicole watched her with her child, envying her the kid, a cute three-year-old with curly hair. But she did not envy her life of daily outings to the park.

I wonder what's happening at the studio? she thought, unable to break herself of the habit of checking in. Whom was she kidding? She'd told Doreen that she was running out for a quick lunch, but she could have taken the whole afternoon off without missing a phone call.

Just then she heard the sound of a Porsche driving up and turned to see Kevin in his Cabriolet. In spite of the beautiful golden day, the top was up. As he crossed the street, she noticed he seemed troubled, and then it hit her. This was it; she was being officially fired. The job of axing her had fallen to Kevin and he thought telling her outside the office would make it easier for her.

"Nicole," he said. No "hi," no other salutation.

He joined her on the park bench, though his gaze was off in the distance.

"I know what you're going to tell me," she said. "I just

don't understand why this is happening. Was my job security solely in the hands of Lance Burton all along?"

He shook his head. "I'm not here to fire you, though I expect sooner rather than later you'll be out of a job."

"What's going on?" Nicole said, and then lowered her voice as two joggers ran by. "You've shut me out, Kevin. Ted's shut me out."

"I had to. It was Lance's call."

"Why? When?"

"I shouldn't even be telling you this. The only reason I bring it up is so you'll know I didn't volunteer for this assignment."

Nicole was more confused than ever. "I've never known anyone to pull your strings, Kevin. That's not the way you operate. How could Lance coerce you? How could he coerce Ted?"

Kevin smiled in spite of his dour mood. "As far as I know, Ted's not part of this. If he's been shutting you out, it's probably because you and Lance are at odds and he wants to keep his distance."

"Part of what? I don't get it."

"Lance wants you out of the picture."

"And how did you end up on his team?" Nicole asked.

Kevin took his time with this question. "Blackmail. I guess you could call it that, though Lance would probably say the opposite. He'd probably say he was trying to protect me. Lance is all about whatever is expedient. The scary thing is, it seems to work for him."

Nicole was enraged. "He's the slime of the earth."

"Who knows," Kevin said philosophically, "maybe karma will win out in the end."

Nicole was too worked up to be philosophical. "He is so completely vile."

"Anyway, Lance's moral shortcomings are not what I wanted to talk to you about," Kevin said. "I came to tell you I'm leaving Millennium."

By the look on his face she knew it wasn't because he'd gotten a better offer.

"You may be reading about it in the papers, and I don't mean the business section."

"And I guess you're not talking about the society page either?"

"No. This is page-two-gossip kind of stuff."

"Don't tell me you're having an affair with some ingenue?"

"The board of directors wouldn't mind that. It's more complicated."

"Are you going to make me guess?" Nicole asked. "I'm not good at this. I never was."

"Let me put it this way. What's the classic shrink explanation for an obsessive conformist? Hiding something, right?"

"I suppose. They'd say out of fear, insecurity," Nicole replied. "It all comes down to that with shrinks, doesn't it?"

Kevin put down the key ring he'd been fiddling with and shifted his body so he was facing her. "Most people probably have a couple of episodes in their lives that they leave behind as they get older. They chalk them up to growing up, exploring, whatever. One of mine came back to haunt me recently. Apparently the news bulletin about my past doesn't fit in with the image of our parent company, particularly when they're looking to sell."

"Is it drugs?" Nicole asked.

"Sex," Kevin replied.

"I don't get it. Did you do pornos?" she asked, throwing out the most ludicrous possibility she could come up with.

"Not intentionally," Kevin said wryly.

Now it was Nicole's turn to gaze out across the park. This information made no sense to her. Kevin in a porno? No way.

"Could you explain how someone unintentionally makes a porno?" she asked.

"The point is, I don't feel bad about anything I did. I didn't hurt anyone. I was innocently trying to figure out who I was, what I wanted. The thing is, sometimes being a nonconformist means you're giving people ammunition they can use against you."

Nicole had too much of a liberal background not to jump on this. "Wait a minute. I don't know what you did and I don't need to know. Sex with some stranger, we'll leave it at that. I'm assuming you weren't a closet John Holmes case. And you're telling me that you're losing your job because the board of directors can't live with that?"

"Nicole, they can't live with the rumors that'll run rampant. It's a public corporation. Stockholders take exception to the image of the president picking up male hustlers."

That last statement silenced whatever argument she'd been formulating in her brain. This piece of news was so unexpected; it wasn't something she could instantly program into her picture of Kevin.

"And," he added reluctantly, "since videotapes exist to document the rumors, the board has every right to be concerned. In the wrong hands those tapes might have put me at the mercy of people who could have strong-armed me."

"But that didn't happen?" Nicole asked, seeking reassurance.

Kevin didn't confirm or deny. "Someday I'll tell you the whole story. The one that the board doesn't even know."

"But the one that Lance does," Nicole guessed.

Kevin nodded.

"So," Nicole summed up, "as far as the board's concerned, you're being moved out because you're bad publicity."

"Basically," he agreed. "So far, it's all been very civilized. Chester Baines doesn't mention any of the details. He simply says my past is incompatible with their corporate image."

Having said that, Kevin relaxed against the back of the

bench. He seemed relieved to have gotten his confession over with.

Nicole reached out and touched his arm in a gesture of support. "Will you explain something to me, Kevin? The way I see it, your personal life is your personal life. Millennium's board sees otherwise. Okay, that's their prerogative. But how can they be so morally rigid about you and seemingly so blasé about Lance Burton making *Dirty Dreams.*"

"Because they don't read scripts. And they won't bother with dailies. They assume Ted is running things, and Lance hasn't failed them yet. It's a numbers game. Anyway, it's not the reality they can't tolerate. It's the public exposure. It puts them at risk."

Nicole didn't know what to say. She got up, paced in front of the bench. "Three things, Kevin. One, you've got my support, you know that. Whatever I can do to help, I will. Two, I'm not going to make it easy for Millennium to get rid of me. And three, why the park?"

"No phones here," he answered. His attempt at a smile fell short.

"Oh, God," Nicole said, realizing that this was the start of a nightmare for her boss.

"It's gotten so that each time one rings, I expect the worst. More dirt, more fallout." He said this in a very matter-of-fact manner, like he was trying to get used to the new tempo of his life.

"Fuck 'em," Nicole advised. "Don't let them get to you."

He picked up his key ring and stood up to leave. "Those are fighting words."

"You're a fighter."

"That I know," Kevin said. "At the moment, I'm just a fighter without a plan."

Nicole watched him get into his Porsche, hit the ignition, turn on the radio, and drive off.

She sat there a moment longer, dreading the trip back to the studio. The mom she'd recognized earlier was now wheeling her child in an Aprica stroller. Nicole pretended not to recognize her. She looked off in the other direction. From where she was sitting she could see TV producer Aaron Spelling's colossal new house, evidence of what you got when you hit the jackpot. The joggers who had run past her before were making another lap around the park. Everything looked so safe here, she thought. So on-track. But that was never the case, she knew. There was always trouble in paradise.

It was midafternoon and Kevin was in his backyard. It was hot out but he was wearing long white cotton pants, a Lacoste shirt, socks, and loafers. His hands were crossed over his chest, and although he sat in one of the poolside chairs, he wasn't there to work on a tan. It was the ninth afternoon of his exile. And nine days after having his past spelled out in the tabloids, he was hardly recognizable as the powerhouse executive he had been. Now he was just another man out of work. No matter how vital his spirit might still be, the truth was, there was nothing for him to do but wait.

He'd spent the morning puttering around indoors. Everything he looked at reminded him of what his life used to be. All the pictures on the wall, the needlepoint pillows made by his wife, all the homey touches, created an impression of normalcy that he now believed was permanently out of his reach. For so long he'd tried to blend in, and by his own estimation he'd done an excellent job. Nicole often joked that in Hollywood, everyone was in rewrite, but since Digby's disclosure of the tapes, Kevin believed that his life had become a scenario outside the imagination of even the cleverest script doctor.

How odd, he thought, to be sitting outside in the middle of the day. He thought back over the years he and Peggy had lived in the house, to recall if he'd ever before spent a weekday afternoon by the pool. Yes, he had, a few years ago, when his wife and daughter had gone back east to visit the Carlyles and he'd come down with a twenty-four-hour flu. He'd cured himself then by drinking chlorophyll in apple juice and sweating it out in the sun. Then he was on the phone all day, directing studio traffic from Bel Air. Today his phone list had shrunk from the hundreds of calls he'd gotten weeks before to two, an attorney and a journalist, scavengers surveying the remains. Did he want to sue for defamation of character? Did he want to give the *Herald* an exclusive side to his story? What I want, he wanted to tell them, is to be able to say my name to someone I'm introduced to and not see a look of perverse curiosity cross his face.

He heard his phone ring, and through the window saw Peggy answer the one installed next to the back door. At least, he thought, a ringing phone no longer threatened to be one of those occasional but dreaded calls from his "Italian sponsors." He was of no use to them now, and in fact they were probably as relieved as he that the unraveling of his life story had stopped at the existence of the tapes, not who made them.

He could hear his wife chatting on the phone. Her voice sounded so chipper. She reminded Kevin of June Cleaver, Donna Reed, or any of the other television wives from the fifties. She would have whoever was on the line believe that her day consisted of nothing more taxing than baking a batch of brownies and picking up her daughter from ballet class. But he knew that once she was off the phone, a shroud of icy silence would descend upon them, broken only by polite but terse questions like "What do you want for lunch?"

When he'd been forced to tell her about the tapes, she'd listened with a frozen expression, the look one would have if death came unexpectedly and instantly. All she said when he was finished was, "Tapes? There are tapes? I see. I see." She turned her back on him and left the room. He followed her and tried to explain, to reassure her that when things died down, he'd get a job somewhere. "Fine, fine," she kept repeating, and with each "fine" it was like another trapdoor closing.

"Lunch is ready," Peggy called out from the patio before withdrawing back inside. With effort Kevin stood up. He was suffering from the fatigue that comes from doing nothing, the lethargy of having no deadlines.

Sluggishly he crossed the yard and entered the dining room. He took his seat, unfolded his napkin, and served himself a spoonful of salad. Peggy came in with a basket of French bread. No sooner had she sat down than she jumped up again, remembering something in the kitchen.

Kevin noticed she was wearing baggy khaki shorts and a white blouse and looked very pretty. He'd never been attracted to women who squeezed themselves into tight blue jeans and skimpy T-shirts. He liked the fact that Peggy was a class act but not a stuffy, inhibited one. They'd always been in sync sexually until nine days ago. He put no pressure on her. He understood her coldness, but he was also coming to an understanding about himself. Confronting the past had forced him to dredge up images that for so long, for survival, he'd effectively repressed.

He saw himself at the age of twelve, a loner at an old boys' Catholic school. A priest named Father O'Brien was the only one there who befriended him. He lent him books, discussed philosophy, and once, under the guise of giving Kevin a hug for a job well done (he'd gotten an A+ on his essay "What Confirmation Means to Me"), let his hands travel down his protégés pubescent body. He rubbed the inside of Kevin's thighs and explored, without protest, his student's budding sexuality. As disorienting as it had been for the young Kevin to have his teacher touch him, it caused a stir in his body that he couldn't deny or resist. Father O'Brien had done him the disservice of introducing the possibility that, for him, sexual satisfaction would be found in men. The incident baptized Kevin as "different," and he'd been compelled to play out the role all the way to its conclusion in a run-down New Jersey hotel room, before finally realizing that homosexuality was not his destiny.

Peggy returned with a crock of French mustard. She glanced at Kevin's plate and saw that he hadn't touched his *salade niçoise*. It sat in front of him like a still life from the Côte d'Azur. She took a piece of bread, avoiding his eyes.

"Maybe we should bring books to the table," he said, trying to make a joke about their mutual isolation.

"Don't you like your lunch?" she asked, sounding like a well-trained waitress working in an upscale bistro.

"I'm not very hungry," he replied, pushing the lettuce around the plate with his fork.

She shook her head.

"Is something wrong with not being hungry?"

"It's fine," she said.

The word was beginning to drive him nuts. "Peggy, do me a favor, could you use another word? 'Good.' 'Okay.' Anything but 'fine.' "

She took a sip of her iced tea. "I don't suppose you want any dessert, then . . . which is okay, but I wish you'd tell me these things in advance because then I wouldn't bother. It's all about respecting someone's time."

"You don't have to make me lunch. I can take care of myself," Kevin said.

Her hands gripped her glass of tea. "That's not the point. We're not talking about whether you're capable of fixing a sandwich, we're talking about respecting my time."

"I do," he assured her.

"Obviously you don't," she said. "I am not going to argue with you about it. I am not going to sink to that level."

"You know, Peggy, sometimes you don't have to try so hard, you don't have to be perfect."

She crumpled up her napkin and threw it on the table. Her eyes filled with hostility.

"You're going to criticize me for trying too hard? Is that my crime? Don't bother answering. I am *not* going to get into an argument. I refuse. I have other things to do."

She walked out of the room. Kevin found her in the den at the desk, a stack of household bills in front of her.

"How long do you think we'll last like this?" he asked.

"Don't you dare threaten me." She glared at him. "Can't you respect my time? I have got to get these bills mailed out."

Kevin picked up the check she was writing out. It was for Arrowhead Water. "I don't think the company will fold if they get paid a day late."

She pulled it out of his hands. "Of course you don't think it's important. What if there's an earthquake and there's no bottled water in the house—then . . . then will it be important?"

"Come on, Peggy," Kevin said. "This isn't about respecting your time or bottled water or earthquakes . . . it's about us and it's about me and my videotaped sex life."

"Shut up," she screamed. "Leave me alone."

"I'm sorry about this," he went on. "I really am, but I can't erase it for you, and I'm not John DeLorean. I'm not going to become born-again. I'm Kevin Holberstein and everything I've done I'll take responsibility for, but I'm not going to hide. I'm—"

A leatherbound business-size checkbook hit him in the face. Surprised by his wife's assault, he instinctually grabbed her out of her chair and pushed her against the wall. "Don't you ever," he shouted as she yelled back, *"Don't hurt me. Don't hurt me,"* and then, in a child's wail, repeated, "Please, don't hurt me." Her hands flew to cover her face. Kevin reached over to pull them away. He wanted her to see she had nothing to fear.

"Don't touch me." She recoiled further. "Don't touch me."

Kevin's arms encircled her—his teddy-bear hug, she used to call it.

"I'm not going to hurt you. It's all right, Peggy. Believe me. It's all right. I'll make it all right."

"You can't," she sobbed, finally releasing the tears

she'd been holding back. He cradled her in his arms as she cried for all that was lost. When she got to the bottom of her tears, she dried her eyes and smoothed back her hair as if these gestures symbolized the end of the grieving period.

"I can," Kevin promised. "We can."

She managed a smile and put her arms around his neck. She looked him squarely in the eyes, searching for the Kevin she had married, not the one conjured up by newspaper stories and gossip. For three weeks she'd avoided looking for fear of finding an impostor, but now she was relieved to see his love for her was no pretense. The naked truth of his sincerity was evident in the way he met her gaze. In a way, it was almost too raw a moment.

Breaking the embrace, she took a step back. "How long do I think we'll last like this?" she asked, returning to the question he'd posed earlier. "I'm not leaving, are you?"

"Peggy, you're my girl," he replied. It was something a high-school jock would say, and the tenderness behind it almost made her cry again. She was vaguely aware of the time and knew their daughter wouldn't be back from day camp until four.

"Wait here," she ordered as she dashed off. Seconds later she came back with a bottle of champagne and two glasses.

"A celebration?" Kevin asked.

"For you and me. Who knows, maybe we'll turn out to be stronger than we ever thought."

18

Bambi set her croissant down on her desk and took a gulp of the coffee she'd bought at the A.M./P.M. mini-market near the studio. She wasn't used to being in the office at seven-thirty in the morning. She wasn't used to being out anywhere at seven-thirty. An uncivilized hour, she thought, but also a good time to prowl unobserved through the halls of Millennium.

She put down her Styrofoam coffee cup and proceeded out of her office. As she stole down the corridor, she was enjoying the nervous flutters in her stomach. She considered this early-morning mission not only daring but also unconventional, not only gutsy but also well-planned.

Generally the executive offices were locked, but Monday mornings were the exception. That was the day the florist delivered the weekly supply of fresh flowers.

It was a two-step process. By seven A.M. the guy from Floral Art had come and gone and taken with him last week's rapidly drooping arrangements. Around eight-thirty, he'd return with their replacements. Where he went for the hour and a half in between, Bambi didn't know, nor did she really care. Even if, by chance, he popped in early, she wasn't worried. For all he knew, she had every right to be in Nicole's office.

She kept that in mind as she stepped into the executive V.P.'s inner sanctum and went directly over to Nicole's desk.

She pulled open the top drawer, which was filled with

pens, personalized note cards, gum, a takeout menu from Chopsticks—but no key.

Bambi did her best to check thoroughly without disturbing the order of things. Shit, it wasn't there. Bambi was sure she'd seen Nicole put the key to her personal file cabinet in this, the only drawer of her desk. At the time, Bambi had made a mental note of it, thinking: I bet she keeps her spare house key under the doormat. It was so obvious. But now that she wanted to benefit from Nicole's lack of originality, her boss had wised up. Dammit. Where could it be? Bambi wondered. In Nicole's new secretary's desk? She doubted Nicole would trust Doreen with the key to her secrets. But with no other options, she had to check it out. Feeling like one of Charlie's Angels, she rifled through Doreen's desk, only to find cigarettes, Tic-Tacs, memo pads, stamps—but no key.

Could Nicole have taken it with her? Bambi considered that likely. These were paranoid days at the studio. Anything was possible. She decided to figure out her next move from the comfort of her own office. Not because she feared being discovered—in fact, she was feeling increasingly bold—but because she needed another hit of coffee.

As she hastened down the hallway, she passed Carolyn's closet. That was how she referred to the office that had been delegated to Nicole's reader. Out of a combination of curiosity and a desire to keep tabs on an adversary, Bambi decided to snoop around.

On top of a stack of scripts was a copy of English *Vogue*. Ah, so this is where she gets her ideas, Bambi thought as she flipped through the glossy pages. I'll pick up my own copy after work, she decided, tossing the publication back down on the desk. But her aim was off and a corner of the magazine toppled over a small vase containing one pink rose. Water trickled across Carolyn's desk. "Dammit," Bambi exclaimed as she looked for something to sop up the mess. She opened the top drawer and pulled out a yellow legal pad. As she did, an odd-shaped silver key clunked down on the floor. Immediately Bambi recognized it as "the one."

She was delighted to have located it, though it did occur to her that Carolyn's possession of it might imply a growing trust between Nicole and her reader. I've got to watch this girl closely, Bambi vowed. She may be only a reader, but she's a reader with a key.

Quickly Bambi headed back to Nicole's suite and unlocked the bottom, private drawer of the file cabinet. In a second she had Nicole's personal file out and found what she was looking for: Nicole's studio contract. The expiration date was next November, which meant Bambi had more than a year to go before she could hope to take over Nicole's position. She then noticed the salary—a quarter-million a year. She smiled. If Nicole were a guy, she would have gotten at least three-hundred thousand. She was just about to close the file when she spotted a memo labeled "Confidential." She glanced curiously at the text until she realized what it was. Changing gears, she carefully read Nicole's strategy for derailing *Dirty Dreams*. Bambi could not believe what she had in her possession. This memo written to Ted and Kevin back in July was now a time bomb that Nicole had unwittingly delivered into her hands. Bambi thought about making a Xerox copy of the incriminating evidence but decided to just take Nicole's copy. She folded the memo and put it in her jacket pocket. Standing up, she pushed the file cabinet closed with the toe of her high heel.

Her adrenaline was pumping away. Her whole body was tingling in anticipation of what she was about to do. Helping herself to Nicole's phone, she put in a call to Lance.

"It's Bambi Stern," she said to a very tired-sounding Brett.

"Lance is on another call," he said.

"It's important," Bambi insisted.

"I'll put you on the list," he said.

"No, you don't get it. This is high-priority. The highest."

"The highest?" Brett asked in a campy mocking tone. "Well, in that case, hold on."

Bambi looked out the window and saw that the florist had pulled his van up to the front door of the building and was unloading a particularly exotic spray of flowers. She wasn't worried about his imminent arrival, or even Nicole's for that matter. Yeah, Nicole, she thought, just try to get on my case about something. You'll lose. The paper in her pocket made her feel invincible.

"What is it?" It was Lance on the phone, sounding like he had all of two seconds to give her.

"We have to have an emergency lunch."

"Call my secretary. Book a time."

"No." Bambi was adamant. "We've got to meet today. It's about *Dirty Dreams.*"

Lance was silent for a moment, considering whether or not Bambi and whatever she was onto was worth his time. "Studio commissary at one," he said.

"See ya then," she said, trying to sound flirtatious. But Lance had already hung up.

Lance was grumbling to himself as he pulled into the studio lot for the so-called "emergency" lunch with Bambi. He was in a miserable mood, and had been for days— ever since Digby Butler, whom Lance referred to as that Faggot Scumbag, had leaked to the world at large the secret of Kevin's past. Lance felt that piece of information belonged to him, and that Digby had literally robbed him of a valuable security. "Fucking journalist scum," he mumbled as he strolled across the quad to the commissary. Lance considered journalists, particularly Hollywood journalists, nothing more than bloodsucking parasites who lived life like a spectator sport.

Butler had undone his agenda, destroyed his perfectly

planned itinerary. It infuriated Lance that this lightweight could interfere with his life, and it made him uneasy that no one seemed to know how Digby had gotten the scoop. Joey was freaking out, convinced his family would blame him. Lance tried to cool him out but didn't have a lot of time or patience for Joey's panic. He was much more concerned about the fact that *Dirty Dreams* had lost all its momentum. With the power vacuum in the wake of Kevin's departure, there was a complete paralysis at the studio. He could have had Kevin—the real decision maker—in the palm of his hand, and instead his palms were empty. Worse, with Kevin gone, there was a chance that Nicole could increase her leverage, get some notice from the board of directors. He had to mobilize a new plan of action. First, he resolved he had to move Nicole out. Then he had to prove to the scared Styvie Pell that Millennium was as good a buy as it ever was. That the scandal would blow over and mean nothing in a month. Lance would have to assure Styvie that Millennium would emerge from this mess as the same solid studio but at a lower price. Keeping Ted visible was the key to the stable appearance of the studio. Lance had to make sure that Ted was seen everywhere: screenings, parties, restaurants, George Christy's columns, the *Wall Street Journal*. Events were moving swiftly, so Lance had to seize the initiative. What if the studio was bought by someone who owed him nothing? What would happen to *Dirty Dreams* then?

Lance was already five minutes late, and Bambi was annoyed with herself for showing up on time. She'd planned to be ten minutes late. She considered having her secretary call at ten after and leave word that she was running behind schedule, but as the hour of the lunch date approached, she could hardly contain herself.

She took out her compact and checked to see if the walk over in the stifling heat had made her look flushed.

She was happy to find that she'd reached her destination intact. She snapped shut the compact and went back to the menu. Although the food wasn't memorable, Bambi liked having lunch there. The air-conditioned room with its high ceilings, light wood furniture, and white everywhere . . . the walls, tablecloths, even the flowers at the reservation desk, were a pleasant contrast to her cluttered office, which she complained about constantly. She insisted the thermostat was off, making the temperature either too warm or too cool, and Bambi was too much of a Goldilocks to be happy with that. She wanted the controls in her office.

"Try the meatloaf." Bambi looked up to find Lance settling into the seat across from her.

"I didn't see you come in," Bambi replied. She immediately closed the menu and studied him instead. She looked for some sign of their chemistry, some gesture that would fuel their ongoing flirtation.

"I got here early," he said, forgoing the usual "sweetheart," "baby" lines he automatically used when dealing with any female other than Nicole. "I was sitting with Ted for a few minutes."

"Ted's here?" Bambi asked, swiveling around to locate him in the room she thought she'd thoroughly cased. She spotted him in a back corner with a peppy blond who had on a sweatshirt and shorts. Her hair was in a ponytail and when she talked, it bobbed up and down, accenting her vivacity.

"Who's that he's with? She looks like an aerobics instructor," Bambi commented.

"She is," Lance answered. He didn't have time for Bambi's idle speculations. Besides, he knew about Ted's sex life, including his brief episode with Bambi, and there was no leverage to be gotten from that information.

"So, what's going on?" Lance asked. "Fill me in."

"A lot," Bambi teased, "but no one's supposed to know."

"Sounds interesting." Lance picked up the butter knife

and started tapping it on his fist. He wasn't sure he wanted to hear another revelation.

"It *is* interesting." Bambi smiled, working for Lance's attention. "It all started when Andrew Spencer came in to pitch an idea."

"Andrew who?"

"Spencer. He's English. A producer."

"What'd he produce?"

"Well, nothing yet . . . but he's aspiring."

Lance slouched back in his chair. This better be good, he thought.

"Anyway," Bambi went on, "he and I were talking about this idea, a remake of one of the classics . . ." She paused for a second. "I forget the title, but anyway, we discussed it for about forty-five minutes and . . ."

Oh, God, Lance thought. For the first time he realized Bambi was one of those people who liked to relate every detail of an event—what she'd worn that day, what Andrew had on, what the weather had been like, and what she'd had for breakfast. He could be there for a half-hour before she got to the point.

"Sweetheart, I know how those pitch meetings can be. So what did this Andrew do? Did he bring you the next Tom Cruise movie? Is he fucking Nicole? What's the bottom line here?"

He tried to make it sound lighthearted, but he was speeding her up, and they both knew it. She wondered if he deserved this bounty she was about to present to him, but then Ted walked by with his aerobicized date and she wondered no more. Ted nodded at her, a perfunctory acknowledgment of her presence. She ignored him and concentrated even more on her story. Lance was worth all the effort, she told herself, because he wouldn't disappoint her like Ted did. Ted didn't know how to share his power and she wasn't interested in sharing his bed without it. Partnering with Lance, she reminded herself, would propel her to the next plateau, both in and out of bed.

"The bottom line is this." She stopped, letting her own silence be the drumroll. She pulled her shoulder bag off the edge of the chair, placed it on her lap, and carefully unzipped it. Her moves were so self-conscious they were almost ritualized. She held out the copy of Nicole's memo, hardly able to suppress her glee. "I'd say our executive vice-president is trying to sabotage you."

Lance read it through once, taking in every word. He leaned back and eyed Bambi steadily, trying to determine the best way to reward this act of loyalty.

"Bambi," he said, "you really surprised me. I don't like to admit that. I like to think I'm pretty good at figuring people out, but you're cagey. I like that." There was something of the cowboy in him when he complimented her. It was as if he, the town tough guy, was respectfully acknowledging the "little lady's" spunk.

"It's my job," she tossed off, though in fact spying on one's boss was not part of the job description for a junior executive.

"You're on the right track," he flattered her. "Your instincts are sharp. You're not afraid to go after what you want, and maybe get a little dirty in the process. You understand it's how things get moving."

She loved his praise but wished he'd be more specific. "Where do you think this track will lead?" she asked.

"That depends on you, Bambi. Maybe taking over Nicole's office for starts." He scanned the room. "This place is full of people who only know how to win by default. They don't have your aggressiveness—just ambition —and ambitious freeloaders make me sick. I like people with follow-through." He reached over and touched the side of her neck, and then grabbed a clump of her hair and gave it a tug. If they hadn't been sitting in the studio commissary, but alone somewhere, Bambi was sure he'd have pulled her next to him. This is the beginning, she thought. A surge of determination arose in her and she felt elevated into membership in some exclusive secret club. It was a club where the only order of business was winning. Lance made everything so clear for her. He eliminated all the confusion and conflicts that rendered her ineffectual. With his pep talks and point of view, she felt free to ruthlessly, if necessary, go after whatever she wanted . . . including him.

"Are you ready to order?" The waitress was there, her notebook and pen ready.

Bambi was about to say "Chinese chicken salad" but abruptly changed her mind. "I'll try the meatloaf."

19

Blood Alley is finally bloodless, Nicole thought as she walked down the corridor toward her corner office. The corridor had been so nicknamed by the terrorized writers who waited there to meet with one or another of the executives who would accept or reject them. Even the walls know nothing is happening here, she decided, passing Kevin's office, which had been locked since his resignation.

Last Monday, the furniture movers had arrived, her first bulletin of the ax that was finally falling. Though the movers had skipped her office and loaded all of the carefully selected antiques from Kevin's, the dread had seeped through to her suite.

She sat at her desk and halfheartedly scanned the "Entertainment News" section of the paper. The phones might as well have been disconnected, so little did they ring. It was impossible for her to generate new business. Everyone in town knew that the studio was "in transition," so all the packages were going elsewhere. She despised the condescension she heard in the voices of the few agents who did call, like vultures checking the daily body count. She couldn't take pitch meetings because she couldn't buy anything, so her appointment book was blank. Not only was this lack of activity depressing in terms of work; it also gave her time to think about Steven.

Her perspective on their one night together kept changing. At her lowest moments, like the night she'd called him, she felt like she'd been used and abused. At her best moments she felt: At least we'll always have San Ysidro. But most of the time she just felt disappointed.

Since the night she'd cried herself to sleep, she'd heard from Steven only once—a message on her answering machine at home. He'd called on a weekday afternoon, which was a message in and of itself: he was taking no chance of actually connecting with her. He was "busy." He was sorry he couldn't advise her, but as they both knew, it wasn't appropriate for him to discuss the Millennium situation. He promised to call again soon—but didn't.

It seemed to Nicole that he was hiding behind the cloak of "insider trading." She wasn't asking him to compromise himself. But a few caring words from him would have gone a long way toward healing the pain of rejection.

She should have pegged him as just another guy after a little action and a little information. She wondered if she'd ever learn to read men.

She never called him again. She assumed he was glad about that. Easier all around, she imagined him thinking. Occasionally, when she was tempted to reach out to him, she kept her finger off the trigger by reminding herself that if she'd meant anything at all to him, he'd at least have called her when she was likely to be around.

Restless, she strolled down Blood Alley to Carolyn's tiny space. Lately she found herself stopping by this office for no reason other than that it was an oasis. Unlike the rest of the staff, who looked at her with pity (poor powerless Nicole) or with glee (the bitch is getting what she deserves), Carolyn's respect hadn't waned.

The door was open and Nicole had to smile at the sight of Carolyn in her pink-accessorized office: pink radio/cassette player, a vase of pink flowers, a poster with pink lettering from the L.A. County Museum's exhibit of Picasso sculpture, and extending out along the edge of the desk, Carolyn's feet stuck in pink high-tops. Nicole also less joyfully noted that the shelf reserved for the latest scripts submitted by the top three agencies was glaringly bare.

"Enjoying ghost town?" she asked.

"It has been quiet," Carolyn admitted.

Nicole found it hard to look Carolyn in the eye. She felt responsible for her and wished she could perform the mentor role she had comfortably slipped into.

On the desk were a couple of scripts with notes that Carolyn had prepared for her consideration. Nicole leafed through the top one. How ironic, she thought. Now that I've got the time to read them, I'm not able to get them made. Her only option, to job-hunt, was impossible in the current atmosphere. Besides, it was merely her own job that she wanted, and though she was entirely cut off from the inner workings of the studio, and not privy to the board meetings deciding her fate, she was still officially at work. I have to get to the bottom of this, she decided. I'm a fighter. I have to find someone to engage in battle.

"You haven't seen Ted around, have you?" she asked, knowing the odds of his being around were virtually nil.

"I think I heard his secretary say he's in Malibu getting an early jump on Labor Day weekend," Carolyn answered.

Nicole stood up, tapping her inexhaustible well of determination. "Then I think I'll make an impromptu visit to the beach," she announced.

"Good idea," Carolyn said. "Great! Really!"

They both laughed at this display of enthusiasm.

"We'll see," Nicole replied. "Just my luck, this'll be a day he decides to come into town."

Nicole had no game plan. She was coasting on her nerve, a high-priced commodity. She parked her car behind a red Mustang convertible in front of the wood-and-glass facade of Ted's Carbon Beach hideaway. This section of Malibu was an enclave of million-dollar-and-upward "shacks," north of the Colony on the Pacific Coast High-

way. It was the destination of most of the upwardly
mobile, the sign of complete success afforded by gross
participation in a hit picture or a platinum record. Ted's,
she figured, was from neither, but rather from a proces-
sion of well-negotiated "terminations," Hollywood's version of failing upward. Nothing is what it appears here,
were Nicole's last thoughts before she rang the doorbell.

She brushed back her hair and breathed deeply,
anticipating Ted's shock upon finding her at his door.
However, it was not Ted who greeted her, but a perky
blond in a ponytail whom Nicole found deliriously
healthy-looking.

"I'm Joy," she answered, as though she'd been asked.

I don't believe this, Nicole thought. Her name is actually Joy.

Ted sauntered into the room and saw his surprise guest.
"My God, Nicole. What the hell are you doing here?"

"Can we talk in private, Ted? I really need to see
you."

"Shit, Nicole, Joy's been cooking for hours and I'm on
the phone to New York. What the hell is up?"

"I'll wait," Nicole replied. "It's not like I'm missing
anything at the office. It's completely dead."

Ted knew when he was trapped. "Okay, Nicole, let's
talk on the porch. I'll be back in a few minutes, Joy.
Please hold lunch."

Nicole and Ted sat facing each other on his off-white
Brown/Jordan lounge chairs. He had no trouble looking
her in the eye, or looking off over the horizon. All the
same to him.

Nicole jumped in. "It's really important that you hear
me out, Ted. We've worked very well together over the
past few years, and you've been wonderful support for
me, so you can't pull the rug out from under me without
any conversation. I can't just roll over and play dead."

Ted shifted to find a comfortable position. "You're
way ahead of me, Nicole. What is it that's got you so
worked up?"

"Are you putting me on? Could you possibly not know what I'm referring to?"

"Nicole, the president of the studio resigned. This makes for tumult. You've got to be a pro and roll with the punches. You've got to stay cool."

"How can you talk of staying cool when I don't know what's going on anymore? I've been cut out of my own meetings."

Ted smiled. "I know how close you and Kevin were, but there was a Kevin none of us knew. Now we have to take the consequences and see what the wind sweeps in. That's the name of the game."

"As long as I can still take my roll at the dice, Ted. I'm more than Kevin's protégée. I know more about every project this studio has in development than anyone else. You'll lose continuity with our entire inventory if you fire me."

"Nicole, you're talking like things happen for logical reasons around here. Change is in the air, and you have to smell it out and do what is best for you. You are who counts, not your projects."

"What are you telling me, Ted?" Nicole asked pointedly. "Am I finished, with no recourse? There's nothing to discuss?"

Ted sat up and leaned forward. He was growing earnest, mellow-style. Nicole prepared herself for the ridiculous prospect of Ted's waxing philosophical about the way things were. Here we go, she thought.

"Nothing is forever. Friendships aren't forever. Alliances aren't forever, even enemies are transitory in our business. You gotta play for the long run, and in the long run you can find yourself working and making deals with someone you hate, or in major competition with someone you think you love. It's time to examine your options, Nicole. Take it from me. I've been through this more times than I care to remember, and it doesn't even bother me anymore. You can't take these things personally. They're not about you, or how good you are or aren't. They're about power, and who's got it." Ted relaxed, proud of his presentation of his world view.

"Okay, Ted. I'll bite. Who's got power at Millennium now? You? Lance? Surely not me."

"None of this is quite clear at this point, Nicole. But if you want my advice—and take this in the friendly way that it's meant, because personally I'd love for you to stay—I'd start looking for another job now, if you haven't already."

Nicole felt the rage building inside her. She stood up and paced back and forth on the redwood-plank porch. "Of course I could get another job. I'm not stupid. I know how people behave in this town the minute they feel their power base begin to erode. They run. That's what they do. That's what you always did, and that's why you can afford this fabulous beach house. But I'd like to believe in something more than self-preservation. I want to be able to look a writer in the eye when he pitches me an idea I love and tell him that I'll do my best to be there when the script comes in. I care about the things I buy and I believe that one idea is intrinsically better than the next one . . . one will make a better movie than another. And the ones I love are at Millennium and they deserve to get made. How do I know that some jerk who occupies my office will give a damn about any of the scripts that I've worked two years to make right?"

Ted hated women on tirades. He had no patience for their inability to be ultimate pragmatists. "Get a grip, Nicole. So you buy back the scripts in turnaround. I didn't think I'd have to explain these things to you. I thought you were a professional, but I can see that I was wrong. You personalize all of this to make yourself a heroine. There are no heroes here."

"It may be okay with you to live your life in turnaround, Ted," Nicole responded. She felt herself going in for the kill, and forced herself to back off. "It probably makes you more secure to know where to appropriately place your allegiances. But right now I want to fight for my job. My allegiance is clearly to Millennium and to the writers and directors under contract there to whom I have committed myself."

At that moment the glass partition to the porch swung open and Lance strolled in. He was looking robust and irrepressible in long baggy denim surfer shorts, a sleeveless gray shirt, and a denim jacket. "Nicole, what the fuck are you doing here? What's the matter? No one returning your calls? Can't get a lunch date with any of the execs over at U.A.?"

Ted barely held in a laugh, while Nicole was caught totally off balance. Just what she didn't need, to have her career slights become fodder for Lance's perverse humor. His mere presence there confirmed her most paranoid fears of what had brought her career down. She had nothing to lose, now that she knew how the sides were drawn.

"What a shock," she said. "I wasn't expecting to run into 'the dark force of Millennium.' The man who can fell an entire studio with a single whim."

"What does that make you? The force of light? Joan of Arc in a garter belt?" Turning to Ted, he smiled. "I've always appreciated the weight of Nicole's egomania. It amuses me." He looked again at Nicole. "Why are you visiting with us on the beach when you should be job-hunting? I've placed a couple of calls on your behalf already."

There was a momentary standoff, disturbed by Joy's entrance onto the porch. "Smoothies? I've made the most delicious pineapple protein smoothies."

Nicole was stricken by the fact that to everyone else here, this was just a routine day. The surrealism of the smoothies being offered to them as though they were on a yoga retreat whipped her into a personal frenzy.

"You make me sick, Lance, you really do." Nicole spoke to him as if no one else were anywhere near. "You think you're so fucking powerful, but none of it's personal power. It's power that comes from money and your current ride on the top of the charts. Without hits and bucks, you wouldn't have the magnetism to attract any of your so-called friends."

"Is that what got you wet at Sushi on Sunset? Were you hot for my hits and bucks?" Now it was his turn to laugh.

"Why do you debase everything in your life?" Nicole shot back. "Why must you reduce it all to one big common denominator called screw them before they can screw you? It's a lovely way to live."

"We can't all be role models like you, Nicole. How old are you now? Over thirty-five, is it? No man, no children, and who knows . . . maybe no job. Now, that's a record to be proud of." Lance picked up his smoothie from the tray, smiled at Joy, and casually leaned against the banister, sipping it.

Nicole knew this verbal war would go nowhere, but she wanted to make one more point. "It'll all come back to you someday, Lance. Karma. Learn what the word means. It really exists."

"Interesting sermon coming from you, Nicole."

"Whatever, Lance, whatever you say. But it is true: no one gets to skip steps. No one."

"Is that right?" He put his glass down on the porch ledge and reached into the pocket of his denim jacket. He pulled out a neatly folded sheet of paper and turned deliberately toward his audience. Joy was watching carefully, and Ted. Nicole stood up to leave.

"I'm actually quite glad that you came here today, Nicole," Lance said. "The meeting we were going to have is about you, and now we can bring all this to a head." He handed her the unfolded paper. "Does this look familiar?"

Nicole felt her body go rigid, and her thoughts crystallized as if in a dark hallucination. Her mind raced to find the culprit who had betrayed her. For a moment she thought of Carolyn. Was it possible her own judgment could have been so wrong?

Lance put an end to her train of thought.

"See what Bambi gave me? A play-by-play description of your plot to undermine a viable movie property by lying and deceit. You tried to draw your superiors into a conspiracy to dupe the strongest producer on the Millennium lot. I've been wondering how Ted should respond to this move. I was going to discuss it with him today. Miss Ethics. Ha!"

Lance handed the memo to Ted, who read it as though he had never seen it before. After a minute he looked at Nicole.

"Never put anything in writing," he said. "Lesson number one."

"Thanks, Ted," she said. "I must say you're consistent. Not only do you refuse to take a stand, but you advise me to refuse to take one. It's been a true experience, guys," she added bitterly as she grabbed her purse and walked out.

The three witnesses to Nicole's performance looked at each other in amusement.

"Lunch?" Joy asked.

"Absolutely," Lance agreed. "Let's have it out here. Ted and I have our futures to arrange."

Joy went indoors to set up their healthy meal. Lance sat erect on the lounge chair.

"You know," he reflected, "I'm going to kind of miss Nicole. She made so much noise."

Ted was not up for reflection. He was relieved that the confrontation was over. But now he had Lance's emergencies to deal with.

"What's up, Lance?"

"I am going to make this short and sweet, Ted. Neither of us has any time to waste. I'm hoping I can get Styvie Pell to buy Millennium, but nothing's definite. If he doesn't, there's no telling who's going to be calling the shots. You want your security and I want to get my movie made. The chances of these things happening without Styvie on board are considerably lessened."

"So what can I do?" Ted knew this was finally the right moment to contemplate taking a stand.

"Stay in place. Stay visible. I want to be able to assure Styvie that the transition will be smooth. If the administration becomes more unstable than it looks now, his family might block the purchase."

"That's it? That's all?"

"And your word that, Styvie or no Styvie, you'll push for *Dirty Dreams.*"

"I'll pay or play you now," Ted answered. It was the most decisive Lance had seen him all year.

"No way. So you'll pay me my producer's fee and my director's fee whether or not you make the picture. That's not good enough. I want you to pay me and make the picture."

"So I'll pay and play you."

"Sorry, Charlie. That's no guarantee. I need the studio to get so pregnant with this project that they can't turn back, no matter who's in charge. I want a line of credit to begin crewing up. I want approval on my current budget, and a start date in six weeks."

Ted silently considered his options.

"Listen to me, Ted," Lance continued. "It's a gamble. You could go out on a limb here, and then some uptight asshole could buy the studio and we'd both find ourselves out in the cold. But if Styvie's in charge, I promise, as soon as *Dirty Dreams* wraps, I'll make sure you get that golden parachute you've always wanted. The biggest, most luxurious parachute package that this town has ever seen."

"Assuming Styvie's interested, that doesn't mean the sale will go through," Ted said. He was really just thinking out loud, inching his way closer to a decision. Should he be on or off Lance's team?

"And when *Dirty Dreams* is green-lighted, I'll guarantee you more perks. Car and driver. You name it." Lance was pushing hard.

Ted picked his favorite spot on the horizon to gaze upon. "You must want this pretty bad."

"Are you with me, Ted?" Lance asked. "Yes or no?"

It had been a while since it had come down to those two little words for Ted. He drew on his instincts for the answer. Instincts honed by his twenty-five years in the business. "I'm with you."

20

The Aegean Sea sparkled like the diamonds Christie Collins had seen at Bulgari's. The fresh air and warm sun revived her after the string of smoggy days she'd left behind in L.A. Cruising the Greek isles aboard a 150-foot yacht was an extravagance that far exceeded anything she had known. Although she'd been around, until she met Styvie Pell she'd had no idea what it meant to have the kind of wealth found in the top third of the Fortune 500.

The trip to Europe had been her idea. Styvie would have preferred a vacation on Nantucket or a few weeks up at his house in Bar Harbor, Maine. He was such a stuffy Wasp sometimes, she thought, but his bank account made him the kind of boyfriend she'd always wanted. She felt protected, rich, pampered. But most of all, she felt restless.

The Labor Day weekend had passed and she felt an urge to be back "in traffic." It was the season for cities now. As far as she was concerned, summer was over. But until she could get Styvie on the move, she was going to loll about in luxury.

She adjusted the tie on her string bikini and applied more Lancôme body lotion. The sun was an aphrodisiac for her, and she liked nothing better than rubbing oil all over, basking in the rays (though of course, not her face), and then making love. She supposed she could go downstairs and pry Styvie away from the movies he spent his day watching, but the thought didn't thrill her. She had known the first time she saw him that under all his properness was a man who wanted to be a stud but wasn't. She could never be attracted to that quality, but she knew she could take advantage of it.

When they first became lovers, Styvie had delighted in relating his fantasies to Christie. When she offered to stage them for him, he reacted as if he'd reached a new sexual frontier. In bed, she made him feel like a king of men. The next morning, he'd strut around as if he deserved the Don Juan award for consummate lovemaking. Christie was amazed at his self-deception. Doesn't he understand, she wondered, that his calling card is money, not sex? But then she reminded herself that it was her ability to deceive and his inability to see that kept him so attached.

She caught the eye of one of the staff and pointed to her glass in a signal that meant she wanted a refill on her Coca-Cola. It was brought over by Dimitri, a twenty-two-year-old waiter, half Greek, half Italian.

Yesterday while taking in the sights on the island of Santorini, she'd seen him relaxing on his day off. He was sitting in an outdoor café having an ouzo with a girlfriend. He was very affectionate toward his date, touching her hair, pouring her a glass of water, every gesture a caress. Christie had seen him on the yacht without his shirt on, and his muscular arms and strong back tapering down to thin hips made her ache for his youthful passion.

"Thank you," she said with a smile as he set the Coca-Cola down in front of her. She noticed that for a quick second his eyes traveled over her body and liked what they saw. Christie thought about what it would be like to have a pure overwhelming desire for someone, a desire with nothing else involved, no other credentials needed, just a physical connection. It had been a long time since she'd had anything like that. Maybe she'd never had it. At thirteen her mother's boyfriend had seduced her in the back of his pickup truck. By sixteen

she was seducing middle-aged men who drove Mercedes.
She couldn't remember a simple crush, a simple flirtation. It had gotten complicated awfully fast.

When Styvie finally came up to the deck after watching
a double feature, the best hours for sunbathing were
over. Christie was dressed in one of her Gianni Versace
outfits, reading the latest Sidney Sheldon novel. Styvie
had taken a shower, been handed a perfectly blended gin
and tonic, and was feeling quite content.

"How was your afternoon?" he asked, as if he had just
returned home from the office. Styvie's behavior wasn't
affected by the environment. In his corporate offices or
on a cruise, he was the same.

"I can't believe how blue the water is here," Christie
gushed.

"Did you go for a swim?"

"No," she replied, annoyed with him for asking. She'd
explained to him days ago that she had a phobia about
the sea. She couldn't remember what trauma she blamed
it on, but she'd made it clear it was a sensitive subject.
The truth was that she wasn't a skillful swimmer. She
managed to stay afloat but looked so desperate doing it,
she'd given up the sport altogether.

"Is that a gin and tonic you're drinking?" she asked,
changing the subject.

"Would you like one?"

"Just a sip of yours."

He offered her his glass and then let his hand slide
down to her thigh.

"Do you want to take a nap? A siesta?"

This was Styvie's way of asking her if she wanted to
make love. It bugged her that he couldn't come right
out and say it. She gave him back his glass.

"Look at the sky. It's going to be an amazing sunset."
To keep him happy, since she didn't exactly jump at his
request for sex, she moved over on the deck chair to

make room for him. Sweetly she kissed his ear. "I've been thinking. Maybe we should start talking about the kind of movies we want to make," she suggested. "I've got some ideas. What about an adventure story?"

"There's plenty of time to talk about that. It could take months, even years, before I buy into the right setup," he said.

"Is Millennium off the block?" Christie had just recently added that bit of business lingo to her vocabulary.

"No, it's still a possibility, but I'm not rushing into anything."

Styvie didn't need a base in Hollywood. Acquiring one was an appealing thought, not a necessity. Admittedly, he'd grown bored with his role on the board of directors of his family's automotive company, an organization that ran quite efficiently without his input. A new enterprise might be an interesting challenge, but he wasn't desperate.

For Christie, waiting a few months meant living in purgatory, and even if the fringe benefits of that purgatory were glamorous, it was still a halfway house for her. Hollywood was her only chance to gain some financial independence. She knew TV stars who weren't any more talented than she was who were earning huge sums of money. The acting classes she'd been going to for a year made it obvious she was no Meryl Streep. But neither was Joan Collins. Christie had no doubts that given the right role, she could succeed in the same way Joan Collins had. At his B-B-Q, Lance had slipped Christie a copy of *Dirty Dreams*. Five pages into it, she realized this could be her ticket to stardom. She also realized that her flimsy résumé would be no match for the more experienced actresses Lance was considering. But they were no match for her determination. The only options Christie saw for herself were making it in Hollywood or marrying a wealthy man. Unfortunately, most of the rich men available believed in prenuptial agreements or had lawyers shrewd enough to protect their clients from their romantic impulses.

Styvie was adamant about not getting married again. He had told her so the first night they spent together, and hadn't weakened in his resolve in spite of her considerable efforts to get him to do so. When they had been in Aspen last winter, she had made a big deal about how cute the preschoolers looked all lined up for their first ski lesson. He acknowledged their cuteness the way he would a shelf of stuffed animals at FAO Schwarz. He clearly wasn't thinking about an heir.

God damn him, Christie had cursed silently. He was taking away from her the most powerful weapon in her arsenal. Getting pregnant wouldn't assure her of anything other than money for an abortion and, once the operation was performed, a "feel-better" trinket from Cartier.

"Well, I'm going to rest before dinner," Styvie announced. Christie got the message. He meant he'd be there waiting for her.

She hated that she was forever "on call" with him. Sex on demand was part of their unspoken agreement. Only wives could beg off with a headache, she realized. Girlfriends like her were expected to take two aspirin and remove their clothes.

She watched Styvie march off toward the master suite and procrastinated in following him. Five more minutes, she bargained with herself, five more minutes of being left alone in peace before she had to succumb to his weight on top of her.

"Telephone, Mr. Pell," Dimitri announced.

"Thank you," Styvie said in Greek. It was the only expression in that language he'd bothered to learn. He continued toward the bedroom to talk privately while Christie, her curiosity piquing, sought out Dimitri for info.

"Mr. Biton," he told her.

"Burton, Burton," she corrected.

Dare she listen in? She weighed her chances. Could she get away with it? Probably. Over the years, she'd perfected the art of eavesdropping, a talent she considered necessary to her survival.

"Thank you," she said to Dimitri, dismissing him.

As soon as he exited, she turned her back to the door and carefully picked up the receiver to the extension phone on the bar. Lance's voice was clearer than that of the dressmaker she'd called in Paris earlier that afternoon.

"It's the exact instability you were looking for," Lance was saying. "Call Steven Lloyd. He'll tell you that you'll never get a studio at a per-share price like this again. It's the same studio, the same library, the same inventory. The only difference is that a couple of interchangeable executives are playing musical chairs. You can see through the current instability. You'll look like a genius. There'll never be a better time. Trust me. If you don't move fast, Wall Street will be praising some Texas wildcatter for his cunning Hollywood takeover."

"I hear rumors that the asking price will be high," Styvie said.

"High?" Lance repeated. "That's what they said when Marvin Davis bought Fox. Do you know how much he made on the real estate alone? This is not that different a deal," Lance pointed out.

"I'll be in New York next week," Styvie said calmly, too calmly for Christie.

At that moment, from behind her Dimitri called out her name. She turned to find him standing in the doorway. The wine list for dinner was in his hand. Christie put her finger up to her mouth to silence him, but it was too late.

"Christie?" It was Styvie. "Are you on the extension?"

"Sorry, hon. I didn't know you were still on the phone. I told my dressmaker in Paris I'd call her back today."

It was a lame excuse and they both knew it.

"Christie, honey," Lance greeted her. "You could be Mrs. Mogul."

She couldn't tell if he was making fun of her, but she did like the notion of being the wife of a movie tycoon.

"Really?" She acted surprised. "Is the deal happening? That's very exciting."

"We'll meet up in New York, then, Lance," Styvie concluded. He was trying hard to sound calm in spite of his rage over Christie's eavesdropping.

"Make that call to Steven Lloyd," Lance repeated.

"Will do," Styvie replied.

Christie hung up and braced herself for Styvie's wrath. As for Dimitri, he was oblivious of the problem he'd created.

Christie walked over to him and yanked the wine list out of his hand. At her request, every evening he'd check with her about what bottle would be served with dinner. Ordinarily it was a task she enjoyed. It made her feel like she was in charge of things and not just along for the ride. Today she randomly pointed to a chardonnay and returned the list to Dimitri along with a dirty look.

As the young Greek headed back to the kitchen, Styvie reappeared.

"I've ordered us a great bottle of wine," Christie said demurely.

Styvie grabbed her arm and pulled her inside near the bar. He picked up the extension she'd listened in on and ripped it out of its radio transmitter.

"This wasn't put here for your use, Christie. My business is *my* business. Can you comprehend that? If I choose to include you, that's my choice, and if I don't, you're out. It's very simple. You're part of all this by invitation only, and if you're a bad guest, you'll be asked to leave. That's the arrangement. If you don't like it, you can fly back to L.A. tomorrow morning. My rules. You understand?"

She understood, all right. Once again she'd have to apologize and appease someone because his money made her need him. But now her career was at stake, and at the risk of further offending him, she had to make a point.

"I understand, Styvie, don't worry. I'm not trying to pry into your private affairs. But maybe I'm curious about your business because I care about you. I don't know anything about the numbers being discussed, but it sounds like the studio is available, it's cheap, and Lance is your ally. What more do you want? Why don't you just say yes? Take a stand. Why can't you be more aggressive, for God's sake?"

She knew her remarks had hit a nerve because Styvie got defensive.

"It's not that easy, Christie. It's not fucking pool jewelry. I can't make a false move. It's a lot of money and I've got my family judging every step I take."

Christie saw that he was getting worked up over his own indecision and knew from experience he'd ultimately take it out on her. He hated to have her witness his weakness.

"You're so fucking stupid sometimes, Christie. You've got a five-and-dime mentality. It's impossible to deal with you. This kind of thing doesn't work for me," he warned, "and if it continues, this relationship will be short-lived."

Christie understood exactly what she had to do. Her directness had made him withdraw; her submission would bring him back.

"I'm so sorry, honey. You're right. I just get so scared sometimes and say things without thinking."

She embraced him, tears welling up in her eyes. "Please forgive me," she begged.

Her confession brought no words of forgiveness from Styvie, but he did let her kiss his neck, and he didn't push her away when she rubbed his lower back. He was enjoying this passive role. It became her job to work him, and the more aloof he appeared, the more skills she had to employ to win him over. Slowly she slid her hands inside the waist of his pants and felt the erection she knew she'd find. He looked over toward the open door and wide windows. Christie knew he was worried that one of the servants might see them. "Fuck me right here," she dared him.

He pushed up her shirt and grasped her full breasts, squeezing them together. She stooped lower and placed his cock in the cleavage.

"Right here, right here," she moaned.

"You fucking whore," he said.

"That's right," she agreed, "and I'm the best whore you've ever had."

Just as she sank to her knees, ready to take him in her mouth, Dimitri appeared outside. They could hear him singing a Euro-trash disco song. His back was to them as he cleared off one of the tables, picking up Styvie's empty gin glass and placing it on a tray.

Styvie pushed Christie back, but she held on to the inside of his thigh.

"Take a chance," she purred. "Come on, don't you want it as badly as I do?"

He thought he'd indulge her for a few seconds more before carting her off to their bedroom, but once he felt her mouth engulf him, he knew he wasn't going anywhere. Christie took her time, her pleasure coming from the knowledge of how well she manipulated him and the thought that Dimitri might walk in. She didn't mind being an exhibitionist in front of an audience as cute as the young Greek. She aroused Styvie until she knew he was ready to explode and then she pulled back, slowing things down. She stood up and lifted her skirt, inviting Styvie to penetrate her. As he gave in to the moment, he kept tabs on Dimitri, who was straightening out deck chairs. The danger of discovery thrilled Styvie, and Christie urged him on.

"Goddammit, you feel good," she said as she began to fake preorgasmic delirium. She adjusted her breathing, forcing herself to pant. She reached back and dug her fingers into his leg. The sound she made was a repressed scream, implying that if she could she'd let out a shriek that would be heard all the way to Mykonos. Styvie's climax was, as usual, silent.

Zipping up his loosely fitting boat pants, he saw that the deck was empty. He convinced himself they'd escaped Dimitri's notice. Next time . . . on the yacht's bow, he fantasized.

Christie ran her fingers through her snarled hair.

"You look like you've just been ravaged by an entire football team," he proudly told her.

Together they sank back on the couch.

His caress told her she was back in his good graces. Even so, she had to proceed cautiously.

"It'll be sad to leave the islands," she said. "It's such a paradise."

"We'll come back again," he promised her, "but this business in New York can't be put off."

At that moment he was in the mood to play daddy and Christie was smart enough to complement his mood by playing dumb. "We have to go back? Right away? Can't you just telex or something?"

"These things are complex, Christie. As a matter of fact, I've got to make some calls right now."

"Will it take long?" she asked, as if his being out of sight for five minutes would be a hardship on her.

"I've got to call Steven Lloyd," he replied, checking his watch and calculating it was ten A.M. in New York, "and I've got to call Medair Travel."

She cozied up to him. "I thought all our travel plans were already taken care of."

"I'm hiring a jet," he explained, "departing Athens at nine A.M. I want to get to New York before another business day closes. Can you be packed and ready early in the morning?"

"Sure I can." She smiled, and this time the scream she was repressing was a cheer. I'll get what I need out of you yet, Styvie, she thought. Hollywood, here I come, and fuck you, William Morris Agency, for not signing me before. You'll be begging for me now.

Styvie rose, and then, before going off to phone, stopped, took her face in his hands, and really looked into her eyes. "Take nothing for granted, Christie, and we'll get along just fine."

"I promise," she said meekly.

"Don't promise," he replied. "Just don't forget."

THE
MUD
SLIDES

21

"Maybe you'll win a car, Andrew," Carolyn exclaimed. "Wouldn't that be great?"

They were at the entrance gate to Disneyland, which was in the middle of a month-long promotion that included giving away a different car each day. Carolyn had suggested this day trip as a way of combating mounting pressures. Ever since Kevin's resignation, Nicole's control at Millennium had been shaky and Carolyn had had to face the fact that she might be hitched to a falling star.

But more unsettling was the tension she felt around Andrew. There were moments when she looked at him and he seemed a different person. He was guarded, almost secretive. As she watched him at parties and saw how he effortlessly manipulated people, she couldn't help but wonder if she too were being manipulated. Only at night, in bed, did they regain the trust and openness that disappeared in the morning light. It made Carolyn sad to see that the playfulness that had initially attracted her to Andrew had begun to wane. For the last few weeks Andrew was so focused on his business—or lack of business—that he treated fun as a luxury he couldn't afford. It was only after they got into a stupid argument over whether movies about rock-and-roll idols had any future in Hollywood that Andrew acknowledged that their relationship was moving off track. As a conciliatory gesture he agreed that maybe a break from their normal routine wasn't such a bad idea.

*   *   *

They bought their tickets and passed through a turn-
stile. No buzzer, lights, or bells went off.

"I guess that means we didn't win," Carolyn said.

Andrew tossed away his stub. "I prefer my Fiat, even
with its leaks."

He looked over at the car on display, an orange Pinto.
"An orange one. Do you believe that? Anyway, I spoke
to Milt Friedman Leasing, and as soon as my deal closes,
I'm getting a Monte Carlo," he cynically joked. Despite
his attempt at covering it, Carolyn could see he was
feeling the strain of being on hold.

Though Bambi hadn't officially passed on Andrew's
idea, she'd come up with a dozen reasons for stalling.
She wanted him to come up with a list of writers for the
project. She wanted to check with marketing and research about how commercially viable they thought *Wide
Sargasso Sea* could be. She wanted to read the book
herself instead of having a reader write up a report on it.
Though that sounded promising, Bambi was working her
way through the slim novel as if it were *War and Peace*.
Carolyn had witnessed Andrew's annoyance with these
delaying tactics, but he hadn't yet written Bambi off
completely. When Carolyn brought up the subject, Andrew was quick to say he had the situation under control.
What did that mean? Carolyn asked herself. That he was
confident of getting the deal eventually? Andrew didn't
elaborate. He was more vocal about his backup plan.
He'd also met with Alan Greer, a Canadian producer
who seemed interested in the project. Andrew sounded
upbeat about this possibility but Carolyn was skeptical.

She'd had her doubts ever since she'd been introduced
to Alan at the Beverly Hills Coffee Shop, Andrew's
favorite breakfast spot for soft-boiled eggs and hash
browns. This past Sunday, Alan had been seated at a
counter stool next to theirs. Andrew made the introductions and mentioned that Carolyn was a writer. Alan
sighed deeply, as if the effort it took to respond was a
gross imposition. "Not on weekends," he replied.

The Fall River girl in Carolyn clamored to break out. Growing up in a working-class, ethnically mixed neighborhood had given her a fighter's reflexes. If she felt pushed, or insulted, her instinct was to strike back. She wanted to say: Fuck off, Alan, you jerk. No one is shoving a script in your face. Instead, she bit her lip and kept the street-fighting girl under wraps. She couldn't have the luxury of expressing her opinion. Andrew needed the money.

A Disneyland employee checked Carolyn's ticket stub and informed her she had won, not a new Ford Pinto, but a pin that said "Fantasyland."

She fastened it to the lapel of her jean jacket, next to the other pins she called her "coat of arms"—a Statue of Liberty, a small American flag, and a signet pin from Brown University. "A memento of our date at Disneyland," she said. "Kind of corny, I know, but hey, I'm just a girl from the provinces."

Andrew didn't comment. He might have agreed to come to Disneyland, but now that he was here, he questioned why he had let Carolyn talk him into this nonsense. He was still recovering from the hour drive down to Anaheim along a stretch of freeway not known for its beauty. Billboards depicting giant tacos were not his idea of visual stimulation.

As they walked through the park, Andrew stared at "Middle America" with their Instamatics. Many of them wore floppy sandals, cutoff jeans, and stretched-out T-shirts. He watched as parents chased after their kids, who all seemed to screech when they talked, bump into each other when they walked, and drop ice cream all over themselves and whoever was in their vicinity.

"What ride do you want to go on first?" Carolyn asked.

Andrew came to an abrupt halt. "Ride?" He wasn't amused. "We have to stand in one of those lines to go on a ride? I can hardly bear to stand in line at the bank, and at least there, I get money. Here all I'll get is sick and dizzy from sitting inside twirling teacups."

Carolyn sighed. She was not going to get into an argument with Andrew, no matter how bad his attitude.

"Andrew, where's your spirit? You're the one who's gone parachute sailing and been on African safaris."

Andrew had forgotten he'd told her his safari story. It must have been in the early days of their courtship when he'd felt the need to use all available impressive facts and enticing fiction to win her away from Paul. It made him uneasy now to think about his lies. Well, not lies, he rationalized. He had been to Africa, but it wasn't anything like an Isak Dinesen novel.

"Let's sit a minute and plot this out." Andrew settled himself on one of the benches that ran alongside a picturesque manmade stream. A second later, a Disneyland employee in a Minnie Mouse costume, complete with an oversize mouse head, also took a breather on the other end of the bench. A five-year-old girl wearing Baby Guess overalls, without ice cream stains, pulled her mother over to get a better look.

"Hi, Minnie, where's your husband, Mickey?" the girl asked.

The mother, looking out-of-place in a navy-blue suit, fiddled with her imitation Louis Vuitton bag and pulled out a camera. The little girl asked whether Minnie knew Ernie from *Sesame Street.* She was a curious, bright, precocious child, and after posing for two snapshots, insisted on taking one of her own—a photo of Minnie, her mother, Andrew, and Carolyn.

"Sweetheart, don't bother other people," her mother reprimanded.

"No, it's perfectly all right," Andrew said. Something about the child reminded him of himself at five. She had the kind of independence that comes from being alone a lot at an early age. She was a child being taken to an amusement park by a polite, guilt-ridden, but uninterested parent. It could have been a page out of his own book of memories.

The encounter with the child had put Andrew in a pensive mood. He kept his thoughts to himself until fifteen minutes later, when, standing in line to buy popcorn, he surprised Carolyn by saying, "I think we should have three children. Three spirited, spunky children . . . and we should raise them on a farm in Scotland."

"The three spunky kids sound good to me," Carolyn replied, "but a farm in Scotland? I'm too much of an American girl for that. How about a place out at the beach, up the coast?"

"How about both?" he compromised. "Malibu and Scotland. Then our children will be bicontinental."

Carolyn was glad Andrew was back on one of his tangents. It was a good sign. Even though she was aware a lot of what he said was embellishment, nobody embellished better. Taking advantage of this break in his gloom, Carolyn guided him over to the line for the Thunder Mountain railroad.

"This isn't one of those roller-coaster rides, is it?" he asked.

"You mean like the Matterhorn? No, this is just a spirited train ride," she assured him as they climbed inside the front car. A teenager behind them let out a whoop and yell as the ride got under way.

Andrew threw Carolyn a look. "A train ride? I'm going to kill you."

His attention was pulled away by the acute angle of the rails they were ascending, a hint at the plunge that awaited them on the other side. Seconds later, piercing screams could be heard as the riders were jerked around corners, shot up, and thrown down hills of steel. When Carolyn wasn't closing her eyes, she looked over at Andrew, who was swept up in the excitement in spite of his belief that it was undignified, and that at twenty-five he was far too old for this kind of diversion.

"All right, all right," he said when the ride was over.

He took her by the hand, ready to meet the next challenge. He sought out the Matterhorn and this time patiently waited in line, his attitude turning playful. He was beginning to succumb to the spell of Disneyland. He was being seduced by an environment dedicated to fun and make-believe, a sanctuary from the bill collectors and rejections he'd left back in L.A.

Temporarily letting go of the pressures and concerns that he'd been fixated on, Andrew allowed himself to think about other things. He knew that lately he'd been neglectful of Carolyn, and sought to correct the mistake. He affectionately slipped his arm around her.

"Magic is an interesting thing, isn't it?" he said. "Think about it. You and I believe there's something special that binds us, something indefinable. Our backgrounds and personalities are entirely different. A computer-dating service would consider us seriously mismatched."

"We're playing the hard eights," Carolyn said.

Andrew looked at her quizzically.

"It's a gambling expression," she explained. "Crap-shooting. It means betting on double fours, which is the riskiest way to play an eight bet."

"Are you a gambler?" Andrew asked.

"Not till I met you," she said.

"Are you ever sorry you didn't stay with Paul? I wouldn't have blamed you. Even I admit he would have been a safer bet." Andrew searched for the right metaphor. "More like playing black or red in roulette."

She took his arm. "There's no magic in that, is there?" she reminded him.

After the Matterhorn, a dozen other rides, and time spent just strolling around the park, Andrew insisted they ride Space Mountain, the scariest roller coaster in the park. They were now fully into the swing of things. Three hours in Disneyland had transformed them. They'd indulged in top-of-the-line junk food, even sampling the sweet Mexican *choritas*, so different from the raspberry tarts of Hollywood dinner parties. They'd splashed each other while riding through the Pirates of the Caribbean. They'd bought Mickey Mouse sweatshirts, mugs, and rings in a spurt of souvenir shopping. They'd had an uncomplicated good time in Disneyland and Carolyn felt their relationship was cleansed by the experience in Americana.

Before leaving, Andrew dragged Carolyn over to the teacup ride. "We have to," he argued. "If I don't do it now, believe me, I will never ever consider getting on that contraption."

The crowd was thinning out and soon they were in a blue-and-white cup doing their best to twirl it around as fast as possible. Their efforts left them plastered to the sides of the giant teacup like clothes to the sides of a washing machine during the spin cycle. When they finally stepped off the structure, feeling, as Andrew had predicted earlier that afternoon, a little sick and dizzy, he didn't say: I told you so. Instead he embellished. "It was great. It was an experience in team effort for delirium."

I love this man, Carolyn thought. Anyone who can describe the teacup ride like that will never be boring. Poor maybe, boring never. And if I have to, I can deal with being poor.

It was sundown as they drove off, and Carolyn felt the day had delivered more than she'd even hoped. She felt innocent pleasure again, which gave her some objectivity about life in Hollywood.

"I've been thinking," she said to Andrew. "I'm too old to be cynical for style and too young to be cynical for real. You've got to promise me you'll remind me of today when I start bitching about some moron's three-picture deal."

"Periodic doses of Disneyland it is," Andrew said.

They drove through the darkening night, past the billboards of giant tacos, now all lit up. As they neared the city line, Carolyn sensed Andrew's anxiety return. She could feel him moving away from her as his mind clicked into its strategizing gear.

Breaking the silence, he offered a suggestion he'd been considering. "I think you should pitch your *Party Doll* idea to Bambi."

For a millisecond Carolyn's mind connected Bambi with a deer—she was, after all, still dazed by the world of Disney.

Party Doll was Carolyn's latest idea for a screenplay. Set in the sixties, it was the story of a girl from a factory town who took advantage of the era's social fluidity. She ended up going to New York and hanging out with the young, rich, and restless, meeting the kinds of people she used to read about in magazines and finding them considerably less interesting in the flesh. It was a coming-of-age story with a moral dilemma and a very atypical heroine. It was perfect for Molly Ringwald.

Although Carolyn was anxious to get a real writing assignment, she was not in the mood to discuss work. Lately it was a topic that caused friction between her and Andrew. He found her too passive and idealistic, and she found him too driven and political. But since he'd met her halfway by coming to Disneyland, she was determined to try to see things from his point of view.

"It's an interesting thought, but I don't think Bambi likes me very much," Carolyn replied.

Andrew knew this was true. "But she needs product."

"She hasn't yet come through for you," Carolyn gently pointed out.

"I need to switch tactics. I played her wrong. I played on her ego, not her fears. She might be a fear buyer. If she thinks David Beach will beat her to the material, she might go for it."

"You think she'll even meet with me?" Carolyn asked.

"You're on staff there. Make it awkward for her to refuse you."

Carolyn mulled it over. When it came to her writing, she wasn't very good at asking for favors. "Do you think she'll get it? My heroine might be too offbeat for her. I think most of the time her taste runs along the lines of remakes of old musicals."

Andrew summed it up. "She probably *won't* get it, but if you credit her with intelligence she doesn't have and imply that someone suggested you also talk to David Beach about it, she might pretend to get it. And her pretending might get you a development deal."

"How do I credit her with intelligence she doesn't have?" Carolyn asked.

Andrew was ready for this one. "She likes to feel smart. The other day on the phone, she referred to Jane Eyre as one of Henry VIII's wives. I didn't correct her. I just said something like 'English history is fascinating' and let it slide. It allowed her to feel brainy."

Carolyn laughed but didn't reply. Instead she snuggled up to Andrew. She wasn't ready for Bambi Stern to intrude on her peace of mind. Not yet. Not until they were back in L.A. No, not even then, she decided. Not until Monday morning at the very earliest.

22

Nicole was prepared to argue her case. What she was not prepared for was a secretary who coldly informed her that her request for a meeting with the board of directors had been denied. "On such short notice, it's impossible to assemble the board," was the official line.

"Well, could you have Chester Baines return my call?" Nicole asked. She'd settle for a call from one of the members.

"I'll try," the secretary said.

As Nicole hung up, the insult spread within her. The board was treating her like "Nicole who?" Every day, she came to work expecting to be fired. The word hadn't yet come down from Ted, but then again, neither had any other word. No input inside the studio and no input from without. She was officially "out of the loop," thanks to Lance.

How long can this suspended animation go on? she wondered. She did a quick calculation. Could it be that Kevin had been gone almost two and a half months? There it was, October 1, in bold red print on her desk calendar. Where had the summer gone? And what, she wondered, would the upcoming season bring besides mud slides?

She glanced down at her Filofax datebook, which lay open on her desk. The page was blank except for a dental appointment and a relationship-maintenance lunch with an agent.

Her only phone call so far that morning had been her

mother. She'd called to say she loved *Phantom of the Opera* and that the house seats had been fantastic. Better than anything Aunt Sophie could have gotten. Nicole was struck by the irony of her mother's belated approval. Now that she was on the verge of losing her job, her mother had started to luxuriate in the perks of her career.

Finally the phone rang. Nicole, desperate for company, almost grabbed it on the first ring. She held herself back and let her secretary take it.

"Charlie Dooley on one." Doreen had maintained her jaunty tone through all the turmoil. What did she care? She was in the union.

Nicole perked up. She hadn't seen Charlie since that awful night at the Peter Gibson screening, and knew that, as always, he'd have some good gossip to distract her with.

"Honey," she said. "Nice to hear from you."

"Honey . . ." His drawl mimicked hers, but with an edge. "So we're moving on?" His tone was insinuating.

Nicole's automatic defense system began to crank up. "What have you heard?" She was exhausted by the charade and wanted some facts on the table. Now. She sucked in her breath.

"Well, honey, I heard you were fired."

The dread word. "Who told you that, Charlie? Because it's certainly not true. At least not as far as I know."

"Bambi." He paused. "She said it was common knowledge."

"Fascinating," Nicole blurted out. "I'll have a chat with Ms. Stern. Thanks, Charlie. You're a pal."

"Just don't tell her I'm the one who told you. Tell her you heard she's been saying it all over town."

"Don't worry, Charlie."

Abruptly the call was over and Nicole was punching in Bambi's extension.

"Bambi Stern's office." It was the secretary's voice.

"It's Nicole. Put her on."

"She's at the Ivy having lunch and isn't expected back until late this afternoon. If she calls in for messages—"

"Forget it," Nicole said.

She slammed down the phone. Bambi at the Ivy. Nicole was sickened at the image of her holding court while lunching on crab cakes and Perrier.

She felt herself weakening. She needed to cry . . . but no way. It was her number-one rule. No crying in the office. She had to get out of there. She wanted some privacy. After four years of abstaining, she wanted a goddamn cigarette.

The ladies' room. It was the only choice, though it irked her that even there she wouldn't be safe. Unlike men in her position at other studios, she didn't have a private facility. Her only hope was that she could pull herself together without witnesses. In the worst-case scenario, she decided, she'd retreat into one of the stalls.

She slipped out of the office and made it down the corridor unobserved. Now she studied herself in the ladies'-room mirror while wiping away the tears that rushed into her eyes. Bravely she moved in closer to inspect every flaw. I really look my age today, she acknowledged. This is not what you'd call *Harper's Bazaar*'s version of "over thirty and better than ever." Her fatigue and tension showed. Reapplying some lipstick and rouge helped, but the eyes were a dead giveaway. Maybe I can pretend I have conjunctivitis and keep my sunglasses on indoors, she considered. But no, that was the kind of thing Bambi would try to pull.

She was brushing her hair when the door was pushed open and Carolyn appeared. Nicole meant to saunter by, tossing off a token greeting, when she saw a mirror image of her own disintegration. Carolyn's poised spirit was clearly broken. Less skillful than Nicole at disguising her misery, it was apparent she was unable to hold back her tears.

"What's wrong?" Nicole asked.

"Nothing," Carolyn answered, unleashing more tears. She reached for a paper towel and dabbed at her eyes.

Nicole handed her another towel.

"Are you sure you don't want to talk about it? Or scream about it? Get it all out. I'll understand . . . especially if it's about Millennium."

This elicited a glimmer of a smile from Carolyn. "There's really nothing to say. I pitched an idea to Bambi and I guess I'm not professional enough to handle rejection."

Nicole knew how traumatic her own early failures had been, and in retrospect, how meaningless.

"Carolyn, these things happen to everyone. I remember how done-in I was when I failed in the beginning. Now I don't even remember the names of the people who did me in. You've got to develop a tougher skin. In this business people are always saying no. You've got to learn to say yes to yourself." I should listen to my own advice, Nicole thought. "So what if Bambi doesn't like your story? Someone else might."

Carolyn leaned against the wall. "It's not just my idea she trashed, she trashed me too. She told me everyone in Hollywood thinks he's a writer. She asked for my credentials. She said the illegal alien who washes her car tried to sell her a movie-of-the-week. Her exact words were, 'If I don't take a meeting with him, why should I ever meet again with you?' "

Nicole's rage was building. "She actually said that? And what else?"

"That my story didn't have any inciting incident, the concept didn't have scope, where was my second-act crisis . . . and did I realize that writing was a craft?"

Nicole sighed. Bambi talked like someone who had taken a one-day seminar in screenplay structure and now considered herself a seasoned critic. It was so typical, she thought. After one session of introductory French at Berlitz, Bambi had started sprinkling her speech with *"ça va?"*

"I don't know, maybe she's right," Carolyn said. "Maybe

I'm delusional." She tried laughing it off, but the giggle stuck in her throat. "Maybe . . ." She choked on the possibility. "Maybe I'm not talented."

Nicole took Carolyn by the shoulders.

"Listen to me. Bambi wouldn't get behind a project of yours if it were *Gone With the Wind*. First of all, she's mediocre when it comes to recognizing a good idea. Secondly, there's nothing she can gain from promoting you. As junior-high as it sounds, she's not about to help another girl look good. Bambi only plays up to the boys. Always has."

"But it went way beyond not helping," Carolyn pointed out. "Bambi became samurai critic."

Nicole smiled at the apt description. "Let's just say her expectations exceed her potential and she's practically psychotic about competition."

"I'm really confused now," Carolyn said. "If you think so little of her, why haven't you fired her?"

Nicole strode over to the other side of the room. "At first I didn't fire her because I thought we could work together, and now I can't fire her because . . ." She hesitated; getting into this subject was an acknowledgment of her own powerlessness. "Well," she continued, "as I said, she plays the boys, and at Millennium the boys she plays are in high places."

"How high?"

"Top."

"How friendly?"

"That's the part I'm not sure of."

Nicole's expression grew more somber. Consoling Carolyn had briefly distracted her, but now the reprieve was over.

Carolyn noticed the change. "Is there anything I can do? I'll run a kamikaze mission, sacrificing myself if it means ridding Millennium of Bambi," she joked. "It's justified. After all, she did draw blood first."

Nicole smiled at the suggestion. "It wouldn't work. The Bambis of this world always survive. At best, they lie low for a few months and then resurface with no guilt or even recollection of any of the damage they've done."

The two of them ruminated over this truth, staring off into space their countenances reflecting their sadness. Nicole broke the brief trance. "Is this what it always comes down to . . . crying in the ladies' room?"

Carolyn forced a grin. "I think I'll write a book about it someday. A research book. *Hiding in the Ladies' Room: A Collection of Experiences by a Cross-Section of American Women.*"

Nicole laughed.

"I must say," Carolyn continued calmly, "Bambi did tap right into one of my nightmares. I worry that I'll turn into one of those 'professional secretaries' who dabble in writing. I worry that at fifty I'll still be locked into a nine-to-five job and at an office party, after a couple of drinks, I'll pull out one of my short stories and talk about 'the collection' I'm working on. You know the type I mean?"

Nicole could picture the scenario, but not with Carolyn in it. "I don't think that'll happen to you," Nicole reassured her, "and I used to be known for my good hunches." Suddenly an idea struck her. "Why don't you give me a copy of your treatment and I'll take a look at it. If I can help you, I will."

"Would you?" Carolyn asked excitedly. "I thought about giving it to you in the first place, but then I thought, no, this is a company and there are procedures and all that. But I'd love for you to read it, and I've got a copy in my—"

"I can't guarantee I'll read it immediately," Nicole said, tempering Carolyn's enthusiasm.

"Whenever," Carolyn replied.

"And," Nicole added, "I'd like you to do a couple of things for me."

"Sure," Carolyn agreed.

"After leaving a copy of your treatment on my desk, I want you to take the rest of the afternoon off."

Carolyn started to protest this generous offer, but Nicole insisted. "Do something fun. Don't let Bambi ruin the whole day. And"—Nicole smiled—"just so my reputation as a demanding boss stays intact, make sure Doreen has your home number in case I need to reach you while I'm out of town."

"I didn't know you were going away."

"I just decided. If I'm going to fight for my job, I might as well go up against the real big boys. I'm taking the red-eye to New York tonight."

23

What the hell is an inciting incident? Carolyn slammed the door to her white VW in front of Andrew's apartment, still mulling over Bambi's words. The thought of seeing her boyfriend soothed her spirit. She was taking Nicole's advice and trying to have fun. To this end she'd stopped and picked up a bottle of wine and splurged on a beautiful bouquet of flowers. She looked forward to the late afternoon and evening ahead in the cozy living room Andrew had decorated in a style she referred to as young fogy. She pictured a fire blazing and the wonderful smell of domesticity that would lull her back to normal. Maybe he'd make some tea as she changed into his Eton rugby shirt. She longed for the sound of his voice that reminded her of every English actor she had idolized in her youth. Andrew would comfort her and laugh with her about the horrors of her meeting with Bambi.

She counted on him to tell her that formulas like the one Bambi had mentioned—the so called "inciting incident" of a screenplay—inhibited real writing. He'd tell her that they were the props of the untalented, the craftsmen and not the artists. He'd insist that they must stay pure in this town, where people's best intentions were betrayed by the price they paid for their dreams. Finally he'd urge her not to give up, and remind her that whereas others had money and power—both transitory—they had love.

She raced up the steps to 2B, put her key in the lock, and turned the knob. The door opened only a crack.

How odd, she thought. Why would Andrew put the chain lock on? She rang the bell. No answer. Fearing for his safety, she rang again and again. Relieved, she heard the padding of feet down the hallway and into the living room.

"Carolyn," Andrew said with surprise as he let her in.

Right off she noticed that his hair was tousled and his expression drowsy.

"Why are you barricading yourself in here, with the shades down?" she asked as she gently placed her packages down on the coffee table.

"My darling," Andrew said, sinking down into his favorite leather reading chair, "I'm an utter mess. I have the most crushing headache and we're out of aspirin."

Carolyn went over and sat on the arm of his chair and caressed his shoulder. "I'll go to the drugstore and get you some right now."

"Would you? You're my savior. What time is it, anyway?"

"Three. Nicole took pity on me and gave me the afternoon off. I'll explain when I come back from the store."

She reached out to hug him before going off on her errand, and felt slighted by how tentatively he hugged her back.

"I'm afraid I'll be a bore tonight," Andrew apologized. "The only cure is aspirin and sleep."

"That's okay," Carolyn replied, though she was disappointed. It would have been nice to give or receive some solace.

Impulsively she reached for the phone. "I think I'll give Lou a call. Maybe she can meet me for dinner later."

"Yes, darling, why don't you?" Andrew said as his head bowed as if with unbearable weight and his hands clasped behind his neck.

His movements were deliberate, commanding attention, even as they tried to fend it off.

Carolyn sensed something strange about him and about the room. As she slowly started to punch in Lou's number, her eyes darted about, looking for anomalies. Immediately she found one. A book lay open on the coffee table. It was a collection of Yeats from which he'd read to her on their first date. She saw that it was open to their favorite poem, *When You Are Old,* the ultimate pledge of undying love. Andrew quoted from it when he was being especially romantic. She realized that what she'd thought was their sacrament was now looking like his modus operandi. She had taken all this in while making her call, and with every number, her pace slowed. Andrew stood waiting for her, looking as though he found it increasingly difficult even to stand up. His behavior, always on the verge of acting, was bordering on overacting. On the last digit, intuition took over. Carolyn placed the phone back on the hook and stepped decisively down the hallway toward Andrew's closed bedroom door. He tried to interrupt her path, but his timing was way off this afternoon.

In bed, her long legs under the covers, Bambi Stern pretended to be startled by the sound of the opening door. Feigning either modesty or her version of appropriate behavior, she drew the sheets over her exposed breasts. Otherwise she was unfazed by Carolyn's arrival. In fact, she glorified in the high drama. She tossed her head forward, fluffed her hair out, and asked, "Carolyn, what are you doing here?"

For Carolyn, the sight of Bambi in the bed she and Andrew slept in was a stab that punctured forever her faith in Andrew's magic.

"I live here." She wanted to add "you cunt," but held on to her last shreds of self-control.

Bambi looked behind Carolyn to Andrew. "You didn't tell me that Carolyn actually lives here."

"Lived. Past tense," Carolyn said, tears flooding into

her eyes. She turned to leave and Andrew reached for her wrist. She flew by him.

"Don't come near me," she said. "And don't ever call me again."

Then she ran through the living room, toward the front door. For a millisecond she stopped and considered the open book. She picked it up as Andrew approached her. She hurled it at him, ignoring his conciliatory sounds. He ducked, and it hit the wall.

Andrew had to think fast. He knew he had few options. He had to finesse Bambi in the bedroom while handling Carolyn's rage. "I'll be right back, darling," he called out. "I've got to clear some things up."

He headed after Carolyn. Though he had no plan, he was proud of the reserve of poise he had to draw from. At his weakest, on those bad nights when he couldn't sleep and panicked at the thought that Carolyn might leave him, he could hardly breathe. Those feelings reduced him to the little boy chasing after his mother's gowns. But tonight he felt powerful. He could keep Bambi in place and placate Carolyn. He was confident that Carolyn truly loved him and that all he had to do was convince her that he loved her too—still and always. Convincing was his specialty.

From the stairs he saw her wipe the tears from her face with angry sweeps of her forearm. He ran to her, wanting to console her. She looked so small.

When he reached for her shoulders to brace her to listen, she turned her head away.

"Come, come, Carolyn. Something like this doesn't destroy a great love. Great loves withstand—"

She slapped him furiously. "Fuck your great loves, Andrew. I could have done with real love. No lies. No bullshit promises and pretense. You're so busy talking about love, you don't know what it is."

"Darling . . ." His voice was cajoling, pleading. "You know what I think of Bambi. You must know how completely meaningless this is to me. It's just a lunch date gone out of control. She called me this morning and invited me to meet her at the Ivy. She probably heard I met with David Beach last week. During lunch she told me she'd lost her copy of *Wide Sargasso Sea* and asked if she could come by and borrow my copy. I admit I should have sent her off to a bookstore and that neither of us should have drunk so much wine, but something insignificant like this doesn't betray what you and I have together."

Carolyn was appalled. "This doesn't betray us? Fucking someone else in our bed doesn't betray us?" She sounded shrill and didn't care. "You phony. I can't hear any more of this."

She started to walk away but Andrew kept pace with her. "Don't you know you'll always come back? We're destined to be together. Don't you know that?"

"Your talk of destiny makes me ill, Andrew. You and your highfalutin phony destiny. Why can't you just have a future like everyone else?"

She clutched for the Fantasyland pin on her jacket. She undid the clasp and yanked it off. She didn't want anything reminding her of happier times and her own bad judgment. She threw it down on the street. As it hit the pavement it made a tinny sound. "Perfect," she said. "A tacky dimestore memento from a flimsy make-believe romance."

"Just a lunch date gone out of control? Do you believe that?" Carolyn asked.

The question was directed at Lou as the two of them sat at Lou's kitchen table.

"He makes me want to scream," Carolyn continued. "He tried to make it sound like his only sin was that he'd had a little too much wine. What did he expect me to say—'Oh, well, Andrew, boys will be boys,' and leave it at that?"

"Probably," Lou chimed in. "But you're not his mother. It's not your job to give him unconditional love. My own particular fantasy," she elaborated, "is to go to Europe and hopefully meet a man who doesn't want to be a little boy or my daddy. That's not easy to find in this country."

Lou noticed Carolyn looking at her quizzically. "I'm just trying to distract you, Carolyn. Get you off the details that'll hurt to remember. If you generalize and philosophize, it's easier on the heart."

Lou had a point, Carolyn thought. It was true that she became unhinged whenever she dwelled on some sweet little thing that Andrew used to do or when she pondered the logistics of the move that lay before her. Her exit had been so swift and dramatic, she didn't even have her toothbrush.

"Damn him," Carolyn said as she got up to get more Kleenex. She knew that this breakup was going to be more horrible for her than for him. Men always handled this stuff better than women.

I hate him, she thought, the tears starting again. How can someone who claimed to love me more than anyone would ever love me, betray me like this? The words of Paul's warning came back to her like a prophecy: "Watch out for guys like Andrew Spencer. They're in love with the idea of love." Unable to heed Lou's advice, she zeroed in on a poem Andrew had written in the beginning of his campaign to make her fall in love with him. She'd memorized it and now tortured herself with the duplicity she found in every line.

Just then the phone rang. Carolyn checked the clock. It was nine-thirty. A slow smile grew on her lips. "It could be him," she said.

"Shall I just let the machine get it?" Lou asked.

Let him ring, Carolyn thought. Let him wonder if I'm here and suffer. She prayed that it was Andrew, begging her forgiveness and pledging his undying love.

At the fourth ring, she couldn't postpone her satisfaction any longer.

"Answer it," Carolyn said.

She watched Lou's face for a sign.

"Hold on," Lou replied into the receiver, and then, handing it to Carolyn, dashed all her hopes with three words: "It's some woman."

Reluctantly Carolyn took the call. "Yes," she said.

"Carolyn? This is Nicole. Is that you?"

Carolyn readjusted her voice to one appropriate for her boss. "Of course, Nicole. What can I do for you?" Her heart was sinking, but she kept herself afloat.

"I've been trying to reach you all evening. I've been calling the number you left with Doreen, but no one was there until now. Finally Andrew answered and suggested I try here. Is everything all right?"

"No, but . . ." Her voice became shaky. She wasn't ready to get into the details of this afternoon with Nicole. "No, but I'm dealing with it," she managed to say.

"I wanted to talk to you before I boarded the plane," Nicole blurted out. "I've just finished reading your treatment and I want you to know I think it's wonderful. It's like a girls' version of *Diner*. I love the relationship between the two leading characters. It's a coming-of-age story without any sappiness. The sex is hot and the situations are real. I love the factory-town backdrop and the title, *Party Doll*. Very commercial. It's exactly the opposite of *Dirty Dreams*. It's about making choices that keep you clean. It's a wonderful vehicle for talent, easy to package. When I get back, I'll see what I can do about helping you move this along," Nicole promised. "Obviously things at Millennium don't look too bright, but I still have some credibility left in this town . . . somewhere."

Things were happening too quickly for Carolyn to register. She hung on the phone, speechless.

"Did you hear me, Carolyn?"

"It's been a shocking night, Nicole, but I hear you loud and clear. This may not make sense, but I feel like a crash-and-burn victim who's just been saved. Oh, never mind, it's complicated."

Nicole laughed, comprehending Carolyn's reactions more clearly than Carolyn could have known. "It's the nature

of our business. I like to think of it as one big good-news/
bad-news joke. Anyway, I'm glad at least to be the
good-news part of the equation."

"Believe me, Nicole, there's no contest for that spot. I
can never thank you enough for this support . . . and
your timing. This is exactly what I needed tonight."

Both women hung up, thinking about how much they
liked each other. If only men could be so easy to get
along with, they both thought as they drifted off in their
separate, lonely realities.

24

Elaine searched for the TV's remote control, which she'd lost somewhere in the folds of the bedsheets. When she found it, she switched from *Good Morning America* to the *Today* show to CBS. It was seven twenty-five. She'd already heard the weather report three times and the news report enough times to quote it verbatim. She'd been up since six, when Steven awoke. Insomnia had become a part of their existence, a manifestation of the uneasiness they both had felt since that night in East Hampton.

She took a sip of her lukewarm coffee and then pressed the intercom extension and ordered her maid, Olga, to bring a fresh pot. As she waited for her refill, she gazed out the window of their New York town house and wished she was still back on the island. The Indian summer Manhattan was suffering through this October didn't help her state of mind. The humidity outside was unbearable. After even a short two-block walk, surrounded by sweating irritable people, she felt trapped. It was *No Exit* set in a sauna.

For the last week she'd stayed inside her air-conditioned spacious home and held telephone court in bed. In the evenings she and Steven would either have a simple meal at home (Olga did a decent poached salmon, asparagus in hollandaise, and raspberry sorbet) or Elaine would accept one of the several dinner invitations they'd received. She chose only those that reinforced the roots she and Steven had established together. Old friends and family were a yes. A fund-raiser for the library, a yes. But an opening at a gallery, a no. She didn't want Steven running into any nouveau-riche Hollywood arty types who frequented Madison Avenue to shop for a little respectability.

She switched back to channel four. Willard Scott was talking about the rainy season in Southern California. He mentioned that the brushfires that swept through the canyons in July could mean dangerous flooding and mud slides. "Isn't that a shame?" Elaine said sarcastically, and switched back to *Good Morning America.*

Olga came in with a fresh pot of coffee on a silver tray.

"My husband hasn't left yet, has he?"

"No, ma'am, Mr. Lloyd's in the kitchen with Alison. They're having breakfast."

Nice of them to invite me, Elaine thought, though in the past she'd insisted on having time alone in the morning. "My hour of peace," she called it.

"Tell him I want to speak to him before he leaves for the office."

Olga made a move toward the hallway, when Elaine called her back. "No, wait, Olga. Tell him I'd *love* to see him for a minute before he leaves."

"Yes, ma'am," Olga replied.

I mustn't sound bitchy, Elaine cautioned herself. I've got to be agreeable. But once this is past, once Steven is over his wanderlust, I swear I'm finding myself another Brando and treating myself to a Nassau vacation.

Alison was juicing oranges and Steven was making a list of people to call once he got to the office. There were several L.A. numbers on the list, among them Nicole's. He wasn't sure she'd even take his call, and he understood why. After San Ysidro, he'd hesitated, and that hesitation had set off a chain reaction of doubts. He was sure she doubted him. God knows, he doubted himself. Then he doubted her, and he imagined she probably doubted herself. The good feeling found in Santa Barbara had dissipated to a disturbing sense of failure. He took the blame for it. He'd dropped the ball, cutting her off and not even explaining why.

Over and over he'd told himself that his involvement in the Millennium takeover made it impossible for him to get involved with Nicole. But he knew the real reason for his withdrawal was that he needed time to reevaluate his own intentions. Now that the deal was closed and it was apparent that he and Elaine had nothing left of their marriage but a social facade, he wanted to see Nicole again.

Today his plan was to call her to inform her about Millennium's new regime. He knew the new administration would want Nicole out. He wanted to offer her assistance, guidance, do whatever he could to help her find another job. He also had to admit, he was glad he had a legitimate reason to make contact. It would break the ice more easily.

"Daddy, you've been working too hard," Alison admonished him, noticing his intense concentration and furrowed brow. She had a delicate face, high cheekbones, and warm brown eyes. It was a face that looked younger than fourteen, but her attitude and dress said she had both feet firmly planted in teen territory. She poured some juice and pushed aside her notebooks. Steven picked up one of them. It had been bought at the start of the new school term, and though it was hardly a month old, its cover was covered with rock-and-roll stickers and half its pages were filled with doodles.

Geometry. World history. The categories made Steven nostalgic for his own school days until he came to an unexpected addition to the curriculum.

" 'Young Adult Relationships in a Changing World'? What's this about?"

Alison giggled. "We call it Modern Romance. It's an elective. It's Mrs. Scott's class about dating, what love is, why it doesn't always work out. She should know." Alison giggled again. "She's been married three times."

It suddenly struck Steven that his daughter wasn't just a schoolgirl, she was a ninth-grader, a high-school girl. "Three times," Steven reiterated, surprised that it didn't sound as outrageous to him as it used to. "So they teach you what love is? And do they test you on it? Are there multiple-choice questions? Is love: a) never having to say you're sorry, b) a joint bank account, or c) intoxicating optimism?"

" 'Intoxicating optimism'? Daddy, sometimes you come up with the weirdest things."

"Let me know what Mrs. Scott says," Steven kidded.

Alison gathered up her books and packed them inside a canvas shoulder bag. "The class is supposed to get kind of interesting toward the end. It's also about divorce and stuff."

"From young-adult dating to divorce and stuff, all in one semester?" Steven was trying to keep things light until he looked over and saw that Alison seemed troubled. She finished packing her supplies, slung the book bag in place on her shoulder, then slumped back down in her chair.

"A lot of my friends have parents that are divorced . . . and it's all right," she said. "It's different but it's all right."

Her words caught Steven unprepared. He saw that she had a determined look in her eyes, as if she were readying herself to get through a shock, and Steven realized that she knew what was going on. Maybe she didn't know the specifics, but she'd probably heard snatches of her mother's phone conversations and had witnessed the formal politeness between her parents.

Steven didn't know how far to go. Was this the time and the place for this talk? Would Olga walk in? Would Elaine? Would his office call in the middle of a sensitive moment? Did he even know how to begin?

He moved over to the chair next to hers. She was now playing with her little gold-cross earring. Noticing the cross made him wish he were religious. Then he'd have someone else's answers to fall back on.

"I wish I could guarantee you some forevers. But the only forever you can count on is that your mother and I love you very much. The rest of the world is out of my control. Things happen. Things change, but change isn't so bad. It can be exciting, stimulating, fun."

"Daddy, you don't have to give me a pep talk. I can handle things. I'm not a little girl anymore."

And in fact, with her spiky haircut and jewelry, she was trying hard to look like a young adult. But in Steven's eyes she was still the child he wanted to shelter.

"Okay, okay," he said. "No pep talks, but just one more thing."

"If you have to," she agreed, feigning impatience. This was familiar ground for them, good-naturedly acknowledging the generation gap and their different sensibilities.

Steven struggled to put things in perspective for her. "I had a philosophy professor in college who used to say, 'We make plans and God laughs at us.' "

Alison had to grin at that one. "You really are weird sometimes . . ." She paused. "But nice weird."

She got up to go and planted a kiss on his cheek.

"I'm serious," he insisted. "Think about what I said."

"Why do grown-ups speak in so many clichés?" she said, but he could tell she felt better. She gulped down the rest of her orange juice and dashed out the door as Olga entered the kitchen and relayed Elaine's message.

"Thanks, Olga," Steven replied as he stood at the window and watched Alison head off toward high school. It's time, he thought, time to make some decisions.

The TV was still on, but Elaine had moved over to her desk and was poised over the red leather book that served as her social calendar. When Steven walked in, she looked up. "What about the Rosses next week? Friday night? Maybe I'll invite another couple. Giuseppe said he would personally oversee the menu."

Giuseppe was the proprietor of Elaine's favorite Italian restaurant. It served the best bellinis, the only cocktail she drank, and the best risotto, which she claimed she'd never get tired of. "So I'll invite them for Friday night," she concluded when Steven didn't answer immediately.

"No, I don't think so." He removed his jacket from a hanger in the closet.

His wife picked up a pencil and held the tip of it up to her lips, but, exerting self-control, did not bite it. "Well, what do you suggest, then? The Allans?"

A button was missing from the front of the jacket, so Steven took it off and rummaged through his closet for another. "I can't make plans right now."

Elaine was not in the mood for this kind of evasiveness. Since she'd woken up at six, everything had bothered her. For over two hours she'd been fighting a black mood, and at best she was holding her ground. "Well, if we don't decide now, it'll be too late. People plan ahead here. It's not informal, like California."

Don't start on this California thing, Steven thought. "So we'll do it another Friday. Have you seen my gray suit?"

"We're not talking about suits now," she said.

Let the issue slide, she told herself, turning her attention back to the TV, where an attractive woman was rushing to catch a plane. It was a deodorant commercial geared to appeal to young professional women. It struck a dissonant note with Elaine, tapping into her paranoid fears. She tried to assess whether Steven was paying attention to the ad and if he seemed attracted to the model in it. She decided he was, and the irritation that engendered made it impossible for her to let any issue slide.

"We're talking about having dinner with the Rosses or the Allans," she pressed.

He gave up looking for his gray suit and picked up his buttonless jacket. "I'll call you from the office," he said as he headed downstairs.

She followed him. "It's not that difficult, Steven," she said. "The Rosses or the Allans. If you're having trouble deciding, flip a coin."

The sarcasm brought no reaction from Steven. As he walked away, Elaine had to stop herself from throwing something at him. She grabbed a cigarette from a lacquered tobacco-leaf box on the living-room coffee table but didn't bother lighting it. She bit down hard on the end of it, tightly retied the belt to her Fernando Sanchez robe, and pushed open the door to the dining room.

Olga was sitting at the table threading a needle, Steven's suit jacket on her lap. He hovered impatiently nearby.

"Olga, you can do that later," Elaine instructed. "Run upstairs now and bring me my phone book."

Olga looked at Steven and he nodded.

"So, sweetheart," Elaine said, softening her tone, "shall we say a nine-o'clock dinner Friday night? I'll call Ginny Ross right now."

Steven shook his head in dismay. "I'll talk to you later. I've got to be at the office early." He moved past her, heading for the door.

"Before noon," Elaine insisted.

Once on the street, Steven felt a wave of intense humidity and looked up at the partially clouded sky. He didn't go back to get the umbrella he kept in the hall closet. He didn't go back to get the list of phone numbers he'd left on the table, or the suit jacket Olga had draped over the back of the chair. With a mixture of uncertainty and relief, he hailed a taxi.

Down below, Madison Avenue was a sea of unavailable yellow taxis. Nicole looked out the window of her tenth-floor suite at the Carlyle at the harried people fighting over cabs. Letting the curtain drop into place, she stepped back into the sitting area of her suite.

She glanced over toward the phone, hoping that somehow its red message light would be on, even though it hadn't rung. All afternoon she'd been waiting for a call from Chester Baines, who she suspected was her only ally on the board of directors. Chester's secretary had promised to call back with an appointment time this afternoon.

Nicole couldn't decide if fighting for her job was brave or crazy. All she knew was that she needed to do something. Mentally exhausted, she threw herself down on the bed. It had been a long time since she'd felt this alone. It reminded her of rainy Sundays in L.A., when the gray mist enveloped her hillside guesthouse and made her feel cut off from everyone else. On those mornings it didn't matter that a half-mile down the street were twenty-four-hour supermarkets, twenty-four-hour instant-teller banks, and twenty-four-hour coffee shops. Then she felt as isolated as an islander who had just lost the bridge to the mainland.

This image brought a chill and a craving for a cup of hot Irish breakfast tea. She dialed room service and impulsively added a bowl of minestrone and a small green salad. Not exactly a power lunch, she thought. Not her usual New York lunch either. In the past, unless she was sick, she would never order room service. How could she when there was Azzurro, Mezzaluna, Arcadia?

She thought about calling her friend literary agent Erica Spellman, her connection to the pulse of the city, but Nicole couldn't cope with being "out in traffic." Erica would try to convince her to come play. The evening would begin relatively quietly with dinner at around ten for about eight at Orso's. Then the group would move on to some party, where it wouldn't be surprising to run into one of the Kennedy kids or some of New York's young movie stars. Maybe three of the original eight would drift off, and the remaining five would pick up another four before going over to Nell's. By three A.M. they'd all be up at someone's apartment off Park Avenue drinking champagne. By four o'clock the men flowing in and out

would be kissing Nicole, once on each cheek, and calling
out *"Ciao, bella,"* and the women would be sharing tales
of their love crises.

It was fun for Nicole to be out in a town where no one
talked movie business. A night in New York felt like a
vacation even when it was a business trip, because though
the days might belong to Millennium, unlike back in
L.A., the nights belonged to her.

On this trip she could hardly motivate herself off the
bed to answer the door. When the buzzer rang, she noted
that room service was awfully quick. She straightened out
her skirt and unlatched the lock. To her great surprise,
there in the hallway stood Steven, jacketless, his clothes
drenched from the rain.

"Do you happen to have a spare towel?" he asked,
grinning. His question, as intended, conjured up memories of San Ysidro.

"Cute, very cute," Nicole said. She didn't close the
door or invite him in, so Steven took it upon himself to
enter and shut the door.

"You're dripping on the rug," she pointed out.

"Sorry about that," he said, not taking his eyes off her.

The hurt and frustration resurfaced in Nicole. "It's
very *déjà vu*, isn't it? But then . . ." She stopped to
control her anger. "It isn't at all the same."

She went into the bathroom, grabbed a towel, and
threw it across the room at him. "What are you doing
here?" she demanded. "How did you find me?"

"Your secretary said you were in New York and I
remembered you'd mentioned that you always stay at the
Carlyle . . ."

"So you've tracked me down. Aren't I lucky?" Nicole's sarcasm was cold and biting.

"I had to see you."

"Why?"

Steven decided to just put it all on the line. "Because it
doesn't work when we're apart."

Nicole sank into the chair she'd been leaning on and

closed her eyes for a minute. When she opened them, she spoke in a soft weary voice. "Don't do this to me. I've worked too hard to put you out of my mind. And it wasn't easy. I had to find my way back from your passionate 'whatever it takes' at San Ysidro to the quick impersonal message you left on my answering machine. I'd call that the grand kiss-off. How could you have done that to me? If being lovers wasn't what you wanted, couldn't you at least have been a friend? Couldn't you have taken five minutes out of your busy day to see how I was doing? And now you say it doesn't work when we're apart? I don't have the energy to fall in and out of love as quickly as you seem to do. I've got to straighten out my job situation. I've got to be in control. Do you understand that? I can't afford to be on some champagne cloud in some emotional fog. I don't seem to function very well when the cloud moves on . . . so, do me a favor. Leave me alone. Let me do my work—at least that's something I'm good at."

Steven sat on the edge of the bed, next to her chair. "Let me help you. I know my actions over the last few months may not have shown it, but I believe you and I have a chance at something here. I'm forty years old. Falling in love wasn't on my agenda. It doesn't fit in with—"

"Don't you dare use the L word," she shouted.

"The L word?" Steven hadn't heard that expression before.

Nicole sat forward, on the edge of her seat. "The L word. The word that's been overused and abused. I'm sick of it. Maybe if I don't use it or hear about it for a while, it'll mean something again." She rested her forehead on her hand. "What am I doing? I can't do this. I have to stay calm."

Steven leaned back on his elbows, giving her all the time and room to get the anger out of her system. For an interminably long moment, neither of them spoke.

"I'm sorry I yelled," Nicole finally said. "I'm under a

lot of pressure and I'm not interested in being the girl you have after work, before you go home to your wife." She looked at her watch. It was a quarter to two. "Actually, it's a little early. Don't you New York businessmen usually stick around the office until at least five? . . . Then you taxi over to some hotel, get there by five-thirty . . . a quick fuck and a shower, and you can still make a seven-thirty dinner with the family." She was glaring at him now. "Well, I don't need that in my life. What I need is a cup of tea, ten minutes with the board so I can plead my case before Lance and Ted do me in, and a good night's sleep. That's all."

Steven sat forward. "Nicole, it's over. Millennium has been sold to Stevie Pell. There's nothing Chester Baines can do for you." He watched her carefully to see how she was taking the news.

"So that's it," she said softly with equal parts relief and concern.

"I want you to know," Steven said, "that I'll help you find another job. I've been thinking about this all afternoon and I've come up with a couple of strong possibilities. It's still early in Los Angeles and I've got some friends out there you should talk to."

A wry smile crossed her face as she shook her head. "Burton. God damn Burton," she said. She thought of Ted and Lance out at Ted's beach house, drinking pineapple smoothies, sealing their deal with a health-food toast. I'll never eat another pineapple, she decided as there was another knock at the door.

Steven answered it. Nicole heard him taking the tray from the room-service waiter and sending him off.

Suddenly she was crying. It came over her without warning and she hid her head in her arms. Steven came over to her side. He put his arms around her and let her cry into his already damp shirt. She embraced him, glad for the company and worried he wouldn't understand what was going on. It wasn't that she couldn't cope; it was just that she had to go through a moment of collapse before drawing on her resilience.

"I feel so inconsequential," she sobbed. "Like no matter what I do, I can't make a difference. No matter how hard I try . . . no matter how tough I try to be . . ."

"I wouldn't downplay your talent to make a difference, Nicole. I'm a pretty stubborn guy, and you've managed to shake my life up." He was going for a touch of levity.

"But I feel so old," she replied. "So hard and cynical and old. Is this the way it has to be? Is this the price you pay to survive? Alive but joyless?"

"You can hope for a lot more than that."

"No, I can't," she sobbed. "I am too tired of being disappointed to be hopeful again."

Steven held her until she was all cried out and pulled herself away from him.

"I'm all right," she reassured him.

"Nicole, I didn't come here just to talk about your career. I want to explain something. I know I let you down. The fact is, I'm crummy at ending a marriage. I wasn't prepared for how difficult it was for everyone involved. It's not a Noël Coward play, that's for sure. I swear, I've developed a new appreciation for the angst in country-western music."

The thought of Steven getting into Tammy Wynette made Nicole smile.

"What I'm trying to tell you," Steven continued, "is that I'm leaving my wife."

Nicole sighed. "Why does this make me feel like I'm in a soap opera? Why do I feel like my script for next week's episode will be 'I thought you said you were leaving your wife'? I don't want to be part of any triangle, not even one where the wife is an ex. I'm only interested in straight lines these days."

She knew she sounded cold, but she was still in love with him, and fake detachment was her only defense.

She got up and poured herself some tea.

He took the cup out of her hand and placed it back on

the tray. He pulled her up against him. Roughly he dug his hands into the small of her back and moved up to her shoulders. She quivered at his touch and knew she couldn't bring herself to resist him. He sought out her mouth, and when they kissed, their bodies interlocked. They fell back onto the bed, grappling with buttons and zippers. She slipped her hand inside the waist of his loosened trousers. He cupped his hands around her breasts. She pulled him closer, and closer, until he made her slow down, pinning her hands back on the bed. He gazed in her eyes and let himself feast on the sight of the face he'd missed so much. Then he lowered his head to her neck and began to kiss her all over. She ran her fingers through his hair and gripped the muscles in his shoulders.

"I need to feel you next to me . . . inside me," she moaned.

He lifted himself off her and stood at the end of the bed. When he was completely naked in front of her, she undressed for him. Her blouse was tossed on the floor, her skirt slipped off, she undid her stockings and unhooked her garter belt. All that was left was her slip. She was about to take it off, but Steven stopped her. He took her hand.

"I want to look at you," he said, pulling her up.

She stood there in the late-afternoon light, her ample chest heaving beneath her eyelet satin bra. He took in her beauty, his heart beating wildly. Gently his hands slid up her body. They seemed to be everywhere at once, on her back, her thighs, caressing her nipples. She reached for his hard cock as he pushed her up against the wall. She was ready for him, her nails digging into his back. She wanted him to take her body right there against the wall, then the bed, the floor. Her hands slid around him and she pulled him deeper and deeper inside of her. She felt ready to explode when he pulled out.

"Not yet, not yet," he said.

Even without contact, she was a second away from exploding.

"I can't hold back," she said.

"Look at me," he said.

As she complied, he lightly touched the bottom of her chin, saying her name softly over and over. Except for that touch, no other part of their bodies was connected. She felt her desire recede from an orgasm, but only slightly. In that state of being, a step away from peaking, she let him take control. Nothing in her life had ever felt as intimate as that moment, or as erotic. Even the slightest shift of movement created an electric sensation. When he reached for her hand, she felt the desire build.

He led her back to the bed. "We have so much time," he said. "And so much to explore."

Carefully he lowered himself over her, spreading her legs apart and entering her with one thrust.

"I love you," she whispered . . . and whispered, no longer worried about what the L word portended.

The rain stopped. It was seven-thirty in the evening and Steven's offices were practically empty. Nicole sat alone behind Steven's desk, going over a list of people to call about a job. She could have phoned from the hotel, but she and Steven were not about to allow even a half-hour of separation anxiety until they had to.

Nicole felt bold as she picked up the phone. Although her stock in L.A. was low now, at the moment her self-esteem wasn't affected by the west-coast rating sheet. A form of intoxication? Maybe, she thought as she punched in 1-213 . . . and then stopped as the door opened. The woman who entered was wearing a tailored black suit, a lot of expensive gold jewelry, and an Hermès scarf around her neck.

"Is my husband here?" she asked, enunciating each syllable.

"In the conference room with one of his associates," Nicole replied.

She dropped the receiver back into place. If she'd been

caught in Steven's bedroom wearing his pajamas, she wouldn't have felt any more awkward.

Elaine's sharp intuition picked up on how cozily Nicole took to the territory. This was no secretary using Steven's desk. A secretary wouldn't relax back in her seat and play with the miscellaneous personal objects—paper-weights, calendar—in front of her. A secretary wouldn't have a mass of hair tousled around her face, making her look like she'd just gotten out of bed. Well, a California secretary might.

Elaine thought about proceeding to the conference room, but changed her mind. She leaned against the wall next to the Sam Francis she'd contributed to the decor and set her handbag down on the side table as if to say: I'm not going anywhere. "Are you borrowing this office for some reason?" she asked.

Nicole didn't cower. "I'm making a few calls."

Elaine smiled coldly. "There are pay phones in the lobby."

Nicole saw no purpose in being a sitting target. "I'll tell Steven you're here," she said, getting up from behind the desk.

Elaine waited till she was at the door before asking, "Are you Nicole?" The question brought them eye-to-eye.

"Yes."

Elaine was holding a small piece of paper in her hand, Steven's notes that he'd left at home that morning. "You're on his phone sheet today," Elaine announced. "I see he found you." She crumpled the paper and tossed it on top of the desk. "So you must be Steven's California girl."

Nicole didn't like cat fights and she tried defusing this one. "I don't know what to say. This is not an easy situation."

Elaine gave her a blank stare. "Nicole, I doubt very much that you have any idea what this situation *is*." She reached for her handbag, pulled out a cigarette, and went over to Steven's desk for a match. Top drawer, right side; she didn't even have to look. "Men like Steven must occasionally have their diversions. While they're in the middle of them, they can convince themselves it's love. As a matter of fact, it's not a real diversion if there's not a point in it when it seems genuine, but it passes quickly. Three thousand miles, separation will keep it going awhile longer, but not for too long."

"You're not describing the Steven I know," Nicole countered.

"That's because you don't know him." A smile broke on Elaine's face. "Amazing, isn't it? Some women work so hard to appear intelligent and yet they can be taken in by the most obvious lines. It's almost emotional retardation."

Nicole felt the sting of these words. "You and I don't have anything to discuss," she said. "It's not about me, it's about you and Steven."

Elaine stubbed out her cigarette. "That's right, my dear. It's not about you."

Her smugness made Nicole look away.

"What are you thinking?" Elaine demanded. "What Steven will say? He'll be very gallant for about three weeks and then he'll get confused. He'll call less. His office will suddenly get terribly busy. He'll promise you a getaway weekend once things quiet down, but they never will."

"If you think so little of your husband, why are you clinging so desperately to him?" Nicole asked.

Elaine laughed. "Oh, that's right, you California girls believe in endless love, just as you believe in endless summers. You obviously don't have the frame of reference to comprehend what a fifteen-year marriage entails."

Now it was Nicole's turn to smile. "I guess I don't . . . and yet somehow, in spite of your advantage, I wouldn't want to trade places with you. I want to enjoy the person I'm spending my life with, not tolerate him because he makes a good accessory."

"Bravo." Elaine applauded. "A pat little answer . . . meaningless, but it has a certain spirit."

Footsteps down the hall put an end to their sparring. Steven approached, stopping short as he took in the scene.

"I'm sorry," he said to both of them.

"Apologies aren't your style," Elaine said.

She was right, and for him that was part of the problem. Steven believed in action more than words. He was used to solving problems.

"Nicole, could you excuse us for a few minutes? I'd like to talk to Elaine."

"I'll leave. I'll go back to the hotel," she offered.

"No." It was Elaine who protested. "Steven, I think you should straighten things out right now, right here, so there are no further misunderstandings."

She was pushing him to choose, a bad move, and she knew it. But she despised this Hollywood creature before her and was overwhelmed with a need to wipe that dewy, falling-in-love look off her face. Elaine was counting on Steven to try to placate both his women, and in doing so, unwittingly mar Nicole's romantic fantasies. That deflation would give Elaine the foothold she needed to wedge a wider separation between her husband and his paramour.

"Elaine," Steven said, "I really don't think you want to have this conversation right here, right now."

"I'm out of here," Nicole said, heading for the door. The dissolution of a marriage was definitely not one of her favorite spectator sports.

"No, I'm the one who is leaving," Elaine said, pushing her way past Steven, confident he'd follow. The sound of her high heels digging into the polished hardwood floors conveyed her mood of assumed superiority.

Steven and Nicole exchanged glances. His said: I've got to go talk to her; and hers said: I understand.

He caught up with his wife in front of the elevators. A secretary working late was also waiting there. When the down light lit up and the doors opened, Steven held on to Elaine's arm and she let the elevator depart without her.

"I can't . . . no, *we* can't keep on like this," Steven said.

"What do you propose?" Elaine asked. "A divorce? Why? Irreconcilable differences? Adultery? Really, what's your reason, Steven? Boredom? Is it the new trend to rejuvenate yourself through a romp with some vacuous Hollywood parasite? What is she, a producer? That's a euphemism for hustler. Or is she an agent? I hear they call themselves career architects. What an unbelievable joke this all is."

She was getting louder, so Steven reached out and pressed the elevator's down button, which infuriated Elaine even more.

"I am tired of living with a man who's constantly threatening to leave me," she shouted.

Steven wanted to punch her, not to hurt her, just to derail her tirade. He couldn't completely blame her for it, but he also couldn't tolerate it.

"I'm not threatening," he said. "I'm trying to end this in a way that'll do the least damage."

"Aren't you a saint? What a pair you make with what's-her-name . . ." Elaine paused for effect. "Oh, that's right, her name is Nicole. I must say that is a name that rates right up there with Shauna, Debbi with an I, Alana, and Kristy with a K. *Nicole?* That's perfect," Elaine shrieked. "Where'd she get that name . . . from a Jackie Collins novel?" She laughed. "What's her last name? You've got to tell me. Starr? St. John?"

The elevator arrived and Elaine marched in. Steven stepped in front of the door to keep it from closing.

"I'm not coming back tonight. It's over," he said.

"You bet you're not coming back tonight," she replied. "You can't get in. Five-five-five-eight-one-seven-one—the number of a twenty-four-hour locksmith. I've been memorizing that number for a while, in case I needed it."

She hit the button for the lobby and shoved Steven aside, but his extended arm kept the door from closing the whole way. They stared at each other through the narrow gap. "You always were incredibly efficient about the wrong things," he said. Then he drew back his arm and allowed the elevator doors to shut.

"Mr. Baines will see you now." Nicole thought the secretary's monotone was patronizing, as if she were reproaching her for the inconvenience caused by setting up this appointment. Nicole was not prepared for this attitude or for the meeting. After staying up till three in the morning talking and making love to Steven, she was not the jacked-up crusader she wanted to be. In fact, when the call finally came in at nine A.M., she had been on the verge of saying to herself: Fuck it. My days at Millennium are over. Why bother?

What got her out of bed was her determination to defend her reputation, not allow herself to be pushed over by a flippant wave of Lance's hand.

Baines's secretary led her into his parlor suite. It was burgundy and mahogany—what Nicole imagined the Princeton Club to be. A plate-glass window overlooked the East River, and the Chippendale chairs around his massive desk were assembled to facilitate intimate meetings only. Baines looked almost lost behind the desk, his blue eyes bleary as he weaved a hand through his thinning silvery hair. His complexion looked sallow and his shoulders slouched forward, giving the impression that power came at a cost. Stacks of reports were piled high on his desktop. He looked beleaguered, or sour, or both.

Nicole walked purposefully toward Baines and shook his weakly extended hand.

"Thanks for agreeing to meet on such short notice, Chester. I know how busy you've been. This means a lot to me."

"Sit down, Nicole." His tone was grim. "Would you like something to drink?"

"Nothing, thanks. We can dispense with any amenities. I don't want to take up too much of your time."

"Go ahead, Nicole. Tell me what's on your mind. I know you well enough to know you're going to tell me anyway, or otherwise you may burst." He smiled with a vestige of patience.

Nicole got up from her seat. It was hard to be impassioned from the seat of a Chippendale armchair.

"I think you should know that Lance Burton's crusade to get *Dirty Dreams* made is undermining Millennium. For the past few months he's used his connections to the board to try to intimidate me into making decisions against the studio's best interests. I want to set the record straight about this project. It may have been developed while I was at Millennium, but never with my enthusiasm. From the start I had major reservations about the idea. Unfortunately, my opinion carries little weight when it comes to Lance. It's gotten to the point where Millennium is practically his little fiefdom, his own personal bank. The entire studio operation is based on his whims."

Silence filled the room.

"Does Ted know?" Chester asked.

"Ted is very much aware of Lance's agenda." She took a deep breath. Her intention was not to get off on a discussion of Ted's role. Lance was the culprit. Ted was just the willing pawn. "The point is," she continued, "right now you've got some wonderul scripts in development, with very talented directors attached. What'll happen to those projects when forty million dollars is spent making *Dirty Dreams?*"

He raised his hand as if to still her. "First of all, I want you to know that I appreciate how difficult this is for you, and I want you to know that I take what you've told me very seriously."

Nicole sighed with relief as Chester stood up from his chair and walked around to the front of his desk.

"But Lance has played a critical role in the sale of the studio. He has gotten Styvie Pell to buy Millennium outright. Last night Styvie asked all of the board members to resign so he and Lance can constitute a new board."

Now, for the first time, he looked her in the eye.

Nicole thought he was trying to penetrate her core. Was she really tough? Could she take bad news on the jaw?

She would let him see the answer.

"I had been forewarned," she said calmly.

Baines gave her his most avuncular smile. "I'm afraid the battle for Millennium has been won, but not by us. I'd be happy to make some calls for you. Let the right people know how terrific I think you are, and explain the context of your . . ." He paused. "Resignation."

"I'd really appreciate that, Chester," Nicole answered gratefully. She wondered if he was sincere.

Baines called to his secretary over the intercom. "Remind me to call Larry Winters after Nicole leaves." To Nicole he explained, "Larry's an old friend of mine. I understand he's looking for someone."

As he spoke, he led her to the door. He kissed her on both cheeks, European style. There was something about the way he ushered her out that answered her question. He was being polite, not sincere, Nicole realized sadly.

So this is what it's all about, she thought. You rise, you rise, and suddenly you hit the glass ceiling of the boys' club's inner sanctum.

As Nicole left the office and headed down the long corridor to the building's elevator, she remembered a phrase her father used to quote to her when she was young and wounded by love or friends. Bloody but unbowed. That's what she felt now. Bloody but unbowed.

Alone in his office, Chester Baines returned to his pile of corporate portfolios. His thoughts were interrupted by his secretary calling to him over the speaker.

"Do you want me to get Larry Winters in L.A.?"

"Don't bother," Chester responded. He owed Nicole nothing.

*   *   *

The next morning, Nicole and Steven took the first plane to the west coast. It was an American Airlines flight, stopping in L.A. on its way to Hawaii. The atmosphere was festive, even with the usual group of business travelers hunched over their open briefcases, preparing for their next meetings.

The first-class section was only two-thirds full and the seats across from Nicole and Steven were empty, allowing them a sense of privacy.

After weeks of nonstop negotiating on Styvie Pell's behalf, Steven allowed himself some mindless entertainment. He was reading one of those paperback techno-thrillers that airport bookstores carry. Nicole was busy working on a draft of her resignation letter.

"What do you think?" she asked.

Steven read the copy:

To Ted McGuiness:

It's become obvious that my usefulness at Millennium is over.

For the past few months I've been working in a vacuum, making decisions the only way I know how—on merit. However, the political machinations, complicated by the sale of the studio, have made it impossible for me to do the job I was hired to do. Rather than perpetuate this unproductive arrangement, I've decided to make a clean break. I hearby resign, effective today. I wish you luck in restructuring the studio and I hope you wish me luck as well.

Steven handed it back to her. "This is the season for clean breaks. Are you worried about what comes next?"

"No," she was quick to reply. "Are you?"

He thought about it before answering. "I can't remember the last time I couldn't predict the broad strokes of my life. This is a whole new thing for me."

"But," Nicole gently pressed, "that doesn't answer my question. Are you worried?"

He lifted up the middle partition between the seats and pulled her closer. "Relieved," he replied.

They ordered mimosas, not bothering to articulate exactly what they were celebrating. They didn't have to. It was a toast to their future. The details of how it would all work out had not been discussed at length. Would theirs be a bicoastal relationship? Would she move to New York? Would he open up a west-coast branch of his New York office? Could Steven Lloyd, born, raised, and entrenched on the Upper East Side, move to a suburban city like L.A.? The discussion would come later, and neither worried about the outcome too much. They were, in fact, "intoxicated with optimism."

25

This was the moment Nicole had dreaded. Leaving her office was—like divorce—the tearing of the book from its cover. The drive to the studio felt ritualistic: This is the last time I'll ever pass this corner bodega and pick up a *Herald* and . . . the studio logo at the main gate tugged at her heart, and Nicole said good morning to the studio guard with a wistful look that she was sure he caught. Administrations come and go, she thought, slipping into her prestigious parking space for the last time, but the guards forever hold down the fort, just like at Buckingham Palace.

Nicole had picked the moment of departure from Millennium as best she could. She'd waited until three days after her resignation ran banner headlines in *Variety*. The past week with Steven had fortified her. His confidence in her had coated her raw nerves. She felt immune to local toxins, notably Bambi and David Beach, and almost up to the task of packing her life to get on with it.

She noticed on her arrival that today was not business-as-usual. Moving boxes were stacked on the floor, enough to evacuate a small village, compliments of the studio. Nicole found this "generosity" insulting. She wanted to think of her leaving as a private, profound moment, but the studio's well-oiled machinery had forced it out into the open.

First she tackled her desk, mindful that it contained personal notes she was anxious to discard. In her top drawer she found the emotional mementos of her years at Millennium: a baseball card of her jock heartthrob, Cal Ripkin, that a writer had given her for good luck; a promotional pin designed by Tiffany's from Kevin, commemorating their first hit together; an old George Christy column in which she looked particularly swell (she'd meant to send it to her mother); loose change amounting to thirty-seven cents; a pack of Camels she'd bought a few months ago during a particularly nerve-racking day, but never opened.

On top of her desk was her favorite office accessory: a crystal ball given to her by a friendly journalist to celebrate her promotion. If only it could reveal something of her future now. Her eyes stumbled upon an early draft of an evaluation she'd made of Bambi for Ted: "Bambi seems to prefer the game to the work. Full of knowledge about deals around town, she seems less than conversant with the scripts we're discussing in weekend read meetings. I know you prize her skills as a golden retriever, and she does seem fairly plugged-in. However, I don't know if she has any real point of view. She can be talked into or out of any position, depending on what's political." Without a thought, Nicole shredded the note into long even strips, rendering it unreadable to the vultures who would go through her garbage in the wake of her departure.

Thinking of Bambi eroded her goodwill. If Bambi gets this office, I'll gag, she thought to herself. It would be another chapter of Hollywood's favorite morality play: *When Good Things Happen to Bad People.* What she wished for more than anything now was some equal time for good people, like Carolyn. Nicole would love to see her get a break.

Facing her reader was the most painful part of moving out. Nicole hated to give up the newly acquired role of mentor. For years she had kept herself aloof from the many hopefuls who'd solicited her for meetings and friendships, feeling their emotional manipulation would undermine her objectivity as a buyer. But Carolyn was different.

Nicole saw her own lost creative self reflected in her, less pushy to be sure, but surefooted and original. It was precisely because Carolyn had never pushed that Nicole wanted to help her, and she was humiliated by the prospect of letting her down.

Nicole decided not to buzz her over the intercom. One last time she'd stroll down to the tiny office at the end of the story-department corridor that she'd grown accustomed to visiting.

As she passed her secretary's desk, Doreen handed her a piece of paper. "You want to take a look at your phone sheet?"

"I didn't think I had one," Nicole replied. She glanced at the list, expecting to find only a couple of personal callbacks. Instead she found the names of four of the best writer/directors in Hollywood: Nora Ephron, Barry Levinson, James Cameron, and Jim Brooks. These were writers and directors she had longed to work with. Whose talents she had always nourished with special attention. "Don't they know I'm out of a job?" Nicole asked.

"Yes, in fact they do." Doreen smiled. "But they want to meet with you anyway."

Nicole was astonished at this evidence of loyalty. With a lighter heart she proceeded down the hallway to Carolyn's office.

She opened the door to her reader's small space and found her busily typing script notes to the beat of Edie Brickell and the New Bohemians on the cassette player.

Carolyn looked up, startled to see Nicole standing in front of her. "I didn't know you were here. I looked for you when I got in, but you weren't around."

"I sort of slipped in late. You got a minute?"

Carolyn lowered the volume on the cassette player while Nicole shut the door.

"As I'm sure you've heard, Carolyn, things didn't exactly work out in New York."

"The news has hit the studio grapevine."

"I'm sure it has." Nicole sighed. "I can just imagine what version."

"The new buyer is an asshole to let you go," Carolyn said.

Nicole shrugged. "Can't say it surprised me. Lance likes the squeeze play."

"I may not know very much, Nicole," Carolyn said, "but from my limited vantage point, it's obvious that the studio will go under with Lance in control. You're better off out of here."

"I can't argue with your perceptions." Nicole was heartened by Carolyn's strong response but didn't want to dwell on Millennium madness. "But more to the point, what I really stopped by to say was, I still believe in your *Party Doll* treatment. Obviously I can't do anything for you here, but I've got a few contacts around town. As soon as I regroup, I'll try to help you set it up somewhere else."

"I'd like to write it for *you,* Nicole. You understand it," Carolyn said. "If I set it up just anywhere . . ." She stopped and nervously sought the right words. "Don't get me wrong, I'm overwhelmed by your support, but without you attached as producer, it could end up being just another script left sitting on the shelf while clones of *Dirty Dreams* get made."

Nicole smiled. "I'm flattered that you want to work with me, but I don't want to slow you down. I know you need money, and it's not fair for you to wait until I'm well-placed again."

Carolyn sat up straight. "I've thought about this a lot, Nicole, knowing you might have to take some kind of stand in New York. I've thought about it ever since you called me that night and changed my . . . well . . ." She let that train of thought drift away. "Anyway, I've found a new job. For the next few months I'll be working for Tom Hedley. He's going to help me with my writing, so I can spec out this script for you and I'll do his typing and research."

Nicole had to laugh. "You won't learn how to write fast from Tom Hedley, but you *will* learn how to write well."

She threw her arms around Carolyn. "Look at this," Nicole said, beaming. "A team is forming. A writer's loyalty is the only thing worth having in this whole damn town. While you're working on *Party Doll*, I'll get myself a job somewhere, and my first order of business will be to buy your script."

As they walked out to the hallway, a thought occurred to Nicole. She blurted it out to her protégée. "The key to this town is not being afraid. I've seen talented people fail because they didn't know how to sustain a belief in themselves, and I've seen the mediocre rise to the top because they weren't intimidated."

"How do you think they get that way?" Carolyn asked. "The fearless ones."

"Some people are too dim to be frightened," Nicole said, "but for the rest of us it comes down to jumping off the high diving board and not worrying about whether or not you can swim."

"What if you're phobic about heights or water?" Carolyn asked.

"Jump," Nicole insisted.

"Jump?"

"Jump."

Just then, Bambi emerged from her own office at the other end of the hall and walked toward the reception area.

"One of the dim ones?" Carolyn suggested.

"Forty watts," Nicole agreed.

There was no anger in these comments, only mild amusement at the absurdity of things. They both knew Bambi's role as nemesis had peaked.

"Tell me, Nicole," Carolyn asked, "how do you feel when you've jumped and you're free-falling through the air?"

Nicole smiled as if sharing a secret. "You feel alive. Very much alive."

Bambi had been waiting for Nicole's exit and had finally witnessed a gushy emotional scene with Carolyn, which baffled her. What's that all about? she asked herself. They can't possibly be friends. Carolyn's only a reader. What perplexed her even more was that Nicole seemed happy.

From a third-floor window she watched Nicole's Maserati peel out of the parking lot for the last time and was thrilled by the pace of the changes around Millennium. Nature abhors a vacuum, Daddy always told her, and with Nicole's departure, Bambi's path was finally clear.

She headed toward Nicole's old office, pushed the door open as if making a territorial claim, and danced around the large room. I can decorate this far better than Nicole did, she thought. Her musings were interrupted by David Beach, who waltzed in as if he owned the place.

"What are you doing here, Bambi?" he asked. "The body's not even cold yet."

"The better question is: what are *you* doing here?"

They looked at each other, two coiled cobras equally capable of striking, but preferring for the moment merely to bare their fangs.

"To be frank, Bambi," David Beach said while strutting around the room, "I'm checking out the office. I'm going to need some real space now that *Wild Horses* has been green-lighted."

Bambi felt like she'd been nuked. David Beach had a project that had gotten a green light? Where had she been? She might have been able to block it if she hadn't been too busy burying Nicole.

"Aren't you going to congratulate me?"

She tried hard to keep a lid on her jealousy. "Congratulations, David. But if I'm not mistaken, this office is reserved for whoever the new executive vice-president will be."

"Well, maybe I'm next in line," he gloated.

Bambi gave him a patronizing smile.

"What, Bambi? You don't think so? Don't think I'm qualified?" He was playing with her.

"I didn't say that," she replied. "But from what I understand, Lance will have some input on the decision."

"I hope so," David Beach said confidently.

"What do you mean by that?" Bambi asked with a note of panic creeping into her snotty tone.

"It just means that he's a fan of *Wild Horses*. He told me today that he thought I had a winner."

Bambi stuck her hands in the pockets of her suit jacket. Was it possible her promotion was in jeopardy? Adopting her best businesslike voice, she fired off a question. "What's the start date of your movie?"

"Check the production sheet, Bams. I don't have time to keep you updated." David laughed, and turned to exit. "Late for lunch with the director," he said as he left. "Gotta crew up."

26

David Beach drove down the tail end of Beverly Boulevard as it turned into Silver Lake. This odd, somewhat bohemian industrial neighborhood, populated mainly by Mexicans, was located on the outskirts of Hollywood. He took this route every Friday night in his leased black Porsche cabriolet, to meet up with a spicy mix of the week's best friends at Helena's. He was proud that he'd been an early member of the exclusive dance/dinner club and had only had to pay five hundred dollars to join. Many of his peers, agents especially, had had an awful time trying to become members, some paying upward of fifteen hundred dollars, only to have Helena return their checks in the mail.

Tonight he was in a particularly good mood. Being in preproduction on a movie he had developed was, for him, what this business was all about. As soon as the news hit the streets, his daily incoming phone list had increased. He felt like a serious player. It was fucking exhilarating.

To celebrate, he'd pulled together a high-profile group. He'd invited the director of *Wild Horses,* whom he'd whipped into a frenzy about the finest bimbos in L.A. —all of whom would undoubtedly arrive during the course of the evening. It would be pretty much an all-male table, he had explained, as the girls would eventually provide themselves. In addition to the director, he had invited some hot new comics in town for another "Comic Relief Show."

When his party arrived at nine forty-five, the parking lot was empty. The lack of cars made David Beach jumpy, as though this were a party at his house and he was somehow responsible if no one showed up. But he reminded himself that within the hour the warehouse street would be filled with limos and Porsches, and like the Ma Maison of old, the parking lot would soon display its finest Rolls-Royces out front.

As he waited for the cars in his group to unload, David Beach warmed his crowd with some standard Helena's lore. "Parking is such a nightmare here that Helena had all these heavyweights call the people next door, begging to use their space on Friday nights. Finally, rumor has it, Jack Nicholson called and spoke to the guy's wife, who then called Helena and said of course they could use their lot. But, she added, she and her husband wanted to be members. That was that. Helena said absolutely not. So the valets drive around all night in your car looking for a space."

David Beach checked in at the door and then led his guests past the deejay booth and the bar, through the still-empty dance floor, to the elite dining room inside. At the entrance the maître d' marched around with a portable phone, taking orders from somewhere about the celebrity seating plan for the night. Helena, thin, dark-haired, and Mediterranean, in a white cocktail dress, darted about the room, preoccupied. She was scowling at the guests she didn't know, nodding to the ones she did know—unless they were movie stars, in which case she sat down with them. David Beach passed her, waving sweetly as she talked with Madonna and her entourage.

He was relieved to see that he had a well-placed table for eight near the fireplace, ablaze in the late-October coolness. Above them, the canvas canopy was cranked open just a bit, coaxing a small breeze inside. Soon the garlic bread arrived, with Coronas and limes. "Helena designed and built the place herself," David Beach intoned, playing the hip tour guide to the one or two New

Yorkers who were first-timers. Everyone chomped garlic bread, oblivious of the smell, as the whole place seemed to have been sprayed with a garlic atomizer. David Beach wondered whether it did something to the sex vibes in the air, and if that was why it was the only high-class hetero cruise joint in L.A. Tramp was for aging play-boys, Vertigo was for young Euro-trash, Stock Exchange was for yuppies, and all the other public spots were filled with his past secretaries. Helena's was his only viable option.

Lance was basking in the glow of the hottest table of the night. He wasn't at the hottest table, he *was* the hottest table. Wherever he went, the heat followed. He was the man of the moment, the maverick, the one who made up his own rules.

Styvie had green-lighted *Dirty Dreams*. The budget was being finalized, and casting was under way. Every-one at Helena's knew Lance had scored, and having Styvie and Christie as his guests was his way of flaunting it.

The only downer of his evening was his date, Jasmine. Lance had become bored with her. Girls like Jasmine were only stimulating when he was getting them to break through their sexual inhibitions. Once that was accom-plished, there was nothing else there to intrigue him. Jasmine was also a minor problem because she was not hitting it off with Christie. In addition to the understand-able animosity between two would-be actresses both eyeing the same part in *Dirty Dreams,* there was another source of tension. With very little effort, Jasmine was charming the pants off Styvie. The financier couldn't take his eyes off her dress, which consisted of satinized strips of adhe-sive tape strategically misplaced. Not that Styvie flirted. He was too much of a gentleman to do that in front of Christie, and too sober to forget what a gentleman he was.

Just then Lisa popped up and squeezed herself in between Lance's and Jasmine's chairs. "Everyone having fun?"

"Hey, Lisa," Lance said warmly. "You remember Styvie and Christie. You met at my Fourth of July party."

"Of course I remember," Lisa said. "Nice to see you again." Styvie nodded. Christie managed a smile.

Lisa rested her hand on Jasmine's shoulder. "How's the star of *Dirty Dreams* doing?"

Immediately Lance's face tightened. "That part hasn't been cast yet," he coldly pointed out.

"I'm fine," Jasmine said quickly to cover the awkwardness of the moment.

Lance noticed how thrilled Jasmine was by Lisa's presence. She's got a crush, he thought. Figures. A girl like Jasmine would need to conventionalize her sex life with emotional baggage.

What he didn't have a beat on was why Lisa had gone out on a limb with her *Dirty Dreams* comment. Surely she knew Christie was in contention for the part. It wasn't like Lisa to say something that would alienate the girlfriend of a studio head, nor had she ever before tried to force a client on Lance. Could she be attached to this model-turned-actress? Lance wondered.

"Gotta get back to my friends," Lisa announced to the table. "See you on the dance floor."

Christie coolly eyed Lisa's departure and then turned toward Lance with a questioning look on her face.

He was not about to deal with her paranoia.

"Have another glass of champagne," Lance suggested, refilling Styvie's glass. He thought it might be amusing to watch Styvie loosen up and see how Christie handled it. In fact, all evening Lance had been entertained by watching Christie try to camouflage their past affair.

"Have you always been in the movie business, Lance?" she'd asked, as if they'd just met.

He'd responded in kind, pretending they were merely acquaintances filling in the blank spaces about each other. "Did you grow up in Los Angeles?"

"Southern California," was her ambiguous reply. No mention of her youth spent in a trailer park or her formative years spent hanging out in Miami, or her fling with a younger, less successful (but still rich enough for a poor girl), wilder Lance. He wondered what it would be like to fuck her again. Would the fact that she was now Styvie's girlfriend make her desirable? She was even prettier now than she had been when they were together. Now she had money for Jose Eber haircuts and Aida Grey facials. She had a great body—those long legs, narrow hips, and full breasts were his ideal—but the answer was no. He knew her too well. He didn't need a rerun of her repertoire of seductive tricks. Besides, she faked orgasms.

Styvie finished the last piece of feta cheese off his salad. "Someone told me that Helena is Greek."

Who cares? Christie thought, but she kept up the act. "I heard that too, sweetie, and that she used to be an actress. She was in some movie called *Five Easy Pieces*. I never saw it. It was before my time."

"How old are you?" Lance asked.

"Twenty-two," Christie answered.

Lance was impressed that she could look him in the eye. She'd been twenty-two when he met her four years ago.

Suddenly two arms reached from behind to embrace him. He looked down to see perfectly manicured nails and wrists weighed down with costume jewelry. "Hi, boss," said the familiar voice. It was Bambi, slightly drunk.

"Hi, sweetheart, having a good time?"

"I feel gr . . . eat." She looked over at Styvie and smiled. "We haven't been officially introduced. I'm Bambi Stern."

Styvie shook her hand. "Styvie Pell," he offered as his introduction. "And this is Christie Collins."

"And you've met Jasmine before," Lance said, trying

to speed up the hellos and good-byes and get Bambi on
to someone else's table.

"Uh-huh," Bambi replied, not bothering to look over
in Jasmine's direction. She was too busy looking for a
chair to pull up. "Helena really should invest in more
chairs. I mean, this is ridiculous," she said, surveying the
room. She had her damsel-in-distress pout on her face,
but no knight came to her rescue. She was left leaning on
the back of Lance's chair. "I'm so excited about all the
changes at Millennium," she gushed, trying to connect
with Styvie. Her attempt at playing up to him was obvious to everyone present.

Styvie smiled but said nothing.

Bambi kept going. *"Dirty Dreams* is going to be a
gigantic hit . . . I really feel that, I really do." She was
tossing her hair around as she spoke.

"I think we all feel that way," Styvie said, while Christie calculated. It took her a second to size up Bambi. Not
Styvie's type. Too forward. But the kind who could wea-
sel her way into his life because of his weakness for
women who flattered him.

Christie caught Lance's eye across the table. The demure debutante was gone. She was silently communicating to him for the first time since their paths had crossed
for the second time. It was a language they both understood, the language of sharks. Get that bitch away from
this table, is what her fiery glance said. His grin said:
You owe me one.

"Who are you with?" Lance asked. He realized if he
wanted Bambi to move on, he might have to personally
escort her back to her friends.

"Andrew Spencer, an English producer. I don't think
you know him. We're at the agents table." She gestured
across the room. "I'm over there doing my homework,
casting our movie." She directed this to Styvie.

Lance pushed his chair back in an effort to rise, but
Bambi, still standing right next to him, was oblivious of
his intentions.

"Do you like musicals, Styvie?" she asked.

"Some."

"Don't you think a remake of *Singin' in the Rain* is a winning idea?" she asked.

"An interesting idea," he said.

"What is your name again?" Christie asked, determined to keep tabs on this piece of business.

"It's Bambi, Bambi Stern," Lance informed her. He stood up and gripped Bambi around the waist. She was clearly out of her league here. "I'll be back in a minute," he said, and then pulled his tipsy junior executive toward the other side of the room.

"Bambi. That's an unusual name," Jasmine commented.

"Yes, it is," Christie agreed. "An unusual name for a very common girl."

Andrew Spencer sipped his champagne and gazed around the dining room. He had already worked the three agents at the table, who were by now prowling for new clients and prospects. Bambi had gone off to talk with Lance and the new mogul in town, Styvie Pell.

Andrew was glad Bambi had decided to flirt with Styvie. In fact, he had suggested it to her, in his new role as her career adviser. For an ambitious player on the make, Andrew discovered, Bambi had remarkably dull instincts. Andrew had explained to Bambi that Lance only looked like the center of the power constellation at Millennium, when the truth was, much of his leverage came from his proximity to Styvie's money. Andrew felt that he understood Hollywood in his bones. Everything was positioning. And what he was doing this year was getting into position. He accepted as truth a line an agent had once told him: You have to get a place at the table in order to get a roll of the dice. And though baccarat would have been more his style than craps, he appreciated the aptness of the metaphor. He rationalized his cynical maneuverings with a dose of Marxism. Hollywood was a town adept at justifying means. Sometimes it seemed that Bambi

was his robot, that he could program and operate her by
remote control. They functioned effortlessly together,
working the same people—and her access was a perfect
match with his sophistication. Not a bad alliance, he
thought, sending a public smile to Bambi as Lance marched
her back to her table.

Only one agent from William Morris and one from
Triad were still at the table when Lance arrived. Within
seconds, however, two CAA agents were back at their
seats for the Lance/Bambi introductions.

"Do you know my friends?" Bambi gestured toward
everyone at the table.

"These are your friends, Bambi?" Lance teased. "Agents
don't have friends, do they? They have transitory allies,
am I right?" He stared charmingly into the eyes of one
overachiever making his mark early from the Morris
mailroom.

"Lance alone knows," the young agent responded,
pleased that Lance had picked him out of the crowd.

"And this is my date, Andrew Spencer. Andrew? Have
you met my mentor, Lance Burton?"

Andrew hated when Bambi went "on the nose" in her
descriptions—"this is my date . . ." . . . "my mentor"—but
he'd been waiting for an introduction. Casually he turned
his head and pushed his chair away to stand. "Charmed,"
he said.

Lance glanced at the Englishman for a moment, then
looked down at Andrew's shoes, the telltale sign of a
man's sense of self. Lance smirked as he saw Andrew's
tasseled black velvet slippers. "Nice shoes, Spencer. Did
you bring your bathrobe too?" He laughed and left the
minor-league table frozen, agape.

Carolyn ended up at Helena's at the end of a Friday-
night caravan. It began at the Dong Bang Bar, where she
stopped for a drink with Tom Hedley and a bunch of his
Venice artist-type friends. Predictably, part of the party
inched east to the popular Friday-night hangout. Carolyn

would have preferred Vertigo because it drew a crowd more interested in dancing—preferably to the live sounds of a reggae band—than zooming agents and studio executives. Helena's was too Hollywood for Carolyn. In the post-Andrew stage of her life, she had become a workaholic. Only real work, not zooming, interested her, and as she confessed to Hedley, she was "losing all social skills."

"I think you need a break," he'd suggested.

"I think I'm going through the twenty-five-year-old crisis," she'd explained. "I'm too old to cruise on my potential. I'm hungry for some results. I should stay home and work on my screenplay." But in the end, she was talked into a night out.

There were five of them, including a downtown conceptual artist who had some weird name Carolyn kept forgetting, a USC student named Michael, and Stacey, an aspiring producer who interpreted the scene for Carolyn.

"See that woman over there? The one wearing earrings that look like chandeliers?"

Carolyn searched the crowd.

"Over there," Stacey pointed. "The one staring at Justine Bateman because she'd probably love to attach her to a 'movie-of-the-week' she's trying to sell."

Carolyn finally spotted the target.

"Well," Stacey went on, "I pitched her a story a few weeks ago. Two minutes into the meeting, when I was talking about the saga of a teenage girl who survives cancer, this woman interrupts and says to her assistant, 'I'm starving. Are there any pretzels in the office?' " Stacey shrugged. "It's depressing. They only listen when you're pitching *Rambo*."

"Very few people in this town recognize a unique story," Hedley said. "They choose projects based on a precedent, and the precedent comes from reading the weekend box-office totals in the *Hollywood Reporter*." He said it casually, understating his own profundity. He'd

had enough "adventures in the screen trade," especially
with his script for *Flashdance,* to give him perspective.

When Stacey got up to go to the ladies' room, the seat
next to Carolyn was immediately occupied by Michael,
the preppie-looking grad student. His complexion was
fair and his hair was the kind of light brown that turns
blond in the sun. His eyes were friendly and his smile
slightly crooked. He was wearing a black linen Perry Ellis
suit, white T-shirt, and Avia basketball high-tops. Though
it was Carolyn's favorite look for guys, she still wasn't
ready to end her self-imposed flirting boycott.

"I feel sorry for the waiters," he said, obviously trying
to open up a conversation with Carolyn. "I mean, how
can they keep track of who orders what, what tab be-
longs to what party? By the time the pasta's ready, they're
serving all new faces. It's musical chairs in here."

"I think they do approximate billing," Carolyn said.
"They look at who is at the table, then count the glasses
and plates, come up with a round figure, add seventy-
eight cents to the bill to make it sound authentic, and
then drop it in front of the person who's got the biggest
expense account."

"I like that theory." Michael smiled. "Tell me some of
your other observations."

Carolyn eyed the prospect of this flirtation wearily.
"Can't think of any right now," she said.

She was going through an "I-don't-date" phase. She
wanted no part of any of it. Not the getting-to-know-
each-other stage. Not the are-we-or-aren't-we-having-a-
serious-relationship stage, and definitely not the dramatic
denouement. Based on her experience with Andrew, she
had come to see that in Hollywood the news of another
romance gone sour hit the streets like caffeine pouring
into the bloodstream.

She'd been amazed at the calls she'd gotten. The first
was from Jay, a lawyer she'd met only twice. His token
"sorry about you and Andrew" couldn't camouflage his
delight. Ever since his wife had left him ten years before,

Jay had enjoyed hearing about other people's failures. It encouraged him to believe that all marriages/relationships fell apart sooner or later and that he, the fast-tracker, had just gotten his breakup out of the way early.

"You should come by Tramp tonight," Jay had said, "now that you're a single again. There's a party for Rod after his concert. All the guys will be there, Nick, Rick, Stan." At first she didn't know who he was talking about, but then it came to her. They were the group that Lou referred to as "emo-homos." Emotional homosexuals. They tried to fashion themselves as an American version of the infamous European playboys, but not only didn't they have a drop of charm, they also didn't have the essential spirit for the playboy role. They liked pretty faces and young (twenty-six tops) tight female bodies and liked passing these girls around as if they were a piece of cake being offered at the dinner table. This sharing created a fraternity bond among the emo-homos that was more important to them than any relationship. Occasionally they talked about finding the perfect wife, settling down, having a family, but the mother of their children wasn't thought of as a whole person as much as she was a fetal envelope for their progeny.

Who are these men and who do they think they're kidding? Carolyn had thought when Jay tried his best to add her to his inventory list.

"Carolyn, don't become a bitter woman over this Andrew thing," he'd said.

Interesting, Carolyn thought. If I don't go out with him, it's because I'm bitter, not because he's a jerk.

Later she'd heard he was telling people that she had a castrating personality, was possibly a lesbian, and Andrew had been right to find someone else.

Lou had laughed when Carolyn repeated that gossip to her. "What do you care?" she said. "My advice is go out with young men. Nineteen, twenty, twenty-two . . . twenty-three is a perfect age. They're not damaged souls like Jay's crowd. They don't use romance for revenge. Sexually they're uninhibited, not perverted, and they don't need money to look good."

"But Andrew's young," Carolyn reminded her. "He's only twenty-five."

"Andrew was never young," Lou replied.

But this one is, Carolyn thought as Michael continued to seek her attention. "Well, I've got a theory," he said. "Actually, it's more of an observation. It's about hyphen-ates. Have you noticed this club is filled with writer-directors, actor-singers, producer-directors, and actress-producers? I guess it's the way of the future. I hear the regulars here don't mate anymore, they hyphenate."

Carolyn laughed. She liked his sensibility. He was funny, smart, and, she had to admit, very cute.

Her laugh had encouraged Michael. "I figured," he went on, "that non-pros hyphenate for identity, pros do it for power, and in both cases it makes good copy."

"I've got one," Carolyn said. "A non-pro, Stephanie of Monaco: princess-singer. Or better, the ultimate hyphenate—Frank Wells, studio chief-mountain climber."

"That's pretty ultimate," Michael agreed.

A waiter-actor piped in, "What about star-alcoholic-coke fiend? We get a lot of them in here."

"A triple hyphenate," Michael said. Suddenly he stopped. "Am I getting carried away? Has this joke peaked?" He wasn't really worried. Carolyn could see that he was comfortable and confident. She wondered just how young he was. Still in college? She hoped he wasn't studying film, or another actor trying to break into the Brat Pack.

"I wouldn't worry about it," she answered, "unless you're a stand-up comedian and this is a rehearsal for your act."

"Not only am I not in show business, I'm conservative. I'm only interested in one career."

Carolyn's curiosity was growing. "And what career is that?"

"I'm studying to be an architect."

Thank God, Carolyn thought. I've met a builder, not another destroyer.

She was about to ask him a dozen questions when she was distracted by a familiar-looking sport jacket. It was the gray-and-black one she'd encouraged Andrew to buy. Her eyes caught the familiar tweed as Andrew stood up, his back to Carolyn, to allow Bambi to reach her corner seat.

Carolyn managed a flustered "Excuse me" as she left Michael and headed toward the disco area. She wanted a few moments to think. She thought of the ladies' room but there was a line of four waiting outside the door. She moved toward the bar, pretending she was about to order a drink. Her mind was racing. Should I leave? Stay? Ignore him? If she were with her Fall River girlfriends, they'd say, "Slash his tires."

"What can I get you?" The bartender was waiting for her order.

"Ah . . . nothing right now." She moved closer to the entrance, thinking about going outside. But where? Her keys (she'd self-parked) were in her bag, which was back at the table, and she couldn't exactly take a walk on streets that felt like the dark side of New Jersey. To her right she saw a friend of Andrew's, an agent, whose main contribution to guiding her clients' careers was picking out their wardrobes. From behind the agent, she glimpsed Andrew approaching. Quickly she spun around, and though the front door was blocked by a new wave of revelers, she pushed her way through the crowd.

Outside, Carolyn found a fairly quiet spot at the far end of the club's front-porch area. She leaned against the wall and observed the parking-lot action.

Feeling emotionally fragile, she took a deep breath. Get tough, she told herself. Big fucking deal. So Andrew, the man who broke my heart, is in there with Bambi. So, Paul, who was the only security I ever had in my life, is doing just fine without me. So, I'm alone in a parking lot in East L.A. watching an egomaniac have temper tantrums because there's no room for his BMW. Big deal. That's not so hard to take.

What would Nicole say? she thought. "You're a writer"? "Everything's research"? Probably. And maybe, she considered, at least for now, that's exactly the perspective I need.

When Andrew's agent friend told him that Carolyn was there, he immediately went looking for her. First he wandered through the dining area, then the disco, back to the dining area, and then back through the disco. Standing in the middle of the dance floor, he took one more look around the room. In front of him, half a dozen people were gyrating to a sixties song. It was not Andrew's favorite music or his favorite decade. Helena needs a new deejay, he thought. Someone who'll play Simply Red, UB 40, and Pet Shop Boys. He glanced up to the alcove where the deejay was set up and there was Carolyn, off to the side, alone, looking right at him.

He crossed the dance floor and ran up the steps to where she was sitting.

"Carolyn, why haven't you returned my calls?"

She looked at him, refusing to respond, but saying more with her silence than any words could convey.

"Carolyn, darling, this silent approach of yours is really juvenile."

Approach? she wanted to yell. It's not an approach. It's self-defense. It's not getting involved in a debate with someone who's more in love with the sound of his voice than he is concerned with the point he's making. She kept these thoughts to herself, said nothing, and focused on the crowd below. Andrew tried again.

"It's so frustrating when you won't at least tell me what I can do to make things better. I'll grant you that I'm responsible for breaking the trust we shared, but trust can be restored."

She looked at him, thinking: How? By reading me poetry? By telling me fictitious bedtime stories?

"Just tell me," he insisted. "Can't you just tell me that?"

She leaned against the railing. "I'd like to see you not be so political about everything in your life. Burn a bridge for a change."

"You mean Bambi? You want me to stop seeing Bambi?"

"Stop seeing her?" Carolyn was enraged. "No, I don't want you to ever-so-charmingly ease your way out of your affair with Bambi. I don't want you to leave her thinking she was the one who dropped you. I want you to burn a bridge, *burn it*, Andrew, don't just light a cigarette match to it for five seconds. Don't preserve your connection to Bambi because it's good for business. Reject her and do it in a way that's public and humiliating. I want her to hate your guts, not just now, but forever. I want you to hurt her so much that if you ran into her on the street twenty years from now, she'd spit on you."

Carolyn vented her revenge fantasies, not caring that she wasn't being cool or that Andrew would find this display of anger too crass for his refined taste. When her emotion had been spent, they were both silent. With a Madonna song filling up the dance floor below them, they remained stationary, both painfully aware that the link between them had snapped.

Carolyn wrapped it all up. "Maybe there's no way to get the trust back, or maybe it just takes time, lots of time. Maybe someday we'll see each other at a party or something and you'll walk over to me and ask me to dance. I don't know."

"And what if your dance card is filled?" Andrew asked.

Carolyn thought about that. "I don't have any answers, Andrew. I don't know if there are any. Maybe all that 'magic' wasn't enough to keep our romance from being another Hollywood casualty."

Andrew backed off. "All right, Carolyn. If that's the way you see it. It's your call, my dear. If you don't want to see me, if you want to shut me out of your life . . ."

He was at the top of the stairs, ready to make his descent, but still facing her. "You want me to leave you alone?" he asked, calling her bluff. "I will. I'll leave you completely alone."

"Yes," she said, though her voice was shaky.

He let that sink in. He leaned over the railing and stared at the festive crowd reaching peak-one-A.M. party frenzy. Then he looked directly back at Carolyn.

"Bad call," he said as he turned and disappeared down the stairs.

27

The rain had been coming down all night, and by morning the news was full of reports of traffic accidents. Christie felt snug inside her Jaguar as she passed drivers moving more cautiously than she through twisting slippery canyon roads. She snapped on the radio in time to hear that the Pacific Coast Highway was closed due to mud slides.

Up until this morning she'd been glad she'd arranged to meet Lance at the Equestrian Center. If the weather had been better, it would have been a perfect spot—public enough to appear proper. "I ran into Lance today and we got to talking about *Dirty Dreams*," was how she'd put it to Styvie when he asked what she'd done all day. Styvie was not only possessive but also concerned about appropriate behavior. "Where'd you meet?" he'd drill her. "At the Equestrian Center," she'd reassure him, and then he'd relax. Since she frequently took riding lessons and Lance occasionally visited the horse he boarded there but never rode, it was not inconceivable that their paths would cross. Besides, Christie had chosen this site because she knew she looked great in riding pants. But now Mother Nature was messing up her plans, and a change in locale wasn't possible because, as usual, no one seemed to know how to reach Lance. So there she was all decked out in her riding gear, scanning the sky for a break in the clouds.

By the time she drove through the white-fence gates of the Center, the rain had subsided to a drizzle. As she pulled into the parking lot, she saw that Lance's Ferrari was not among the handful of cars present.

She had forgotten her umbrella, so she hastened over to their designated meeting spot—the arena where the polo games were held. She felt conspicuous in spite of the fact that there were a few other people around, going about their business, tending their horses and checking out the posted schedule of upcoming events. Suddenly this arrangement was starting to feel to her—and, no doubt, could appear to others—more like a tryst than a business meeting, and that was the last impression she wanted Styvie to have.

I've got to do something to assure Styvie will be in a good mood tonight, she decided. She remembered that there was a French bakery close by that sold Styvie's favorite strawberry cream-cheese cake. I'll pick up dessert, then swing by the video store and rent a porno, she thought. That'll put him in a good mood.

In spite of being rained on, she felt good. Things were moving right along. Since returning from Greece, she and Styvie had been getting along well. Insecure about his new undertaking, he seemed to need her more and was inclined to keep her happy as a way of ensuring she'd stick around. He didn't even protest all that much when she announced that she wanted to read for the part in Lance's movie. In a calm voice he said he was concerned that such an artistically ambitious script might be too big a challenge for her to take on. He also said he wasn't sure it would look right, the boss's girlfriend reading for the lead, but she worked on him. She made him watch *Woman in Red* and informed him that at the time, the star, Kelley Le Brock, had been married to the film's producer. She told him that Lance had agreed to let her read, not as a favor, but because he thought she had a certain quality that might translate on film. Besides, the intention all along was to get an unknown for the girl. She overcame Styvie's objections to "his woman" taking on such a provocative role by pointing out that whoever got cast in the role would become a symbol of an evolved healthy sexuality. Never coming right out with it, she implied that if she became an object of desire, it would make him seem more macho for having her. Eventually he agreed to let her audition. Yes, things were definitely looking up, Christie decided as she stepped inside the arena. But that was no reason to get careless.

The place was empty except for two old men standing to the right of the entrance, chatting and drinking coffee out of Styrofoam cups. Christie turned all the way to the left, and that's when she saw Lance, in the second row of the bleacher seats.

She stepped up to sit beside him. "I didn't see your car out there."

"I drove my Jeep," he replied.

"Ah, right." She smiled. "Four-wheel drive for a little rain. That's the California way." She hoped she sounded smart and cute.

"A red Ferrari is a liability when you're trying to be low-profile," Lance pointed out.

"Maybe I should think about getting myself an old Datsun, then," Christie joked.

"Maybe you should, sweetheart. I don't know what you're juggling these days."

Lance said this lightly, not meaning to insinuate anything, but it made Christie nervous just the same.

"I'm all work these days," she replied as she opened her leather shoulder bag and pulled out the *Dirty Dreams* script.

"I've been a very good girl, very studious," she boasted. "I've been learning it all. The Stanislavsky method. The Uta Hagen approach, and the Milton Katselas technique. I've read up on Strasberg and Olivier, and I'm working my way through the biographies of Hollywood stars. I've been to improvisation workshops and speech coaches. I've been looking in and projecting out. I've been—"

"Commendable," Lance interrupted. "But you can forget about all that. You'll be glad to know your screen test came back today. You look good on film. That's what counts here. The camera loves you. I didn't know you were so photogenic."

"Well, I guess I never got around to taking Polaroids when we were in Miami together, back in the early days. No nautical shots of you at the bow of the boat. No snaps of me sunbathing. No mementos of our picnic lunches."

It was the first reference she'd made to their past, and it had been sanitized to sound like *Ozzie and Harriet Go Fishing*.

Christie turned to face Lance, and continued in a more serious tone, "I've been doing a real selling job on you lately. You'd be proud of me. Last night Styvie and I discussed how sharp your instincts are and how good you are at handling people, which is what a director must do."

"You've got a talent for handling as well, my dear. You've certainly got Styvie's number."

"So do you," she said. "Let's face it, Styvie's a fairly conservative guy and you've got him making a controversial film."

"Styvie's not a conservative guy," Lance argued, "just confused. He can't figure out if he's supposed to be the personification of the elite staid society he grew up in or if he's the family rebel whose duty is to conquer new territory. When he's in a conquering mood, he makes *Dirty Dreams*."

Christie looked at him steadily. "Whatever his reasons, he *is* financing the picture and I *am* the one he discusses things with."

"So you have the king's ear," Lance said.

Christie laughed. "You could say that, and the king would like his queen to be the star of your movie."

Lance crossed his arms over his chest. It was time for him to rein in this pretender to royalty. "It was my idea that you test for this part, and I don't give a fuck who's writing the check. This is my movie. I'm calling the shots or I'm taking the project elsewhere. You get this part because I say so"—he paused—"if I say so." He sat forward, in a friendly posture, to extend some advice. "Christie, there are lots of people in Hollywood who have goals that exceed their grasp. Don't become one of them. It's not a pretty way to grow old."

The truth was, Lance wasn't anxious to go studio hunting for a new home for his project, and after a wide search for the right girl, he'd finally resolved that Christie was a good choice. Lance knew he could control her, and recalled she took instruction well. Besides, physically she was perfect. She had the kind of face and body that men masturbated to. He was going to take that wholesome face, the face of a girl who could have been a Miss America, and show this country what their innocents really craved. He would create a world on the screen that was familiar, clean, classy, civilized, ordered, and then he'd seduce his audience down a road of sexual adventures. The critics who had always panned his movies for being devoid of anything other than a comic-book concept would be forced to revise their opinions of him. He'd be tapping into the essence of what motivated people, their drives, their passions. He knew how to pull it off, and Christie would do just fine, provided she understood her place.

"That's not what I wanted to see you about anyway," she said, changing her tack. "Last week when I was in Styvie's office, I saw two notes on his desk, dated consecutively, both from Bambi Stern. She seems to think she needs to stay in daily contact to keep him updated on her plans for a 'musical remake.' Now, I'm not familiar with how things work at the studio, but it occurred to me that a junior executive doesn't usually send the owner of the studio memos about her stupid half-baked ideas. Plus, they were cutesy-playful notes, which, I'll tell you, Lance, made me sick. She is so obvious. This girl is a joke."

"And," he said, "it's not your kind of humor."

Christie got to the point. "Styvie has a blind spot about

certain kinds of women, and I'm not interested in having him stumble into the likes of her."

"So you want her exiled," Lance guessed.

Christie laughed again and composed a demure response. "It's not up to me. I'm powerless," she lied, "but you know how to 'handle' these things."

"Christie, Christie, Christie, haven't I always tried to help you?"

No, she thought, you haven't, but she nodded yes to encourage him to continue what she hoped would be a declaration of, if not friendship, at least a temporary alliance.

"We've known each other a long time," Lance said. "Of course I'll help you out. I like being able to do favors for special people. That's really what success is all about. Not the money. What? I need another goddamn real-estate investment? I own a place in Aspen I haven't even seen, and I just bought a house in Florida and I hate Florida. The more money you have, the more money people want from you. I get hit up for every charity west of the Mississippi and then some. And politicians. They're greedy. You give a thousand dollars to somebody running for Congress in Iowa because the guy votes the right way on the nuclear issue, and you get calls from his staff bitching 'cause you didn't give five thousand. The money can get to be a headache, but the success gives me the muscle I need to take care of things, and that's the part I enjoy. Bambi will be no problem."

This last statement was made with such finality, Christie got nervous. "I'm only asking you to keep her away from me and Styvie. I just don't want to see her face in my face. You know what I mean?"

Lance smiled. "Christie, do you know that every so often a trace of the girl you used to be comes through? The tough girl from the wrong side of the tracks."

"Thanks a lot, Lance."

"No, I mean it as a compliment. It's interesting."

Christie relaxed a bit. "So Bambi is out of the picture?"

Lance leaned across the table. "Listen to me. I said no problem."

"And no one at the studio will object?"

Lance laughed. "She means less to the studio than she does to me."

Christie was relieved. "Thanks, Lance." This time she really meant it.

"My pleasure." He pulled out a folded piece of paper from the pocket of his jean jacket. "You know what this is?"

Christie checked out the itemized list. "The budget for *Dirty Dreams.*"

"The revised budget with different locations, more exotic ones, a pivotal extra scene that must be shot on a tropical island, a must for the authenticity of the work . . . and estimated costs for a crucial, unprecedented ad campaign. This is not an ordinary film. The public has to become aware of it while we're still in production, and that awareness has to hit a frenzy by the time the movie comes out. This will not be inexpensive, but I must have it. I'm submitting this list to Styvie late this afternoon, so tonight during your pillow talk you might want to 'handle' him. Make him agreeable to the new terms. Bluntly said, I know," Lance confessed, "but I respect you enough to shoot straight, and the additional money will benefit both of us."

"Both of us?" Christie asked.

"It's your movie too."

"Is it? *My* movie? Like in 'starring Christie Collins'?"

"Tell your agent to put in a call to my office this afternoon. We'll get a deal memo out by tomorrow."

"I'm in between agents," she admitted.

"Call Lisa Sapien. She's a personal manager." Lance jotted down Lisa's number on the cover of the *Dirty Dreams* screenplay. "She'll arrange everything."

Christie was overwhelmed. She reached out and touched the script in front of her, seeing it with new meaning.

This was her "starting line," and she was determined to finish a winner.

"I'm sure Styvie will go along with the additional costs. As I told you before, I've been doing a real selling job on you."

Lance put the list back in his pocket. "So let's all have dinner this weekend. To celebrate. We'll do the west end of town this time. We'll go to Rebecca's in Santa Monica. Have some tequilas. Styvie will love it, lots of arty types."

Christie was ready to accept when something came to mind and all the excitement vanished from her face.

"Will you be bringing that model with the dress made of adhesive tape?"

Lance got the message. There was another candidate for exile.

"Don't worry, Christie. You're the star. Jasmine didn't survive the team cut."

28

Bambi was dressed for a big night at Spago. She'd spent the day on Rodeo Drive because she believed it was good luck to buy something new for an important evening, and she'd dropped seven hundred and fifty dollars at Lina Lee on a sleeveless black suede dress with a linen turtleneck collar. The Bulgari gold hoops that Daddy had gotten for her birthday complemented the outfit perfectly.

Lance had invited her to join an A-list dinner crowd tonight. He'd said that she could bring a date, so she knew she was needed for some business purpose, and she was more than happy to oblige. She loved being his player, and relished the thought of Andrew watching her in her mogul guise.

Strolling down the steep incline leading from the parking lot to the restaurant, which was set high above Sunset, overlooking the heart of the Strip, she held on to Andrew's steady arm. The great thing about Andrew was that he was always appropriate. You knew that he would always dress correctly and could converse with whatever surprise guests Lance might materialize.

A throng of freakish celebrity hounds pretending to be paparazzi hovered at the restaurant's entrance, hungry for anything but food. They either mobbed the passing guests or dismissed them. Bambi despised them for their pathetic *Day of the Locust* hysteria, and wished that moguls, rather than television stars, were recognized by the masses. Little did they know who really owned this town. The actors are the pawns, she thought. We are the bishops, queens, and kings.

The bar was packed as always, as Andrew and Bambi made their way in. Bambi approached Bernard, the maître d' she remembered from her Ma Maison days with Daddy. "Hello, Bernard darling. You look so well." From the look on his face, Bernard clearly didn't remember her. "Bambi Stern," she reminded him. And then she mentioned a name she knew he'd recognize. "I'm meeting Lance Burton."

"But of course, my dear," he replied. "Follow me."

With a sweep of her hair, reminiscent to her of Ava Gardner, she strode past the twenty or so impatient patrons in front of her.

"Excuse me," she said over and over, to no one in particular. "Please excuse me."

Lance was seated and surrounded by agents. Bambi sized up the crowd in a flash. "Casting *Dirty Dreams,*" she explained to Andrew. "Lance needs a big name to play against Christie, and a lot of stars don't want to work with an unknown. We have our work cut out for us."

Lance was so distracted when they arrived that Andrew, who found himself frequently appalled by the lack of manners in Hollywood, had to introduce himself to the seven others at the round center table. He decided to relax and not try so hard. Casting *Dirty Dreams* was not his problem. He leaned back in his chair, gazed out the window at Tower Records, and thought of Carolyn. She loved rock and roll so much that often she would make him get out of bed late at night so she could find a record he'd never heard and play it for him. She was like a rock-and-roll missionary, he thought, smiling at the recollection. How he missed her good company.

"What are you thinking about?" Bambi asked.

"Nothing important," he lied. "What are you thinking about?"

The conversation at the table had still not opened up sufficiently to let them in.

"I keep thinking about David Beach. He doesn't even know where the soundstages are, and his picture really did get a green light."

"What's his picture about? And what do you mean by *his* picture? What did he have to do with it?" Andrew found the proprietary relationships of executives to pictures baffling, as he considered executives no more than paper shufflers with expense accounts.

"I don't know . . . it's some sleazy musical he calls the *Purple Rain* of the nineties. I hope it's as successful as *Under the Cherry Bomb.*" She giggled at her adjustment of the title of the least successful of Prince's movies, *Under the Cherry Moon.* "I don't know what David Beach actually did on it, besides slip it by me. I'm sure that if Nicole were still in power, this never could have happened."

Andrew had to laugh. "I never knew you to speak so highly of Nicole. Could this be nostalgia, Bambi?"

She glared at him. "Nicole only cared about getting her own projects through, with her own pet writers. She got so distracted trying to block *Dirty Dreams* that she forgot to block David Beach. That's all."

Lance's voice boomed across the table. "Who is blocking *Dirty Dreams?* What are you talking about?"

The focus of the table turned to Bambi. She flashed a sweet smile and forged ahead. "Ancient history, Lance. I was talking about Nicole's unsuccessful attempts to get in our way."

"Nicole wouldn't know a good story idea if one woke up with her in bed, and it's the likeliest candidate to wake up with her too."

The men at the table thought Lance's biting comment was hilarious.

Bambi sensed an opening, and trusted her instinct to surge forward. "I remember those story meetings with her on Monday mornings. There was no sense of direction. She wanted so badly to be 'hip' that she paid no attention to what goes into good old-fashioned entertainment."

This declaration quieted the crowd, all of whom relished the prospect of being on the inside of studio politics.

"Well, Bambi," Lance said, "tell us what you think is
a great idea. Somebody at Millennium has got to be
coming up with stories besides me."

"As a matter of fact, I've been dying to tell you an
idea I had at the manicurist. I hate waiting for my nails to
dry so I was using the time to concentrate on some future
projects, and the cutest premise hit me."

All eyes were on Bambi.

"Then tell me, Bambi," Lance chuckled, "before the
pizza comes. In twenty-five words or less."

Bambi brushed her hand over Andrew's thigh as though
she were rubbing a good-luck rock.

"It's a coming-of-age story about a party girl who
grows up in a small New England town but is always a
fish out of water there. It's *Breakfast at Tiffany's* before
Holly Golightly gets to the big city." She was proud of
how easily the log line rolled off her tongue. "It's young,
fun, and offbeat and can be done in a very commercial
way. Kind of a blue-collar John Hughes piece with a
female protagonist."

Andrew violently threw her hand off his knee. His
heart was pounding. At that moment he didn't care who
thought what of him or what happened to his chances for
a damned development deal at Millennium. His sonorous
voice boomed all over the room.

"You're out of your fucking mind. Who do you think
you're kidding? That was not your idea and you know it.
That idea is Carolyn Foster's and she's been working on
it for six months. She pitched it to you and you passed."

"That's not true," Bambi protested. She looked to
Lance for assistance, but his eyes were set on Andrew,
who had stood up abruptly, knocking his chair over in
the process. She looked back to Andrew, intimidated by
his rage.

"How dare you try to steal Carolyn's ideas? How dare
you even steal her phrases to try to sound articulate for a
change?"

"What is your problem tonight, Andrew?" Bambi tried
to sound indignant, not defensive.

"I'm sick of all the lies. I'm sick of all the goddamned desperate lies . . . mine included," he added. Then he turned to the rest of the dinner party and, in his most civilized voice, said, "My apologies, and good night."

Once outside, he headed on foot toward Sunset Boulevard. He was glad to be out of there and into some fresh air. He felt charged. He'd come up against a line he wouldn't cross, and that discovery was invigorating.

As he neared the corner, he saw that Book Soup, his favorite bookstore, was still open. The thought of browsing through its shelves was very appealing. Then, he considered, maybe I'll go over to Tower Records and buy a couple of new releases. He wished Carolyn was with him. They could take their new books and records back to his place, make some pasta marinara, and—

This fantasy was interrupted by a conversation behind him. A young couple, obvious newcomers to L.A., stopped at the corner to wait for the streetlight to change.

"Sunset Strip," the girl said. "I can't believe I'm actually on Sunset Strip."

Her boyfriend said, "Look at those fuckin' billboards."

The girl looked back over her shoulder and freeze-framed on the window of Spago, where the elite could be seen dining at their VIP tables. "Must be nice," the girl said, obviously longing for that privileged life-style.

Andrew smiled as the light turned green. "Not really," he announced. "Not as nice as you would imagine."

Bambi watched the million-dollar shacks along the Pacific Coast Highway rush past as the speedometer in Lance's Ferrari hit sixty-five. Ever since they'd left Spago, she'd been unusually quiet. Andrew's outburst had shocked her. What had she done to deserve such betrayal? Could Andrew have harbored anger toward her because she'd ended up taking an upcoming actor to the black-tie fundraiser she'd initially invited him to? She quickly dismissed this possibility. They were grown-ups. Surely he understood it was a business decision. On the other hand, what he had done tonight was cruel and unjustified, she fumed. Where was his loyalty? Where was his professionalism? Everyone borrowed ideas from everyone else. How dare he call it stealing and how dare he accuse her of it in front of people she worked with? She'd wanted to throw a cup of cappuccino at him.

She gazed out the car window. Everything resembled a set. At any moment MacGyver might come running out of the Malibu supermarket in pursuit of some television criminal. The houses didn't seem permanent. And, given the shifting shoreline, cracks in the earth, and the occasional boulders that tumbled down from the canyons above, they weren't.

She looked over at Lance. He was consumed with his reckless speeding and seemed in no hurry to start a conversation. He too had disappointed her tonight because he hadn't defended her in the face of Andrew's accusations. Lance should have hit him. Nothing brutal; just a swift upper cut to the jaw would have been fine. At the very least, she'd expected Lance to threaten Andrew. Even a token "You'll never work in this town" would have been something. But Lance had let her fend for herself. All he contributed were some meaningless words about how she shouldn't worry about it and "by tomorrow it will be old news." Then he offered her a ride—not a ride home, she was quick to note, but one of his infamous rides. With mixed feelings she'd accepted. This was not the way her night with her dream lover was supposed to begin.

Although it was a cool night, Lance opened his window. As Bambi reached for her jacket that had fallen on the floor, her watch caught a thread in her stocking and caused a run. Get off my case, God. I've had enough to deal with tonight, she silently cursed. She crossed her arms and hugged them tight, hoping Lance would take the hint and buzz up the window or turn on the heat. But he paid no attention to her.

The Ferrari swung off the main highway. Lance drove

past his four "Do Not Trespass" signs and stopped before a tall wooden security gate that blocked the rest of the driveway. He punched a code into the computerized lock near the driver's side and the gate swung open. He sped up to his third and most remote house, the infamous gazebo, and came to a screeching halt.

As Bambi stepped out and got a whiff of the sea air, she was reminded of that night months ago when she'd made her unscheduled visit to Ted. That seduction was to have been her rehearsal for this one. As she followed Lance into the gazebo, she tried to recapture her "unconventional spirit."

The place wasn't set up for entertaining. There was no champagne on ice, the Jacuzzi was flat and cold, and the Levolor blinds were raised, an intrusion on their privacy. After flicking on a light, Lance lowered the window coverings.

"You want something to drink?" he asked.

"A margarita, no salt," Bambi replied as she wandered around, eyeing an expensive Fabergé egg mixed in with the drug paraphernalia left on the coffee table. Without apologies, Lance handed her a beer and took one for himself.

She reluctantly settled for what she considered a pedestrian beverage and sat down on the white divan.

"I don't know how I should handle this Andrew thing. I'll have to counter the damage somehow. I should make a list of people to call. Give them my side of the story before they hear his." She was babbling to buy time until she could tap into her elusive unconventional side. "Lance, what exactly do you think my story should be?"

Lance wasn't interested in helping her devise a strategy.

"Bambi, let it go. You've got to be able to smile at these things."

"Smile? Lance, betrayal is a painful thing."

"Enjoy the pain," he said, taking his place next to her on the low couch. His presence, so close, accelerated her breathing. She wanted him to take care of her, talk to her, calm her down.

322   *Lynda Obst and Carol Wolper*

"Enjoy it?" she asked, cozying up.

He played with her shoulder through the suede fabric and then abruptly unzipped the back of the dress so he could feel her skin. "Yeah, enjoy it. It'll teach you some things about yourself. It'll make you tough."

"I am tough," she said. "I've got a reputation at the studio for being tough. That's why I'll be so good at Nicole's job."

Lance pulled her head into his chest in a boxing maneuver as if he were playfully fighting with her. "David Beach is executive vice-president," he announced.

Bambi's face was pressing into his shirt when the news hit her, and for a second she felt like she was suffocating.

She yanked her head back. "You told me that I was going to get Nicole's job."

Lance touched her knee. "David's been working his ass off while you've been off having your little affair."

"He has affairs too," she pointed out like a kid justifying her errant ways.

Lance was unmoved. "Bambi, David's got a go project."

This incensed her, and she pulled her leg away from his touch. "You didn't say I could be vice-president if I had a go project. You said . . ." She was sputtering now. "I gave you that memo. I helped you. I played on your team." She stopped and then added, "I'm going to talk to Styvie."

Lance grabbed her arm. "Oh, really? What are you going to do, Bambi? March into his office and complain because you didn't get promoted? The first thing he'll ask you is why you think you should be. What are you going to tell him? Because Lance said this or that? You'll look like an idiot. It didn't work out, Bambi. These things happen. It's a setback. Everyone has them. Roll with it. Anyone can cruise through tranquil waters. This is what I mean by getting tough and hanging in there. Personally, I wouldn't blame you if you left Millennium. Maybe it's not the right situation for you. But you've got to learn to handle change. If you can't handle this, you can't handle running a studio. I'll tell you this, Bambi. David Beach knows how to roll with it."

This last comment left her utterly defeated. Seeing this, Lance loosened his grip and softened his tone.

"Sweetheart, you'll get over this. I know you will. You've got a great future. There are a lot of job possibilities on the market for someone like you. Don't sabotage yourself."

"Why is there always another test I have to pass?" Bambi moaned. "Is there ever a last test and then a 'Hooray, you've made it'?" She looked to Lance for some sign of what to do. He embraced her, and though she wanted to cry on his shoulder, she decided to go for the one thing still available to her.

It's time to perform, she decided as she got up and walked to the other side of the room. As she strolled over to an open wall console, she moved her hips to a made-up tune she was humming. She did a quick inventory of Lance's record collection, seeking the best beat. She hit the stereo system's power button and the sounds of a radio deejay filled the room. From behind her Lance reached over and shut it off.

"We don't need that," he explained.

His interruption of her planned striptease infuriated her.

"But maybe I want it, Lance," she shouted. "Maybe we don't *need* it, but it'd be nice." She shook her head, exasperated because nothing was working. "Okay, okay, Lance. We'll do it your way." She stormed across the room to pick up her bottle of beer, and took a swig. "Come on, Lance, whatever you're into," she taunted him. "Maybe you've got some leather around here you want me to wear. I'm a size eight. I'm a thirty-four B. Come on, show me your stuff. Are you ready? Come on. Show me all your gadgets and toys." She started searching around for Lance's hiding places, opening drawers and closets, rifling through his belongings.

Sensing him right behind her, she turned to continue

her tirade, but in a second he'd locked a pair of handcuffs on her. "I'm ready." He smiled.

Bambi was horrified. She stared down at the serious-looking police handcuffs. They were tight. They hurt. Oh, God, she thought. I want a vacation. I want to go home. I want to go to the country club with Daddy on a Saturday morning, play some golf, and have grilled cheese sandwiches.

Lance picked up a scarf that had been lying on one of the couch cushions and twisted it tight like a rope.

This isn't the way I imagined it, Bambi thought. This isn't bringing out my unconventional side. This is . . . This is . . . She forced the tears down. She wanted Lance to kiss her, thinking that maybe that would get her going, but he led her over to an empty space on the floor and made her lie down.

She started to say something.

"No talking," he commanded. "The new rules. You've got to learn, Bambi," he said, sounding like a stern taskmaster. "You've got to shut up and learn some things."

I don't want this, she thought. I definitely don't want this. But she didn't say anything. She shut up and tried to concentrate. She strained to hear the ocean instead of the sounds of this man who was shoving her dress up and tying open her legs. He unzipped his pants. Can't you at least put on some music? she wanted to scream. She made herself think of something pleasant so she wouldn't break down. She thought about the manicured lawns and lazy safe afternoons in Scarsdale. She thought about going home.

29

"When you pitch *Party Doll*, try to concentrate on the theme, not the small details. Mention that it's a modern Cinderella story but with the magic being determination."

Carolyn was trying to jot down Nicole's ideas as they passed the last light on Pico before Metro. But glib sales-type phrases like "a modern Cinderella" stuck in her throat, and she suspected that she was as prepared as she was going to be. Quickly she added a few notes of her own on the piece of paper she'd arbitrarily ripped out of her notebook. She realized it was her grocery list for next week's Christmas dinner. She and Lou were cooking for ten people. The single life wasn't as unbearably lonely as she'd imagined.

"Do you think you could do the selling part, Nicole? You're much better at it than I am."

"I'll do the windup, introduce you, and then, as Joan Didion says, we play it as it lays. I'll try to create a relaxed atmosphere. Larry Winters and I have always liked each other. I don't know whether Jim Canker will be in the meeting. It'll be interesting either way. And don't be upset if Winters doesn't give us a definitive yes or no. He doesn't usually take pitches and may need time to talk to Canker, see what existing deals are on the development slate, so that if he has to, he can blame him for the pass."

Nicole's Maserati breezed up to the guard gate, and with her priority pass visible on her windshield, was allowed through.

She had chosen her first pitch as an independent producer very carefully. She'd always felt comfortable with Larry Winters and was thrilled when he was promoted to chairman of the board of Metro Studios. She felt he was an untapped ally. And because his regime was fairly new, they weren't overburdened with inventory, and were anxious to establish new relationships in the community. She wasn't so sure about Jim Canker, the head of production. She didn't quite trust him, though he always kissed her on the cheek when they met. He spent too much time in George Christy's column for Nicole to take him seriously.

"I heard rumors Canker was in trouble at Metro, around the same time there were rumors about me," Nicole said to Carolyn.

"Do you think they're true?"

Nicole smiled. "You never know what's really going on when you hear rumors about a marriage. But when you hear rumors about a studio, they're usually true."

Unable to find a visitor's spot close to the executive building, Nicole seized a good spot nearby, belonging to a director she knew was away on location.

"I can't promise anything," Nicole suddenly said as they walked toward the main building. At times they both could palpably feel her loss of power, though neither ever mentioned it.

"Would you like something to drink?" Larry Winters' secretary asked from behind the red poinsettia plant on her desk. She was making the appropriate meeting amenities available.

"Nothing for me, thanks," Carolyn said. She was too nervous.

"An Evian," Nicole crisply answered. She glanced at the time. In Hollywood you could calculate the gravity of an insult by the number of minutes you were kept waiting. Nicole counted ten, exactly. Insult began now.

Just then the door swung open and Larry Winters appeared. Slim, fortyish, and balding, he wore a cardigan sweater, fine tweed slacks, and a jacket. The no-effort power look. He was tall, ruddy, and subtle, like a fox.

"Great to see you, Nicole. Come on in. Millennium's loss is my gain." He smiled hello to Carolyn and led them proudly into his office, as if it were a trophy den.

"So what are you doing with your leisure time?" Winters sized Nicole up closely through squinty eyes.

"I'm impersonating relaxation," Nicole answered. "I'm in the last stage of working out a lease/option agreement on a house I found with my boyfriend, and preparing myself for the first stage of decorating it. I've discovered that all decorating costs come in two units, "two thousand dollars or twenty thousand. Anything you need—tables, plumbers, wallpaper. It's beginning to make running production look easy."

"So you haven't lost your appetite altogether for this side of the desk?"

"Not entirely. But I'm excited about giving hands-on production a try. I always envied producers being able to lead a project from beginning to end."

They nodded at each other, in commiseration.

"As an executive," Nicole continued, "it's all about the deal. When the fun really starts, you're on to the next deal. It's enervating."

She glanced over at Carolyn to include her in spirit if not in fact in this professional minuet. Carolyn seemed fascinated by her first real look at her former boss in action. Nicole took her rapt attention as a compliment. She was beginning to feel back in her element.

"Tell me about it," the studio head responded. "This is why we can never find good talent to run production. The ones that can, won't. The ones that will, shouldn't."

"I don't know what category I fit into," Nicole continued, "but I know I'd love to make a movie for you guys. At Millennium we envied your distribution apparatus, and I believe we made an unsuccessful raid on your venerable marketing department."

"I'm flattered you chose to come here first with your

pitch." He looked at his notes. "I'm not familiar with your writer. Carolyn Foster?" He stretched his hand toward Carolyn. "Nice to meet you."

"Carolyn used to be my secretary," Nicole explained. "It quickly became obvious to me that she had better taste than my creative staff, so I promoted her. Turns out her own ideas were both mainstream and fresh. So, rather than rounding up the usual suspects for my first pitch, I wanted something original. *Party Doll,* the idea we're going to tell you about, is my favorite of Carolyn's. It's about a factory-town girl who bootstraps herself into the Upper East Side café society of the late sixties. A kind of Sabrina set in the world of Andy Warhol."

As Carolyn began to tell her story, her voice was soft, firm, poised. The sharp details of her own Fall River background provided an edgy but touching sensibility to the well-worked-out saga.

Nicole looked like she was listening, but she was really watching Larry Winters' face for signs of impatience. But he was laughing at all the right beats and appeared to be genuinely charmed. At the end of the piece he was smiling broadly.

"Who do you like for the girl?" Larry asked.

"This is a wonderful opportunity to discover an exciting new talent," Nicole answered.

"And sign her up for three more options with the studio."

"Four, if she can carry a picture."

They laughed at the mogul perspective they shared.

"A piece like this is dependent on the writing, and I have no sample on Miss Foster."

"I'll guarantee the writing," Nicole assured.

Carolyn's stomach twitched. She was the potential stumbling block.

"You've got a deal. Call business affairs. Let's make this one and find the new Molly Ringwald while we're at it."

Larry Winters stood up and walked around the room,

indicating the meeting wasn't quite over, that there was something else on his agenda.

"Carolyn," he began, "would you mind waiting outside for a moment while I talk to Nicole about something confidential?"

Carolyn shot out of her chair. She was so elated by the deal that she would have worked at the guard station or answered phones if he'd asked her to. Well, maybe not answered phones.

"Sure, no problem, Mr. Winters." Then, without thinking, she added, "I won't let you down."

Larry Winters shut the door behind him. There was deliberation in his actions, as if he were thinking out each motion for the first time. He sat back down in his crackly green leather armchair. He looked straight at her.

"Are you happy?"

"I'm not unhappy," Nicole replied. "Which I always assumed I would be without a fancy title behind my name. It's actually making me more secure."

"I don't know any secure producers." He sort of laughed.

"For the first time in a while, I have to rely on my own strengths, not my logo, for a sense of worth. Being Nicole Lanford of Millennium gave me power, but it was borrowed power. People returned my calls because I was the studio."

Larry Winters agreed. "I know men of sixty still handing out business cards at Beverly Hills coffee shops, pitching their guts, trying to nestle up to the young V.P.'s, hoping they'll take their calls. It's pathetic."

"Sounds pretty bleak."

"Are you getting your calls returned these days?"

"I place them carefully. I know who my allies are. It's really all about talent. I don't care if I get a piece of material out of the agencies if the writer will give it to me."

Larry was watching her every gesture. He got up from

his chair and rolled his head around his shoulders. He picked up a thick computer printout from his desktop.

"Do you know what this is?" He answered for her: "It's our upcoming production slate. Twelve movies will be released by us this year and I like two of them." He paused for a moment. "One, really."

"Not a good percentage."

"I don't know why these scripts were ever put in development. Obviously Jim Canker and I do not have the same taste."

Winters leaned his back against his desk. "I've been thinking about something since you called. Then I checked you out with Ovitz." Nicole wondered what the top agent at CAA might have said. "But it was something else that made up my mind," Winters added.

"You've made up your mind?"

"I decided something watching you pitch and listening to your point of view. I love your intensity. You know what you like. You're not afraid to express your opinions. That's what I need in a president of production. I need someone with the courage of her convictions. I'm too damn tired of second-guessers."

Nicole's heart was still. She wasn't pushing, angling, cajoling, or striving for a job. Now that she could live without it, she saw it was within reach.

"Are you offering me Jim Canker's job?"

"I'm offering you Nicole Lanford's first real opportunity. What do you say? Would you be ready to start after New Year's?"

She stood up and shook her new boss's hand. "Call my lawyer in the morning," she said. Then, as an afterthought, she asked, "Did Chester Baines ever call you about me?"

"Chester Baines?" Larry Winters seemed confused. "I haven't spoken to him in over a year. Why?"

"I just wondered. He once mentioned something about calling."

"I never got the call."

Nicole smiled. "It's not important," she said. It was better this way. She liked owing Chester nothing.

Nicole found Carolyn waiting for her by the elevator. "We did it."

"I can't believe it," Carolyn exclaimed. "Thank you so much. This never would have happened without you."

Nicole downplayed her influence. "Deals like this get made all the time."

"I don't just mean the deal," Carolyn explained. "You really believed in me, treated me like a professional. No one ever has before."

"Well, you may not be thanking me when the studio starts asking for endless drafts and rewrites." Nicole smiled.

"Development, hell," Carolyn replied. "I'm ready for it."

Nicole gave her a congratulatory hug. "For better or worse, Carolyn, you've just launched a career."

30

Carolyn, her date, Michael, and Lou were among the first to step onto the cordoned-off area of Millennium's back lot for the postscreening festivities of the *Dirty Dreams* premiere. Ever since Lance had announced the plans for his movie one year ago, at his Fourth of July gathering, the town had been abuzz with rumors about how the project was going. Since January, blind items had appeared in the industry columns. Lance had fired three cinematographers . . . they'd been shooting for three days and were already three weeks behind schedule . . . Christie Collins had been through five hairdressers in one month . . . when a storm hit the Philippines and destroyed Lance's meticulously created garden paradise, he moved the entire company to Versailles. All through May, gossip about the postproduction nightmares circulated. Lance apparently insisted his three sets of editors work around the clock to assure a summer release, and was constantly changing his mind about what cuts he wanted. It was said that he had become so alienated from Millennium's board of directors that he'd turned to Joey Martucci, his executive producer, to finance the *Dirty Dreams* ad campaign. His extravagance from the start all the way up to this June 30 premiere had been so well-documented that one paper had dubbed him Cecil B. De Burton. But all the stories combined hadn't prepared Carolyn for this grand finale.

To begin with, the guests were shuttled to the party from the nearby screening room by uniformed drivers in remodeled golf carts. They were brought to an ornate glass door manufactured the night before, when Lance had been appalled by the lack of a proper entranceway. Inside, the poles that pitched the satin tents were draped in swirls of white water-stained taffeta. The area covered the size of five tennis courts, including three soundstages that had been redecorated in two days to resemble an Italian mansion. The effect was completed with marbleized floors and walls stippled with gold and peach, turning the instant pleasure dome into a faded, aging Mediterranean villa. Scores of studio painters had worked golden overtime to accomplish the set, and many had been fired when Lance deemed their speed under par. Nervous waiters garbed in servants' uniforms stood ready to serve the meal, while women dressed as courtesans circulated the room carrying silver trays. Perched on these trays were glasses, real crystal from the executive dining room, filled with Taittinger champagne. The matches and centerpieces on the formally appointed dinner tables had gold-embossed logos, as if announcing a marriage. DIRTY DREAMS, they read in high Roman.

The extreme attention that had been given to the ambience fascinated Carolyn. It was so over-the-top. There was a short story in all this somewhere. She was glad she'd come after all, though this kind of hot summer night made her want to drive out to the beach. "We'll drive out after the party," Michael had said, always ready for a romantic adventure. Recently they'd celebrated six months of "she-wasn't-sure-what." That's how Carolyn casually referred to their relationship. She wasn't ready for anything more specifically defined yet. Especially since so much of her energy went into her work. With a "go" on *Party Doll,* Carolyn was in the midst of a production final rewrite.

As the three friends maneuvered their way across the room, David Beach walked hurriedly past. "Glad you could make it," he called out to Carolyn.

She smiled, appreciative of the invitation he had ex-

tended, but not fooled. The onset of his friendliness
toward her just happened to coincide with the news that
Metro had green-lighted *Party Doll*. David Beach's friendship was blatantly conditional.

Lou plopped down at a table and stretched her legs out
on a chair nearby. "I think the silence after the screening
was staggering."

"Not a good omen," Carolyn agreed.

"I never thought decadence could be so boring," Michael said.

"Can you imagine what the reviews will be?" Lou
asked. "Not to mention how Millennium's stock will drop
when the film dies at the box office."

A wandering courtesan passed their table and Michael
helped himself to three glasses off her silver tray. He
handed one to Carolyn, one to Lou, and set one down
for himself. "Here come your friends," he said to Lou.

Lou looked up to see Digby Butler, the *Tribune*'s
"Hollywood Reporter" and his date/escort/friend, Brett,
making their way toward her.

"I swear," she said, "ever since he bought a couple of
pieces from my store, he acts like we're family."

Just then the journalist, followed by Brett, joined the
trio at the table.

"Well, I know what the title of my review is going to
be," Digby announced. " 'The Unbearable Heaviness of
Hubris.' Now I know why the movie cost forty-eight
million."

"It was only thirty-eight," Brett countered.

Digby went on. "They admit to thirty-eight. Lance
doesn't know how to compromise."

Brett nodded. "That's true. You should see how he
flips out if the sheets and towels aren't folded right. His
linen budget could keep me clothed for a decade."

"And even if it were thirty-eight," Digby said, showing
off his expertise, "the movie would have to gross around
one hundred million just to break even."

"What about videocassette sales?" Brett asked, trying to keep up his end of the conversation.

"Maybe in the porno section." Digby laughed.

Michael silently mouthed to Carolyn: The beach . . . now. She smiled and whispered back, "Do you really hate it here?"

"No. It's fine. It's a trash novel come to life," he whispered back.

"No secrets," Brett said, trying to be cute.

"Oh, there's Ted McGuiness," Digby announced. "And the one in tight white is Joy. She's an aerobics instructor who is about to be his third wife."

"God," Lou said, aghast. "It's Big Brother in the form of Digby Butler. Do you know all about their sex lives too?"

Digby just smiled and kept his attention on Ted, who was approaching their side of the room. He got up from his seat as Ted was about to pass their table, and sidled up to Millennium's chairman. In his haughty Harvard accent, the reporter asked Ted's reaction to the controversial movie.

Carolyn took mental notes. How does a studio head handle such a colossal public failure?

She focused on Ted as he focused somewhere on the horizon and put his arm around Joy in preparation for moving on. "I think Lance got every penny he wanted up there on the screen."

A noncomment, Carolyn noted as Ted smiled and turned away.

"And you?" Digby addressed Joy, who was shocked to be called upon. She pretended she didn't hear and kept up with Ted's hasty departure.

"No opinion," Digby said, as if he'd just interviewed a beauty contestant and was now doing a summary for the audience. "A necessary quality for a studio head's future wife to have."

Just then an already drunk actor known for getting into fights off-screen and playing the leads in action-adventures on-screen came up to Digby. "If a movie about fucking is a fucking bore, then you've got a fucking disaster. That's what I think," he offered before being dragged off by one of his more sober actor pals.

Digby jotted the quote down and was about to replace his notebook in his jacket pocket when he spotted David Beach with Lisa Sapien beaming at his side.

"Ah . . . the executive vice-president of production," Digby exclaimed. "Is that his girlfriend?" he asked at large.

Brett sat up in his chair. "No way. That's a straightforward deal. Lisa Sapien's a major-league dyke who is going with Lance's ex, Jasmine. David Beach only dates bimbos, but I guess he didn't want to get slowed down by one tonight."

"More data for your computer," Carolyn said to Digby.

"I think I'll go over there and drill him for a few quotes," Digby responded.

He got up and headed over to David Beach's circle.

Brett watched him leave and then he too popped up to cruise the room and take in more of the show.

"Do you think anything could have saved this movie?" Michael asked.

"Saved? No," Lou said decisively. "Helped? Maybe a different actress."

"You know the star is Styvie Pell's girlfriend," Carolyn said.

"Figures," Lou said. "She acts like she's Styvie Pell's girlfriend. No style, no substance."

"What I was shocked by was the inane story line," Carolyn said.

"Not your idea of a sympathetic heroine?" Michael joked.

"I mean, really," Carolyn replied, "here's this woman who travels all over the world looking to experience the ultimate passion. Okay, fine, I can relate to that, but when she finds the man who delivers her to whatever you want to call it—sexual nirvana—she wakes up the next morning with the same vacuous attitude."

"Once a bimbo, always a bimbo," Lou summed up.

"Maybe that's Lance's message," Michael suggested.

"I think Lance thought he was doing a mainstream *Belle de Jour* of the eighties," Carolyn said. "But Burton isn't Buñuel and Christie Collins isn't Catherine Deneuve."

Just then a young agent and two junior executives from Paramount and their dates sat at the next table. Although they'd already helped themselves to food from the sumptuous buffet tables, their desire was to talk shop more than it was to sample the cuisine.

One executive, who was wearing a trendy arty tie, had an especially loud voice and was quizzing his dinner companions about what kind of people would go see this movie. "Personally," he said, "I don't find it sexy to see women get beaten up. Do you? Do you?" He polled the table, getting "of-course-nots" and denials all around. Noticing that Carolyn was looking over at him, he impulsively asked, "Do you?"

"Not my idea of an aphrodisiac," she replied. Then, checking out his plate, she added, "What's for dinner?"

"Carpaccio, veal and angel-hair pasta with caviar," his date answered for him.

"So look at it this way," Carolyn said. "Lance's movie may be a bomb, but you're getting an elegant dinner out of it."

She turned back to Michael and Lou and shrugged. "Sorry," she said softly. "Maybe they weren't being vindictive, but the truth is, if Lance had another movie on the boards tomorrow, those same people would be playing up to him, flattering him, referring to *Dirty Dreams* as an example of what a courageous risk-taker he is. All the negatives would be reinterpreted to add up to an entirely different picture."

"That's their job," Lou reminded her.

"What planet are these people on?" Michael asked.

"The planet power," Lou suggested.

"The planet survival," Carolyn said. She paused a moment, taking in the circus atmosphere of the room. "But you know what? I'm hooked on it."

Digby counted on the fact that David Beach was not a seasoned enough main player to fear a writeup. "Can we chat for a second, on the record?" he asked.

David Beach excused himself from his new admirers with an impatient look toward the ornate ceiling. "The press," he explained. "I'll be right back."

"Perhaps we can sit for a moment so I can take notes," Digby suggested.

"Good idea, Digby. As you know, I've always been an avid reader of your column."

Digby went for it. "And the movie, *Dirty Dreams*. What is your personal reaction?"

"We're all terribly proud of Lance Burton. He's the cornerstone of Millennium Studios. We all think he accomplished his personal vision with *Dirty Dreams*."

Digby saw that the party line was all he was going to get, so he changed tactics. "Some people are comparing this picture to *Heaven's Gate* and *Howard the Duck*," Digby said. "How does Millennium respond to allegations that the movie went twenty million over budget?"

"That's absurd," David Beach responded. "Where did you get your numbers?"

"I was told that Lance insisted that one shot be filmed in Palau, in Micronesia, and then got rained in for a week."

"Well, problems come up. That's a force of God. Nothing the greatest producer could have done to prevent that."

"What about the stories of a team of round-the-clock editors employed because Lance insisted that his movie come out as a big summer release? And, what about the enormous promotion budget? The highest in the history of Hollywood."

David Beach might not have been a seasoned player,

but his instincts were sharp. He knew how to protect himself on record with the right quotes. "A movie like this, with such a delicate theme, had to be handled just right. We had to open this movie, and to do that, we had to make the public extensively aware of it, months before the release date."

"Is it true that so many set dressers quit that you ran out of union set dressers, had to use nonunion help, and got picketed by the west-coast branch of IATSE?"

David Beach pushed his chair back in a move that readied him for a quick getaway. He cleared his throat and kiss-kissed a passing well-wisher. All smiles, he returned his attention to the interview. "This is off the record, Digby. I am getting the distinct impression that your slant is hostile on this film, and I'm not surprised. Subject matter like this often offends the sexually confused. Have a good night, and enjoy our hospitality."

Digby sat at the table smarting from David Beach's insult. Not that he minded people knowing he was gay; in this town it hardly mattered. But members of the press were usually immune to barbs of studio politics. He'd get his, Digby vowed. A man that remarkably shortsighted was not likely to enjoy power too much longer.

As he looked around the room to see whom else he should get quotes from, there was a sudden commotion at the glass door. Dozens of paparazzi snapped away. In a blaze of flowing red silk adorned with more jewels than Harry Winston could ever dream of selling one person, Christie Collins swept into the room.

This is my moment, Christie said to herself. Nothing will take it away. The glare of the flashbulbs was better than any diamond Styvie had ever bought her. She twinkled her eyes at the camera and smiled at the *Entertainment Tonight* reporter who was just that moment stuffing a microphone into her artfully made-up face. Someone was telling Christie how gorgeous she looked, and she was hunting for Styvie in the crowd so that he wouldn't miss it. Fuck him, she thought, where the hell is he when it's my turn?

"People say you got this part because your boyfriend owns the studio." This nonquestion was posed by the reporter from *Entertainment Tonight.*

Christie's face froze. Where were all the publicists who got paid to prevent this? "How ridiculous," she answered. "How sexist of you. It was really much harder for me. I had to overcome the stigma of being Mr. Pell's friend and earn the part. Mr. Burton has a mind of his own, as I'm sure you're aware." With this sentence barely out of her mouth, she brushed past the microphone and grabbed a passing David Beach. She screamed into his ear, "Find Styvie and get me out of here. And make sure that piece doesn't run on *Entertainment Tonight* without my approval." Then she turned to smile at a photographer from *People.*

Styvie was in the furthest corner of the room, hiding from the publicity. Over and over in his mind he was trying to figure out what had gone wrong. I saw the movie a hundred times. Why didn't I know how bad it was? I'll never be able to face my family, who already think I'm a flake. Did Christie make me do this? Was I somehow blinded by a conspiracy hatched by her and Lance? His hiccups of Wasp hysteria were interrupted by the arrival of Christie and her hangers-on.

Though she was smiling, he knew she was troubled by the look in her eyes. For a moment he saw her more clearly than ever before, overdressed and overbejeweled, redolent of perfume and cheap with ostentation. This woman is evil, he realized. She has sheared me from my real values and made herself my family. What power does she have over me?

"Why do you look so glum in the middle of our triumph?" she babbled to Styvie for the benefit of the assembled retinue, all of whom were intimidated by her sullen boyfriend. "Did Mommy leave you alone too long when she was talking to the press? I was talking about *you*, darling . . ."

This made Styvie more gloomy than ever. Visions of his family huddled in the library watching *Entertainment Tonight,* taking in the spectacle of Christie playing the movie star while they dissected his inability to handle the family mantle, played in his brain like Chinese water torture. Grosse Pointe silent torture is far worse, he thought, ignoring Christie.

"Well . . ." Her tone was foreboding. "What's wrong?"

"Nothing. I'm tired. That's all."

"Well, of course you're tired," Christie shot back. "*You* are not the center of attention. You've never been able to let me have a good time, unless you're in control of it."

"Really, Christie," he said. "Not here and not now. I am not in the mood for an argument. Go enjoy your success, and I'll meet up with you at the head table in a few minutes."

Christie dismissed her fans, begging their pardon. In a second the two were alone. "You're not in the mood for an argument because you are a major wimp with nothing to offer but your money." Christie spat out the words she'd been holding in for almost two years. She finally felt free of his financial hold on her. She had status now. There would be other deals for her to make.

Styvie spoke softly. "My money was enough to keep you happy so far, and to get you the lead in your first picture. A picture, I want you to know, I'm ashamed to have had any part in."

"Don't give me that 'ashamed' shit," Christie shot back. "You never complain about being ashamed of anything when I'm getting you off."

She took a step back and tried to adopt a more objective tone. "Styvie, why don't you go find yourself a prim-and-proper girlfriend? One of the girls you grew up with. Someone who has only been fucked by men who think foreplay is getting drunk on gin and tonics. You'll be perfect for each other."

Styvie pulled her closer and continued to speak quietly but emphatically. "Christie, you're pretty but you are not by any stretch of the imagination irresistible. You've obviously and very stupidly decided to gamble on an acting career. Given your upbringing, it was a mistake you were probably destined to make."

He grabbed her by the elbow and headed toward the table in the center of the room. He remembered duty from his stint in military school, and he knew that his role was to go through the motions with erect carriage and head held high.

"You're hurting my arm," Christie said.

Styvie lightened his grip. "After tonight, I don't care what you do or where you go. I don't want to hear from you or about you. But for the next sixty minutes you're going to keep smiling and say as little as possible."

"And if I don't?" she threatened.

"Don't be that stupid, Christie."

Carolyn had finished her pasta, drunk her champagne, and accumulated a wealth of images that she was sure she'd use in something. A book? A screenplay? In the meantime, her journal would store them. She scanned the room as the party began to wane, noting Styvie's stoic countenance and the lack of any communication between him and Christie. She recorded Ted affectionately whispering something in the ear of his aerobics-instructor fiancée and smiled at the sight of Joey Martucci having the time of his life with the two blond ingenues who accompanied him. Carolyn was ready to call it a night when Bambi Stern made her late entrance to the party.

Bambi had been away from the scene for months. She'd taken a leave of absence from Millennium last fall under suspicious circumstances. The gossips said it was because David Beach got promoted. Others said Christie had it in for her.

As Bambi stood near the entranceway, she held on tight to the arm of her Latin companion. A look of anxiety crossed her tanned face. She sought out an anchor, a haven in this world that held such mixed messages for her.

To Carolyn's chagrin, Bambi headed for the table next to hers.

"Honey, where have you been?" one of the agents asked.

"I've gotten married. This is Jorge."

The man by her side smiled weakly in response to greetings from a group he seemed completely uninterested in.

"And," Bambi continued, "I've been traveling, assessing my options." Bambi's prepared response sounded like a press release.

"Traveling where?" the preppie executive asked.

"Well, Jorge's family owns a number of banks in Venezuela, so of course I spent some time there. Then we went on an African safari for our honeymoon, stopping in Europe on our way back. I made it to the collections in Paris, and then decided to spend a few weeks in New York before returning to L.A. and plunging into the work of fall development."

As she finished this declaration, she noticed Carolyn and quickly looked away. But the sight of her onetime competitor clearly threw her off.

"Where will you be working?" the aggressive young agent asked.

Bambi fiddled with the bow on her off-the-shoulder Donna Karan gown. Puffing it out, and taking a breath, she resumed her performance. "Not at Millennium. That's for sure. I left last year because, quite frankly, the power vacuum in the absence of Kevin and Nicole made the place impossible. I couldn't get any of my projects through in that atmosphere of uncertainty."

Lou nudged Carolyn. "Get Digby over here, this girl isn't talking, she's giving a press conference."

"That's Bambi," Carolyn whispered to Lou.

"You're kidding. That's Andrew's ticket to the big deal?"

"As far as I know, he didn't even get a *small* deal out of the alliance," Carolyn said.

The agent found chairs for Bambi and Jorge, but Bambi declined the invitation to join them. "I'm too wound-up to sit," she said. "I just got back into town and there are so many people I've got to see."

"Have you seen Lance anywhere?" the agent asked.

"Lance? Isn't he here?" Bambi swiveled around to view the head honcho table. She spotted Styvie, Ted, but no Lance.

"No one knows where he is," the agent replied.

His date, a girl with pale skin and wild red hair, who looked like she got around, said, "I heard he was in Tahiti. Either Tahiti or the Betty Ford Clinic. I've heard both."

He'll show up again, Carolyn thought. No matter how much money the picture loses. He'll wait a few months, then suddenly reappear, brand-new. As Nicole would say: Old moguls never die, they just repackage themselves for a new market.

Carolyn looked to Michael and Lou for a group decision. "Shall we get out of here?"

"Let's," Michael said.

As the three got up from their table to move toward the door, Carolyn felt a hand tug at her sleeve.

"Hello, Carolyn," Bambi said.

Hello, Carolyn? Carolyn thought. Did I miss something? I don't remember us becoming friends. "Hello," she politely replied.

"How'd *you* manage to get on the guest list?" Bambi asked.

Carolyn smiled. Maybe Lance would come back repackaged, but this was the same old Bambi. Without any guilt about how these two words would sting, Carolyn answered her question. "David Beach."

As crowds from both sides of the room funneled themselves toward the doorway, Lou tugged at Carolyn's sleeve and whispered in her ear, "Oh, God, the great deceiver is here."

Looking through the throng, Carolyn saw that Andrew had spotted her and was going against the direction of the exiting guests to reach her. She shifted her gaze but could not shift her thoughts. Her emotions were a mixture of nostalgia and hate—well, maybe not hate. Andrew didn't have that kind of grip on her heart anymore. Maybe it was just nostalgia and disappointment, she concluded. As he neared, she saw that his face wasn't full of the false bravado she'd seen the night he followed her out to the street to explain the presence of Bambi in his bed. It also bore no trace of the dangerous combination of strategy and charm she remembered from Helena's. It was the face from the quiet times they'd spent together. It was the way he looked when he was immersed in a book or a movie. It was Andrew unarmed and receptive, and it stirred those old memories.

Catching up to her, he took her hand and gently pulled her away from the people traffic. Carolyn signaled to Lou and Michael that she'd meet them outside.

"Yes?" she asked. "Is there something you want to say to me?"

"Will you dance with me?" he asked.

She shook her head. "I don't think so, Andrew. We don't make very good partners."

"Well, will you talk with me?" He was smiling, trying to pull her in as he had when they first met.

"You're too good at talking," she said.

He laughed, thinking she was flirting with him.

"My dear, I'm sure there are a few things you'd like to say to me."

She'd often thought that she'd like to say: Andrew,

you worked so hard to win me—if only you'd worked half as hard at keeping us together. But now that they were face-to-face, she no longer wanted or needed to tell him anything.

"No, there's nothing left to say," she stated.

He looked concerned. This was clearly not a flirtatious line. "So, that's it? Time apart hasn't helped? What we had means nothing? Am I disposable? Are you on to the next?"

"I'm not looking to repeat what we had somewhere else," she said. She thought to herself: I own Andrew's twenty-fifth year and he owns mine. Nothing will change that.

"Do you ever think about those times? Lawry's? Disneyland? Neiman-Marcus?" He reached out for her, his hand caressing her shoulder. He forced her to look at him.

She knew she had to be curt. "Things are different now."

"Meaning?"

"Our breakup made me see things. I've created a place for myself. I'm not afraid anymore."

"That doesn't surprise me. I always knew you could." His response was full of pride, as if he deserved credit for her independence.

"We tried, Andrew. Let's leave it at that."

He wasn't about to settle for her conclusion. "What about the connection we have?" He gripped her arm again and searched her eyes for the answer he wanted. "It's something, you know. It is."

Carolyn cracked a smile. Yeah, it was something, all right. For a while it had summoned everything she had, every feeling, every pleasure, every need. But once summoned, her precious small self was abandoned. Maybe, she feared, she could never bring back that hidden girl/woman again. Maybe she was too damaged by this love. The only thing Andrew's charm could instill in her now was fear that she might never love like that again.

That's what he was counting on, Carolyn realized. That she couldn't live without it, no matter how little it was. No, she thought. Nicole had taught her about jumping from a high board. She had to close her eyes and free-fall into her future without him.

"It was something," Carolyn conceded. "But it's just not enough."

Andrew looked at her for a long moment. "What happened to your spirit, Carolyn?"

"It's there. It's intact. Don't worry."

"If you don't watch out, you're going to turn into another Nicole," Andrew said.

"I hope so," she answered, noticing that Michael had returned and was trying to get her attention. He was holding up a key and mimicking "golf cart."

"If that's what you want," Andrew said, turning cold. "Get ready for a lot of lonely nights. You can't make love to your career."

"I've no intention of doing that," Carolyn said, making a move past him.

With that she left him behind and moved closer and closer to Michael, who was waiting for her on the sidelines.

31

Westwood Village was, as it always was on a Saturday night, teeming with college kids. On every street of this commercial area that marked the southern border of the UCLA campus, there was a myriad of waiting lines.

As Lance aggressively drove his Ferrari through the traffic, he eyed the long line outside Stratton's Grill, a much smaller line in front of the Security Pacific instant-teller machine, a more relaxed line at the checkout register at Tower Records, and a two-block line of moviegoers waiting to get in to see Paramount's new summer comedy. As he turned the corner, he saw another impressive line outside the theater showing Warner Brothers' new action-adventure. But farther down the block, at the Westwood Theater, where *Dirty Dreams* lit up the marquee, the path to the ticket window was clear.

Lance pulled into an illegal parking spot in front of the theater and shut off the engine. For a minute he just sat there, sickened at the sight of so little business at the biggest theater in the area. He had fought hard to get *Dirty Dreams* into the Westwood, where only the most promising blockbusters ever opened. Early on there had been resistance to guaranteeing *Dirty Dreams* the three weekends Lance demanded, but that was when having Joey Martucci as his executive producer had paid off. Lance didn't like owing the mob a favor, but the thought of his movie not getting a chance to play bothered him more.

As he approached the window, a young couple in

motorcycle-chic leather outfits was purchasing tickets. The girl in the glass booth put aside her magazine to make the transaction and then immediately went back to her issue of *US*. The sight of her reading infuriated Lance. To enhance his bad mood, he saw that a line was already starting to form across the street for a United Artists movie not showing for another hour. I can't fucking believe that people want to see that sentimental piece of shit, he thought.

"How's business?" he asked the girl.

She listlessly looked up from her reading. "Slow."

Lance was about to ask her what the exact ticket count was when he spotted a coming-attraction poster on the wall.

"What's that doing there?"

"It's a coming attraction," the girl replied.

"I know it's a coming attraction but it doesn't belong here. This whole area should be nothing but *Dirty Dreams* posters."

She shrugged.

"Where's the manager?"

She pointed inside. "Somewhere. His name's Billy."

Lance walked purposefully up to the entrance.

"Where's Billy?" he asked the ticket taker.

"A . . . I think he's around. Have you seen Billy?" the young man asked the girl at the candy counter.

She looked in the direction of a closed door.

Lance stepped over the velvet rope that partitioned off the lobby and headed toward it.

"Hey, mister, that's not cool," the ticket taker said, though he made no move to stop him.

"Fuck cool," Lance replied.

The girl behind the candy counter giggled. "I think you left your manners at home," she said as Lance knocked at the closed door and then without waiting for an invitation barged in.

Billy, the twenty-five-year-old preppie manager, looked up from the papers he was sorting. "Can I help you?"

"I don't fucking believe you've got coming-attraction posters out front," Lance said.

"Whoa," Billy replied. "Wait a minute." He lowered the volume on his cassette player. "You're . . . ?

"Lance Burton."

"Lance Burton," he repeated, placing the name. "Well, Mr. Burton," Billy continued respectfully and somewhat defensively, "it's customary to advertise what's coming up when the current feature has such a weak opening."

"It's customary," Lance pointed out, "to do your best to sell tickets to the movie currently playing in your theater."

"Well, I'm just doing what I was taught," Billy answered calmly. He was not about to butt heads with this ego.

"Let me give you some advice," Lance offered. "Pick better teachers."

With that he stormed out of the office and went inside the theater to see for himself. Standing behind the last row of seats, he counted thirty-nine people. Thirty-nine people in a seven-hundred-seat theater at an eight-o'clock show on a Saturday night. That said it all.

He felt abandoned, as if the world had moved on and left him standing there. As the curtain lifted and *Dirty Dreams* began, he felt the pain in the pit of his stomach. They didn't get it. Why didn't they get it? He looked up at Christie's face on the screen, remembering how long it had taken him to shoot that scene. The lighting alone had had to be reconceived three times before he decided it was right. Didn't people understand what he was trying to say? How had he lost his audience on this picture, when they'd been there for all his others? Never for a second did Lance, a producer known for his ability to create blockbuster entertainment, consider that maybe his big statement was a big bore.

Fifteen minutes into the movie, Lance left the theater. He noticed that the coming-attractions poster had been replaced by one promoting *Dirty Dreams,* but he really no longer cared. Instead, his thoughts centered on where he could buy some coke. His dealer, Bruce, lived in Westwood but Lance didn't have his number and knew it wasn't listed with information. So fuck it, he decided. I'll just drop by. Lance knew he couldn't get through this weekend without a little artificial stimulation, or, as he used to joke, without a little help from his enemies.

When he reached his car, there was no parking ticket on the windshield but there was a flier advertising the opening of a new nightclub. He crumpled it up and threw it on the ground. Surrounded by all these college students who appeared to have nothing on their minds but fun, Lance became even more depressed. For the first time in his life, he felt old.

Cruising down the alleyway behind a string of nondescript apartment buildings, Lance tried to remember which one Bruce lived in. Spotting his dealer's Honda inside one of the open garage stalls, he pulled his Ferrari up next to it. As he got out, he noticed two suspicious-looking guys walking toward him down the alleyway. Normally he would worry, seeing as this part of town was notorious for car thieves trying to score fancy foreign cars. Come at me, assholes, Lance thought. Just try to fuck with me. His frustration and despair made him reckless. Whatever intentions the two young thugs had, they reconsidered. The look in Lance's eyes told them that there was easier prey elsewhere.

Lance climbed up the narrow staircase that led to Bruce's second-floor apartment. He knocked on the door. After some muffled discussion a girl called out, "Yeah, who is it?"

"Is Bruce there? It's Lance."

More muffled words followed and then the door was opened. Bruce stood there wearing yellow surfer shorts and a UCLA sweatshirt. His girlfriend, sitting on the couch behind him, was wearing a micromini and a denim jacket.

"Lost your number, buddy," Lance explained. "Hope I'm not busting in at a bad time."

"No, come on in . . . but I'm not really dealing anymore," Bruce said as he closed the door behind them. "I'm actually quitting at the end of the month."

Sure, Lance thought. He'd heard that before.

"I'm going to bartend for money and concentrate on my acting," Bruce explained, " 'cause you know," he said, breaking into his Arnold Schwarzenegger imitation, "action movies are my life."

Lance forced a smile and faked some encouragement. "Do it, buddy," he said. Then, without wasting any more time, he added, "Got anything at all for me tonight?"

"I'll see," Bruce said as he stepped into the bedroom.

Lance was left alone with the girl, who looked at him provocatively. He knew her type. Aren't I sexy? she was trying to say. Aren't I mysterious? Don't you want me? Lance ignored her. He picked up a surfing magazine from the table and flipped through it aimlessly until Bruce returned with a small clear plastic box—half full.

"Five hundred," he said.

Lance took out his checkbook.

The girl, annoyed that he'd turned his back on her, jumped in. "Cash only," she said.

Bruce gave her a look that warned her to stay out of this. Turning to Lance, he smiled. "No problem."

As Lance wrote out the amount, Bruce measured out a few lines for him to sample.

Rolling the check into a makeshift straw, Lance snorted the cocaine. It went down smooth and easy.

"So one more month and you're out of the business? Got a referral for me?" Lance asked.

Bruce hesitated. "A . . . I'll . . . Call me in a few weeks."

Lance doubted Bruce would give up this profitable business in a month's time or a year's, but he humored him. "Will do."

Suddenly anxious to get out of there, Lance pocketed the plastic box.

"We're thinking of going to the eleven-o'clock show of *Dirty Dreams*," Bruce said, trying to bring the conversation back around to acting.

"Good idea," Lance replied.

"Will it change my life?" the snotty girlfriend asked.

"It changed mine," Lance said cryptically before he turned and headed back out into the night.

Lance downshifted to second as he reached a steep incline in the Beverly Glen tributary that led to Mulholland Drive—the summit of the Hollywood Hills and an occasional drag strip for teenagers. On one side of the winding peak, the lights from the sprawling San Fernando Valley descended. On the other, lush pine cover camouflaged the pleasure palaces that wound down the canyon into Beverly Hills. His Ferrari could negotiate the tightest of curves within a minute ratio, and Lance often cruised the drag like a subversive adolescent when he needed to purge his frustrations.

At the light at the intersection of Beverly Glen and Mulholland, Lance was at an impasse. Where was he going? Home? To Warren's? Jack's? Don Henley's party? He extended his hand into the glove compartment for some chemical fortification—a "bump" to focus, he thought. His fingernail shoveled out an ample portion of white powder from its clear plastic container. He inhaled it sharply and a bolt of exhilaration surged through him as the light turned green.

I'll go to Warren's, he decided with a flourish. Now he was excited. Seeing his real pals was what he needed after the bummer at the theater. Warren had been through this kind of thing. He'd survived *Ishtar* and the pettiness of marketing types. Lance accelerated to seventy, rounding the curves toward Warren's Mulholland compound. But suddenly he was seized with paranoia. His head started to pound. Warren might be busy. He hadn't returned his call yesterday. Anyway, Warren was in the middle of shooting. He'd be full of optimism and obsession and all those feelings that had engulfed Lance into myopia over the past year.

By now he was idling in front of Warren's driveway, realizing he had to move on. He didn't want to alert the private security or trigger the house's closed-circuit television. Impulsively he threw his Ferrari into reverse and careened into the middle of the winding dark road.

"I'll go to Henley's party." It was as though he were commanding his car, and like a magical chariot, he presumed it could hear him and obey. It's a party, I won't have to talk about work, he told himself. But a rational voice inside him held ground. I've never talked about anything *but* work at a party, he realized. So how could I start tonight? Everyone will look at me and think one thing and one thing only. My movie didn't open. I might as well wear a goddamn billboard that says, "My movie is a flop. Come laugh at me." It was like public pillory. And it was goddamn *unfair!* As he shifted into fourth gear, still without any certain destination, he thought: What am I, a goddamn small fry? A nobody? Big producers can survive a flop, for Crissakes. They survive by having other deals in the works. But not me. No! Where the fuck's my agent? He should be behind closed doors finalizing my next deal this fucking instant. He wasn't even at the theater to see how we did. "I'm firing the motherfucker," Lance bellowed to no one.

He grabbed the handset of his car phone and pressed 07, his code for his agent's home number. His heart was pulsing so fast he could feel it in his throat. Was that the palpable anger for all his wasted work? he wondered. Or was it the coke?

He held the handset to his left ear, pressed between his shoulder and his neck. Sweat beads began to form on Lance's brow as he waited impatiently for the phone to be answered. Five, six, seven rings . . .

In Coldwater Canyon, in the middle of a family barbecue, Don Mayer, Lance Burton's agent, picked up the phone as he flipped a burger. "Helloooooo," he sang.

"Where the fuck are you, you piece of shit?"

"Lance, how are you, buddy! How'd we do tonight?"

"You fucking miscreant. Worse than fucking last night, if it's possible. What the hell are you doing?"

"Cooking dinner for my in-laws, Lance. Flipping burgers. Settle down. What's the problem?"

"The problem is, you're fired because you don't do your job. No one does their fucking job around here, except me. I get the movie made by myself. I cast it. I market it. I have to get my own goddamned distribution for it, and what do I get? I get no support. I'm so fucking exposed, I can't believe it. While I'm traipsing around the world breaking my fucking back trying to make this movie a reality, what are you doing besides spending your ten percent and playing the agent role at the Grill? Why aren't you out there getting me another picture to direct? No. You're fucking flipping burgers by the pool I paid for—"

At this point Don Mayer's phone went dead. He thought Lance had hung up on him—a relief—but the automatic operator came on the line, announcing that the "Pac Tel customer has left the vehicle or is out of operating range."

Around the next bend, two teenage boys, younger and more reckless than even Lance, revved the engines of their souped-up Camaros. Lance heard the sound of purring engines up ahead through the crackling static of his car-phone reception breaking up. Unyielding, he continued to shout, as though his sheer passion and the weight of his will could defy technology. "I'm sick and tired of being exposed like this by two-bit shysters like you. I won't have it. I won't—"

His tirade was stopped by the pair of blinding headlights approaching. His first thought was to hold his speed and force them to clear the road, but his usual confidence had been undermined by the night's failure and he opted instead for what should have been a safer move. He swerved the Ferrari off to the right, to what he thought was a driveway. But at the crucial moment, his timing and judgment were off. His right-front wheel caught the top of a boulder and spun out of control. For a crystallized moment he dangled on the precipice of land and air—the edge he'd always been looking for. That was his last thought, as physics finally overcame him and his car toppled down the edge toward the Valley—not even the chic side of Mulholland.

From a distance Lance and his dream machine were no more than red metallic cartwheels tumbling down the hill, until the Ferrari burst into flames.

32

Nicole sat on the stone ledge of the terrace overlooking Coldwater Canyon. As the sun sank lower in the sky, she welcomed the cooling-off of the three-digit-temperature heat that had made this July Fourth a day to be at the beach. However, she and Steven had decided to forgo the parties out in Malibu and instead spend the day puttering around their new home. We're like newlyweds, Nicole realized happily, we're still at that stage when unpacking the groceries can be incredibly romantic.

As she surveyed the property that had captivated her the minute she saw it, she thought: My first holiday in my new house. It was not the typical Hollywood-Mediterranean villa. Perched on a cliff behind a brick wall, amid palm trees and lush exotic plants, it had more of a Caribbean feel to it. The air around it seemed gentler, as if blown in on a tropical breeze. Nicole could hardly believe she was living here with Steven. She could hear him laughing while on the phone with his daughter, his voice coming from the room that would be the den whenever they had the time and money to fix it up.

As Nicole thought ahead to their dinner that evening with Kevin and Peggy, it was hard not to draw comparisons to the July Fourth of a year ago. To begin with, tonight would be the first time she had seen her former boss since his departure from the studio. Of all the Millennium people who had been at Lance's B-B-Q, only Ted's position had remained unchanged. Lance had set something in motion back then that had shaken up many lives and cost him his own. Though his death was called an accident, everyone in town felt that the demons Lance carried inside of him had finally taken control. If it hadn't been a smashup on Mulholland, it would have been something else.

Whatever the circumstances, Lance's death had deeply shocked Nicole. She had always thought he was too resilient, too smart, too stubborn, and too bad to die young. He had been such a vivid and vital character that his death left a void as well as a kind of legacy. Ticket sales for *Dirty Dreams* had increased sharply after news of the accident spread through the media. Moviegoers were now finding profound meaning in the erotic images and bizarre scenarios that dominated Lance's last work. In a way, Lance had had the last laugh, Nicole thought. But he'd died without learning the most important lesson everyone who worked in the industry had to learn: It's only movies. There *are* more important things in life— like lovers, friends, and family.

This train of thought reminded Nicole to make the call she'd been putting off. She picked up the second line on the phone atop the patio table and quickly, before she lost her nerve, placed a call to New Jersey.

"Hi, Dad."

"Hi, honey. Everything okay with the new house?"

"There are a few leaks in the roof and some chipped paint, but it's perfect, if you know what I mean."

"If it's home, it's perfect," he agreed.

"I've got some other news. Is Mom there? Could you tell her to pick up the extension?"

As Nicole waited for her mother to get on the line, she was well aware that this was a call she should have made months ago. What had stopped her was knowing that once she did, there would be no place to hide if it didn't work out.

"Nicole, what's the big news?" It was her mother's excited question.

"Remember I told you I was seeing someone—Steven

is his name . . . well, it looks like we're going to be together."

"Are we talking engagement ring?" her mother asked.

"Mother, we're talking about meeting someone special and being together."

Nicole was not about to mention Steven's first marriage until the divorce papers were signed. Even then it wouldn't be easy.

"Who is he? Where's he from?"

"You'll meet him on our next trip to New York or when you come out here."

"Are you happy, honey?" her father asked.

"Very."

"You sound happy," he said. "That's all that matters to me."

His words brought tears to her eyes.

"Maybe we'll come out in November," her mother said. "You know how I hate the cold weather back here. A break will be nice."

"Come for Thanksgiving or whenever you want." Nicole felt a remarkable generosity of spirit from being in love.

"Well, I'll call again soon," she promised. "I just wanted to tell you about my guy."

"Take care, honey," her father signed off.

"Make him happy," her mother advised.

With a light heart, Nicole moved inside. She took a seat and admired her sparsely furnished but still homey living room. For the past couple of weeks she'd spent her free time browsing through stores, looking for the perfect little touches: pillows, lamps, vases. Though she was normally an impatient shopper, these excursions hadn't bothered her. Surprisingly, the overtired saleswoman at Saks hadn't gotten to her. When she'd found herself in the middle of a slow-moving traffic jam in the Beverly Center mall, she relaxed back and turned on the radio. She sailed through the weekend store mob scene undaunted, her attitude attracting attention. A young man who worked in cosmetics at Robinson's had flirted with her and wanted to give her dozens of free perfume samples. She sensed that there was a glow about her these days that people noticed. She had "the self-assured radiance of a well-fucked woman." It was a line by one of her favorite screenwriters.

Her lack of anxiety couldn't be credited solely to Steven. The last couple of months had been unpredictable and crazy and she had finally, after initial resistance, learned to go with whatever came her way. And things seemed to be working out, dreamlike.

First there was her new job at Metro, which was turning out to be challenging in a healthy way. And now there was Steven's recent decision to open an L.A. branch of his investment banking company. Though he'd still have to spend time in New York overseeing his east-coast office, a bicoastal existence was manageable. This decision had quieted Nicole's concerned girlfriends who doubted Steven's intentions. They'd made her nervous with comments like: "Fifty percent of men like Steven [though what they meant by "men like Steven," Nicole wasn't sure] end up back with their wives." She couldn't think types, odds, probabilities on this one. All she knew was that so far, since they'd found each other again in New York, Steven had been unfailingly committed in spite of the difficulties he'd encountered. His wife was trying to freeze all his assets until the property settlement was final, and threatening to sue for total custody of Alison. His east-coast friends joked about L.A.'s cultural wasteland and warned him he'd lose five IQ points for every year he spent in what they called the "land of sham." And, at best, his business associates were skeptical about his expansion to the west coast. Nicole felt that at times the two of them were like village idiots. No matter what turmoil was going on around them, they were happy.

She heard Steven laugh, and looked up to see him through the open door. He was still on the phone amid a half-dozen cartons of personal possessions he'd had sent out from New York. He eased back into his leather armchair, the only piece of furniture he had taken from his Manhattan town house.

Nicole loved his laugh. She was hooked, she had to admit. She wanted to flaunt her newly found passion the way other women flaunted their jewels and Mercedes 450's, and yet she didn't want to diminish the purity of her feelings by introducing a competitive spirit into her consciousness. Anyway, she knew the jewels and cars would get more attention. How ironic, she thought, in a town obsessed with power, that the power of love was so little appreciated.

This was so different from her past relationships. She used to analyze her dates as if she were analyzing a script: "He's got a good job, no ex-wives or kids to deal with . . . he's a little short, not a great dresser, but I can change that. We like the same restaurants. He doesn't expect me to cook for him. The sex is okay and he's got a decent sense of humor." No such evaluations took place with Steven. There was only one thing to consider. They were bonded. Everything else was secondary to that.

"Alison's coming out either the twenty-seventh or the twenty-eighth," Steven announced as he emerged from the den. "She'll call us back in ten minutes to let us know."

"Great," Nicole replied. She opened the drawer of the pine coffee table, pulled out a scrap of paper, and jotted down a reminder to herself. "I want to call the Geffen Company to get tickets for the Peter Gabriel concert. Think Alison would enjoy that?"

"I'm sure she would." Steven leaned against the fireplace mantel. "I don't want you to worry about this visit. You don't have to entertain Alison or try to impress her. She's a smart kid. She'll see what a terrific person you are. Don't worry about it."

"I'm not worried," Nicole said as she slipped the note to call David Geffen into her daily calendar book. As she did, the check for next month's mortgage fell out. "Dream houses are expensive," she thought aloud, not regretting for one second their decision to go for it, in spite of its being more than what they really should have spent.

"Nicole, it's not as if we're investing in hundreds of thousands of tulips. This is a house. It'll be here for a while. The worst that can happen is that after owning it for a few years, we'll have to sell it."

This made her laugh. Steven had a way of defusing any potential panic by his steady clear logic.

Nicole beamed. "Oh, I get it. You're going to intimidate me by being the perfect man."

"Don't worry," he replied. "I'm a real dud when it comes to hang-gliding."

She laughed as they walked out onto the terrace arm in arm.

They leaned on the railing listening to the faint sounds of a reggae band playing somewhere in the canyon.

"Someone's having a reggae Fourth of July," Steven said. "That's what I like about this place, it's eclectic."

Nicole snuggled closer. "Living here takes some getting used to, especially for a New Yorker."

"It has its charms: warm weather, a great basketball team," Steven countered.

"It also has a major drawback," Nicole insisted.

"Well, aren't you being a gloomy Gus," Steven kidded.

Nicole burst out laughing. "I guess I do sound a little negative. I'm just trying to let you in on the pitfalls of this place."

"Like?"

"Like there's no point of view here. There's no debate about anything. People are afraid to risk alienation, so they don't really judge anything but failure. It may at first seem liberating, but it encourages a lot of irresponsible actions."

"The wild west." Steven smiled. "It's going to be an adventure."

An adventure. Nicole liked the sound of that. Why not

a new love and a new vocabulary? Forget "obstacle," "drawback," and "hurdle."

"Adventure . . ." She smiled back. "Okay, I'm game."

When the doorbell rang, Nicole leapt to answer it while Steven headed for the kitchen and a chilled bottle of champagne. Nicole hadn't realized how much she missed Kevin until she saw him and Peggy on her doorstep. She proudly led them into her new home, while they all apologized for not getting together sooner. As she gave her visitors a quick tour of the place, Nicole noted Kevin and Peggy's deliberate manner. It reminded her of people learning how to move around again after being bed-ridden or, in their case, after a self-imposed exile.

"It's good to see you again," Steven said as he poured the champagne.

"Unfortunately, we didn't get a chance to talk when we met last July at Lance's B-B-Q," Kevin replied.

Right off the top he brings up Lance's name and all that implies, Nicole thought. He's not hedging anything.

"That seems like such a long time ago," Peggy said.

"A lifetime ago," Kevin agreed.

For a moment they were all silent.

"Sometimes Lance is more present in his absence," Nicole said, "if you know what I mean."

"Not to mention," Kevin added, "that he just died and there's already a movie-of-the-week in the works based on his life."

Nicole shook her head in dismay. Changing the subject, she asked, "Have you heard the latest rumors about Millennium?"

Kevin nodded. "Styvie Pell is going to sell the studio to a consortium of Japanese companies. It'll happen. It makes you kind of wish for the old Hollywood, when a green light for a movie didn't have to be a decision made by committee."

"All I know is that all I can do is fight for the projects

I believe in," Nicole said. "And so far at Metro, my voice is heard."

When all the glasses were filled, Steven lifted his in a toast. "Up the rebels," he exclaimed.

They savored the celebratory drink. No one was in a hurry to terminate the peacefulness of this canyon oasis.

"Let me call the restaurant and tell them we'll be late," Peggy suggested, reaching for the phone just as it rang.

"You can use the phone in the kitchen," Steven suggested as he answered the call. "Hi again, sweetheart," he said as he stretched out the long phone cord and moved toward the den.

"His daughter," Nicole explained to Kevin.

Kevin nodded. "Family," was all he said, as if that one word said everything.

Now that the two of them were alone, Nicole wanted to express a thousand thoughts about what had transpired since they'd left Millennium, but she started off simply.

"How have you been, Kevin?"

"I'm pretty good. Got through the year, body and soul intact. Peggy's been great. It's been hard on her but she jokes about it. Says it saved her from all those awful ladies' lunches at the Bistro Gardens. Actually freed from my routine, I'm even feeling creative. I've been working on some ideas that I'll do as soon as I can set up an indie-prod deal somewhere."

"Somewhere?" Nicole wouldn't hear of it. "You'll do them for me at Metro. We're a team. You taught me my job, Kevin. We have the same tastes. It's decided. Done."

Obviously pleased, he continued, "I think you'll like these projects. One of them is a nightmare Peggy had. When she told me about it the next morning, I realized it was like a Stephen King story. It'd be perfect for Jim Cameron to direct, and not half as expensive as *Aliens*. I'm at a stage when I can translate nightmares into something constructive." This declaration was accompanied by an impish grin, his Irish humor resurfacing now that his Jewish resiliency had gotten him through the crisis.

"I'm so glad you're here, Kevin," Nicole blurted out. "And I don't just mean here this moment. I was worried you might move away."

He got up and wandered over to the window. "I thought about it. I thought about going to Austin. Can you see me in Texas?" He shook his head. "Don't ask me why. Makes no sense, but I considered it. I guess because I've never known anyone who went there, so it seemed safe."

He gazed out across the rugged canyon. "But I couldn't leave L.A. Somehow, and I don't know exactly when it happened, I've gotten attached to this city. Besides, my daughter would miss the beach. She's fallen in love with volleyball. She's only eight but she's already dreaming about the Olympics."

Peggy joined them and slid her arm around her husband's waist. Turning to Nicole, she said, "Kevin's an amazing coach. This morning he taught our daughter how to spike the ball."

Nicole saw the hard-won intimacy the two of them shared and was deeply touched by it. Behind them, she saw Steven approaching, still engaged in conversation with Alison.

His eyes sought Nicole. At that moment it hit her: there was a harmony in the room, a point of synchronization. I'll never forget this, Nicole promised herself. I'll never forget that this kind of joy can thrive here even for a moment. It reminded her of a wildflower on a parched prairie. No matter what follows, she told herself, this is what I need to remember.

ᗭSIGNET

DRAMA & ROMANCE

(0451)

☐ **FLOWERS OF BETRAYAL by June Triglia.** Tiziana D'Eboli risked everything to free herself from a ruthless mafia bond. Here is a novel of passion, shame, deceit, and murder—and the stunning woman who took destiny into her own hands. (402472—$5.99)

☐ **BOUND BY BLOOD by June Triglia.** Two beautiful sisters overcome brutal pasts to become successful and prominent women. From Pittsburgh to Paris, from Manhattan to Milan, Angie and Nickie learn just how far they can go. "Masterful storytelling that will keep you turning pages!"—Fred Mustard Stewart (401832—$4.95)

☐ **VEIL OF SECRETS by Una-Mary Parker.** In this sizzling novel of mystery and seduction, Una-Mary Parker vividly interweaves the *haut monde* with affairs of art and finance, giving full reign to three beautiful women who become tangled in a triangle of love, passion and greed. "A glitzy romp with the rich and famous."—*Booklist* (169328—$4.99)

☐ **DOCTORS AND DOCTORS' WIVES by Francis Roe.** Greg Hopkins and Willie Stringer, two powerful and dedicated doctors, find their friendship shattered by personal and professional rivalries. A masterful medical drama, this novel vividly portrays the lives and loves of doctors and their fascinating, high-pressure world. (169107—$5.50)

**Buy them at your local
bookstore or use coupon
on next page for ordering.**